THE DROWNING STREET YEARS

A Lifetime of Survival

The inside story of how the Establishment and vested interests fleeced the public and who got away with the money.

RAI HAMILTON

First edition published in 1999

Reprinted with corrections in 2025

The Drowning Street Years is written in three parts:

PART ONE – LEARNING TO SWIM

Percy Vere, born in the aftermath of World War II, was expected to follow in his family's footsteps and uphold Establishment values. He navigates the complexities of his own identity, experiencing a worldwide crisis of greed and injustice.

PART TWO – THE WINDS OF CHANGE

Percy strikes out to build a global presence, forging alliances in the cut-throat world of finance. He is swept along in the tsunami of arrogance and extravagance with a chip in the game. He fences with hidden vested interests that align the media to promote a culture of globalisation.

PART THREE – TRANSHUMANISM

Violence takes hold as individual nations make a desperate attempt to reassert sovereignty. Rogue scientists are paid by influencers to engineer killer infections to depopulate the world. Peoples in areas of deprivation migrate to swamp the economies of the West. Islamic forces sabotage cultures and the world erupts into mayhem. Ownership of agricultural land and food processing is centralized requiring ID compliance. Satellites providing a constant source of energy for robotics are armed with a pulse for galactic destruction. A handheld version becomes the sidearm of choice to control the survivors on Earth.

Part 1: Learning To Swim

To Sally

A people and their King
Through ancient sin grown strong,
Because they feared no reckoning
Would set no bounds to wrong;
But now their hour is past,
And we who bore it find
Evil Incarnate held at last
To answer to Mankind

Rudyard Kipling

Contents

Prologue..1
Chapter One HERITAGE.......................... 5
Chapter Two DISCIPLINE....................... 35
Chapter Three TRADITION....................... 65
Chapter Four EDUCATION...................... 85
Chapter Five ASSIGNMENT CAMBODIA.. 141
Chapter Six HERITAGE....................... 169
Chapter Seven WELCOME TO WORK......... 221
Chapter Eight WELCOME TO THE CITY.... 279
Chapter Nine TWISTING THE TRUTH....... 329

Prologue

Miles Long was in his sumptuous office suite on the seventeenth floor of Banque Longchamps in Zurich when he got the call on his private line.

"Mr Long?" a voice enquired. "My name is Anton Pillar, Percy Vere's solicitor. I'm instructed to tell you that your friend Percy has disappeared."

Miles swivelled his giant leather chair round to face the window with its birds-eye view of the Bahnhofstrasse.

"Disappeared?"

Miles knew exactly what Anton had said, but a man in his position needed time to think about the implications of such a call.

"He has disappeared," Anton repeated clinically.

"Disappeared?" Miles stalled again as he recalled the last time he had spoken to Percy. He wondered if they were on good terms and whether the secrets he had imparted to his friend were likely to have been leaked.

"Is this a 'concrete,' as in shoes, kind of disappeared or just a 'not interested in being seen around for a while'?" he asked in an even voice.

"I am instructed only to say that you will not see him again."

"Thank you for being so helpful, Mr Pillar," said Miles without sarcasm. "Now, if there's nothing else, you will forgive me."

"Mr Vere left a letter for you."

"Is it possible to fax it over?" Miles asked.

"As you wish, Mr Long," Anton replied.

Miles put down the phone and walked across the plush, hand-woven carpet within a few feet of his private fax machine. He gazed up at the Renoir he had acquired for what he considered a song at Sotheby's the month before and frowned as an image of his lifelong friend, Percy, clouded the masterpiece.

Thirty seconds later, a one-page fax slipped silently into the tray.

Dear Miles,

You will only have received this letter because we won't see each other again. I hope you are suitably sad. We had some great times together.

It was you who told me that we are all pawns in a global game and that nothing will stop the vested forces at work. I now know that no matter who wins the power and the money, we are all destined to be slotted into our little compartments. Democracy cannot crush greed, and the poor will never be free.

I am not a conspiracy theorist, but the future we have talked about for so long is approaching fast, and whether you call it '10 Island 2030' or anything else, I am no longer interested in being part of it.

I have stood by and watched the manipulations, the payments, and the disappearances, and my conclusion is that, in the absence of any truth or benevolence in the corridors of power, these are the inevitable dynamics of forward motion.

I wrote a story of all the events that led me to this point, but it is too late to change anything, so I left the only manuscript for you behind the old millstone at our prep school. I confess I wanted to expose your awful plans to a few honest men of influence, but I couldn't find any.

Percy

The following afternoon, Miles Long's customised Boeing 727 glided into the private jet park at Heathrow, and he took a last look at his new hand-picked stewardess. He eyed up her legs and mused that the extras he would demand on the way back to Geneva would be worth the wait.

An hour later, Miles' stretched Rolls-Royce cruised through the iron gates of Abra Cadabra. He signalled for his driver to stop halfway up the drive towards the main buildings. Getting out of the car slowly into the warm afternoon sun, he stood for a few moments to allow childhood memories to seep through.

'This is progress,' he thought as the soles of his handmade shoes stuck irritatingly to the surface of the hot tarmac.

Miles walked deliberately across the manicured lawn and through the trees towards his first classroom, where there was an old granite millstone against the wall, unmoved for decades. He slid his hand behind it to pull out a thick plastic envelope. And in the sunlight, he carefully wiped off the dirt and two spiders with his calf-skin glove.

Miles couldn't help but grin at the sight of his name written across the front in Percy's distinctive looped style. He glanced up instinctively at the curious stares of small faces gathering against the inside of the classroom window.

"Where was the Magna Carta signed?" he shouted through the glass.

There were blank stares.

"On the bottom, of course!" he grinned.

Miles walked deliberately back to the car and dialled a Swiss number from his portable phone.

'I've got it,' was all he said.

Chapter One
HERITAGE

Key Witnesses:

PERCY VERE	*Author*
MOLLY CODDLE	*His nanny*
COMMANDER VERE	*His father*
MRS. GRIMM	*Kindergarten headmistress*
PEREGINE FROMAGE-POTTS	*Percy's classmate*
MELODY LINGERSON	*Music teacher*
STIG MATTIK	*Ophthalmic surgeon*
CHESTER DRAWS	*Carpenter*
DAME EMILY VERE	*Percy's grandmother*
MAJOR CORK STOPPER	*The lodger at Cudgel Manor*
DOUG ROSEBED	*The gardener*

"Why is Percy looking at Woolworths and Boots at the same time?" enquired Molly.

"Don't be silly; they're on opposite sides of the street," pronounced Mrs Vere as she leaned over the pram to gaze at her one-year-old little boy.

Molly Coddle, Percy's sometime nanny, was right. Percy's round blue eyes were stuck in a wide angle.

"Are all babies able to do that, Molly, or do you think Percy's got something a bit special?" Mrs Vere asked. "It may be genetic because his father rammed the dock gates in Gibraltar with one of His Majesty's destroyers. Later on, he lost a convoy of 47 merchant ships he was escorting across the Atlantic."

Percy's eyes seemed to move independently, which in later years would be described as an example of self-control.

Mrs Vere moved aside to allow two shoppers to pass.

"I think it's an asset," she concluded. "He can see around corners."

Mrs Vere looked slightly detached, like a software update stuck at 87%.

Percy enjoyed surveying the Oxfordshire village scene from his pram while the two women in his life prattled on. He saw a good-sized Adelphi cinema playing 'The Lone Ranger' flanked by the grocer on the left and the butcher on the right. Further on, past the Post Office at the far end of the street, was the sweet shop and then a row of cottages, each with its neat front garden and slatted fence. From this point, the high street turned into a picturesque country lane meandering through the lush English countryside.

Percy's eyes wandered independently in their sockets until one or the other was prompted to take command. Then his head, with its curly blonde locks, would tilt as he focused to establish whether there was anything exceptional going on. There never was, but that was no reason to give up.

"Look, he wants a cuddle," muttered Molly mistakenly. She looked down at his little face with its squashy nose and two large dimples in the front of each cheek. Then she dragged Percy out of his pram to her ample bosom, smothering him whilst she continued to chat away.

Percy, avoiding suffocation, fought his way up for air and scrambled up Molly's breast to look over her shoulder. He fixed his left eye on two local farmers chatting outside the National Bank. One of them was stuffing a wad of banknotes into his trousers, and a red-faced woman in a thick woollen coat coming out of the bank handed half a crown to the diminutive man waiting for her.

'People are coming out of there with money', Percy noted. '*Enter poor, exit rich – fantastic!*"

"And don't be long, Henry," the woman commanded as her man sidled off towards the grocers.

Meanwhile, the taller of the two farmers started tapping his shepherd's crook on the corner of a cobblestone. His left jacket pocket was half ripped off, so when he lifted his arm to touch his cap at a woman barging past with a heavy shopping bag, his tin of Old Holborn nearly fell out. He caught it just in time.

"Buggerarf," he spat at her two grubby children who were dawdling behind.

They picked up their pace quickly like ducklings.

The womenfolk in the village seemed uniformly plump in their tweeds and woolly hats. They jostled in the shop doorways like sheep queuing up to be dipped on the farm.

Mrs Vere and Molly were ready to leave, so the viewing time for Percy was over. Molly unceremoniously removed Percy from her shoulder and dumped him back in the pram. He grimaced, squinted at his mother, and shook his favourite stuffed lamb by the throat.

Mrs Vere always seemed quite anxious, like a flickering street lamp. She was clearly detached from everything going on around her, not unlike a tassel on a remarkable tapestry. She was thinner than most of the local shoppers around her, wore no make-up, had her hair tied back in a ponytail by an elastic band, and wore a patterned frock. It would have dragged along the pavement, but for the two tucks of material around her belt.

"She looks like a runner bean sticking out of the top of a wigwam," concluded Percy.

"Look!" exclaimed Mrs Vere more dramatically than necessary. "He's lost his bottle."

While looking for it, Percy lobbed his lamb over the side.

Molly Coddle was a rounded woman with short auburn hair and a happy twinkle always in her eye. She never had a bad word to say and always ended her sentences with an indisputable, “It’ll all turn out for the best; you mark my words!”

Molly was married to the Vere farm manager and lived in one of the cottages on the estate while the Vere family occupied the dilapidated manor house. The next occupied building was over two miles away, and ensured that the two of them were friends. Molly didn’t consider herself responsible in any way for Percy. She just helped out because it seemed the natural thing to do.

“Here comes the Commander,” Molly smiled, pulling a blanket over Percy as Mrs Vere dumped her shopping on his legs.

Molly pushed Percy’s pram over the edge of the pavement and started to wave at the small black 1946 Ford Popular weaving its way towards them. Percy lurched because the shopping was cutting off the blood supply to his feet. He fell sideways, tipping a bunch of bananas and a tin of baked beans out of the bag.

“Now look what you’ve done!” Mrs Vere chastised her baby son.

Percy focused on his father steering the car down the street. He was hunched over the wheel and peered left and right like a searchlight in a sea rescue. Even so, he missed them and drove straight past.

Commander Vere was impeccably dressed as usual in a white shirt, starched white collar, and his Royal Navy tie with its little gold crowns on a royal blue background. It was knotted in a tiny knob at the front. His hair was immaculately Bryl-creamed back off his weather-beaten face, and a fresh red rosebud with a couple of leaves around it poked out of his suit buttonhole.

“He’s missed us again,” sighed Mrs Vere, grabbing the pram from Molly and pulling it back onto the pavement so a bus could pass. “Shall we wait here or chase after him?”

“I’ve got to cut out potatoes,” Molly declared as she staggered backwards.

“Where did you tell him to meet us?” asked Molly.

Molly paused to wipe the beads of sweat from her forehead.

“Outside the Adelphi,” replied Mrs Vere without looking at her. “Even he can’t miss that!”

Percy’s legs were numb from the groceries, but the two ladies stopped for nothing as they headed down the pavement towards the cinema. Then Molly saw the Ford Popular coming back up the high street on the wrong side of the road. She seized the moment and pushed Percy's pram straight across the nearside traffic and into the path of their car.

"Undiscovered talent and child protégé wasted in village slaughter," thought Percy as his father accelerated towards them.

Mrs Vere jumped forward with her arms in the air. She was only just in time as Commander Vere had stamped on the brake pedal a little too late and, with squealing tyres, stopped only a few feet short of killing his son and heir.

Mrs Vere tossed Percy onto the back seat, and Molly got in the back with him. With the pram tied onto the open boot lid, Commander Vere drove off and somehow negotiated a safe way to where the fields began.

As the hedgerows trundled by and the car swerved down the lanes, Mrs Vere issued instructions to avoid potholes as if her husband had never been to their house before.

"Watch out!" she would repeat as Molly in the back was clutching Percy's head against her chest.

"It'll all turn out for the best, you mark my words," she mumbled as Percy grappled inside her cardigan.

"These feel rather nice," he thought as his hands explored her breasts.

Percy snuggled closer and went to sleep just as they turned the last corner home. During the war, the house had suffered from neglect. The paintwork was cracked and faded, and the brick chimney stacks had half collapsed.

* * * * *

By the late 1940s, pre-preparatory day schools were bulging with babies born precisely nine months after the cessation of Second World War hostilities. It seemed that every sailor had berthed and every soldier discharged in the same 24-hour period.

Mrs Grimm's day school for four-year-olds was four miles away from the Vere home. It wasn't exactly a school; it was the right-hand side of a large Victorian detached house hidden by trees. It was part of a parade of buildings occupied initially by successful merchants but now occupied by Mr and Mrs Grimm and 20 screaming children. It housed the educational model Britain had clung to for decades.

The Grimm family had been downsized by the two World Wars, and with money tight, Mrs Grimm had taken control. She had bricked up two internal doors, sold off the left half of the house, and created an income by taking in local children. The unsuspecting parents thought it was a school because the front room had twelve small writing desks in three rows and a blackboard, as if it were a classroom. An old upright piano, a set of drums, and two large cymbals were in the corner. Bolted on to the back of the house was a playground and, at the side, a small brick extension, which needed no introduction because it gave off the distinctive smell of disinfectant.

A large portrait of Mrs Grimm's father in a military uniform sporting an array of medals was positioned prominently in the entrance hall. The picture had him standing with his nose in the air in front of a scene of carnage, presumably his regiment in battle. They seemed to be in hand-to-hand combat. This was the legendary Captain Phileas Grimm, who led the First Lancers out of the trenches at the Somme, as evidenced by a clipping from the Illustrated London News, yellow and faded and glued to the corner of the canvas. If you got close enough to read it, this testified that Phileas Grimm had survived with 17 of his 6,700 men. A higher authority had ordered them over the top for seven consecutive days of heavy German machine-gun fire.

In plain view at the end of the hall, there was a more recent oil painting of Mrs Grimm's brother-in-law, Major Lucius 'Lucy' Grimm of the Grenadier Guards. Again, a yellowish piece of newsprint confirmed Lucy had been awarded a Military Cross posthumously for being the first British officer to reach the top of the cliffs at Normandy on D-Day. Later that same day, he was cut down in front of a pillbox, waving his men forward. There was a smaller second picture of him jumping enthusiastically out of a landing craft onto the beach, and next to it a copy of a page from the mess book of the Guards just before the invasion. It read, 'There was an air of expectancy in the mess, rather like on sports day.'

Mrs Grimm assured the Commander that honour was paramount in these troubled times.

"We are keen to impress on our children that duty without question is the order of the day," she confirmed

"Hopefully, Percy will survive," muttered Mrs Vere as Mrs Grimm barked the command, 'In you go, Percy. Join the others!"

In his new green blazer topped with a peaked green cap with a badge on the front, Percy looked like an enormous greenfly. He stared without moving, first at his parents, then at the other children, and finally at Mrs

Grimm's flabby biceps wobbling like ocean waves. She seemed to have the personality of a filing cabinet.

After the parents were all out of sight, the children were put under the command of the man standing next to the stove, adding some small logs into the fire. His sleeves were rolled up, and both his arms were covered in old and faded tattoos. His look was bitter, and his lip quivered as if remembering his battlefield injuries. That was the same look he adopted to avoid re-enlisting. Instead, he had gone on a fishing trip only to find himself scared of water. It cannot have helped that his wife had cut the family home in half to accommodate all these screaming children.

Arthur Grimm was lean with long black sideburns. Percy thought instantly that he was the spitting image of one of the scrawny servants at Castle Frankenstein.

"Did you say goodbye to your mum and dad?" he growled morbidly as if they would never return.

Dragging his satchel, Percy moved two steps towards him and stopped in trepidation as Arthur Grimm started to scratch his crotch. Percy blinked, and a vision of Arthur Grimm with vampire teeth appeared and disappeared in the same instant. Percy froze and held back the tears as Arthur Grimm pushed him into the front room with what looked like a cattle prod.

Commander Vere never visited the place again.

* * * * *

After stencilling, drawing, and trying to learn the alphabet as the morning routine, the children would settle down to eat or swap stuff out of their packed lunches. Percy had a steady diet of biscuits, lumps of cheese, fruit, and anything that needed no preparation, whilst Peregrine Fromage-Potts gorged himself on Marmite sandwiches with the crusts taken off, slices of chocolate cake, and iced buns. At precisely 2:00 p.m., they cleared up every trace of wrapping and crumbs and stood to attention before being dismissed in alphabetical order and herded for games into the chain-link cage. This procedure was unbroken summer and winter unless there was a Force 10 gale or more than 18 inches of snow. Anything less, and the children were cold and shivering, especially those without coats. This extended to an hour break after the music period.

Every day, with accompaniment from Mrs Grimm on the piano, the music lessons included turns with tambourines, drums, cornets, recorders, and triangles. Then, at 4:00 p.m. precisely, the cooing mothers arrived to take their little ones away.

Mrs Vere had never been a keen timekeeper, and Percy had always missed the 5:00 p.m. beginning of 'Watch with Mother' on the television. It used to be a matter of Mrs Vere forgetting the time, but, after a while, it seemed she was fearful of leaving the house. Percy was resigned to never knowing what Bill and Ben, the Flowerpot Men, were getting up to with the beautiful Little Weed.

Mrs Vere was at least consistent. She was late picking Percy up from Mrs Grimm's every day for the following two years. Percy assumed punctuality was a rumour, as he would sit at Mrs Grimm's kitchen bench sometimes for hours, as all the other children were collected.

'My mother must have had an accident' was something Percy stopped saying after the first week.

Percy didn't know what his parents actually did because his father rarely saw him, and when they were together, it was for a few seconds as their paths crossed. Anyway, Commander Vere left the house before Percy was brought down for breakfast, and he arrived back after Percy had been tucked up in bed.

* * * * *

Percy's grandmother had spent twenty years in China, and her stories of situations and places were like children's coloured books, especially as she travelled alone, spoke their language fluently, and became fond of opium. Nevertheless, she was a devout Christian, and her most urgent mission was to instil the truth of the life of Christ in her grandson. Her voice was intoxicating, and her words stayed with Percy even from an early age. She wanted to make her presence felt as backup when Percy ever needed clarity on his own journey.

"Jesus suffered himself to enter the natural world," she related quietly. "In doing so, he took on the evil that is part of all natural bodies. He defeated evil and overcame temptation. He showed the way forward by his own good deeds based on love and wisdom. He paved the way for all Mankind to have the potential of understanding a future beyond understanding."

"That is very clear, Grandma!" Percy said just as convincingly.

She pushed the envelope by teaching him the ways of faith and the possibilities of 'Eternal Life'.

"Jesus of Nazareth was publicly executed by Roman authority. This was a state-sanctioned death penalty, delivered with maximum shame and finality. He was buried in a known, accessible tomb by Joseph of Arimathea, a wealthy member of the Jewish council. This wasn't a myth; it was memory, and the only reason to report this detail is that it actually happened. Why would some 500 witnesses proclaim his resurrection and themselves be stoned to death for saying they had seen the risen Christ? If the tomb still had a body in it, Christianity would have been instantly exposed as a hoax."

Percy's grandmother's words would become the basic reason for Percy's oftentimes relying on his faith in times of confusion and despair. Her simple explanation covered the certainty that Jesus had risen from the dead.

"Do you mind if I keep this on the back burner?" Percy requested it so he could bring it to the boil when needed.

'Dear Jesus, if you get me out of this, I swear I'll never do it again' would come in handy.

* * * * *

Percy's mother had been in the Women's Royal Air Force, serving alongside the future Queen Elizabeth in driving trucks and packing parachutes. She moved on to plotting small model aeroplanes on a room-sized chart of the coasts of France and England, either side of the English Channel. She had a stick like a croupier at the roulette table to push little model planes as they came to attack our country.

Mrs Vere became an officer in Bomber Command and was witness to horror by accepting a ride on one of the infamous bombing runs over Dresden. She felt the void of friends failing to return. Then there were those who did return with their faces burned off. Mrs Vere was stationed at RAF Stradishall, home of the Stirling bomber, when bombs fell through the hangar roof, and her back was lacerated. In her recovery, she became an assistant to Archie MacIndoe, a burns surgeon in East Grinstead. Working with MacIndoe and the burned pilots he affectionately called his 'guinea pigs', her own faith became useful in the rehabilitation of all those unrecognisable airmen.

During this time, Mrs Vere compiled the recordings of the war in the air that went out daily on the BBC and were collected for posterity by the Imperial War Museum.

Percy remembered his mother primarily as the lone person sitting naked and distressed day after day on the carpet on the first-floor landing of their home. She faced the wall, continuously scratching her right eyebrow. Blood always ran down her face until she looked like a crucifixion. She would say repeatedly, 'It'll be alright' when it was undeniable that it was not.

Percy was experiencing that humans were complicated, especially women. He learned not interrupt when a woman was speaking, especially about something that had nothing to do with him. Mrs Vere didn't read books or talk to anyone on the telephone, and often she had the milk bill on the carpet beside her. Percy configured that she was absorbed in working out the number of pints left outside the door, and that was the reason she forgot the time.

Nevertheless, Percy was a sympathetic soul, and he was fighting for an answer, so one day, without prompting, he said to her, 'Mummy, don't worry, you've done your bit.'

* * * * *

Percy ended up enjoying being away from home. Mrs Grimm didn't bother that he waited every day in the kitchen, and he spent time nosing around the kitchen and the adjoining music room. He worked out how to reseal a new packet of chocolate biscuits after taking one out and how a small smudge of strawberry jam on the middle C of the piano keyboard solved the problem of finding it later.

Regrettably, the cleaning lady noticed the little red blob and started wiping it off, so Percy had to think of a more permanent solution. A little scratch with the kitchen knife seemed appropriate, so, in trepidation, Percy launched his first tactical strike.

Placing his satchel carefully under the kitchen bench, he checked on the location of Mrs Grimm upstairs and tiptoed back into the music room. He positioned the sharp point of the knife on the back of Middle C and pressed down. Immediately, a chip of ivory flicked into the air.

Percy stood transfixed with his heart stuck in his mouth. He shut the lid and dropped onto all fours.

"Cripes!" he panicked as he searched across the carpet.

After an agonised two minutes, Percy found the ivory chip and ran back into the kitchen. He threw the knife back into the drawer, grabbed his satchel, and ran out to sit on a chair at the side of the brick outhouse. He started chewing the strap of his satchel while the chip of ivory burnt a hole in his clenched fist.

After a short while, his insides twisted in a terrible knot in case Mrs Grimm might appear. He jumped up and ran down the garden path into the street and crouched over the street drain cover. Percy opened his hand and dropped the evidence through the grill.

"She'll never find it in there," he thought until he stood up and looked backwards, and there was Mrs Grimm at her upstairs bedroom window full frontal, holding the curtains back and looking straight at him. Percy was thinking about running away to a foreign country when Mrs Vere arrived, only an hour late.

Percy spent a terrible night, knowing that retribution was inevitable.

Despite his protestations about feeling sick enough to die the following morning, he was delivered to school late in the usual way. The piano had not magically disappeared as he had hoped, and no one said a word about it.

The morning was spent trying to write letters of the alphabet, but Percy's crayon stayed pressed on one spot, making a bigger and bigger red dot. In intense concentration, and his tongue gripped firmly between his teeth, he tried to get the letter 'S' the right way round. The only respite was the sniggering around him as Mrs Grimm publicly announced that he was a 'witless boobie.'

Percy knew that being a witless boobie was nothing to being a piano-chipping maniac.

At 3:01 p.m., Mrs Grimm opened the piano lid to start the music lesson. Percy stood like a statue with a red and green painted drum hanging around his neck, his heart in his throat. His knuckles were white as he clutched the drumsticks. He could see right through the back of Mrs Grimm's head as she leaned forward and peered ever closer at the keyboard.

Percy was hoping against hope that she would somehow keel over and be taken away in an ambulance.

Then Mrs Grimm's biceps started to wobble out of control while her right hand picked at middle C and confirmed her worst fear. She stood up and turned.

Percy's stomach did its typical twisting as she lifted the long ruler from the top of the piano, the ruler that whacked the back of little hands that tried so desperately to play the right notes. The sequence, 'Eat Good Bread Dear Father' or more appropriately, that afternoon 'Every Good Boy Deserves Flogging' was a mystery with any connection to music.

Mrs Grimm pointed to the keyboard and grabbed the ruler in an early demonstration of how institutions deal with non-compliance.

"Will the boy who is responsible for this step forward?" she barked. "We will all stay exactly where we are until the culprit owns up!"

"What's a 'culprit'?" whispered Peregrine Fromage-Potts.

Percy had no intention of moving, but he didn't need to own up. His face lit up scarlet red. Mrs Grimm's piercing eyes focused on him, and despite her huge bulk, with biceps flapping, she pranced forward and pulled Percy out of his seat by his right ear. Every little person in the room was braced for what was to come.

Percy's first thought was to confess to other crimes he had not yet committed. That seemed stupid, and there was nothing that was going to save him from the inevitable prising open of his right hand, palm upwards.

"Hold his arm, Melody!" she ordered her music class assistant, Melody Lingerson.

Melody was the shrill old spinster who was in charge of singing lessons, and she held Percy's wrist in a vice-like grip.

"It was only an accident!" screeched Percy in terror before the first blow.

The ruler whacked down the first time, and a searing pain cut through Percy's hand. He screamed out of control as a further five whacks followed.

"This piano is my most prized possession," shrieked Mrs Grimm as Melody released Percy's mutilated hand. "It has been passed through my family for two generations."

Percy started jumping up and down and broke the string on the drum around his neck.

"Take your punishment like a man!" ordered Melody Lingerson.

But Percy wasn't a man. He was only four.

Peregrine Fromage-Potts ran forward, picked up the drum as it bounced across the floor, and handed it back to Mrs Grimm. Percy never spoke to him again.

The Vere parents never had a clue that this torture was going on. Percy would arrive home with various confirmations that everything was progressing well. The evidence would be calculated to ensure the school fees continued. A good example was a cardboard square with his handprint on it in green ink with a poem printed alongside.

Sometimes, you get discouraged.
Because I am so small
And always leaving fingerprints
On furniture and walls
But every day I'm growing up
And soon I'll be so tall
That all those little fingerprints
It will be harder to recall
So, here's a little handprint
Just so you can say
This is how my fingers looked
When I placed them here today.

* * * * *

After leaving Mrs Grimms, the terror that is not supposed to be part of childhood continued for Percy because he had a squint.

In the late 1940s, medicine was still mainly carpentry done in Latin. Surgeons were magicians whose knives were sharper than their predictions, and Harley Street was the closest Britain had to a temple of transfiguration. Far away in 2030, men would pay fortunes to have their retinas replaced with sensors and their memories backed up nightly. Still, Percy's first upgrade was cruder: two eyeballs forcibly realigned by a Scandinavian with a god complex.

Percy should have known something was coming. His mother had re-buckled his sandals four times at breakfast - the domestic equivalent of a military drumroll. Then there was the brown paper bag she fetched after remembering his pyjamas. In family traditions, a bag behind the back usually meant someone was going to throw up.

If there had been any doubt about where they were going, it was dispelled as his mother told the commander to stop the car because she had forgotten Percy's pyjamas.

"Silly me!" she was muttering as they set off again.

"Where are we going?" asked Percy in a begging tone.

"It's for your own good!" she replied.

After the pioneering procedure, Percy woke to find he was blind. Not metaphorically - that would come later courtesy of the Establishment. This was literally as his face was wrapped in gauze and panic. His little hands clawed at the cardboard Elizabethan ruff fastened around his neck, a device designed to prevent self-harm in dogs.

His screams brought a nurse hurrying in.

"There, there," she cooed, deploying that classic British medical reassurance used when there is absolutely nothing to be done.

Percy thrashed until exhaustion became a release. Only after two days did he regain the kind of composure that later allowed him to sit in boardrooms and committee meetings full of men lying about their intentions. He learned early that fear is limited by stamina and resolve.

When the terror ebbed, he explored, and his hands found familiar shapes: a wooden toy bus with wheels to assist direction when blinded. Percy perched astride the bus and slowly explored his way around the ward, collecting bruises when ramming the steel legs of beds. Swing doors attacked him from both sides as he ventured out, while elderly patients encouraged him as entertainment.

Percy went bed to bed introducing himself.

"Hello!" he started. "My name is Percy. Would you like to hear a joke?"

"Yes, please, young man, said the patient in the first bed - a man with a cough like wet gravel.

Percy obliged with one from his repertoire.

"After a serious accident," he started, "a man in the hospital shouted, 'Doctor, doctor! I can't feel my legs!' The doctor replied, 'I know. I've cut off your arms!"

Percy would then move on.

"Hello," he said again. "My name is Percy. Would you like to hear a joke?"

"Okay," the guy said.

"I went to the butchers the other day, and I bet him sixpence that he couldn't reach the meat off the top shelf."

"And?"

"He said, 'No, the stakes are too high!'"

"I'll look forward to you coming again tomorrow," spoke the unknown patient. "Now buzz off!"

"My friend drowned in a bowl of muesli," Percy tried to tell the occupant of the next bed. "A strong current pulled him in!"

He performed this ritual daily. The jokes were dreadful, but in his defence, he was four, blind, and not yet aware that humour would one day be humanity's last defence against its own invention.

When the bandages finally came off, light hit him like a revelation. Shapes resolved into colours, colours into forms, and forms into the large blur that was Stig Mattik himself.

"I am thinking you will soon be alright," the surgeon pronounced in the tone of a man who believed improvement was a personal compliment.

"Doctor, would you like to hear a joke?" Percy asked automatically.

Stig looked bewildered and didn't answer.

"Okay," said a patient behind him with one arm.

"A man goes to his eye surgeon with a strawberry growing out of his head", Percy retorted. "And the surgeon says, 'I'll give you some cream to put on it!'"

"And do you know what the doctor said to me this morning?" said the one-armed man.

"No?" replied Percy.

"I told him I get exhausted when I go on a diet, so he gave me some pep pills, and you know what happened?"

"No?"

"I ate faster."

"I have other patients!" Stig said as he hastened away.

"You can take my place in the joke-telling department!" Percy whispered to his one-armed friend. "I'm going tomorrow, and I'm scared."

"What is there to be scared of?" came the answer as his remaining arm came across and put a hand on top of Percy's head. "Remember that a life with no obstacles doesn't lead anywhere."

"What's an obstacle?" Percy muttered.

Years later, Percy would recognise this episode with tech pioneers unveiling retinal implants and memory-editing algorithms. They all sounded like Stig: humourless, benevolent, and, they hoped, successful.

Percy went round the ward to say goodbye to his audience. He saw his friend and only then felt the impact of losing an arm because he was used to his comic book heroes surviving torture by extra-terrestrials and Desperate Dan, who regularly lost arms and legs. Still, somehow, they were replaced before the next issue.

"I didn't really think it was gone," Percy mumbled. "I'm sorry!"

"Never be sorry," he replied, resting his remaining hand on Percy's head. "One of the secrets of happiness is not to try to be a man. Just continue to be a great boy."

They exchanged smiles, and Percy left the hospital with newly aligned eyes and a slightly misaligned idea of what counted as progress.

For reasons lost to time, Percy remembered 'never be sorry' more clearly than the operation itself. It would still echo faintly in 2030 when he would watch grown men trying to upload themselves into machines, convinced that silicon immortality was superior to decency.

When Stig Mattik was knighted shortly afterwards, the Vere family dutifully joined the crowds outside Buckingham Palace. Dozens of Percy's former fellow-patients squinted in post-operative loyalty as Sir Stig's limousine glided out of Palace Yard.

* * * * *

After this blinding experience, for whatever reason, Percy never minded being left alone, even for long periods of time. He found a million ways to amuse himself, blissfully unaware that child psychologists were gathering evidence to excuse grown men for fiendish behaviour. No one knew that this would spawn an army of social workers to ensure that children would run wild rather than suffer any punishment, so there was no memory of any savage retribution.

Like every other child of his generation, Percy became curious about why he was expected to do everything on command while grown-ups did precisely what they wanted whenever it suited them. Life was obviously a leisurely affair to be conducted between frequent cups of tea. So why did he have to jump to attention every five minutes? If Percy wanted anything, like food, he would always have to wait.

'Can I have a biscuit, please?' was met by 'Wait until supper, or you'll spoil your appetite.'

Percy's reaction was simply that he wanted everything done immediately, if not before. Methodology or caution would be unacceptable. Acting alone and on impulse became the only way to behave.

Percy rarely saw any children of his own age outside school because there were no houses close to his home. There were some local boys from the village who seemed to gather on the riverbank, throwing stones at the ducks, but Percy was scared of them, and there was no reason to mix with 'their sort'. Anyway, there was no teatime at the Vere house. Percy's only friends were the twins, Stan and Dee Liver, who lived on the farm up the road.

"Would you like to join my club?" Percy asked the six-year-old Stan. "And I suppose your sister can join, too."

So it was that Percy arranged for the twins to attend their first and only meeting in an empty pig sty. Percy and Stan pricked their fingers with a rose thorn and became blood brothers, and Dee swore to do whatever Percy wanted.

"We need to communicate", Percy suggested to Dee Liver. "You are in charge of making a walkie-talkie. You get two cans, make a hole in the lid, and join them together with a string. Then we can speak in the dark."

"It doesn't work!" she cried the next day, throwing two cans of baked beans and the string on the pig sty floor."

Percy picked it all up.

"You have to take the beans out first!" he suggested.

Their only mischief as club members was conceived with no evil intent, like Robin Hood, in a way. They went to the pub at the end of the lane and hid Chester Draws' bicycle behind the outside lavatory. Chester was a carpenter working on the local farms, and he was usually drunk. When he stumbled out of the pub and found his bike gone, he went nuts. He complained to the father of the twins, and when it came out that it was Percy's idea, they were banned from seeing him, and that was the end of the club. Years later, Percy reminded Dee Liver about her oath to do whatever he wanted, and she told him to 'bugger off'.

Seniority was apparently a yardstick. Anyone older, and therefore more senior, both in school and in the community, should be obeyed without question.

"It's a system they use in the army," advised Molly authoritatively.

"Is that why the dog gets his dinner before me?" asked Percy.

Everyone Percy met was senior to him, and whilst he had no plans to be a rebel, the never-ending flood of commands was enough to drive anyone off the rails.

'Do what you're told!'
'Don't argue!'
'Don't contradict me!'

'Don't answer back!'
'Come here!'

There were occasions when Percy would go and hide. There were other moments when his face would fill so tightly with blood that teachers thought he might burst like an over-ripe tomato. Then there were his tantrums when Percy had to be physically restrained from smashing his head against the wall. On formal occasions, when Percy was on parade, he would hear himself being described as a 'problem'. This must have been an illness that would be 'straightened out' later on by four years of National Service.

* * * * *

Percy's father had been sent to the Royal Naval College at Dartmouth at the age of 12, and he would progress with a commission as the youngest ever lieutenant in the Royal Navy. His mother assumed that was the natural order of things.

Duty was everything, and it came as a surprise to him to be awarded medals for individual acts of gallantry in the course of battle in World War II. He believed it was ordinary behaviour.

He progressed quickly to command a tribal class destroyer with orders to protect the convoys carrying food into the Mediterranean through the Straits of Gibraltar. No number of attacks by U-boats or waves of German dive-bombers was going to stop him. After months of miraculous escapes from torpedoes, a screaming Stuka eventually dropped a bomb down his funnel as his ship refuelled in Valetta harbour. He found himself the only officer left alive, but instead of jumping ship, he felt his way below decks into the cauldron of the engine room to rescue a remaining engineer.

Commander Vere's new ship's orders were to run the gauntlet from Alexandria to Malta, delivering ammunition for the anti-aircraft batteries. As it happened, on his third run, his ship was spotted in open water approaching Malta in the dawn light and subjected to sortie after sortie of enemy fire. With his boat berthed and stationary against the harbour wall, it was inevitable that one shell would find its way to light up his cargo and the ensuing fire from stem to stern. With the deck ablaze, Commander Vere took a rowboat over the side and secured a depth charge to the hull below the water line. He triggered a fifteen-second fuse and rowed away in a hurry. The hole in the hull sank the ship, and the people of Malta spent the next two days bringing up the 10,000 unexploded shells. Such lunacy was mentioned in papers called 'dispatches' and was the way of an officer and a gentleman.

After the successful troop landings in Sicily, Commander Vere was reassigned to patrol the Atlantic. The Mighty HMS Hood, the largest battleship in the English fleet, was blown away by the new monster German battleship Bismarck.

With Hood gone, it would take every other ship in the whole Navy to attack Bismarck at the same time for any possibility of sinking her. No single boat had any chance against such massive firepower.

Some master-brain in the Admiralty decided that Commander Vere was the one who should go and search for her.

It was by some miracle that a stray Fleet Air Arm plane on the way home spotted the mighty Bismarck and dropped its one torpedo. It was a terrible shot because it missed the whole boat and just caught the rudder. In the bad weather, the pilot didn't realise the significance of his encounter and failed to report the incident. It was Commander Vere who accidentally renewed contact with the disabled Bismarck, able only to cruise around in a circle. The Commander went in close to attract the U-boats away from the advancing English battle fleet. It was another attempt at suicide, but with what could only be some Almighty intervention, the wounded Bismarck was overwhelmed and sunk. Everyone in war has a 'worst' experience that will haunt them, and for Commander Vere, it was three thousand German sailors bobbing around on the surface of the open ocean to be burned to death, while his orders were to sail away from the U-Boats that he had attracted.

Commander Vere was summoned to break a bottle on a new battleship paid for by the City of Blackpool. Somehow, in a miraculous effort of selling homemade scones and tarts, Blackpool had raised £1.3 million, the cost of building a battleship at the time. The whole city turned out to wave her 'Godspeed!'.

Commander Vere, still in his twenties, sailed back into the war, this time across the Atlantic. He found himself in charge of escorting convoys of up to a hundred ships at a time with millions of tons of supplies to feed a starving England. After months in the fog and freezing cold of peering into the darkness, he started to lose his sight – his hearing had already suffered from the years of explosions – but he never lost his sense of humour. He even followed the example of the youthful Nelson, who used to hang six eggs over the side of his ship in a hairnet to signify invincibility. It may have been that gesture that qualified him to lead the fleet to the beaches of Normandy.

* * * * *

At the end of hostilities, Commander Vere drove to Blackpool to thank the people for their incredible fundraising effort. He was so moved by the welcome that he decided to stand as the Liberal Party parliamentary candidate. It would not be accurate to say he 'represented' the people of Blackpool because he could neither see what the people looked like nor hear what they had to say.

The Labour Party's choice in that election contest was Ryder Ramsbottom, who had cut off his trigger finger in 1913 to avoid being sent to the front, and in 1939, he cut off his middle finger next to it just in case his records had somehow gotten lost. He spent the War in Blackpool packing parachutes until the Ministry of Defence opened an investigation into why so many parachutists were dropping a mile to the right into enemy hands.

Ryder Ramsbottom gesticulated during his campaign with two of his remaining fingers, and the Blackpool electorate, shorn of so many sons, would have none of him. The end contest was then between Commander Vere as the Liberal candidate and the Conservative, Matt Grey.

Political argument in those days was a gentlemanly affair, with the Liberal and Conservative candidates staying in the same hotel. They would chat over their second cup of coffee at breakfast before going out and slagging each other off. Commander Vere was too polite for his own good, and the slagging was all one way. Matt Grey was elected, and the Commander turned his attention to promoting the idea of the people of the world working together. He conceived a new political model of federalisation with plans of action and notes on individual responsibilities for every participating nation. It was a prelude to a 'globalisation', and his books were considered a ludicrous and delusional fairy story.

The Commander was always a reflective soul, and he never spoke about his feelings in warfare except the one time Percy went with him to an anniversary of the survivors of his ship's company in Portsmouth. The next morning at breakfast, he showed Percy a photograph of their boat, HMS Penelope, stranded in Valetta Harbour. She was nicknamed HMS

Pepperpot for good reason. The photograph attested to the hundreds of holes in her superstructure from wave after wave of the airstrikes. The back of the photo was signed by the survivors with their official rank. There was one that stood out, 'Billy Stokes - engineer', who had held his position below decks alongside the ammunition without flinching.

"No one who has not been a fighting man in war can imagine enduring the madness, the terror, and the brutality of doing what is necessary to survive", his father winced with his eyes clouding over. "Killing other human beings because they're the enemy is killing or being killed. The scars are forever entrenched in the brain that will never forget."

Percy reflected that was why his mother sat with her memories, because it hurt too much to remember.

* * * * *

In his effort to acclimatise to a life of peace, Commander Vere enlisted the help of his friend Piers Round. Piers had survived the War underwater in submarines, and he told wonderful stories about how he had stalked German battleships. Now, he lived by the sea, and he continued to look around, but now it was at the local girls on the beach.

Piers Round was an alcoholic, and while he was waiting for the pub to open, he sat on a deck chair with a glass of beer, directing Commander Vere in his effort to help create flowerbeds amongst rusty treacle tins, bicycle frames, and broken glass. Percy would gaze in amazement at his father digging for 12 hours straight, still wearing his Royal Navy tie in a tight knot around his throat, with the sweat pouring off him. The bees and flies buzzed annoyingly around his ears, and he occasionally swiped at them with a spotted blue handkerchief from the top pocket of his suit.

Percy enjoyed his time on the beach. Whenever he was told, 'Don't bother me,' it was a great excuse to disappear. The wind would lash the water, and the rollers pounded the beach as he watched other parents making encouraging noises like, 'Go on in. It'll do you good.' Those who believed such a deliberate lie jumped out of the water immediately, their bottom jaws juddering with cold, their lips white and bloodless, and their arms clasped across their chests.

Like gramophones and scooters, sandcastles were 'in', and whole families competed to build the finest on the beach. Percy loved it when other children gathered around to admire the supreme examples of medieval architecture with minarets and battlements. At the critical moment, Percy would open a channel from the sea up to his efforts at a castle to fill the moat and then watch the approaching tide engulf his masterpiece.

Percy inadvertently was the reason the visits stopped. He ran away in the middle of the night.

Percy had woken up from a howling noise like a dog in pain. The howling got closer, and he pulled the blanket over his head. However, when the howling was right outside his window, he leapt up and ran into the next carriage, but there was no sign of life anywhere.

'A werewolf has got Mummy and Daddy, ' Percy thought.

In his pyjamas and Wellington boots, Percy set off down the lane and reached the bend at the end where he saw lights in the window of a cottage. He went through the wicket gate, up the garden path, and reached up to ring the bell. A short, plump lady came to the door, and Percy explained that his parents had suffered a gruesome end and he was looking for a new home.

Suddenly, he was in a massive bed with four girls.

"What's your name?" they enquired, rubbing their eyes against the sudden light.

"I'm Helen," said one.

"I'm Judy," said the next.

After the formalities, the lights were switched off, and everyone fell asleep and jumbled together.

Unfortunately for Percy, the local police were informed about a missing child, and he was plucked out of bed before he could explore the opportunities.

"Come again," invited Helen as the hysterical Mrs Vere whisked him away.

* * * * *

Every summer after that, the Vere family went to Cornwall to visit Commander Vere's parents at their old manor house. For the Commander, there were gardens to tend, stable doors to mend, and they even delivered The Times. Percy was instantly absorbed in visiting the animals on the farm, playing in the swaying corn, and jumping all five bar gates. Mrs Vere sat for the most part in her bedroom overlooking the undulating hills down to the sea with one eye on the combine harvester.

Percy often spotted her staring anxiously out of the window, still scratching her eyebrow. He assumed she was worrying about whether the milkman would tell his friends that their home was empty.

Cudgel Manor was built out of huge white bespeckled granite blocks hewn before the arrival of William the Conqueror. Inside, the musty smell of 900 years of furniture polish and the attitude of his grandparents impregnated the air.

The old General came from a long line of service in the Scottish regiments. He was committed to the military way, and every movement was by the book. There was simply no other way to behave. Percy's instructions were to say 'Good morning, Sir' and 'Good night, Sir'.

At Cudgel Manor, breakfast had an established chain of command, and the legendary cocktail parties were always arranged with canapés from Harrods. These were delivered from London's Paddington Station aboard the Cornish Riviera, and the guests wore their military regalia. Percy was displayed formally, and he seemed to be a hit with the old ladies who, to Mrs Vere's relief, used to croon, 'What a perfectly charming little boy. With his hair groomed neatly to the side for those occasions, Percy would complete a painstaking circuit of the extensive drawing room until, squinting deliberately, he would stick out his hand and say, 'Good evening, Sir' to the suit of armour in the corner.

Mrs Vere would smile nervously, hastily put down her unfamiliar cocktail, and reassure the guests.

"We've tried to instil him with the good grace to tell everyone minimal about himself," she apologised as Percy was ushered down to his bedroom underground.

Percy stayed out of General Vere's way because everyone was judged. On those few occasions that their paths crossed, Percy would hear him muttering something about 'the cause of all the trouble'. This became an unfortunate reality after the so-called 'murder' of the farmer's sheepdog.

Percy was required to get up at 6:30 a.m. and report to the farm to help with the morning chores. He was woken by the ship's bell, engraved 'HMS Beagle', hanging outside the back door. He would carry pails of pig food, collect eggs, and herd the cattle for milking under the watchful eye of the tenant farmer, Si Lage. Si accepted Percy's presence under sufferance and often made unjustified snide comments to the General, intended to get Percy banned from his domain.

When a few eggs were broken outside the pigsty, and a pail of milk was spilt in the dairy, Si Lage exaggerated the incidents and reported how an unbolted steel door had let his two prize boars wander down to the village. Percy overheard his unequivocal continuous complaint, 'Perzee be a bluddy noozance.'

Si Lage's sheepdog, Bessie, always sat around in the rickety old barn where the cows were tethered in a line waiting their turn to be milked. Percy had to collect hay to feed them.

The only way to collect a bale of hay was to tip it off the top of the haystack. Percy would cut the string and spread clumps of hay down the length of a long wooden trough. That process continued until the fateful morning when a bale toppled off the pile onto the back of the cow at the end of the line. The cow reacted and kicked the bitch to death.

It took minus one-tenth of a second for the General to be informed, and Percy was summoned to the drawing room. He brushed his hair, washed his hands, and cleaned his shoes before he knocked at the drawing-room door, prepared for execution.

"It was an accident, Sir," he admitted as the General's blood surged through his neck into his face. Fortunately, before he had time to explode, Percy's grandmother dragged him out of the room by his ear and back down to the dungeon.

"You will wait here!" she ordered.

Not long afterwards, Commander Vere arrived with a belt.

"This is going to hurt me more than it hurts you," he lied.

Percy got 12 stripes across the bottom, and he was confined to his underground room for three days.

The floor of Percy's bedroom was solid granite without any carpet, and the walls were obviously built with a view to constructing the West Country's earliest deep freeze. The bed frame was metal with a thin mattress and topped only with a pile of scratchy army blankets. During those three days, meals were brought in by either Vera or Primrose, the two young kitchen maids.

Thereafter, during the days, Percy went for long walks far away from Cudgel Manor. He felt for the first time the gusts and sighs of the early morning winds, the ghostly sea mists, and the sudden rainfalls. He explored overgrown footpaths and ran down the fields with his arms outstretched like an aeroplane. He lay on his back for hours watching the swirling clouds and counted the seconds that it would take a dewdrop to fall from its precarious perch on a bent blade of grass. He found a lump of amethyst in a quartz outcrop and was so amazed at its structure that he appointed it his lucky charm forever.

In a new array of colours, Percy travelled the world. The pinks and the reds in the early morning skies above him, the greens and the browns in the woods, the yellows and purples in the flowers, and the greys and the blues in the stones. His armies marched noisily across the hills, and the field commanders invited him to inspect the troops. A button was missing here, and a beret was crooked there. Faster than light, his spaceship visited the moon, and Martians made him their King. He ran a four-minute mile and was acclaimed Victor Ludorum for his third consecutive Olympics. He knew all these feats were within his grasp.

The ship's bell sounded in the distance.

A cheering crowd around Percy on a plinth, wearing a garland of leaves on his head in the amphitheatre at Delphi, turned instantly into the reality of a bumblebee in a buttercup.

Percy started to run back to the house for lunch. He jumped the gates, verily flew up the drive, and started across the lawn like a fighter bomber, keeping low to avoid radar detection.

The old General had built a duck pond in the middle of the front lawn. Percy never saw a live duck on it, but no matter. There was a handsome stone duck on a pedestal in the middle. The General had ordered the duck months before from Plymouth. Percy accelerated, as he knew for sure he could jump over the whole thing. Unfortunately, his foot caught the beak of the stone duck on the way past. He came to a halt by the front door and turned slowly round to face the awful truth.

Lunch that day seemed quieter than usual, with the clanking of heavy silver cutlery on porcelain echoing round the granite dining room.

After being excused from the table, Percy went outside, took off his shoes and socks, waded into the pond, and found the beak. He put it in his shorts pocket, and it felt as obvious as if he had the whole duck in there. He then wandered down to the sea and sat on the cliff's edge.

"Here we go again," he mused, watching the mackerel fisherman prepare for sea in the tiny harbour below.

Dinner that evening was Si Lage's pigeon pie, but Percy was too anxious to eat it. After prodding around, Percy put a pigeon kidney in his mouth, but he couldn't swallow it. He forked it out and onto the side of his plate, put his knife and fork carefully together, and asked to be excused. He went out of the front door onto the lawn and glanced at the stone duck, who glared back accusingly.

'Own up!' it quacked beakless. 'It's the only way."

Percy got 12 stripes across the bottom, the duck got its beak glued back on, and the General frowned every time he saw Percy.

It was apparent to Pecy that these irritations were meant to be a guide to a myriad of dramas that were a training for accidents in adulthood.

* * * * *

One summer, quite a few years later, there was a new face at Cudgel Manor. Major Cork Stopper, known as 'Corky'. Corky had appeared out of nowhere, and the General was suddenly less in evidence. He started missing meals, and there were days when Percy didn't see him at all. Whilst it was a relief for Percy that he had lost the urge to bother with things like the duck's beak, it was upsetting in a way to see him limping around in obvious pain.

Corky arrived in Cornwall from India after having stayed on for a few years after the war to enjoy the polo, the games of whist, and the depravity available in Jaipur. He described England's viceroy as that 'frisky Mountbottom'. Percy had no idea what frisky meant or who Mountbottom could be.

Percy's grandmother was president of the Cornish Country Club at Carlyon Bay, and before the General knew it, his wife had Corky as Cudgel Manor's first paying guest. The old house cringed.

From a practical standpoint, it was a sensible arrangement as the General had long since been unable to cope with supervising the running of the place. The moment of truth arrived when weeds appeared in his precious orchid house in the shingle between the pots.

It was surprising that the General's health had not deteriorated earlier. In World War I at Gallipoli, he had been shot through the head, but the bullet somehow negotiated a way around the critical parts, and the only evidence was a jagged scar at the front and the back of his head. In World War II, on the outskirts of Tobruk, a shell from a German tank found his jeep and blew it into the air, and it landed on top of him, spilling his guts onto the road. As the evacuation of Tobruk was a hasty affair, a conscripted Libyan surgeon with a sense of humour crammed his insides back in reverse order. As if that wasn't enough, his left leg was useless from an old rugby injury. It would have been out of character for the General to complain, and apart from the ugly scars and a severe leaning to the right, Percy always thought he was in good shape.

When Corky arrived, he came with three threadbare Indian rugs as a present for the household, rather like his stake for a game of poker. He must have thought he had a good first hand because, as he gained favour with the General's wife, the rugs were moved from the landing to the morning room, and as he extended his activities to servicing her. After that manoeuvre, the rugs reappeared in pride of place on the drawing-room floor. The General, being in no position to cope with his wife's insatiable appetite for physical attention, said nothing.

Eventually, it was a knowing smirk from the local postmistress that prompted him into the only honourable course of action.

"And how's the good-looking Major Stopper this morning?" she enquired breezily as the General limped in for his specially ordered cigars.

That same evening, as Corky crossed the landing to go into Emily's bedroom, the General blew the remains of his brains onto the bathroom ceiling with his .45 calibre service revolver.

His last dispatch was left hooked on the handle of the cistern. It gave a glimpse of the frustration that he had been bottling up for so long. It read simply, 'SOD YOU, MAJOR, CLEAR THIS UP.'

"Well, Corky, do as you're told and scrape him off the ceiling," Emily ordered in a manner that left no doubt where the cork fitted.

A number of unidentified ladies attended General Vere's memorial service. Mostly, they declined to sign the book as they went into the church, but their anonymity was short-lived as they all came forward to claim chunks of the General's estate as soon as the will was read.

"We were promised," they all cried. "There were services rendered!"

Everyone was a little taken aback at this group sighting, at least everyone except the old petrol pump attendant at the local garage. He was recognised by everyone because of his giant red nose.

"A real gentleman of the manor in his day", he announced as if he was reading the lesson. "The general was takin' care of many a lady in the village."

Percy assumed he meant the General opened their car doors and helped them fill up.

The service was a military pageant to equal a royal passing. The church was stuffed with huge sprays of flowers jostling for attention between regimental banners, taking up every available space, and many of the guests in uniforms were either bedecked with row upon row of campaign ribbons or loaded down with the medals themselves. The lone trumpeter, representing the General's regiment, played the Last Post at the back of the church, and as the notes echoed in the vaulted ceiling, Percy looked at the General's old pals crooked at attention. Here was proof that the lucky ones who had survivedbayonet charges into machine-gun fire were qualified to teach colonialism to the incoming generation.

That was the only time Percy saw his father weep. A few unashamed tears escaped and rolled down his proud face, which was more than could be said for the General's wife, who, acting more as hostess than a widow, was preoccupied with the unveiling of the massive new stained-glass window. Her prearranged signal would draw back a red velvet curtain to reveal, in immortal-coloured panes, 'Emily Vere, Dame of the British Empire, erected this window in memory.'

Commander Vere scattered his father in the gardens of Cudgel Manor, mercifully resisting the old man's request to be sprinkled over the Dardanelles from a light aircraft.

Dame Emily Vere and Major Stopper were confused that the orchids were not self-propagating for decoration at their wedding.

The ashes aren't cold!" Commander Vere frowned. "They've already left for a year-long honeymoon.

In feudal tradition, the faithful retainers stayed on at Cudgel Manor and considered it a duty to follow their daily routine without a break.

As far as the rest of the Vere family was concerned, the re-arrangement was a relief. The old bat could stay in Cornwall, which was almost another country. The alternatives were unthinkable. Percy's mother would have had to submit daily menus and answer the dining room bell.

The painters and decorators who tidied up Cudgel Manor in the absence of the newlyweds were locals who were the product of centuries of inbreeding. They said very little for fear of being ridiculed.

"Put all the General's bits and pieces in the stables," Corky had ordered.

"And put another lick of paint on the bathroom ceiling," Dame Emily had added.

In the event that one of the painters knocked a leg off Emily's dressing table stool. He thought it was better to stay quiet and balance the stool so nothing looked amiss.

So, it was on returning from Scotland that Percy's fatigued granny went upstairs to bed, and the stool collapsed.

In spite of her years of athletics in the bedrooms of Scotland, her injuries were severe, and she was unable to walk again; her demands for attention became unintelligible, and her memory disintegrated.

For Corky, for whatever he had received, he was grateful until the general's full pension stopped. There were no secreted savings and, apart from Doug Rosebed in the garden and Vera and Primrose in the kitchens, all the slaves had to go. This left Corky to cope with his wife and the impossible day-to-day upkeep of Cudgel Manor. It was inevitable that the strain of being summoned every few minutes to attend to his wife was traumatic. Feeding her, bathing her, dressing her, carrying her, and doing ten errands a day for her left him too exhausted for night manoeuvres.

Corky took to the bottle, only a little at first, but a little many times a day, and Doug Rosebed became too scared to stay. He had continued without pay, but Corky, built like an Indian buffalo, was now crashing about with a bottle of scotch in the greenhouse. This was very different from the old General asking Doug's opinion about which blooms were best for the hall table. For Vera and Primrose, they were gone with Corky shouting 'Allo Vera' and 'Evening Primrose' and going for a grope in the larder.

When Corky tripped over an electric heater and fell down the stairs, breaking his ankle, it was Commander Vere's turn to be summoned. He dutifully put the garden back into shape, cleared up the greenhouse, and looked after his mother as best he could. After two short weeks, which seemed like another lifetime, Corky was up and about, limping and swaying. Since he looked precisely like the drunk Corky everyone loved, Commander Vere assumed he was back to normal and drove 250 miles home. As he put the car keys down on the hall table, the phone rang. It seemed that before going to bed, his mother had a cigarette, and the lit butt had fallen down the side of her chair. Corky, drunk and not noticing that she was smoking an empty cigarette holder, had dumped her in the nearest bedroom in the basement. He must have returned to the drawing room and poured himself another stiff one. He clearly failed to smell the smouldering horsehair in the chair behind him.

In spite of active service in India, including the slaughter of an entire brigade of Poona infantry, firefighting under the influence was not one of Corky's strong points. The chair burst into flames and ignited the huge drawing-room drapes, and the best Corky could manage was to spend vital seconds trying to save his carpets. Si Lage had seen the smoke and called the fire brigade, but it was already an inferno. Corky must have pulled his carpets over him, and the only remains were Corky's teeth and his steel watch strap.

Dame Emily survived because the walls of the basement were three feet thick of granite. She was found mumbling that the vicar should have the first melons grown that year.

As the orderlies put Emily into the ambulance next to Corky's watch strap, she was asking how many asparagus canapés should be ordered from Harrods for the weekend.

Emily Vere, Dame of the British Empire, died shortly afterwards and, as requested in her will, she was afforded the rare privilege of burial at sea from a Royal Navy frigate. She was suitably bedecked for the occasion, wrapped and bound in the giant flag that had fluttered for the last time on the battlements at Cudgel Manor. It was her own insignia that boasted two maces with large spikes that accompanied her to the bottom of the sea.

After the service, Percy walked hand in hand with his father through the gardens. The fire had disembowelled the house, and the air was ghostly still. They wandered round the flower beds, through the rose garden, and down the terraces. Commander Vere, as if in farewell, occasionally paused to look at mature trees that he had planted as acorns and pips.

Percy never went back to Cudgel Manor. Appropriately, it was converted into a mental institution.

Chapter Two
DISCIPLINE

Key Witnesses:

DRAGONARA SLASHER	*Headmistress – St Abra Cadabra Prep School*
MILES LONG	*Percy's school friend*
STU POORE	*School "wet"*
MERCY LORD	*Matron*
LOU PLUNGER	*Plumber*
ISAAC HUNT	*School bully*
FERDI LISER	*School groundsman*
WILLIE DUCK	*Captain of cricket*
OBERON FAIRY	*School pervert*
BUSTER JAWS	*School boxing champion*
MURRAY MINT	*Pupil, St Abra Cadabra*
JIM LADD	*Sports master*
AARON A. G. STRING	*Lead violin – school band*

St Abra Cadabra Preparatory School was named after the venerated son of Hilary of Poitiers. It was an upmarket stepping stone for young gentlemen aged six, not because the name conjured up expectations of learning, but because it was conveniently close to the Vere home.

Boys boarded for three terms a year, with a week's holiday for half-term breaks. There was no escape from the tightly regimented schedule. All activities followed the same timetable day after day, week after week. The boys even washed their feet each night at 7:30 p.m. in strict alphabetical order, and the whole procedure ground to a halt if anyone was out of turn.

All new boys were 'debagged' at St Abra no sooner than their parents had said 'goodbye' – a word that conjured up a finality. The boys would be seized by gangs of older boys, pushed to the ground, and held by their legs and arms. Their shorts were pulled down, their private parts exposed, and each member of the gang laughed mercilessly while they pulled, poked, and prodded. Then, one of them would throw the boy's underpants into a hedge or up a tree before running away. The new boy, on his first day of school, was left terrified, clutching his bruised little penis and blubbing in terror.

There were horrible moments throughout Percy's preparatory schooling, and he handled the worst moments as best he could. Foster Child, a boy who found it difficult to make friends and spent most of his time alone, was found underwater in the shallows of the lake. He was discovered by chance, lying face down in the mud by Ferdi Liser, the kindly school groundsman. Ferdi picked him up by his ankles and shook him upside-down back to life. He then headed to sick bay, shouting, 'Mercy!'

Mercy Lord was the matron, newly arrived from New Zealand. It was Mercy who pumped Foster's stomach and dragged him back into the land of the living that he was clearly trying to leave.

The story of Foster being saved became exaggerated.

"When Matron started to pump Foster's stomach, a fish came out with the dirty water."

Ferdi told everyone, including the school plumber, Lou Plunger. Lou took this as an opportunity to visit the sick bay, pretending concern for Foster, but Lou had been touching Matron's rounded buttocks at every opportunity. She had hardly objected after realising there were no other likely candidates. She actually seemed flattered, answering, "Oh, Mr Plunger, you are a one!"

Foster Child shared details of Lou's visits to sick bay. These gave him a status with his classmates. It also confirmed that live-in staff at boarding schools couldn't get enough of whatever Matron was hiding in the examination room.

"Shall we try swapping positions tonight?" Lou Plunger whispered as Matron prepared Foster's medicine.

Foster also reported that Lou had arrived in the middle of the night and started bashing on Matron's door.

"Let me in!" he whispered as loudly as he dared.

"She wouldn't open it," Foster said excitedly. "Then Mr Plunger started shouting.

'Since I first laid eyes on you, Mercy, I've wanted to love you as badly as anything,' he pleaded.

'Jumping on my back when I was asleep wasn't making love,' she responded from behind the locked door. 'Now fuck off back to your workshop!'

After he was released from sick bay, Foster went to the workshop to thank Lou Plunger for visiting him. On the door was a sign, ANYTHING REPAIRED. Pinned to it was a note, 'The buzzer is broken. Please knock.'

Foster Child remained a loner during his time at St Abra, so much so that when he didn't return after half-term the following year, no one noticed.

For the boys, communication with the world outside was limited to Saturday mornings when they all were herded into classroom 4A to write to their parents.

A teacher arrived and quelled the usual Saturday pandemonium and then stood by a table at the front. "Good morning, boys," he started.

"Good morning, Sir," the boys replied politely, waiting for him to sit. On the occasions they had loosened his chair leg or put a rubber spider under the papers on his desk, they suppressed laughter until the chair creaked a warning and there was a grappling for the master to regain balance. Then the rubber tarantula would be revealed, and the boys dissolved into hysterics.

"Vere, get me another chair from 4B, and on your way out, be good enough to remove your spider."

"But, Sir, I am scared of spiders with eight legs!"

"Vere, all spiders have eight legs."

"I know, Sir, that's why I'm scared of them."

The mandatory messages to their parents all began 'Dear Mummy and Daddy', then everyone got stuck, chewed their pencils, and stared at the ceiling, trying to think of something to write.

Percy Vere quickly accepted it was no good pleading by post to be released from all this. Each of the letters would be scrutinised by Dragonara Slasher, the headmaster's wife. She was appropriately referred to as the 'Dragon'. Whoever complained about the food, the perversity of the teachers, or any other indelicacy would have to spend Saturday afternoon rewriting a more acceptable appraisal of conditions.

Percy sat next to Miles Long. Percy had noticed him on their first morning at St Abra because the wool overcoat he was wearing was different from all the others. It had a little fur collar.

"There's some animal stuck on your coat!" Percy ventured, as if it were there by some accident.

"It's a mink," Miles replied in a tone that implied everyone should have one.

"What's a mink?" asked Percy.

"A mink is the collar of a coat made by Balmain of Paris, silly," replied Miles. "Don't you know anything?"

With that initial exchange, Percy and Miles became friends. Percy listened to Miles because Miles had an air of authority about him, not diminished by the fur collar on his coat and the red and blue striped school tie made out of silk. Everyone else's was made of common wool.

Miles was a stickler for accuracy, and he punctuated each session of letter writing with a string of spelling requests. 'Excuse me, Sir?' he asked.

"Yes, Long, what is it?"

"How do you spell 'prune,' Sir?"

The whole class sniggered.

Miles sometimes put up his hand to ask questions solely to ensure that he was perceived as their leader.

"Excuse me, Sir. Have you heard about the cross-eyed teacher who couldn't control his pupils?"

The response was automatic. "An hour's detention after class, Long."

"But, Sir," Miles protested as if surprised.

Miles was never scared of detention or anything else, for that matter.

"Sir?" he continued.

"Yes, Long. What is it now?"

"How do you turn a cat into a dog, Sir?"

"I'm sure the rest of the class will be fascinated to hear."

"You pour petrol up its bottom and light it, Sir. Then it goes 'WOOF!"

Percy and Miles spent many Saturday afternoons in detention, being lectured that their parents were not interested in how regularly they were punished. There was to be no mention that the lean and loathsome headmaster, Daley Slasher, pulled their shorts and underpants down around their ankles. Parents wanted to know how perfectly they were doing in class and at games.

Incoming letters and comics for a few lucky pupils arrived in the post and were distributed at breakfast. Percy assumed that he did not get any mail because his parents found letter-writing as tricky as he did. Miles Long, on the other hand, received comics in a foreign language and magazines protected in round cardboard sausages. On top of that, he got long letters on thick parchment in crested envelopes bearing foreign stamps. He used the stamps to bargain for sweets.

* * * * *

Miles Long was a year older than Percy and, as far as Percy could see, he lived the good life in Switzerland. Whatever was in the Swiss air meant he was always busy during his holiday breaks. He learned to ride, went shooting pheasants, and sailed a catamaran. At Christmas, he went skiing and even bobsledding. Miles attended various weekend parties with the children of castle owners in central Europe. He already spoke three languages while everyone else was having trouble with the eight words that kept cropping up in French lessons.

Percy's holidays were, by comparison, spent in the relative boredom of Oxfordshire. The Veres did not have parties, and Percy was left to find his own entertainment. His favourite days were scavenging around the country lanes and delivering anything he saw to the shoe repair shop. The cobbler had a front window full of unwanted rubbish for a penny. There was a sign where the cobbler had written:

WE EXCHANGE ANYTHING. WHY NOT BRING YOUR WIFE AND GET A BARGAIN

It was almost as good as the sign in the field behind their house, where Percy wiled away hours teasing the bull. On the gate, it said:

THE FARMER ALLOWS WALKERS TO CROSS THE FIELD FOR FREE, BUT THE BULL CHARGES

Percy liked signs.

Percy's holiday situation was undoubtedly better than the unfortunate Stu Poore, whose parents were far away in the foreign diplomatic service. Stu spent his holidays with an elderly aunt in the highlands of Scotland. He returned to St Abra at the beginning of each term, shivering with a cold and with a terrible fear of the torturous term ahead. He was fat and always spent the first week in sickbay, snivelling and crying. He was afraid to come back to class because his weight made him a legitimate target for ridicule.

Stu's finest moment was on the first day of his second autumn term at the assembly. He had arrived from the *Flying Scotsman* and by taxi from King's Cross. During the hymn, his stomach was gripped in a terrible contortion of fear in anticipation of the bullying, and as the whole school sang 'Amen', his mouth opened, and he jettisoned his British Rail egg, bacon, and sausage – now a mixed grill – over the backs of the boys in front of him.

Stu stayed in sick bay for his usual week, and then he feigned a headache to get a few more days of isolation.

* * * * *

Bullying was a traditional school activity and part of the process of developing individualism and initiative. Percy was slightly built and small for his age. He hated being tackled mercilessly on the football field and beaten up behind the dustbins. He quickly learnt that it was better to stay beaten up and not say anything. Someone told him it was good training for prison. So Percy hid his misery and walked around inquiringly, as if an answer to being bullied would appear on the noticeboard.

A bashing-up did not have to be provoked. It just arrived. Having a big nose or just pale skin was reason enough to be left out of any gang and plagued by the day-to-day horrors of being strip-searched for pocket money or sweets or having a stinging nettle prodded up the leg of your shorts. The worst was being tied naked to a goalpost on the playing fields just as it was getting dark. The teachers would rarely intervene. They perceived grouping into gangs as a collective initiative.

Unfortunately for Percy, no one wanted him in their gang, and he would regularly be cornered. He would first try to talk his way out of the situation, and receiving only a punch in the cheek was a good result.

Percy's Sundays were, therefore, mostly spent inside a particularly thick holly tree or lying flat on the carpentry shed roof. He watched everyone else creeping around corners and leaping out of hedges until close to 6:00 p.m., when he slipped into the safety of the main building.

Mercy Lord had been credited with saving Foster Child, and she was needed for a second time when Foster fell out of the copper beech tree and broke his leg.

Matron took Foster to the local hospital in her little red car. Percy avoided making this trip for a long time until, one Sunday, he was spotted looking over the edge of the carpentry shed roof. The war-like shrieks of the horrible Isaac Hunt gang made him leap down onto the ground. He ran through the trees and into the back corner of the bicycle shed a hundred yards away. He pressed himself into a small ball against the corrugated metal sheets. Cries of 'Search and kill!' rang out. Percy peeked through the gaps in the metal to see the gang fan out, poking sticks into the bushes and hedges. As they came closer, he felt his heart vibrating against the sheets of tin.

"He could be in there!" he heard from a voice far too close, and he jumped out in panic, flew up the driveway, and dived down a passage leading to the safety of the kitchen door. As he rounded the last corner, there stood the grinning red-haired Isaac Hunt, who smashed a tin dustbin lid into his face.

Matron squeezed herself into her car and dropped Percy off in the long casualty queue at the hospital.

"Call me and reverse the charges when you're finished," she ordered before disappearing.

Percy was seen relatively quickly, and with six stitches across his eyebrow, he was told he could go home.

"Couldn't I stay in here for a week or so?" he enquired.

Percy didn't phone. He was free and started to walk the two miles back to St Abra, smiling proudly at passers-by who noticed the yellow iodine-stained bandage around his head.

"That looks nasty!" frowned the road-sweeper.

"They say I'll live!" replied Percy, puffing out his chest.

Closer to St Abra, Percy found a rubbish dump filled with odds and ends, and he stopped to rummage around. There were old wheels, springs, cans, and all manner of cast-off toys. He wanted to stay to hunt for something interesting, but it was getting dark. He needed to get back for supper.

Every teacher in each classroom asked Percy the next day about his injury, but Percy never mentioned Isaac Hunt's name. Isaac respected that, and so it was that Percy learned the value of favours, particularly the value of being owed a favour by the most significant and meanest person around.

With Isaac onside, Percy's years at St Abra went by with less aggravation. He became interested in playing games like Monopoly and chess, and he started painting in watercolours. In between, he climbed trees and made things in the carpentry shed.

At the age of ten, Percy and Miles were finishing making model animals in a Nativity scene as Christmas presents for their parents when Percy mentioned all the bits and pieces he had seen in the rubbish tip.

"There were prams, bed frames, bits of cars, and a whole lot of old radios," said Percy as he accidentally cut the tail off his donkey.

Miles was interested to see the rubbish tip for himself, so the two of them sneaked out the following Sunday to have a good look. The upshot was they came back with several lengths of rope, a bicycle frame, and some pram wheels.

"What are you going to do with these?" Percy had asked as they hid them under the hedge.

"Next Sunday, we need a car seat and a steering wheel," answered Miles. "We're going into business!"

'We need an expert,' Percy thought, so he suggested to Miles that they ask the carpentry master to help.

"Oh yes!" Miles said. "And how are you going to explain all the stuff we've stolen?"

"Stolen?" asked Percy.

"Well, it's not ours, is it?"

"Let's put it all in the bicycle shed and tell him we don't know where it came from?"

The carpentry master wasn't interested in asking questions, so they set about using their spare time to complete a go-kart. The unveiling was a world-class affair, with every boy staring in wonder as it zoomed down the sloped lawn. It had a chair seat screwed to the frame with a rope attached to the ends of a pram axle for steering. Miles went first on a test run down to the lake, and after an hour of runs, even when it tipped over, it hadn't fallen apart.

Isaac Hunt saw the potential and started charging a penny a time to ride down the hill with the order to pull the go-kart back up the slope after each run. Then he thought up the first leasing transaction at St Abra for a half-day Sunday rental for three pence and a Mars Bar.

There were numerous crashes, and sometimes a wheel would come off, or the seat would dislodge, but they stole back to the tip as necessary to find spare parts. All was fine until Percy and Miles were caught out of bounds. They were told that dire consequences would follow if it happened again.

The word 'expulsion' was designed to conjure up permanent rejection from society. The threat of it caused a nasty sinking feeling in the stomach and groin.

These were the same symptoms that accompanied the ritual presentation to parents of the school report at the end of each term.

* * * * *

The Vere parents only once got close to receiving a good report about Percy. It was the last day of the summer term, with Percy aged eleven, and all the boys had been collected. Percy was sitting alone on a bench outside the front door, waiting for Mrs Vere and Molly Coddle.

The boys always referred to the headmaster as 'Slasher', and 'Slasher' usually hovered to greet the parents in turn with his half-attractive twenty-five-year-old daughter Rosie at his side. Rosie had all the reports in alphabetical order, and as the boys' trunks were loaded in turn into the cars, she handed them out to the proud parents.

Slasher became exasperated as his last pupil sat looking up the drive with Rosie holding the lone report.

"It's teatime!" he tutted, thrusting the envelope at Percy.

Percy picked at the glued flap. He could feel the abrasive words trying to get out. Ten minutes later, he had found a similar envelope in the master's standard room and was back on another bench halfway up the drive.

He opened his report and scanned the list of subjects. Phrases like 'Does not concentrate' and 'Could do better' predominated.

There was only one thing for it. Percy took out his fountain pen.

Algebra was first with 'Does not have a grasp of his subject'. He added 'Good'.

Against Art, he wrote 'V. good'.

His additions looked like Sonny Liston attempting needlework.

Percy read the headmaster's final comment, 'If Percy absconds from the boundaries of St Abra once more, we regret that we shall be forced to consider expulsion.'

Percy could guess what 'abscond' meant. He carefully folded the report along the same fold marks and put it in the new envelope. Half an hour later, Mrs Vere and Molly drove up the drive.

Percy panicked. He quickly put both envelopes in his satchel and ran towards the car.

"Hello, Percy," beamed Molly.

"Have you got your report?" enquired Mrs Vere.

"Slasher says he's going to put it in the post," groaned Percy.

"You mean, 'Mr Slasher'," corrected Mrs Vere, grinding the gears.

After arriving home, Percy copied 'Master Percy Vere' in spider-like capitals onto the new envelope. He looked at his handiwork. Somehow, it didn't look right. Percy then lost his bottle, took the matches from the kitchen, and lit up his report together with the two envelopes in the middle of the lower field. Miraculously, Mrs Vere forgot about it, his father was too busy to think about it, and that was the last Percy heard about it. More importantly, he now knew how to get out of St Abra permanently. If things got too bad, all he had to do was jump over the boundary fence or even walk out of the gate.

* * * * *

Time at St Abra was less scary in the summer because so much more time was spent outside. There was the notable exception of Wednesday afternoons, which were set aside for cricket-net practice.

The cricket nets at St Abra were chain-linked fenced alleys, and there was no way out. The bowlers lined up in turn in the full knowledge that this was a licence to kill. Percy was not keen on cricket, and it was a nightmare to be called into the nets. To survive net practice without severe bruising was unusual. The opening bowler in the school's First XI was Willy Duck. Percy used to watch in disbelief as Scottish Willy walked back fifty yards and turned for a run-up. As Willy gathered speed and unleashed the leather ball, Percy would drop the bat and leap back against the wire. There followed a sharp 'thwack' as the ball hit the back-netting.

If Percy pleaded, 'Please do a slow one, there always followed a ball that was even more vicious than the last. After pounding down the runway, Willy's left spiked shoe would be level with his waist before his arm hurled the ball deliberately at head height.

Willy sometimes even hit the wooden stumps, which clattered wildly on their steel springs.

'Bliss,' thought Percy, as he used this as a signal that he was finished and had dropped the bat.

"Not yet, Vere, three minutes to go!" shouted the Latin master, whose only connection to cricket was that he had a round head.

"But, Sir!" Percy exclaimed.

Willy smirked with pleasure and bowled directly at Percy. Then, after practise, Willy challenged Percy to arm wrestling. Percy didn't stand a chance, and Willy crushed his arm onto the table-top.

"There you go, Spazzo' he shouted for all to hear.

The nickname 'Spazzo' continued because Percy took every opportunity to join the cissies playing French cricket beside the nets.

Even though Percy played cricket deliberately unnoticed, he was listed to play in the Second XI as the last batsman. This was just before the inter-preparatory school match against the neighbouring William Pitt School for Young Gentlemen.

In that game, Percy was daydreaming in his usual position by the boundary, when suddenly everyone was shouting 'Spazzo!. Percy put up his hand as if to say, 'Here, Sir, and the cricket ball landed as a full toss with accompanying internal haemorrhaging of his hand. This brilliant piece of fielding sparked a disaster. Percy was awarded his Second XI colours and promoted to the First XI for an away match against Caldicott School, and parents were to be invited.

Mrs Vere and Molly knew more about nuclear physics than about cricket, and the scoreboard might just as well have been in Arabic.

While his side batted, Percy tried to explain the game to his mother with the proverbial, 'while one side is in, the side that is out tries to get out the side that is in, so then their side comes in, and the other side would then be out'. Mrs Vere hitched up the waistband of her skirt and said she understood.

Percy then carried on to the critical matter of how empty his tuckbox was, and he took little notice of the game. He would never be called to bat at number eleven.

"Vere, pad up!" shouted the Latin master.

Percy looked up in disbelief at the scoreboard: 33 runs for eight wickets. He ran over to the pavilion to get ready and looked over at the game. He stopped dead in his tracks. Caldicott had an even bigger version of Willy Duck with all flailing arms and legs as he stormed up to the crease. It was a miracle that St Abra had got even 33 runs.

Percy grabbed hold of the Latin master's trousers. "Sir, Sir, can't we declare now?"

"Just put on the pads," came the reply. "You'll be needing them!"

A great cheer went up from the Caldicott crowd as the next wicket fell, and Percy found himself being pushed out onto the pitch. Willy Duck was out, and despite being hit three times by high-bouncing balls, he had scored most of the runs and was clapped as he hobbled off. Mrs Vere and Molly joined in enthusiastically, thinking the applause was for Percy going in.

Percy paused to get the dubious protection of rubber-backed batting gloves from Willy. Willy peeled them off slowly and fumed in his Scottish accent, "Dinna worrie, Spazzo, wheel get them afterwards!"

Percy couldn't believe it. Willy had actually spoken to him. He flushed with pride.

"Middle and leg, please," he squeaked in terror.

The umpire's finger went up, and Percy made a deliberate mark on the turf. He looked up.

"Crumbs!" he muttered as the lunatic bowler was walking so far back that, for one blissful second, Percy thought he was leaving the game.

Percy watched, dazzled, as he thundered back and unleashed the ball, which flashed past at shoulder height. Percy was still standing in wonder as the St Abra batsman opposite was running towards him, screaming, 'Run, run Spazzo!' at the top of his voice.

As the scoreboard recorded two byes, Percy could see Molly in her bright frock on the boundary, bouncing up and down and clapping wildly. Percy noticed that many of the visitors were watching what was happening in her blouse.

Caldicott knew what was going on. There was no one left in the outfield, and silly mid-off was moved in nearly on top of Percy.

“Silly place to stand!” said Percy as he disguised his trembling by tapping nonchalantly at a worm cast with the bottom of his bat while the bowler was making his long trek and turning to run up.

Percy’s bat was halfway up its backswing when his leg stump was smashed flat. He walked back to his mother, jubilant that his life had been spared. Molly confirmed that he was terrific. Well, everyone was clapping as the game ended.

“It was nothing really,” Percy agreed modestly.

In all sports, the boys were programmed to do their best, but sometimes things went wrong. Such an incident occurred when Miles Long was participating in the javelin on Sports Day. He inadvertently flung the ancient weapon at 45 degrees to the right. All those who were paying attention held their breath as it headed in an arc towards the rows of seated parents. The javelin somehow crashed on the platform between two astonished women. Six inches either way would have killed one of them.

“Please stop screaming while they measure the distance!” Miles shouted towards the women.

Then there was the annual swimming gala, during which all the boys had to swim two lengths at the local swimming baths to gain their swimming ‘colours’. Percy always kept his eyes closed and veered to the right, so it was inevitable that he could never complete a length.

“Two widths equal a length?” he argued.

Mrs Vere wondered why everyone else swam up and down in lanes.

Before the diving competition, the headmaster announced what was to happen.

“Each diver will perform two dives,” he explained. “One from the fixed high board and one from the springboard.”

“Yeah, one into the pool and one onto the concrete!” smiled Miles.

“Detention, Long,” whispered the French master.

Slasher then asked all the competitors to stand together and tapped the microphone before calling their names to dive in turn.

None of the parents noticed Slasher’s voice rise a few tones as he watched all his boys in their swimming costumes.

Percy approached the end of the high board and looked around at the guests with their faces upturned towards him. The glory of the moment was short-lived as he allowed himself a glance downwards and felt his knees turn to jelly. It was like looking off a church roof. He’d never been so high up in his whole life, and there had been no practise on anything higher than the stone cube beside the pool they called the 'puddle' at St Abra. As Percy hesitated, an array of encouragement came from the boys below.

'Get on with it!'

'We haven't got until Christmas!'

'Come on, Spazzo!'

Percy leapt into mid-air with his eyes closed tightly and belly-flopped into the water below. There were hoots of laughter as he surfaced in panic with a searing pain across his stomach. He just managed to doggy-paddle to the side, where he hung onto the edge for a full minute until Miles leaned over the side to help him out.

"Miles, how was it?" Percy gasped urgently.

"Spazzo!" Miles smiled. "Nobody dives in sideways!"

Molly and Mrs Vere were sitting in the front row watching until Molly jumped up, ripped a towel off a passing boy, and wrapped it around Percy.

"It'll be all right, you mark my words!" she comforted him.

When the weedy Hugo First lunged into mid-air off the board, there was a hush of impending doom. He hit the water in a contortion of arms and legs, and the equally fragile Mrs First then jumped up and tripped over her own feet. She landed in a stunned heap at the side of the pool.

The lifeguard retrieved Hugo, and Slasher retrieved the unconscious Mrs First. They left the swimming baths in the same ambulance.

* * * * *

Detention was usually in the classroom next to where the teachers had their end-of-the-day cup of tea and a biscuit or slice of cake. It seemed to be the time to air complaints and problems.

"Teaching geography to 3A is a total waste of time, you know that little swine, Vere?"

The maths master would groan sympathetically.

"It's no use. He can't count, and as for multiplication, he gets as far as three times something and seizes up. It's hopeless."

"Anyway," the geography master went on. "This morning, they all had an atlas open in front of them, and I asked Vere for the capital of Australia. Do you have any idea what he came up with?"

"Moscow?" enquired the sports master.

"No, Bombay!" the geography master winced audibly. "What the hell are we going to do if he puts that on his Common Entrance paper into a famous school like Eton or Harrow?"

"He'll have to stay here another term and resit the whole thing," smiled the headmaster.

"God forbid!" all the others exclaimed in chorus.

"And look at this!" butted in the sports master as he held up a card:

THIS IS AN AUTOMATIC WASHING MACHINE. REMOVE ALL YOUR CLOTHES WHEN THE LIGHT GOES OUT

"I put that up," snapped Matron in her strongest Kiwi accent. "We have to set an example."

"And this one, too?" cringed the sports master:

AFTER TEA, TEACHERS WILL EMPTY THE TEAPOT AND STAND IT UPSIDE DOWN ON THE DRAINING BOARD

The antics of the headmaster became more intrusive in their last year at St Abra. He would cite the dangers of 'catching a cold' after the swimming period. It was an excuse for them to take off their wet costumes so he could help dry them off. Worse, he would insist on allowing the drying when he supervised evening bath times.

The boys were listed on a bath time rota. Each of them had one bath a week under the watchful eye of either Slasher, his daughter Rosie, or Matron. Whoever was supervising sat on a stool beside the tub, presumably to stop anyone from drowning.

Sweets often changed hands to swap bath times to avoid Slasher. Four sweets would secure bath time with the docile Mercy Lord, and a Mars bar would buy five minutes naked in front of Rosie. The oldest and bravest would stand up in the bath water, eager for her hands to soap them down. She would not be persuaded even by enticements like, 'Your father does it like this, Miss Slasher.'

As the years went by, Miles Long lived up to his name, and whenever his turn came, the headmaster would roll up his sleeves and grab the Lifebuoy with glee. But Miles was less timid than the rest, and he swore to stop the older man's pranks.

So it was that his dormitory devised a plan for Miles to 'masturbate' in the soapy water when Rosie was next on duty.

"It's a spiffing idea!" joined in Percy, anxiously avoiding admitting that he didn't know what 'masturbate' meant, except it might mean everyone speaking at the same time in debating.

It was inevitable that Rosie Slasher would report back to her father, and Miles would be summoned. Thus, the plan was that Miles would confront Slasher and tell him that his daughter didn't know how to wash the boys properly. It was to cost everyone in the dormitory a whole week's worth of sweets in advance.

'Brainy' Leaks, the school swot, commented that he didn't think that it was such a big deal because Byron did it with his nanny when he was only nine, and Onassis played with his chambermaid at the age of ten. Genghis Khan was doing it with everything that had breasts before he was Miles's age.

Brainy was showered with pillows.

When the fateful moment came with Rosie on duty eight days later, all the dormitories were buzzing with excitement. Miles was given a hero's send-off with Matron in charge of the foot baths that evening. She couldn't work out why so many boys were packed in the one dormitory nearest the bathroom.

Miles came back grinning from ear to ear to a hail of, 'Tell us what happened', 'Did she touch it?', and 'Did you give it one?'

Miles' version was that he had stood up in the bath and washed it energetically, but the drama of the occasion had done him in, and the blood had gone the wrong way. He had blushed, and their great hope had remained miserably lifeless.

There followed a chorus of, 'Give us our sweets back!'

Percy was too scared to even talk about it, but he was jealous of Miles for his balls. Percy had to content himself with his own secret sex life.

Late in the summer afternoons, Rosie, often with her girlfriends, all of whom had better bodies than faces, used to swim in the 'puddle' which was encircled by a thick hedge. Percy found a hiding place in the middle of the hedge from where he could spy out between the leaves and soak up the vision of clinging swimsuits containing forbidden fruits. Percy did not know what the fruits were, but he knew that when he grew up, he would be a swimsuit salesman.

Percy was never caught peeking from the hedge. Still, he was punished for a variety of other mischief, ranging from crossing the public road to the playing fields unsupervised to defacing textbooks and carving his initials PV on various wood surfaces.

"That was pretty stupid!" Miles told him. "You must sign SPAZZO so it's there forever and everyone knows it's you without you announcing it to Slasher!"

Percy had become quite used to the cane, so what was one more whacking? Anyway, Percy was careful to avoid the venomous six of the best from the French teacher who blamed the English for invading his country at 100-year intervals.

"Does that include Normandy?" Miles asked.

That made the French teacher order Miles to stand in the corner facing the wall for thirty minutes.

"Don't look round, Long!" he was ordered every time he glanced back. "Or there will be more detention."

Percy always wondered why there was a preamble to a beating from Slasher. Shorts and underpants had to be lowered to the ankles, and the toes had to be touched. Slasher must have found a glimpse of young buttocks irresistible, as he would prepare himself with a light stroking of the cane on bare buttocks for a few minutes, and then he would line himself up. It couldn't be called a punishment because there was a long cuddle afterwards with Slasher running his bony hands up and down his legs.

"I'm going to be late for prep!" blurted out Percy as he tried to pull up his shorts.

Percy noticed a big blue vein used to appear in the headmaster's neck.

Miles had taught Percy how a regular bathing of his behind in methylated spirit hardened the skin, and a caning was therefore infinitely preferable to the alternative of being shut for an hour in the tiny cupboard under the sink on the landing. The screaming and bashing of the wretched offender trying to get out echoed through all the dormitories at night. Percy couldn't stand it and held a pillow over his head to shut out the fearful sound.

Miles Long had a younger brother, Fairley Long, who suffered this awful brutality. After twenty minutes of listening to his brother's muffled screams, Miles jumped out of bed and disappeared down the corridor, only to be met by Slasher coming out of the master's standard room. Miles lunged at him and grabbed his tie in a fit of rage. The next second, Miles was knocked flat by a rabid Slasher and suffered twenty-four strokes of the cane. Miles was taken back semi-conscious to the dormitory, his backside and thighs slashed red and purple. Percy could do nothing to help him and hid under his bedclothes, grateful for the small mercy of attractive buttocks.

Unfortunately for Percy, that slight advantage was also seized upon by Oberon, a fairy, one of the older boys. He told Percy that terrible things would happen unless he met him one night in the gymnasium. Oberon was tall and gangly and topped with a shock of red curly hair, which looked like a bunch of bedsprings. When his weapon sprang out of his pyjamas, Percy was scared to death.

"Touch it!" Oberon ordered.

"Cripes!" Percy blurted out, backing up against the wall bars in terror until Oberon smashed him over the head with a plimsoll. Then, Percy started to scream so loudly that Oberon, the Fairy, thought someone in the distant buildings might hear him, and he ran off.

As for Miles, he saw the folly of making a stand against a teacher, and on the next occasion Fairley was beaten, he took the cactus from the telephone table in the masters' common-room and put it under the blanket in the dog basket in Slasher's study. The squeals from Slasher's dog were no worse than his brother's.

Miles was never identified for that, and the following weekend, he was allowed to go by taxi to a cousin's wedding in London. When he arrived back that same evening in the same cab, everyone in the dormitory wanted to know what London was like.

"We got lost, we arrived late, and the church was already full," Miles admitted. "I stood at the back and only realised it was the wrong church when they brought in the coffin. Anyway, I came straight back."

Miles blamed the taxi driver.

"He shouldn't have been a taxi driver in the first place," he explained. "He said he lost his left hand in the War, and he steered with a plastic stump while he used his good hand to scratch himself. I think he had crabs!"

* * * * *

There was no comfort to be had at St Abra apart from the occasional visits to the voluptuous Mercy Lord. Mercy had been moved from sleeping next to the treatment room to her own bedroom on the same floor as the dormitories. The occasional boy ran to her after a bad dream, and even a fake nightmare. A hug from Mercy in her dressing gown or even her nightdress was Percy's first risk v reward choice. There was always a chance that fumbling in a cuddle would allow one of her beautiful breasts to slip out just like Molly.

"There's probably milk in those, Spazzo," Miles remarked knowingly.

"So?!" asked Percy as he and Miles stole a round file from the carpentry shed to enlarge the ancient keyhole of Mercy's door for a better view. It took weeks of sporadic filing on the way past her door to make it possible to watch her getting undressed. During that time, Percy had a recurrent nightmare of the heavy door lock dropping onto the floor. He'd been caught peering through the keyhole, and Slasher would then beat him to death.

At the age of twelve, Miles was moving on. He seemed to get ill in the early morning. He would start groaning and then sneak out of bed and knock on Matron's door. His visits became more frequent and lasted longer. Percy thought Matron was a wizard at curing all manner of complaints because Miles always returned to the dormitory without any side effects and was happy.

"What are you up to with Matron?" Percy whispered one Sunday evening over a game of draughts in 4C.

"Mind your own beeswax!" Miles replied.

"Something is going on," Percy insisted as he failed to spot taking two of Miles's pieces in one go.

"Forget it!" shouted Miles suddenly as he jumped up and threw the board off the table.

"Blimey!" started Percy as the pieces scattered over the floor. "Sorry, I asked!"

Miles walked out of the side door onto the terrace outside and sat on a bench in the fading light. Percy followed him, taking care to close the door quietly.

"Matron's leaving at the end of this term," Miles started in a pained voice as Percy sat beside him.

"So, we'll have a change of breasts," Percy consoled him.

"It's not like that, Spazzo. I'm in love with her!" Miles confessed.

Percy was so surprised that he couldn't think of anything to say.

"She loves me too," added Miles. "She touches me all over and lets me touch her."

"Good grief!" Percy started. "You mean she touches 'it', and you touch her umm ….?"

"I mean, she lets me get into bed with her, and we touch each other, Percy," Miles whispered. "It's called love, and I know that because when I get into bed with my nanny at home, she says, 'You know I love you!'"

Percy couldn't reply because something was stuck in his throat, and he was jealous that he had not progressed to that level with Molly.

"You've got to stop asking me about Matron!" Miles accused Percy after the Wednesday football.

"I'm not asking to join in!" Percy replied in astonishment.

"Two's company, Percy!" Miles said sharply as he pushed Percy into a bush.

Percy made a mental note to make himself first in the queue when the next matron arrived, and that opportunity presented itself rather sooner than he anticipated.

Stu Poore got a fever in the middle of the night. As his temperature rose and he started crying out, no one in the dormitory would let him go to Matron because Miles was in there. In the morning, Stu Poore was nearly dead from German measles, and he inadvertently started talking in his sleep and shouted for anyone to hear that Matron was doing something with Miles. The Latin master happened to have dozed off on the sofa in the standard room and was woken.

Matron walked out that afternoon rather than face an enquiry, and Miles was never questioned.

The new matron arrived two days later. At first glance, Miles said she resembled a mediaeval battle-axe. In the evening, Miles took the opportunity to spy through the enlarged keyhole and came back smiling.

"You know, Percy, I think I prefer the fuller figure!"

Miles admitted he had seen her bend over to put on her slippers.

* * * * *

Percy and Miles shared a dormitory with seven others, including the owl-like Brainy Leaks. As with most clever people, Brainy wore glasses, was at the top of his class, and anticipated every move.

"You only want me to play Monopoly so you can sneak off to the bathroom and steal my French translation!" he would complain.

"So that's where you're hiding it!" Percy laughed.

"And you only invited me to look at your silkworms because you want some of my mulberry leaves!" he added.

"Are you some mind-reader? Asked Miles.

"I see you are ill!" Brainy ventured as he looked at the ceiling.

"It's just a sore throat!" Miles replied. "Anyway, how do you know?"

"You're spending a lot of time with the new Matron!" Brainy admitted. "I'm not a mind-reader, but I have to get up in the night because I have a bladder disorder. So I see your bed is sometimes empty!"

Brainy's bed was rigged up with a rubber blanket and a buzzer so that when he wet himself, which was every night somewhere around 3:00 a.m., he and the rest of the dormitory were woken up. Buster Jaws, their dormitory captain and the school boxing champion, would be the first to react, grabbing his pillow, walking over to Brainy's bed, and smashing him over the head with it.

"Can't you piss before you go to bed, like everyone else?"

"Sorry, Buster, I can't help it!"

"Well, tie some string around it or something!"

Brainy was particularly in favour when there was a difficult Latin 'prep'.

Brainy's translation of Hannibal crossing the Alps would be passed from one desk to another when the supervising master wasn't looking. Urgent whispers of, Pass it on, and 'Don't hog it, would punctuate the silence until Brainy would get in a state to retrieve his work before it was spotted.

On the few occasions when even Brainy was stumped, the abuse was undisguised. Whispers of 'Think harder' and 'Hurry up' would intensify into 'You're useless' and 'Just you wait'. Then there was a scramble to write down anything that vaguely reflected an hour of thought.

When Percy couldn't do his 'prep', he turned his hand to work out silly ditties about characters in the library books. After reading *Wind in the Willows*, he started, 'Mole, if you start badgering me, I'm going to start feeling Ratty,' and, much more seriously, he began writing poems to Marilyn Monroe in Hollywood. She would fall in love with him just like Matron had with Miles.

One horrendous evening after 'prep', Percy had taken his place at the long dining table. As he waited for the *brown Windsor* soup to be passed down, he took his most recent verse to his darling Marilyn out of his shorts pocket and held it out of sight below the table. He started to read it to himself.

Suddenly, a shriek in C above high C tore the air.

"Vere, give that to me!" screamed Dragonara Slasher.

Percy scrunched up the bit of paper and put it into his mouth, but before he could get enough saliva together to swallow it, Dragon leaned over and grabbed him by the ear. She then pinched his cheeks on both sides like a dog and extracted the poem.

The whole dining hall held its breath as she unscrambled the paper and read it out loud:

My darling Marilyn loves me true
I stare into her eyes, so blue.
She says that I'm her only one.
She loves me more than Rock Hudson.

"Who's Marilyn?" she demanded, sneering, as the whole dining hall fell about with laughter.

"No one," stammered Percy, dazed by the speed of it all.

Dragon hauled Percy out of his chair by his hair and led him through the classrooms into the study. Percy couldn't believe that pulling his hair was so painful and screamed every time she yanked him forward.

The Dragon bent Percy over a chair and gave him six of the best with the fat cane rather than the thin, whippy one. It was the first time that Percy had been caned really hard, and even with the unusual protection of shorts, pants, and the vinegar, it hurt really badly.

"Now get back for supper!" she ordered.

As Percy stumbled back to the dining room, everyone looked up from their soup. They were obviously surprised to see him alive. Alongside the tears, Percy felt like a fighter pilot shot down on a mission, limping back to the mess at Biggin Hill for tea.

* * * * *

The financial discussions at St Abra were limited to buying sweets with the sixpence a week that went on the bill at the end of term. Percy liked the idea of making some money, and he turned to gambling as a way forward. That started off by preparing a conker soaked for three days in vinegar to prepare it for action to become a bet-earning champion. His first challenger was Murray Mint, the nine-year-old heir to a confectionery fortune. Murray wanted to win at all costs, and he was perfect for repeat bets at one penny each. Percy was up two shillings when Murray smarmed up to the Dragon and complained.

"What do you think you are doing, stealing from Murray?" Dragon snarled.

"But I won it fair and square?!" Percy replied in a panic.

Six whacks followed, with the order that 24 pence would be deducted from his pocket money for as long as it took.

The premise that it was a perfect commercial arrangement didn't fool anyone.

"Caveat emptor!" smirked Brainy.

"Carve what?" asked Percy.

"You should have known 'caveat emptor,'' Brainy explained. "It means that the person who does the robbing is always right."

"How about a punch in the cakehole?" replied Percy as Brainy fled round a corner.

To make matters worse, after his caning, Percy was walking on the drive when a large black Mercedes came careening round the corner and knocked him down.

Percy's first visitor in the hospital was Murray Mint's father, who introduced himself with a handshake. Percy shivered, fully expecting to be beaten up for taking 24 pennies off his son, but, instead, he got a bag of bullseyes, the kind which had to be looked at intermittently after sucking to see how the colour had changed. Things could have been worse. Percy was at least out of St Abra for a while.

Percy's leg was broken, and his left kneecap was split, so he spent some ten days in the hospital before he was released in a plaster cast. No one else cared that he went to the hospital or that he was injured, so he thought about the 'absconding' bit in the school report. After his cast was off, he would leave, and that would be the end of it all.

Percy borrowed two shillings from Miles for the trip. Miles always seemed to be rich. Anyway, he owed Percy the tidy amount he had gotten from the go-kart rental.

"You have to give me back two shillings and sixpence," demanded Miles. "And just in case you think you're not coming back, we have to become blood brothers, so you'll send me the money."

"Blimey, Miles, we're supposed to be friends," Percy reminded him.

"This is banking!" Miles insisted. "It has nothing to do with friendship, and if I don't get my money back by the end of term, I'll take your chessboard."

Percy agreed because he was confused, and the future could wait.

Both boys pricked their fingers with a rose-thorn until blood seeped out, and then they held their fingers together. Miles swore that he would be friends with Percy forever, and Percy promised that Miles would get back two shillings and sixpence.

"I'm not quite sure why you didn't just take my word for it," commented Percy as Miles handed over the money.

* * * * *

Percy planned to escape from St Abra after breakfast on the first Saturday after his cast was off. He thought that he might get away without being noticed until Sunday night, as Miles would put his pillow on his bed and answer his name at Sunday morning roll call.

Two weeks after he retrieved the money from inside his football boot in his locker, Percy was feeling strong enough to catch the bus that passed St Abra. Three hours later, he was home.

"That was easy!" Percy said to himself as he arrived and knocked on Molly's door.

When she appeared, tears welled up in Percy's eyes, and he started whining about hating school.

"I can't go back!" cried Percy as Molly spun him round and pushed him in the direction of the main house.

At the sound of Percy crying, Mrs Vere appeared at the bedroom window, clutching the milk bill while Commander Vere glanced up from the herbaceous border with a giant purple thistle in his hand.

"It'll all turn out for the best, you mark my words!" comforted Molly as she shoved him towards the car and bundled him into the back. The Commander drove back to St Abra without taking any notice of Percy's screams, enough to choke. The great escape ended with Mrs Vere selecting a suitable gap in the hawthorn hedge to push Percy through. Then it was up to Percy to get back into St Abra unseen.

Percy always wondered why he didn't just walk in the gate.

"Spazzo is back before he's even gone!" scoffed Miles as he saw Percy sneaking past the bicycle shed.

"Don't say anything!" Percy said to Willy Duck as he walked across the lawn.

Willy was sitting on the lawn by the cricket nets, and he jumped up with a nasty grimace. Percy looked the other way because Scottish Willy was still fuming that his parents did not get him the bicycle he wanted for his birthday. Willy had stolen one from the train station car park.

"You don't even need a bike!" Percy shouted across to him.

Percy's leg was still painful, and he was excused from both cricket and gym classes. It was bliss to watch the cricket net practice from afar, but, as it happened, Percy was quite partial to the gym.

* * * * *

The gymnasium at St Abra was a corrugated iron shed set apart from the rest of the school buildings. The windows were stuck up with paint, and the whole gym permanently gave off a musty aroma of young sweat. The gym shorts, gym vests, and plimsolls, all of which were only washed at the end of each term, were left in lockers in the changing rooms.

It was forbidden to wear underpants or vests underneath the gym kit. The muscular young sports master, Jim Ladd, was dressed in his Olympic white singlet and shorts. He was always helping with somersaults and rope climbing, but his favourite help was holding the ankles of someone trying a headstand. If he spotted underwear, the miserable culprit would have to go and take them off to afford him a better view.

There was no mercy for the fat and flabby, who had to try again and again at exercises that were too difficult for them. The overweight Stu Poore would run up to the horse to perform a vault as many times as he could until he collapsed. As far as climbing the ropes was concerned, he was only able to climb without lifting his feet, so he would hang desperately before dropping onto the thick coconut matting in a flabby heap.

Percy, when healthy, was in his element in the gym. He flew up the ropes, swung on the high bar, did handstands on the parallel bars, and performed somersaults on the floor. He thought he would make an excellent cat burglar.

* * * * *

All the boarders at St Abra had to play a musical instrument of some description in the school band. The last thing Percy was going to be was a musician, but he elected to join the string section. This proved an irrational choice as he was tone-deaf, and the violin had no frets. The brass section was by far the loudest, so Percy on the violin was drowned.

In spite of the dreadful cacophony of the whole band together with cymbals, tambourines, drums, and triangles, St Abra arranged an annual Christmas concert for the local older people's home. This event was the highlight of each musical year.

The boys hated the practising, but the occasion was always a giggle, with the most memorable being during the concert of '59. The great day arrived, and the unsuspecting older people started tottering in. For them, too, this was a highlight in the calendar and one of their few trips away from the tedium of institutional life. They all smiled enthusiastically in anticipation as they were handed the Christmas carol sheet and led hobbling to their seats.

Behind the curtain, the orchestra assembled. Miles Long played maracas at the back alongside Isaac Hunt on the kettle drum. Willy Duck was on the left with his bagpipes, and Brainy Leaks and Lou Rolls sat together at the piano. Behind the curtain on the right was Stu Poore, straight out of sick bay. He was on the triangle. In the front were the three violins, Percy, Fairley Long, and a keen musician, Aaron A.G. String.

Aaron was the first violin and the only musical talent in the school. This was the climax of his weeks of practice, and everyone had been made aware of it 100 times.

"Just follow String," the music master would advise as Aaron beamed with self-esteem.

Aaron waited in the wings for his big moment while Percy and Fairley made ready.

"I can't do it!" whispered Fairley viciously as he kicked his violin case and made no attempt to tune up.

"Cripes!" remarked Percy as he grabbed the music stand to stop it from falling over.

Fairley was not in a good state after another spell of time locked in the cupboard under the sink on the landing. He had flicked an ink pellet out of the classroom window with his ruler. Ferdi Liser, the grumpy old gardener, happened to be outside trimming the box hedge at the time, and it smacked him right in the ear. Fairley had arrived on the stage an hour in the cupboard the previous evening, and his eyes were red and swollen, and his hands shaking. Percy had used Fairley's sleeve to wipe his runny nose and helped him to adjust the height of his music stand so that it hid his face.

"Slasher will kill you if you mess up his concert!" argued Percy as he tried in vain to keep control of himself.

Isaac Hunt was warming up on the drums as if he were backing Mick Jagger with the Strolling Bones.

With everyone in position, the curtain was pulled back, and the sanctimonious Aaron A.G. String came out of the wings, smiling and bowing. There was a smattering of frail applause as bony hands tried to clap. Gurgles and hoots of laughter came from the stage as the school band unashamedly focused on the older people.

"Ma God, look at tha one orn tha left!" chortled Willy Duck.

"It's from another planet?" chuckled Miles.

"Well, it's certainly not a Pearson," replied Willy amid general sniggering.

"Don't worry," Percy observed to Fairley. "They're all wearing hearing aids!"

The music master raised his baton for silence as Aaron readied himself with the orchestra poised in concentration behind him.

The music master raised his baton, and off they went into a medley of noise. There was nothing coming from Aaron. Fairley was still fiddling, getting his instrument out of its case, and Percy was the lone violinist.

Aaron then burst into tears.

"What's the matter!?" asked Percy from the corner of his mouth as loudly as he dared.

"Shut up!" screamed Aaron above the brass section.

"And what was in those ships, all three?" murmured the geriatrics.

The music master glared and jabbed at Aaron furiously with his baton while the rest of the band carried on playing in terrible concentration without him.

Only Oberon, the Fairy, knew what was really going on. Aaron had refused to touch his 'thing' in the gym at night, so Oberon had retaliated by wiping soap on Aaron's violin bow. Oberon tittered away with his legs wrapped around a double bass at the back of the stage.

By the third verse, the geriatrics were entirely out of control. Some were already singing the second carol, 'The First Noel', while others in a group on the right had thought the tune was 'O Little Town of Bethlehem' from the very beginning. One old gentleman with an enormous hearing aid hanging on his ear was screaming 'Adeste Fideles' all by himself.

The music master ordered the curtain to come down. He then instructed that the geriatrics should be shown to their coach. As they filed out and shook his hand by the door, they all said how beautiful the music had been and how much they were looking forward to the following year.

"Assuming any of you are still alive!" added Miles.

"Detention Long!" snarled the music master.

* * * * *

The 11 Plus examination was a new form of intelligence yardstick, and Percy had no idea what any of the questions meant. St Abra had provided no preparation because they perceived the 11 Plus as a socialist measure, and their pupils were out of some higher space. Thus, this exam was a mystery for the cream of Britain's youth. Percy couldn't answer a single question.

"Never mind," he said to Miles in the end, not realising that this was a vital part of life's progress. "I'll do better in the Common Entrance. I can repeat history like a parrot."

"You idiot, Vere," the English master remonstrated when Percy handed in his blank 11 Plus paper. "If you don't know the answers, guess."

"He's perfect material for the army," concluded the Latin master.

"For those who understand, no explanation is needed," Slasher insisted. "For those who do not understand, no explanation is possible!"

"What's got into him?" muttered Miles.

The Latin master summed up the Slasher situation at the end of prep one evening. He took a swig out of a flask he had in his back pocket.

"I'd like to fling his new hairdryer things into his bath," he grimaced.

* * * * *

St Abra had built a reputation for getting young dolts into the finest public schools, and the public schools themselves were always a bit surprised about how some of the clods they received could have gotten through the entrance procedures.

Successive years of Common Entrance results at St Abra were successful because the teachers all agreed to disregard the rules. They knew that was essential for the continuity of fees and their wages. Willy Duck had the assistance of notes pinned in front of him on the back of Isaac Hunt's blazer, and as soon as Brainy had finished his first page of the Latin, it was passed around. Lou Rolls was so scared of failure that he took the appropriate textbook into each exam up his jumper. Since the papers were all going to different public schools, no one would ever notice similarities in the mistakes that were passed from desk to desk.

Percy looked openly at the papers of his friends sitting at the desks on his left and right. The supervising master at the front rarely looked up from what he was doing, and Percy relied on them all not to get up until the end.

During the French dictation, where cheating was impossible, Miles put up his hand after, 'Marcel et Denise ont reçu les paquets et les lettres'.

"Excuse me, Sir, how do you spell *reçu*?" he enquired.

"R E C U, with the accent under the C," came the immediate response.

The French master was aware that the combined IQ of his whole class was less than a hairbrush, so he ensured everyone got fantastic marks in French dictation.

Percy's history paper in his Common Entrance exam into a public school was impossible. Percy was not aware that there had been a Revolution in France; he did not know how to distinguish a Roundhead from a Cavalier, and what he knew about the American Civil War wouldn't cover the back of a postage stamp. He, therefore, elected to write his whole answer about Nelson at Trafalgar, which didn't happen to be one of the questions. It helped that Percy's father was desperately interested in the controversy surrounding Lord Nelson's private life.

'Lord Nelson couldn't keep his hands off that '*scheming trollop*, Percy wrote about Horatio's dalliance with Lady Hamilton.

Immediately after the exam finished, the history master asked Percy how his answer fitted any question.

Percy thought fast.

"Do you think that perhaps the Pope and Admiral Nelson were friends?" he asked hopefully.

The teaching staff at St Abra were amazed that Percy had scraped into both Eton, Marlborough, and Harrow with the exact overall pass mark of 55%. They helped the cause with exaggerated reports about his extracurricular activities, including being accomplished on the violin and piano.

They were excited that Percy's name would be painted in gold leaf on a shield bearing the coat of arms of whichever great school he attended. That shield would forever acknowledge that Percy had been afforded a proper education on his way to fame.

Commander Vere was convinced that Percy's success was due to the excellent teaching at St Abra, and he made the appropriate noises to Slasher on Percy's last day. The good Commander would have committed suicide from the dishonour if he had known the dreadful truth of how his son would succeed by bending the regulations. Cheating was a vital component for all St Abra's pupils to move on to a public school. This was the proud reputation that guaranteed future parents would pay good money for their precious offspring to join the bottom rung of life's merry ladder.

The headmaster put his hand on Percy's shoulder as he was handed back in the courtyard.

"You know, Commander," he groaned as Percy moved away from his grasping fingers, "we're very sorry to see the back of Percy. He's been a credit to the school!"

"Abra Cadabra indeed!" Commander Vere nodded in gratitude as he reflected on his luck at sinking the Bismarck.

Chapter Three
TRADITION

Key Witnesses:

EVERARD COCK	*Percy's Grandfather*
CHOU EN LAI	*CCP Politburo – China*
ARTHUR CONAN DOYLE	*Author and Occultist*
APOLLONIUS OF TYANA	*Greek Sage*
LORNE MOWER	*Gardener at Oak Park*
POPPY COCK	*Everard Cock's First Wife*
ANITA BOTTOM	*Everard Cock's Second Wife*
SIR DICK GOLDSMITH WHITE	*Director General – MI5*
ISAAC WOLFSON	*Marketing Guru – GUS*
ARSON BURNS	*Fire Insurance Broker*
CHARLES CLAW	*Retail Magnate – Sears Holdings*
CHARLES FORTE	*Founder – Trust Forte*
MANDY SPLICE-DAVIS	*Escort*
CHRISTINE KEEL-HAUL	*Escort*
JOHN PROFUMO	*Minister for War*
BEN LEIGH-COUPE	*Rolls-Royce Franchise Holder*
MUSTAFA M. PYRE	*Pakistani Property Developer*

Percy's grandfather, Everard Cock, had been a Classics scholar at Oxford and President of the Oxford Union. He then read Law and was called to the Bar, where he flaunted what he loved best: his ability to argue on his feet. In court, he became famous for orating so effectively that his clearly guilty clients escaped retribution. He had astonishing resources of knowledge, wit, and charm. There was no point challenging Everard because, however unpalatable it might have been, he always seemed to be right. If he ever was not, he got lucky, swaying female jurors wherever he wanted during a trial. On occasion, he would engage them in extra-judicial procedures in a hotel close to the court.

Every morning at exactly 9:00 a.m., Everard could be seen in a distinctively colourful bow tie, buying *The Times* from the same vendor on the Strand. He would then continue to his chambers in the Inner Temple. He attracted increasing press attention in front of juries, with journalists lapping it up from the public gallery. His High Court hearings were often attended by visitors enjoying his repartee and cutting wit.

Everard's career was meteoric. He moved on from representing murderers, armed robbers, and arsonists to protecting criminals in the corporate sector. These included bent industrialists and politicians exercising themselves with gay abandon. After a short ten years, unheard of at the time he took Silk, and the press followed his chauffeur at night in his tomato-coloured Rolls-Royce. The rich and famous, many of whom had unmarried daughters, made sure they paraded them as debutantes at glamorous dinner parties whenever Everard was in attendance.

The young Everard was particularly proud to be invited to become a member of the Garrick, where he entertained leading thespians of the day with conversation and fine wine.

Even as a King's Counsel, Everard's fee income was somehow insufficient for his ambition, and so he resolved to travel before embarking on a new career in business. Using his political contacts, he began attending the courts of Europe, hosted by royalty, prime ministers, and leading commercial figures. Such was his personality that he was often invited to stay, enjoying the finest guest accommodation in palaces and châteaux from Lisbon to Budapest.

It was in Paris in 1921 that he first met Chou En Lai, who had previously studied in Japan and had become a key figure in the early political reorganisation of China. In the summer of 1923, Chou invited Everard to join him in China and to meet the tall and steely Chiang Kai-shek. Chiang and Everard became friendly during that visit and, in May 1924, when Chiang Kai-shek was appointed Commandant of the Whampoa Military Academy, he persuaded Everard to return to China to assist with a new policy aimed at unifying the Chinese provinces. The objective was to bring an end to the constantly shifting warlord alliances.

While the politically adept Everard was at the Whampoa Academy, Chou En Lai emerged as a prominent communist and invited him to travel to Moscow to secure military assistance for the new movement.

This demonstration of negotiating skill in the Russian language secured Everard a valuable position as a mediator between competing factions of the Communist Party. It was an influential role for an outsider, particularly in a country that had endured half a century of foreign interference.

Everard was in his element, equally fluent in persuasion in French, Japanese, and several Chinese dialects. He became invaluable to Chiang Kai-shek when foreign warships appeared along the Yangtze River, and Chiang elevated the brilliant and manipulative Everard to unprecedented power.

By 1927, Chiang Kai-shek had gained control of the Central Government and succeeded in unifying much of central China, establishing something approaching a national administration. However, he exercised little authority in the outlying regions, where famine had killed millions during the early 1920s. Millions more, drawn to the cities in search of work, found only corruption, slave labour, and prostitution.

Workers' uprisings were inevitable, and while Everard was advising Chiang in Jiangxi Province, he witnessed the Nanchang uprising, in which newly formed communist-inspired trade unions, striking against severe repression, saw a large proportion of their members slaughtered within a week.

As a foreigner identified with the Nationalists but confronted by the growing communist movement, Everard found himself caught between opposing forces. Anticipating isolation or assassination, he sought the protection of the International Settlement in the westernised city of Shanghai. As a Japanese-speaking negotiator and a friend of senior Japanese generals, he knew their troops were protecting foreigners, particularly those considered useful.

Here, Everard Cock relished political intrigue and was invited to join the secret company of Freemasons by Roger Hollis, a young executive at British American Tobacco. Following his initiation into the Shanghai Lodge at the Masonic Hall on Avenue Road, Everard was surprised to discover that Hollis spoke Russian and knew all about his time in Moscow. Everard took to the exchange of secrets like a duck to water, making a point of passing vital intelligence to Western powers regarding Japanese intentions in a city primed for explosion.

* * * * *

Poppy Cock, Everard's wife, was a scholar and forever enlightened. She admitted to being introduced to opium during Everard's prolonged stay in China, and it was probable that opium influenced her fixation with travelling alone throughout South-East Asia. This was in the 1920s, while Everard was enmeshed in political drama, and so Poppy struck out on her own, spending long periods in meditation with religious leaders. She learned how to separate her spirit from her body and, more importantly, how to re-enter it. Astral travel became her chosen pursuit, and she could visit anyone she wished without having to use public transport.

After years on the missing list, Poppy returned to Shanghai and became pregnant by Everard on the night before she travelled alone to England.

Poppy became an acclaimed author and was best friends with the creator of *Sherlock Holmes*, Arthur Conan Doyle, and the author of *The Water-Babies*, Charles Kingsley. Both men were known to be deeply involved in the occult and gifted with unusual powers.

Poppy herself adopted the role of spirit medium and wrote twelve books, each presented as an exact account of her previous lives. Sceptics questioned how she could describe, in such detail, the drowning of a young boy in Atlantis at its seismic end, or her life as a virginal temple attendant to the Pharaohs. Eminent historians were astonished by her accuracy in relating customs of eras otherwise sparsely researched. Either she had lived in those places, or she had access to an ancient library no one else had discovered.

According to Poppy, long before Egypt as we know it, a sophisticated civilisation existed at the mouth of the River Nile. Excavations revealed monumental structures predating traditional Egyptian civilisation by thousands of years.

"Take, for example, the Step Pyramid of Djoser, built around 2630 BC by Imhotep," she lectured at the British Museum. "This was the first documented pyramid, so it stands to reason that pyramids predating Djoser would have been inherited from an earlier culture. Nor can we refute that the limestone temple of Qasr el-Sagha dates back as far as five thousand years before Djoser's pyramid. Similarly, the outer granite layer of the Small Pyramid of Mycerinus dates from around 4000 BC. We do not know the identity of the builders, but we are forced to recognise that the Egyptians we read about did not start from scratch. They were copying architectural and engineering capabilities that were far older and integrating them into their own civilisation."

Conan Doyle and Poppy Cock were immersed in the occult, and both believed that a cataclysmic event had been experienced by a lost civilisation. Moreover, they perceived evidence of precise technology, interplanetary influence, and even extraterrestrial connection on Planet Earth. The idea that hunter-gatherers represented the starting point of human life struck them as preposterous.

Some of Poppy's more remarkable manuscripts purported to have been produced under the direct inspiration of Apollonius of Tyana, a Greek sage, religious leader, and contemporary of Christ. Apollonius lived to more than one hundred years of age and was honoured as one of the greatest philosophers of his time, with access to ancient knowledge.

* * * * *

As Chiang announced his new 'Republic of China' from Taiwan, Everard Cock set sail for London. He had the ship's hold packed with looted treasures, which eventually found their way to Oak Park, a vast estate he acquired as his base in the wooded expanse of Burnham Beeches.

Everard's return to England coincided with an unprecedented recession that culminated in the summer of 1932, when he met the thirty-two-year-old Isaac Wolfson. Isaac was a hard-nosed Jewish shark and merchandise controller of Great Universal Stores, known as GUS. The business, already floated on the Stock Exchange by Cazenove, operated through mail order and retail.

Isaac Wolfson engaged Everard Cock to assist in manipulating a controlling interest in GUS. Everard was every bit as cunning as Isaac, and together they devised a scheme that would ultimately rock the company.

In January 1933, a series of mysterious warehouse fires at GUS premises resulted in insurance settlements totalling around a quarter of a million pounds. These payouts were followed, in February, by the fire insurance assessor Arson Burns being sent to prison for fraud.

Everard informed Bud Rose, the eldest of the three brothers who had founded and owned GUS, that his youngest brother had been implicated in starting the fires. Bud Rose burst a blood vessel from the shock and humiliation and was persuaded to sell his thirty-five per cent stake cheaply to Isaac Wolfson. This allowed Wolfson to seize control of the board and remove all three Rose brothers as directors. With Arson Burns and his co-conspirators safely imprisoned, and the Rose brothers too frightened to speak out, Wolfson began reorganising the group.

His first move was to issue new GUS shares as payment for hundreds of retail units acquired cheaply in the depressed economic climate of the 1930s.

Secondly, as if to atone for his sins, Isaac Wolfson established the Wolfson Foundation, endowing it with six million GUS shares he had previously issued to himself, an act that cost him nothing but appeared generous. He then awarded himself a bonus and donated a further five million pounds' worth of shares, again at no personal cost, to the Weizmann Institute in Rehovot in a widely publicised gesture of humility. His reward was a plot for permanent retirement.

"One only develops a conscience when one is being watched," observed Everard.

There were no consumer watchdogs in the 1930s. Business regulation extended little beyond stamping letters, and if one asked what a watchdog was, a finger might point to the friendly Labrador outside the Post Office. A new breed of entrepreneur recognised that everything and everyone was for sale.

In the years leading up to, and during, the Second World War, Everard Cock embarked on a campaign of property accumulation alongside figures such as Charles Claw, the moody property and finance genius behind Sears Holdings, and Charles Forte, a milk-bar proprietor turned founder of Trust Forte Hotels. Forte's claim to fame included the customary act of penance in creating the Forte Israeli Foundation, followed by the purchase of a seven-thousand-acre estate in Surrey. The vendor later complained too late that the sale did not include seven Old Master paintings acquired quietly over a decade at Sotheby's. The paintings were promptly resold, effectively delivering the land free, with change to spare.

Charles Claw then developed a taste for indulgence and paid £800 for the Prince of Wales Theatre so he could pursue two sisters in the chorus line. Claw, Forte, and Cock each built property empires driven by egotism, entitlement, and ruthless ambition. In ordinary men, such traits would have been unacceptable, but business rivals appeared anaesthetised. Those unable to keep pace or who made mistakes were left wounded, or worse, in their wake.

The three entrepreneurs offered no apology for their conduct, merely observing that the only way to avoid bloodshed in business was not to enter the fray in the first place.

* * * * *

Charles Claw led the post-war open season on struggling retailers, and Sears Holdings swept up such jewels as Mappin & Webb, Garrard, the Queen's jewellers, and the prestigious Selfridges. At the same time, the Cock empire accumulated a row of freeholds in Fleet Street, seventeen major hotels, and three of the largest residential blocks of flats in Europe. These were all held within a complex corporate structure of offshore foundations and anonymous nominee trustees. There was a pathological and irrepressible force in Everard's head that refused to allow him to follow the straight road of normal accounting procedures and annual tax returns. He ignored the basic safeguard of declaring a reasonable profit based on a vaguely plausible turnover. As a result, it became evident to the Inland Revenue that Everard was, quite deliberately, taking liberties.

Everard knew from early on that there were no safety belts on his corporate roller coaster and no way back.

"There's bound to be a warning sign giving us time to brake," he told his team of accountants.

"They don't like you," they observed, handing Everard a file of demands for tax on capital gains.

"They always have a lot to say, don't they?" he smirked, throwing the inspectors' letters into the bin.

Everard's social life became every bit as adventurous as his forays into business. His chauffeur was often seen late at night outside London clubs, where proprietors would remove other guests from Everard's favourite tables. At the Astor Club in Mayfair, he became friendly with Lieutenant Philip Mountbatten, an impoverished prince who was courting Elizabeth, the heir to the throne. Everard attended dinner parties at Number 10 Downing Street and spent weekends at Cliveden, where, after dinner, he engaged in many frolics by the pool. He charmed them all and even seduced Mandy Splice-Davis in the boathouse while her friend, Christine Keel-Haul, was extracting delicate secrets from the government minister responsible for Britain's security, John Profumo.

After Profumo had his collar felt, Everard bought a number of cottages on River Road in Taplow, on the banks of the River Thames opposite the Guards Club. These were reserved for his ladies. The arrangement ensured him a permanent weekend invitation to the Guards Club rather than Cliveden until the dust settled.

* * * * *

It was Poppy who instructed Everard not to bother with her, and it was she who told him to get on with his life, seek out pleasure on his own, and make sure Percy was safe. Although it seemed miraculous that Everard became the doting grandfather of Percy, he willingly took the cue and agreed to a divorce, allowing him to marry his new secretary, Anita Bottom. Anita always wore silk stockings and suspenders beneath a black skirt, which allowed her calves to be on display.

Anita was much younger than Everard and filthy too, like a hyena in frilly underwear. She had arrived in London at seventeen to attend secretarial school and quickly learned which side her bread was buttered on. She opened the slit in her skirt for a line-up of admirers as she made herself known to property heavyweights and newspaper barons at the Silver Slipper, the Astor, and the Flamingo, where she was often mistaken for part of the cabaret. She was introduced to Everard at tea at the Ritz and, suddenly, her long, attractive legs, tightly crossed, then crossed again, were positioned beside his desk for dictation. From time to time, her skirt hitched up and fell open, occasionally allowing Everard a glimpse of forbidden fruit. Anita was doing a great deal more dictation than typing, and Everard found himself unable to resist looking at her full, young breasts, testing the top buttons of her blouse. He developed a habit of licking his lips. This was no accident but the natural outcome of Anita's resolve to use her perfumed cleavage as bait.

Each time Everard reached forward, he was reminded that there would be no chance of manoeuvring between those succulent thighs until she had a proper ring on her finger. Anita had her own ideas about what constituted a 'proper size'.

Everard resisted as long as he could, but eventually he could not stand it any longer and grasped the nettle.

Poppy appeared unsurprised by the engagement, and Percy assumed this was because she had astral-travelled into Everard's office and watched the bitch in action.

After the formalities, Anita Cock, née Bottom, moved into Oak Park together with her beloved dachshunds. A hoard of these German sausages sprawled across the furniture and even slept on her bed. There was a consequential hoard of even smaller sausages in the corners of every room. The only sausage that did not get a look-in was confined to solitary confinement in Everard's trousers.

Everard was obliged to keep his hand busy on the tiller, so to speak, with his thrills now provided by ducking and diving in the City. He concluded that it was just as pleasurable as ducking and diving in the valley of forbidden fruit, since there was other low-hanging fruit everywhere.

* * * * *

Every Saturday morning during the school holidays, the Vere family visited Oak Park, where, each spring, the grounds became a wonderland. Percy would leave the grown-ups chatting and wander through the tens of thousands of daffodils and snowdrops sprinkled liberally beneath the oak trees lining the half-mile drive to the house. The scene was magical as the daffodils swayed in the breeze, stretching towards the orchards and woods beyond.

As spring progressed, the bushes and shrubs that had stood naked through winter suddenly began to shoot new leaves. Buds split open, creating a profusion of colour. It was a vision that stayed for a lifetime with anyone who experienced it.

The main house was painted white and appeared to have been planted on top of the hill. With its grand white pillars along the front and wings extending on either side, it looked like a transplant from New Orleans.

The typically English lawns, cut each week religiously for hundreds of years, sloped a quarter of a mile from the front of the house between lines of towering Lebanese cedars. In the open fields beyond, Arabian yearlings with legs up to their necks pranced and played.

As spring gave way to summer, the extensive walled kitchen gardens and complex of greenhouses begged to be pilfered. There were hairy gooseberries, juicy, crisp apples, and big, fat strawberries growing in long netted enclosures. Best of all were the peaches in the greenhouses, just ripe and larger than tennis balls.

Everything at Oak Park reeked of wealth and affluence. Antique Chinese furniture and substantial dusky canvases crowded every room. They echoed the grand drawing rooms of Europe, where inherited fortunes sustained generations solid, inbred, and indifferent to the fortunes of lesser beings.

Percy might easily have assumed that everyone had a fairy grandfather. The old man, with white hair brushed neatly to one side, snoozing in a favourite armchair before the French windows, was convincing. He surveyed his domain as if everything were in order.

During these school years, Percy felt no need for long-term worry. It was enough to be enveloped in the aura of this man.

One particular treat was sitting in the front passenger seat of the collection of Rolls-Royce cars during their Saturday warm-up. After the chauffeur opened the concertina garage doors at the appointed time, Everard Cock would spend five minutes in each car, with his grandson staring at the back wall. Percy listened to tales of business adventure while his senses were filled with the smell of leather, soothed by the purring engines, and reassured by the clocks ticking in perfect time.

"The quieter you become, the more you hear," Everard advised.

The stories came out like tales of the Wild West. The only difference was the technique of the Hole-in-the-Wall gang. In the films, the robber was the hero and the sheriff a sanctimonious bore wearing a silver star. If the robbers were locked up, friends in high places would rip the bars from the gaol wall with a rope. If there were to be a hanging, someone would shoot the rope just as the trapdoor opened. Everard insisted it was replicated almost exactly in his property business. Yet he also maintained that true wealth was measured in peace, not gold, as the cars idled in the garages.

Afterwards, martinis were prepared in the 'green room', so named because one had to fight through indoor trees, plants, and flowers to enter. Suitably fortified, Commander Vere would climb into his beekeeping suit and wander up to the orchard to tend his hives. They had been moved to Oak Park from the Vere home after hysterics from Mrs Vere, who was convinced the bees were under instruction to go for her throat. Percy suspected his father had taken up beekeeping partly to assist the flowers in his immaculate herbaceous border.

Percy watched, fascinated, as his father collected honeycombs and filled jars with golden nectar. While he worked in the shed, Percy would creep towards the hives to spy on the bees coming and going. Some were so laden with pollen from the abundance of flowers that they crashed-landed on their own front porch. When no bees were visible, Percy discovered the thrill of waking them by shaking the hive, guaranteeing an eruption of buzzing bodies—and a frantic run back through the orchard, glancing nervously over his shoulder to see if the bees were in pursuit.

Percy Vere's introduction to the world of finance came through digging weeds out of the lawn at one penny each. For particularly large weeds, with their roots intact, he earned tuppence. With pocket money set at sixpence a week, this was a considerable windfall. For his grandfather, it was a cheap way of safeguarding the Chinese vases on the side tables from Percy's running about. It also discouraged Percy from pestering the gardeners or bouncing dangerously alongside the 36-inch cylinder-blade Dennis mower as it swathed dark and light stripes across the lawn.

Lorne Mower, the friendly head gardener, explained that cutting the head off a weed merely ensured its return. He showed Percy how to position the fork precisely to open the soil and remove the root intact.

"That's the same in the criminal world, Master Percy," Lorne added. "That's where the phrase 'root out the problem' comes from."

Percy stored that advice away for a rainy day.

It usually took at least two stripes of pleading and picking up stray twigs before Percy was allowed to guide the mower for a single pass. Lorne would clutch his forehead as a treble S-bend appeared alongside his perfect parallels.

"Don't ever try for work at Wimbledon, Master Percy," Lorne advised as Percy ran back to the house.

From the terrace, the lawn looked glorious until Percy's hand slipped on the clutch at the end of a stripe in front of the rose garden. The mower leapt forward at full throttle before Lorne could stop it. The sharp cylinder blades scythed through the roses before crashing into the wall. Percy watched in horror as a trail of spikes marked where the bushes had stood.

"No damage done, don't you worry, Master Percy," Lorne smiled, creases spreading across his weather-beaten face.

The mower was sent away for repair, the rose bushes replaced, and no one was the wiser. The only consequence was that Percy was denied his next turn at mowing.

Percy could not believe that no one mentioned the decimation of the roses, but he learned that swift repair was preferable to confession. The rush of adrenaline, he concluded, was best headed off at the pass.

"Thank you very much, Lorne," Percy whispered later.

"You take care now, Master Percy," came the measured reply, as Lorne touched his old cloth cap.

Percy was not entirely sure why caution was required when an old gardener with thirty years' service seemed able to fix almost anything.

* * * * *

During the Fifties, at the age of ten, Percy often stayed at Oak Park and would sit with his grandfather in the great library, his favourite room in the house. There must have been a thousand books arranged in rows up to the ceiling, including rare first editions and monastic volumes decorated with vivid red and blue dyes and gold leaf. Ancient Greek and Latin tomes lay open on a massive Chinese scroll-top desk. It was here that Percy listened to stories of political intrigue and business daring, interspersed with explanations of human behaviour and degrees of misery. Everard described life as an adventurous balance of pleasure and treachery, part of an astrologically unfolding mysticism.

"Thousands of years before the history you are being taught," Everard explained, "a mysterious civilisation had detailed maps of our solar system."

There was a quiet pause as he leaned against the desk and lit a perfectly preserved twenty-year-old cigar selected from the humidor of an ancient sailing ship.

"The Sumerians created drawings on clay," he continued, "and those that have survived show the sun at the centre of the solar system, with other planets revolving around it. They accurately depict their orbits and positions."

Everard paused to light his cigar properly and took three puffs.

"Some of their paintings have also survived somehow, and they depict strange images of giant entities with symbols resembling human DNA sequences. To this day, we cannot know how, all those thousands of years ago, the oldest known civilisation possessed such profound knowledge."

Percy drank his milk.

"We can no longer call ancient peoples 'cavemen'," Everard said. "We can see with our own eyes evidence of their extraordinary achievements. They sculpted stones as hard as diorite, which ranks eight on the Mohs scale and is tougher than iron. And here we have diorite carved into a flawless twenty-five-ton statue of Pharaoh Khafre, dated to at least 2500 BC. They achieved sharp edges, smooth finishes, and near-perfect symmetry with no sign of tools. We must accept that these techniques are a mystery, lost even from a civilisation before them."

Everard opened an old book he had taken from the shelves.

"Here is a picture of the Colossi of Memnon," he explained, pointing to the page. "Two colossal statues, each weighing around 720 tons. We know the quartzite was quarried at Gebel el-Ahmar, some 420 miles from Luxor."

He paused to relight his cigar.

"Imagine, Percy," he continued. "Thousands of years ago, how would you move two boulders fifty-nine feet high? You need to understand that ancient civilisations existed with abilities we no longer possess, so that you can understand where we come from, who we are, and perhaps who we might become."

Everard took great pleasure in elaborating his explanations, examples, and ideas.

"Never dismiss the possibility of advanced civilisations out there in the stars," he concluded. "They may have visited us long ago."

He snapped the book shut and returned it to its place on the shelf.

"When you have finished your education," Everard continued, "there will be great opportunities for adventure and wealth. Do not ignore the chances that come your way, but always see how they fit into a bigger picture."

Percy was gazing up at the Matisse above the great Adam fireplace.

Everard was educated beyond most people's ability to comprehend. He believed entrepreneurs were those who possessed the wisdom to blend the Arts and the Sciences. Those who leaned too heavily towards

Art became too creative to be businesslike; those who veered too far towards Science became too clinical to lead. Balance, he insisted, was everything.

Percy's eyes followed the shelves around the room.

"How is it possible for you to know so much?" he asked. "Learning is difficult."

Everard took his hand and led him down the steps out of the library, through the French windows, and onto the lawn. A few yards away, the brick garages appeared between the trees.

"Do you see the garages?" Everard asked.

"Yes."

"Then tell me how they are built."

Percy looked around, unsure.

"Learning is like building a garage," Everard said, as a squirrel darted up one of the Lebanese cedars. "You start with the first row of bricks, which must be straight and level. Each brick takes the same effort to lay. You place them one at a time, and what you are creating gradually grows. Learning works in exactly the same way. One brick at a time and before you realise it, the building is finished."

Percy's fascination with history soon shifted towards politics. It was grounded in Everard's attitude to the Establishment. In that great library, Percy first heard that entrepreneurs were regarded as mavericks indigestible to institutions that demanded conformity. Supervision existed to suppress deviation from traditional methods that might threaten financial control. Everard had created a way to use law and politics to achieve his aims, protecting himself through Law Lords he knew personally. He represented leading industrialists whose manoeuvres might otherwise have been unlawful. Everard was a pathfinder, driven by an unusual determination.

At cocktail parties at Oak Park, Everard often dropped the names of his legal acquaintances and recounted personal anecdotes. He particularly enjoyed describing the excesses and hypocrisies of judges, using shocking detail to underline his point that authority and virtue were rarely aligned.

Everard always stressed that judges were not required to be morally qualified to judge others; they were appointed by politicians. Nor, for that matter, were jurors qualified. They were ordinary citizens selected at random and required to own property, ensuring a bias in favour of the

Establishment. No entrepreneur, he warned, should ever place his life or liberty in the hands of a judge and jury.

"Never forget the words of Chiang Kai-shek," Everard would quote. "A single spark can light a prairie fire."

Although Everard recognised the danger inherent in his path, part of the thrill lay in anticipating that inevitable blaze.

"It's not far from Park Lane to Parkhurst," he would say with a smile, as though already resigned to the outcome.

* * * * *

Poppy Cock devoted herself to shaping Percy's thinking. She lived mainly in her London flat and, although she appeared calm and detached, her divorce from Everard had affected her deeply. After the separation, she wrote constantly and lectured at the British Museum, while receiving only occasional visits from her daughter, with Percy in tow. Mrs Vere adored her father, and Poppy accepted that some greater force had determined both his path and her own.

As Percy grew older and more inquisitive, he pressed Poppy to explain what had happened to her and how she had arrived at her conclusions. Over the course of many visits, she told him her stories.

"I wrote about the structure of the universe and the evolution of the cosmos," she explained, "so that we might explore the possibility of life beyond this planet. Think about the final ray of sunlight striking the Pyramid of the Sun in Mexico at the precise moment the first ray hits the Pyramid of Cheops in Egypt. Beneath these structures are vast underground complexes filled with ceremonial carvings. They are evidence of a forgotten civilisation, and they challenge everything we think we know."

"You mean our lives don't end on this Earth?" Percy suggested.

"Ask your grandfather," Poppy replied sharply. "He will explain the difference between what you are taught and what is true."

"He already has," Percy said.

Without guidance, Percy might have believed that history began with cavemen dragging women into caves.

"Everard believes everything is part of a hidden history," Percy said. "The strange thing is that money and power seem to have taken hold of him."

"I imagine he seats you in those gold-threaded wingback chairs in his library," Poppy replied, recalling her own time in Shanghai. "You are young, and the education system will never explain who truly controls progress. Nations remain in a state of crisis so that they may borrow endlessly money created at no cost by those who issue it. No one explains who owns the gold in the central banks. These are the mechanisms of concealment."

"How can anyone make decisions without knowing that history?" Percy asked.

"In the background," Poppy said carefully, "powerful European families, once known as Templars, arranged international trade and finance. When America gained independence in 1776, one particular family, the Wrathchilds, set out to control the world through money. They persuaded Congress to grant them the right to issue currency under the Federal Reserve Act of 1911. From that point onwards, money was created from nothing and loaned back at interest, binding nations into perpetual debt."

Percy nodded. "I can understand that."

"Everything has been done to disguise this power," she continued. "It determines foreign relations, brings down governments, and decides when wars are fought."

At that age, Percy could not possibly have grasped the scale of what she was describing.

Poppy's beliefs extended even further, linking finance, war, and ideology. She believed Germany's rise before the Second World War had been fuelled by interest-free money, and that banking power later reasserted itself through new global structures.

"Is Everard Jewish?" Percy asked quietly.

"I am giving you foundations," Poppy replied, almost breathless, "so that you can recognise, throughout your life, who is pulling the strings."

* * * * *

Poppy was revered within her circle for her pronouncements, although outsiders regarded her as eccentric. Her lectures, by invitation only, were held in cathedrals and major museums, lending gravitas to her ideas.

She was also remarkably accident-prone. On one occasion, during a rare visit to Harrods to buy a melon, she wandered into the lighting department, tripped over loose cables, and pulled down a standard lamp.

The result was a cascade of exploding bulbs that resembled a Chinese New Year display.

"I could have been seriously hurt!" she scolded the approaching floor manager as she picked herself up from the wreckage.

Her final accident occurred when she mistook an open lift shaft for an airing cupboard during building works. In that moment, her body fell while, as she would have believed, her spirit rose to join the Ancients and the gods she had long contemplated.

Percy attended her funeral and later received a plain envelope containing a pristine Chinese government bond certificate, decorated with an engraving of a steam locomotive. A letter instructed him to keep both until his twenty-first birthday.

"That long?" Percy thought, turning over his first financial instrument and wondering what one hundred thousand shares in the Manchurian Railroad Company might be worth.

At the time, he did not understand the letter that accompanied it.

* * * * *

Percy kept the letter safely, intending to read it properly when the time came. There was, however, one final card enclosed in the envelope, which seemed more appropriate for the present moment:

God is saying to you today,
Your best days are never behind you.
They are always ahead.
You will rise higher, dream bigger,
and go further than anyone in your family ever has.
You are a leader, a difference-maker,
a vessel of My love and power.
Before anyone speaks against you,
I will already have placed a blessing over you.
Walk boldly in that blessing.

From time to time, Percy heard Everard speaking in his sleep.

"Poppy?" he murmured into the darkness, as though she were still travelling.

"I must try this opium business," Percy thought. "I could leave my body at school and spend the day at the seaside."

* * * * *

Then, suddenly, things began to unravel. Everard's intellect gave way to ego, and someone struck a match. The prairie fire was no longer contained.

One of the most complex Inland Revenue investigations of its time was already underway, both at home and abroad. Shareholdings and directorships were tracked with bloodhound determination across continents, unravelling structures that had been deliberately knotted into an impenetrable corporate tangle. Had Everard seen the growing piles of files accumulating on inspectors' desks, his familiar smirk might have faded. Blind alleys were breached, and behind closed doors, the grey-suited men of the Revenue congratulated one another, intoxicated by pursuit and authority.

"This Everard Cock is a real cunning bastard," one inspector confided to Judas Silver, the department's informant, Everard's own company secretary, who was operating in return for immunity.

"We'll get him," they agreed.

As rumours spread, former associates began to offer evidence in order to divert attention from themselves. Men who owed their wealth to Everard's brilliance now joined the chase, eager to distance themselves from his methods. Envy sharpened their enthusiasm.

Above it all hovered Anita Bottom, watchful and calculating.

"Too clever by half," she muttered.

One Saturday morning in the library, Everard spoke quietly.

"It's time to be generous."

Percy watched as his grandfather wrote twenty substantial cheques, sealed them in envelopes, and placed them in his jacket pocket.

"Come," Everard said. "We're going into my office."

The streets were gridlocked by the unveiling of Field Marshal Montgomery's statue.

"That Monty causes trouble even when he's dead," Everard grumbled.

At the office, Everard handed the envelopes to the doorman.

"Make sure these are delivered personally," he instructed.

"Who are they for?" Percy asked on the drive home.

"Organisations that help people in distress," Everard replied. "Sometimes one is given the chance to be sorry."

"Why don't you give them the money yourself?"

"Perfect valour," Everard quoted, "is doing without witnesses what one might otherwise do for praise."

* * * * *

Everard was diagnosed with advanced cancer and given only weeks to live. He refused to go to the hospital; there was too much to finish.

Mrs Vere, unable to imagine her father's vulnerability, signed documents without reading them, trusting the seals, signatures, and assurances that suggested order. Anita watched carefully.

Everard's physical strength faded, but his determination did not. He reversed transactions, created trusts, and shifted assets offshore with diminishing energy. Advisors arrived daily, messengers ran constantly between Oak Park and London, and the Inland Revenue moved from anticipation to fury as activity intensified.

Deathwatch beetles gnawed at the timbers of Oak Park while the Inland Revenue ground its teeth at the thought of Everard escaping them through death.

Anita dismissed gardeners, pocketed wages, and allowed the estate to decline. The dachshunds fouled priceless carpets. Lawns yellowed through neglect.

"You won't have to look at it much longer," she smiled.

"There's one difference between you and a vulture," Everard rasped. "It waits until the prey is dead."

* * * * *

Everard lingered far longer than expected. Associates grew restless. Documents disappeared. Accounts were emptied. Anita burned papers, discarded medication, and spent freely. Jewellery, furs, and cash accumulated.

Near the end, Everard asked to see Percy.

"In life and business, be bold," he whispered. "Remember, Mark Antony."

"What did he say?" Percy asked.

"I did not come here to talk."

Everard died alone.
His chosen epitaph read:

THERE ARE MANY MANSIONS, DID YOU SAY

Within days, Mrs Vere was confronted with legal action. Anita, entirely undeterred, hosted dinner parties and entertained suitors. Among them was Ben Leigh-Coupe, the Rolls-Royce franchise holder, who arrived wide-eyed at the sight of Oak Park's untouched fleet of cars.

He would not last long.

Chapter Four
EDUCATION

Key Witnesses:

DR JAMES DICTUM	*Harrow School Headmaster*
MARK MYWORD	*Harrow School Form Master*
RICK O'SHEA	*Irish Pupil at Harrow*
GRINNAN BEARITT	*Irish Foreign Minister*
TOBY ORNOTOBE	*Nigerian Pupil at Harrow*
TOM BOLAS	*Argentine Pupil at Harrow*
EGOR BEVA	*Czech Pupil at Harrow*
SAM AND JANET EVENING	*Harrow Pupil and His Twin Sister*
SGT - MAJOR MARK TIME	*Head of Cadet Force - Harrow*
ELOVA SHOTT	*Secretary - Harrow Photographic Club*
BITA FLUFF	*German Maid*
MOLLY CULE	*Laboratory Technician*
RED ALERT	*Head of Reel Life International*
ART FARTY	*Features Editor – Reel Life*
VIVIEN DUFFER	*Daughter of Charles Claw*
JOYSTICK STEVENS	*Head of English Heritage*
PHILIP WAYWARD	*Music Entrepreneur*
AARD DIJK	*Son of Hugh Dijk*
JACK HAMMER	*Car Mechanic*
THELMA HOUSE	*Estate Agent*

Before Everard Cock had died, great consideration had been given to the choice of a public school for Percy. Eton had been considered too grand, too aristocratic, Westminster too urbanely metropolitan, and Shrewsbury too remote. Uppingham had an image problem of being situated in England's smallest county, Rutland, and Winchester was far too academic and too much the nursery of bankers and civil servants. St Paul's was too Jewish and, in any case, a day school, and Marlborough and Radley too nouveaux. Lancing was too religious, and King's School, Canterbury, was not quite in the top drawer. Everyone at Ampleforth was fiddled with by the Catholic Fathers, Rugby and Charterhouse lacked sufficient discipline, Cheltenham was too agricultural, and Wellington's academic standards were geared to the lowest denominator, which was pretty low. At this time, Everard Cock was still alive and was entertaining his daughter and her family at his home. "Where then can Percy be groomed as a lawyer and a statesman?" wondered Mrs Vere out loud as the possibilities were explored.

"There were three gentlemen," Everard Cock had recounted as the family discussed the problem, "an Old Etonian, a Carthusian, and a Harrovian. The Old Etonian asked for a chair for a lady, and the Carthusian fetched it, and the Harrovian sat on it!"

"Harrow, of course," confirmed Mrs Vere as if she had made this important decision.

"The fagging system will instil order and respect," confirmed Commander Vere. "Harrow on the Hill is not too far away - but far enough so Percy won't be appearing up the drive every five minutes."

"Harrow created the likes of Nehru and Byron," Dr James Dictum, headmaster of Harrow, confirmed as the Vere parents attended the interview to put Percy's name down for a place.

"What were they famous for?" Mrs Vere asked out loud.

"Nehru was India's first Prime Minister, and Byron was a poet," Commander Vere informed her behind his hand.

When Percy passed his Common Entrance exam, Mrs Vere proudly reported the news to her father.

"Harrow created the likes of Nehru and Byron," she repeated exactly.

"Both as gay as a brush!" Everard replied.

"There's nothing wrong with a little fun," Mrs Vere retorted.

"Not that kind of fun," Commander Vere shuddered.

"I mean, they had the morality of Plato and Caligula," Everard explained to his daughter.

"How wonderful," Mrs Vere glowed.

"And you have to remember that Harrow is the only public school that can field its own team at Lewes Open Prison," added Everard.

"Well, it's too late to change now," Mrs Vere announced. "Percy's got a place, and he's hardly in demand."

Everard sucked on his pipe, and a wisp of smoke curled upward. He smiled knowingly. Of course, Percy had gotten in.

There was only one form worth starting at Harrow: The Fourth Form of the Lower School. Sir Robert Peel, who first regulated law and order in the masses by the invention of the 'police officer,' started in the Fourth, as did Gandhi, who had proved, amazingly, that the peaceful intervention of an individual wearing a loincloth can prevail under the yoke of serfdom without a truncheon.

'Every time I speak, I set off an economic chain that embraces the world!' Gandhi had pronounced.

'And what exactly are you smoking?' asked someone in the crowd.

Winston Churchill was considered a dullard and never got beyond the Fourth, yet he was credited with saying, 'If what you have got to say is not more beautiful than silence, save your breath!'

The Fourth was the lowest form of all, a class apart for those of no evidence of intelligence and specially designed for those who were inbred and indifferent. Some were noted for a particular creative alternative invented by the prep school to gain traction, like 'Horace has a beautiful singing voicc' or 'Horace is particularly good at team sports.' Interestingly, most came up with an occasional memorable quip on entering the Fourth

"Experience is a wonderful thing," a new boy muttered as he entered the basement Fourth Form classroom. "It makes you recognise a mistake so you know when you repeat it."

"My father doesn't have a clue what he is doing," said a second new boy as he chose a desk at the back. "If he did, this is worse than I thought."

It was clearly understood that an annual intake of flotsam was allowed to scrape through the Common Entrance exam by something more compelling, like an endowment to the Vaughan Library, the Speech Room, the Science School, or even to 'Ducker', Harrow School's ever-popular giant swimming pool. Some of this flotsam was desirable because a title looked good etched in gold leaf on the boards. Alternatively, a family's position in industry or politics ensured publicity or clout when necessary.

There was nowhere for these odds and sods to go but the Fourth, so it was definitely the class to be in. Anyway, the school grounds were littered with brass plaques immortalising those who started in the Fourth.

* * * * *

Percy's grandfather had secretly endowed whatever was necessary to ensure Percy had squeezed in, and the lowly Fourth was, therefore, where he started.

The form master of the Fourth was the irreverent Mark Myword, housemaster of Bradby's. The dunces in the Fourth were his pride and joy and, for a reason no one had ever fathomed, he was going to craft them into a recognisable breed both in and out of the classroom. Mark Myword would not have had it any other way, and from his first glance at the assorted faces in Percy's year, he knew this intake was no different.

Amongst Mark Myword's new charges was the young Jerry Mander, son of Sir Jerry Mander, Chairman of Jerry Mander Construction. Then there was Rick O'Shea, nephew and chip off the block of Grinnan Bearitt, the Irish Foreign Minister. Next was Toby Ornotobe, the son of Chief Ornotobe, President of the Niger Oil Corporation, and Tom Bolas, fifth son by the third wife of Lucio Bolas, the Argentine nine-goal handicap polo player and cattle baron.

They all had one trait in common. It was the look of not belonging and not wanting to belong to Mark Myword's branding. History would prove this was a temporary reluctance because all the world's political leaders were feted because they started at Harrow in the Fourth.

Tom Bolas was particularly suited to the Fourth. From his first day at Harrow, he obviously had no intention of staying to be educated. He had been shipped to Harrow from Buenos Aires, like so much baggage. In return for this treatment, Tom considered that he could do whatever he wanted.

"I'm financially independent, and I'm not staying here with you cripples," he announced, flashing his chequebook.

Many in the Fourth had never seen a chequebook, and some had never even touched money. It had been unnecessary, so they were suitably awestruck.

Percy felt comfortable surrounded by the protective cloak of the Fourth.

Mark Myword entered the room twenty minutes late for their inaugural class. He walked deliberately up the steps of his dais, mortarboard and black cape over his arm. He placed them slowly on one side of the raised desk and leaned forward to survey his new charges.

"My God, what a horrible lot," he opened.

Everyone was transfixed by the saliva bubbling at the corner of his mouth.

"Every year," he went on after a long pause, "I've landed with a bunch of horrible worms like you, and it is my misfortune to have the task of turning you into gentlemen."

Mark paused again and stared at Tom Bolas' tanned features and slicked-back hair.

"What are you called, you foreign freak?" he splattered, as his bushy eyebrows rose over his sunken cheekbones.

His words stabbed across the classroom.

Tom was chewing gum, and the rest of the class was transfixed.

"Bolas!" Tom replied.

"Bolas what?"

"Just Bolas", he continued, chewing.

"Bolas, I don't like you one little bit. Bolas, you are scum. Bolas, you are going to regret the day you came here."

"Never a truer word …" retorted Tom.

"Would you like to repeat that, Bolas?"

There was a silence, but Mark Myword was enjoying the ritual of the new class cowering below him.

"Bolas, you will not bring your sweeties into my classroom, and you will address me as 'Sir'. You will not speak unless I address you. Is that clear?"

"That's pretty much what I expected, Sir," Tom answered cynically.

"Then at least we understand each other," Mark retorted with a wry grimace.

Mark Myword surveyed the rest of the class, desk by desk, for a good five minutes. He then picked up the pile of papers in front of him and slammed them down.

"This is a list of books you will be needing, you vermin," he spat. "Go to the bookshop and get them and be here tomorrow morning at 9:00 a.m. sharp."

"You will stand!" he snapped as he swept out of the door in a wave of black cape.

The class stood and exhaled. Bolas made a strange finger sign behind his back.

"I'm buggered if I'm going to put up with that!" he announced.

Everyone else just gawped as Tom then rolled his chewing gum between his fingers, climbed onto the raised podium, and dropped it into Mark Myword's inkwell.

It was very clear to Percy that Mark Myword wasn't fooling around, and though desperate for a pee, he went straight to the Harrow School Bookshop as instructed. He stood in line to order his books and, with his bladder on the point of perforation, his turn arrived. The assistant started stacking books on the counter until she was hidden from view.

"Porter!"

Percy stepped sideways and saw Toby Ornotobe at the other end of the shop. He was balancing a similarly huge pile of books.

"Porter!" Toby repeated over his shoulder.

Some of the older boys amongst the bookshelves behind him started to snigger.

"How did you get here in front of me?" asked Percy.

"Before my father got rich at the Niger Oil Corporation," Toby smiled, "I used to run five miles every day to school and back."

"That's a bit keen!" observed Percy under his breath.

Toby and Percy went back to their respective Houses loaded to the chin with Latin grammars, Greek dictionaries, the finest English novels, and a host of textbooks in Mathematics and Science, including mysterious trigonometry tables and rodent dissection charts.

Percy struggled up the flights of stone steps to his room, choking back tears of loneliness and fear. He dropped the pile of books onto the floor as he hurried to the bathroom. It was a century-old urinal that briefly distracted him from the thought of years of trying to understand whatever was in these weird books.

"What will become of me?" he asked the porcelain.

His grandfather's words, 'One brick at a time,' floated down from the cistern into his head.

"Just as well, I'm starting in the Fourth," Percy answered himself out loud. "You can't get a lower row of bricks than that!"

To maintain what was generally accepted as academic standards, Harrow School had a centuries-old tried and tested routine of inquisition.

What you studied, what you played, and what you were allowed to be interested in were programmed from the very beginning by a series of interviews for all new boys. It included a visit to the gym, the music school, the science labs, the Vaughan Library, and the famous amphitheatre-shaped Speech Room. Then, just in case you managed to manipulate yourself some spare time, the captains of every sport would be looking for new potential at the beginning of every term. The assessment of each new boy was overwhelming.

"Lift these weights!"

"Punch this bag!"

"Sing 'D'!"

"How much do you weigh?"

"Cough!"

"Run round that lake!"

"Shoot that target!"

"Catch this ball!"

"Kick that ball!"

"Tackle that man!"

"Make your bed again!"

"Salute!"

"I understand that you play the violin," said the music master. Percy looked at his feet, unaware that the headmaster of St Abra had written 'somewhat accomplished on violin and piano' under the music section of the Common Entrance questionnaire. He had not qualified the word 'somewhat.'

The awful truth was that Percy had scraped into Harrow on the exact pass mark of 55%, and that level was reached with a percentage credit for his musical talent and accomplishments in the gym. Otherwise, acceptance would have been less than marginal, and he was not sure what they might have asked his grandfather to provide alongside other hopeless cases where complete idiots had wealthy catalysts like Everard Cock.

"It says here that you played in local community concerts," the music master read aloud as he thrust a violin and bow into Percy's hand.

"In concert, Sir?" enquired Percy, looking desperate. "You're obviously confusing me with someone else, Sir."

"Don't be stupid, boy!" he snapped. "We haven't got all day."

"No, really, I can't play it, Sir," insisted Percy, putting the violin on the floor.

"Well, I'll be looking into this!" concluded the music master sternly as he ushered Percy into the next room.

"You're not going to find a violin, however hard you look into it!" Percy said very quietly to himself as he was ushered by a music assistant into the next room.

In front of Percy was a stool and a giant, forbidding twelve-foot Bösendorfer concert grand piano. One of the music masters from before followed him and planted a sheet of music on the stand, while yet another music master folded his black cape over his body as he sat back in an old, battered leather armchair. Then two more masters came in and sat beside him. One of them looked at Percy over his pince-nez in expectation.

Percy felt terror, and his arms failed to respond as he tried to lift his hands onto the keyboard. Impatient grunts came from the line of masters.

"Come on now, boy, no need to be anxious!" they encouraged.

Percy just sat in front of them with his head bowed and felt the tears coming.

"We're waiting, boy!" groaned the assistant music master.

"Perhaps you could start me off by telling me which is middle C?" Percy suggested.

"Don't be impertinent, boy!" he retorted.

"There must be some mistake, Sir!" Percy snivelled, standing up and gently shutting the keyboard. "You'll have to get someone else to play this."

"Where do you think you're going?" another of the masters inquired.

"Excuse me, Sir, but I don't think I'm very musical," Percy choked before running out of the room and down the hill onto the rugby pitches.

"How on earth am I going to get through five years of this?" he despaired as he watched the First XV rugby front row smashing into the scrum machine.

After one week at Harrow, Tom Bolas walked out of 'Back and Sides', the small hairdresser's shop, with his hair slicked back and their radio inside his jacket. The following morning, they all took their places at the appointed time, except that Tom was missing. Mark Myword swept in and sat up on his platform. His first ominous missive left nothing to the imagination.

"Bolas has been expelled. One down, sixteen to go!" he gloated, rubbing his hands together.

* * * * *

In a world of privilege and structure, boys in the Fourth had only one edge. During over four hundred years of Harrow, the boys in the Fourth alone had the obligation of walking in the gutter whenever anyone senior approached.

The preparatory school system at St Abra had ingrained in Percy fear, rather than respect, for everyone in authority. From the park-keeper and librarian to the schoolmaster and especially the policeman, Percy was scared of them, but Harrow was on a different level with an ancient system of routine and discipline and 'fagging' where new boys were allocated to be at the beck and call of senior boys for whatever they wanted. This was up a notch to petrifying, as in being 'turned into stone'.

It might well be perceived in the corridors of power that such a system would keep the colonial foot firmly on the necks of the Empire. However, in Percy's sorry state, it was more like breeding savagery sufficient to confront everyone. Those who failed to win, oppose, strangle, or kill would have a character flaw like 'Spazzo'.

For hundreds of years, all the House prefects, or 'monitors' as Harrow preferred to call them, had the right of first refusal on the new boys as servants or 'fags.' The single blood-curdling scream of 'Boy!' by a monitor echoing through the stone corridors meant that every junior boy had to scramble out of his room. It was a race to win because the last to arrive got the job or errand. Anyone who didn't respond or was found hiding in a cupboard or lavatory, even if he was gripped by diarrhoea, would be thrashed for insubordination by the monitor. Some walked around as if they relished that privilege and called 'Boy!' just for the fun of it.

Additionally, each monitor had a personal slave who would respond to his double call of 'Boy, Boy!'

Percy was selected as the fag of Denny Grate, a new House monitor. Denny made no bones about being a bully. His father was a career army officer, and Denny had been a fag himself. Now it was his turn to make the new boys suffer - as the Harrow School song suggested:

> 'Jerry, a poor little fag,
> Carrying a kettle and tray,
> Feeling his energy flag,
> Let them all fall on the way.
> On him, his monitor dropped,

'Pick up the pieces at once!
Off to my room to be whopp'd,
Jerry, you duffer and dunce.'
Heigh-ho! Heigh-ho!
Jerry, you duffer and dunce.'

Denny Grate immediately issued Percy a list of duties, which included making his bed, washing his 'eccer' socks, cleaning the brasses on his army cadet uniform, and spit and polishing the toe caps and heels of all his shoes and boots until they reflected a mirror-like image.

At the age of 18, Denny Grate was already something of an athlete and a long-standing member of the Philathletic Club, a celebrated group of the twelve top cricketers, rugby players, and Harrow footballers. These muscular specimens were empowered to exact punishment on all junior school unfortunates for breaches of the rules within the extensive school grounds. These included such heinous violations as wearing the wrong coloured socks, forgetting the straw boater, or, in the case of boys from the Fourth, moving into the gutter to let senior boys pass on the pavement.

During his first interview with Percy, Denny had made it clear that there would be no 'insubordination'. To shove the point firmly home, he described the procedure of a Philathletic beating, making particular reference to the gruesome incident where a thirteen-year-old new boy, Lars Gasp, died.

"In the traditional way," Denny smirked, "Gasp's head was placed underneath the table in the Philathletic meeting room in the basement below the Vaughan Library. All 14 members of the Philathletic Club had two run-ups to swipe at his bare buttocks."

Percy had heard what happened to Lars, and he was terrified.

"You wouldn't do that to me, would you?" was all he could squeak.

"You're not kidding, Vere!" replied Denny as he took a bite out of an apple and threw the core at Percy. "And you look so spastic that you'd be a goner for sure."

Less dangerous but equally as memorable as a Philathletic beating was a beating by the head boy in your House for crimes in his domain, the most frequent of which was stealing food from the pantry and being caught by Jeeves, the upstanding and tail-coated House butler.

"Young Sir, may I ask what you have in your hand?" Jeeves would ask politely from a sudden appearance in the kitchen corridor.

Jeeves addressed all the boys as 'Sir' with a different inflexion depending on his opinion of their status.

'It's nothing, Jeeves' was always the answer.

"In that case, Sir," Jeeves would then request calmly, "there will be no harm in taking 'nothing' from behind your back and putting it on the table if you please!"

Jeeves reported the theft of every biscuit.

Another favourite prank worthy of the risk of a whacking was to flick peas at the dining hall ceiling so that they dried and rained down later.

Such in-house whackings would be administered in the monitor's Common Room after 'lights out.'

There was a roster, so only one fag was on duty at night to answer calls. The spectacular and slightly different 'Boy Up!' would rise to a crescendo over some five seconds to summon the night fag. He would leap 'Up' and go to find out who was to be beaten and fetch him to wait outside the Common Room door. The call reverberating down the stairways and corridors woke everyone, so the night fag would rattle all the doorknobs on his way down the corridors so as to scare the pants off those hiding under his horsehair blanket with his pillow over his head for anonymity.

"Get up!" the night fag would entreat the culprit. "Get it over with, then I can go back to bed!"

The offender would get into his dressing gown and knock on the door of the monitors' Common Room.

'Wait!' he would hear above the noise of revelry inside.

Normally, at least five minutes of terrible anticipation would pass.

"Come!"

The unfortunate boy would then be told of his crime by the senior boy in the House, the so-called 'head of house', and instructed to take off his dressing gown, lower his pyjamas, and bend his head under the table with his hands flat on the top. The head of the house would make a selection from a rack of birch and willow canes that had tasted many a famous buttock. It was as if the monitor was slowly selecting a billiard cue, and to prolong the anticipation, he would swipe the air with each one in turn.

That noise of cutting swathes in the air would be remembered by many a future politician and industrialist. It was enough to contract the young heart - not to mention young buttocks.

"What an absolutely pathetic display, boy", would be the response to any snivelling.

"Not since the waters receded from the Red Sea has there been such a display of invertebracy!" was one of the more amusing taunts.

The number of strokes would depend on the mood of the head of the house on the night in question, and it was relevant to listen in advance from outside the door to get a flavour of the mood inside. The number of swipes was often determined by the level of annoyance about some personal situation.

'My father has promised me a Rolex' would be the kind of comment that ensured a right thrashing.

For any new boy singled out because of some arrogance or disrespect, life was a constant parade of beatings. The unfortunate Randall Crawley was such a victim: born of the MP Aidan Crawley with a shock of blond hair and a permanent smirk, he was beaten for 'insubordination' often before he even opened his mouth to speak.

Percy was beaten because he hadn't the faintest idea of what was going on. He had difficulty remembering so many rules, and anyway, they made no sense. He would most frequently make a mistake about the various combinations of the school uniform to be worn at different times of the day for formal or sporting occasions. When questioned, Percy would respond with a vacant look. Randall and Percy crossed each other on the way to the monitor's Common Room so many times that they became friends, and for safety, they each spent much of their free time in the confines of the marble racquets court. It was one of four courts in the entire country, and once inside, it was surreal because the latch to lock the door was on the inside. It was like a rectangular stone cathedral safe from any kind of attack.

* * * * *

Beating by Harrow housemasters would be the appropriate punishment for misdemeanours in class, such as persistent reports of looking out of the window or for any deliberate lack of courtesy to junior masters or local shopkeepers. Housemasters were ranked in order of the pain they inflicted. Mark Myword was a 10 on the 'Beating Scale' and was to be avoided by any means possible, and that included disappearing for a 'family emergency'.

Hair any longer than shaved up the back and sides got twenty minutes in freezing cold showers because it was considered by every level of authority to be an outward show of the Revolution to come.

For anything less serious, the punishment was always cold showers for various lengths of time. Dirty shoes were two minutes, and sniggering during the endless sermons on the Mount from the chaplain, Lars Rites, got ten minutes under the freezing water in the certainty of a better respect for our Lord Jesus.

The cream of England's youth, therefore, spent an average of 15% of their Harrow school days with their balls retracted in the freezing showers. This did not bother Percy because his balls were not yet in plain view, and the water was warm by Cornish standards.

Boys from India and Pakistan and anything with dark skin, were universally referred to as 'tribal trash'.

Percy developed a good relationship with Juan Tanamo, the son of the boss of the Cuban casino business, who was a class above him in the Lower Fifth. Juan wore a gold chain with a gold crucifix, so he definitely was not from Pakistan. He had been told that no jewellery was permitted, but he refused to take it off, and his father wrote a letter. Since it was on Fidel Castro's notepaper, Juan was given a special waiver, and he touched it every minute.

Percy and Juan shared an interest in playing backgammon, and it proved to be a great way to spend time out of the classroom. In the summer, they took the board to play by 'ducker' between diving in and cooling off. Percy didn't notice the colour of Juan's skin, but Juan was continuously being baited as a 'greaseball'.

"You should say you're from Cuba, not Karachi?" suggested Percy.

"They wouldn't know the difference", said Juan as a larger boy wearing budgie smugglers made a rude gesture from the top board.

"Guarro!" Juan shouted back with a smile, showing his set of pure white teeth.

"What's that Guarro?" Percy asked.

"Pig!" Juan laughed, rubbing his cross between his fingers.

Juan had been caned by the headmaster of Harrow, and it was a prestigious event embodying a crime severe enough to be worthy of punishment, announced in Speech Room in front of the whole school. This was only a whisker away from expulsion, a fine line indeed not to be misjudged.

Percy never got Juan to say exactly what 'disrespect' Juan had shown or to whom, but he guessed it was a remark to the headmaster's wife in the street.

"I didn't recognise her," Juan explained to Percy.

“That wouldn’t have mattered as this is Harrow, not Havana!” Percy suggested.

Percy himself received the supreme whacking only once. And he never really worked out what the crime had been. He was told it was for ‘insubordination’, so he assumed it was something to do with an argument in Religious Studies. He had challenged Lars Rites, as their chaplain, about the meaning of transubstantiation of the poor quality wine he served, and whatever he said must have been disrespectful.

Dr Dictum was always courteous, and afterwards he said evenly and quietly ‘Reflect on your catalogue of sarcasm!”

Percy needed that reminder to keep his comments to himself in the school chapel.

Any sarcasm in the regular beatings in the house Common Room would provoke a proper slashing, sometimes even more than 12 strokes, and it was a pyrrhic victory when the head of house broke into a sweat.

Even when blood was drawn and dribbling down his legs, Percy would not cry nor try to make some reasonable objection because, in their excitement, they could not hear.

‘Sir’, he said to his Head of House as he lowered his pyjamas and stuck his head under the table. “I believe your solution of whacking me is like throwing your shoe at the television set and hoping to get a better picture!”

A week after the headmaster’s beating, his wife came to Percy’s study and asked Percy to join her for afternoon tea.

“Madam”, Percy answered. “I am afraid that I shall not be able to sit down, thank you.”

The greatest humiliation was reserved for those who snuck on their mates. Sneaking was, by definition, a low act to curry favour, and the boys would exact terrible retribution themselves. The sneak would be held down and ‘blacked’ with molten shoe polish. It was clearly a life-shattering experience, and anyone who was thought to have sneaked did not get over it for a long time, nor, for that matter, did their genitals.

A good thrashing and being ‘blacked’ were not the only dangers facing younger boys running the Harrow gauntlet. No girls were allowed at Harrow, and some of the older boys who had discovered their sexuality were unable to cope with the outcome.

Percy had first heard the word ‘bugger’ on the farm and had thought it was something animals did. ‘Bugger me!’ was not an invitation to bend someone over a hay bale, but it was because of when the chickens had got out.

The farmer, or whoever was in charge of the Vere farm, was a straight-talking man with an academic bent.

"Anyone who has observed pigs knows that they're not fussy eaters," he would say. "That is why they are called pigs."

* * * * *

For the first year at Harrow, three boys shared a room, and in the second year, it became two in a room. Percy's first year roommates were Don Key and Hugh Midity. Don Key was the son of a Suffolk butcher and a real swot who had gained a scholarship to Harrow. Hugh Midity had been at a day school in the middle of Wales, and Harrow was the first time he had been away from his mother. Hugh only stopped blubbing 36 hours after his mother kissed him 'goodbye'.

Don, at 5 feet 9 inches, was a thirteen-year-old giant and blessed with the world's most enormous uncircumcised prick. All eighty boys in the House had either seen it in the communal cold showers at 7:00 a.m. or had heard about the size of it. Don attracted pointing and laughter and a backdrop of sniggering in the dining hall at breakfast when the sausages were being served.

It was only a matter of time before Percy, Hugh, and Don would have their fair share of trouble.

In the early hours of one dreadful night, their bedroom door opened quietly. Percy woke to a hand clamped over his mouth and another tearing at his pyjama bottoms.

Percy's eyes stared wildly at the outline of the grinning face of Anthony Boffs-Ewe, a three-yearer in the Sixth Form whose own room was on the same corridor. Percy struggled and lashed out and, pulling Boff-Ewe's hand away from his mouth, uttered a blood-curdling scream.

Don Key jumped out of bed immediately and snapped on the light. Anthony Boffs-Ewe was standing with a stiff dick poking out of his open dressing gown. Don grabbed his tennis racquet and whacked it. Boffs-Ewe doubled up, screaming and struggling out of the room. Hugh Midity started uncontrolled blubbing.

Percy was the fag of Denny Grate, the senior boy on that floor, who must have heard the commotion because he arrived to confront Boffs-Ewe in the corridor. Boffs-Ewe told him that the homesick Hugh Midity had woken him with his crying, so he had gone into their room to find him having a nightmare.

"Were you the nightmare, Ant?" asked Denny.

Anthony Boffs-Ewe was going back to his room when Percy shouted to Denny.

"Boffs-Ewe came in here and attacked me!"

Hugh Midity's nose was now running freely as he sniffled.

"Boffs-Ewe is lying!" Hugh tried to say.

Percy had sunk his teeth into the arm in his bed, and he had blood around his mouth.

"Vere, get into your dressing gown and wait outside the Common Room!" ordered Denny. "Key, get back to bed, and Midity, for God's sake, shut up or ask your mummy to take you away!"

Half an hour later, Denny Grate asked Percy to repeat his story to the head boy in their house.

"Boffs-Ewe attacked me!" Percy repeated.

He now realised it was a dangerous thing to say about anyone.

"You sneaky piece of shit!" came the feared response. "You will have to be taught that gentlemen do not tell tales. The very fabric of society depends on the elite sticking together. A sewer rat like you could give the game away, so I'm going to give you six of the best to instil a little moral fibre in that jelly which you call a spine. Now, get into the Common Room, drop your pyjamas and assume the position!"

Percy started screaming as the cane slashed into his thighs.

Denny Grate got his friend 'Ant' to sign the beating's book as the required witness, and Percy hobbled in despair back to his room and moaned at the pain until he was given the relief of sleep.

The following morning, in the cold showers, Anthony Boffs-Ewe moved menacingly towards Percy.

"You're mine," he grinned.

In this case, Boffs-Ewe was mistaken. Whilst Percy might have been considered a soft target, as evidenced by new assailants trying their luck from time to time, he quickly learnt to duck and dive his way out of the gym, the showers, the squash courts, and the appropriately named 'running shed'. This wooden shack was set aside at the start of the cross-country course, and it was well known that the scratch marks all over the inside walls told a hundred-year tale of bestiality.

Percy was not the only boy who had to protect himself in this seemingly endless game of cat and mouse. Since there was no question of complaining to anyone, Percy established the view that this was part of public-school basic training. In life, ducking and diving to avoid being cornered would surely be of value in progress with authorities like the Police, the Fraud Squad, the Drug Squad, and every other squad.

After the slashing pain of this middle-of-the-night punishment, Percy learnt the lesson of settling scores personally, and he hit the ever-persistent Anthony Boffs-Ewe with a cricket bat and broke his shin bone as he came round the corner of the five courts. After the initial piercing scream as Boffs-Ewe fell onto the concrete, no one told on Percy.

Percy had discovered that 'I don't know anything' was the standard response to any question afterwards.

Perfectly normal boys who succumbed to sneaking could never free themselves from a miserable existence.

"It's a nasty habit of the British aristocracy," commented Rick O'Shea, who lived in a castle somewhere near Cork. "They brought their filthy little habits like shirt-lifting over to Ireland. The English always work under the covers to get information, and their spies are supported by their bum-buddies in government because there are more shirt-lifting MP's than you can shake a stick at. That's why they protect each other from any enquiry."

"So they like young, muscled buttocks?" asked Percy.

"They use a code called 'Mum's the word,'" concluded Rick.

"The British Secret Service is staffed almost entirely by homosexuals working for the KGB," Don Key added. "It's called the 'old school tie' network, and it's the protection to save those who fuck-up. It works on the basis that sticking together when you're homosexual or incompetent is automatic. In America, they call it 'circling the wagons.' Wherever you are, it buys you time to make up a story."

"Well put, if I might say so," smiled Rick. "It fills in the cracks, and it works in the colonies with all the tribal trash. The children are all buggered senseless, and if a parent says anything, he gets his hands chopped off."

"But then they can't work?" reasoned Jerry Mander in a world of his own. "My father has been using a new kind of quick-drying cement to build living quarters for the servants in Africa. Now they've found out it's only a matter of time before the walls crack open or the roofs fall in, so he's done a deal with the insurance company to keep the whole thing quiet. That was the easy bit as they gave the only claims manager a two-year holiday with half pay."

"Typical," confirmed Don Key in a resigned tone. "While the slaves are living in a pile of rubble and are regularly beaten, their complaints go in the bin. Then the insurance bosses work out how to share the money they make from the premiums."

"It's a good thing we all get to wear the old school tie," mused Percy.

Don's extraordinary physical endowment ensured he was a continuing target for bullies. Having entered Harrow on a scholarship, he chose to avoid his assailants by burying himself in his work and participating in as few team sports as possible. He achieved this by taking up cross-country running to fill the required daily hour of sport without coming into physical contact with anyone else. A thrashing was the automatic punishment for skipping this hour of exercise. Don was careful to sign his name at the end of every run in the cross-country book in the running shed. He knew what kind of thrashing he would receive because of his endowment, both physical and financial.

Hugh and Percy couldn't help but notice that some of the other boys had Don in their sights because of the endless sniping comments. Percy was scared for Don, but Don himself was sanguine.

"I'll give as good as I get," he said quietly one night when Percy asked him what he was going to do to avoid the inevitable abuse.

Besides Anthony Boffs-Ewe, the most feared bullies in Percy's House were Hertz Van Rental, son of the founder of a van-hire multinational, and Sam Evening, son of the conductor of the Westminster Philharmonic. Both were to be avoided at all costs.

Sam and Janet Evening were twins, and their photographs were often on the society pages of Tatler and the Illustrated London News. Janet visited her twin regularly on Saturday afternoons to watch the First XV rugby matches. Janet was tall, and at only 17, she was remarkably well developed. At least, every boy who saw her said so.

Janet usually wore a low-cut top and a short skirt to add to her brother's prestige.

It was at a home rugby match against Westminster that Don Key had been standing behind Janet Evening as a crowd watched the match. Sam played as a second-row forward and bludgeoned his way through the Westminster scrum, making a number of fine runs to their line. As Janet jumped up and down in excitement, cheering and clapping at her brother's performance, the onlookers pressed forward, and Don, in turn, found himself pressed up behind her. He felt a surge of blood into his huge member as Janet's firm, full buttocks, protected only by a skimpy silk skirt, moved up and down against his shorts.

As Don's membership grew larger and larger, Sam made a spectacular try, and Janet jumped up, clapping enthusiastically. The adoring crowd of Harrow supporters pushed Don firmly forward, and Janet came down on the huge member in his running shorts. She screamed, turned, and fought her way out of the crowd.

The following Sunday afternoon, after tea, Sam Evening and Hertz Van Rental, supported by two of their rugger pals, crashed into Don's room while he had his head down over his work.

First, Percy and Hugh were pushed into the corner and held back out of the way while the three others grabbed Don and dragged him backwards onto the floor. They pulled down the bed and tied his hands and ankles to the four corners of the metal frame. As Percy and Hugh watched the struggle, Hertz pulled down Don's underpants whilst Sam took out a glass phial and removed the stopper.

Sam raised the phial and held it in the air over Don's private parts while Hertz put on yellow rubber Marigold kitchen gloves and took hold of Don's penis.

"Jesus, you're all crazy!" screamed Don. "Let me go!"

"Okay, Key," Hertz replied. "Now we want to see if you can tell the truth. We've got a nice bottle of acid here, courtesy of the science labs, and we're going to pour it onto that revolting piece of meat you call a dick."

"What do you think of that?" enquired Sam.

"What are you talking about? What have I done?" squirmed Don, his voice cracking in fear.

"You stuck it up, my sister, you filthy big-willied pig!" exclaimed Sam.

"You must be crazy. I didn't lay a finger on her!" shrieked Don.

"Not your finger, you baboon, your revolting dick," shouted Sam. "Just admit that you did it. Everybody saw you."

Sam brought the bottle closer, and Hertz held Don's penis in the air by its end.

"You are a filthy liar, Key - from a filthy family!' Sam shouted. 'Admit it, and we might let you go."

"What do you want me to say, Van Rental?" Don shrieked in panic. "I didn't do anything, but if you want me to say it, I was pushed up against her in the crowd."

"You filthy pig!" Sam shouted immediately. "People like you have got to be stopped!"

"You malformed sex maniac," agreed Hertz as he yanked Don's knob. "Now we're going to burn your prick off!"

Hugh was blubbing wildly, Percy was faint with fear, and Don was now screaming wildly.

"Quick, do it, Sam!" Hertz ordered.

Sam poured the liquid over Don's genitals.

Don uttered a hideous scream as the tap water splashed harmlessly on his penis. Percy bit right through his lip as the four bullies dashed out.

"I'm going to get that bastard!" spluttered Don as his whole body shook and Percy's juddering hands tried to untie the bits of rope.

Don took up weight training in the gym, and just over a year later, Sam was lying on the mat getting ready for a bench press when Don appeared in the doorway. He picked up a ten-kilogram dumbbell and smashed it onto Sam's right hand.

"Try wanking with that, you maniac!" said Don.

*****

As the years went by, intakes of new boys entered this process of 'character building', and Don, Hugh, and Percy moved up a few rungs of the ladder out of the fagging system into relative security, where there were lighter moments of taking part in a range of stupid but harmless pranks.

Sergeant-Major Mark Time, who was the odious head of the Combined Cadet Force, had an old Volkswagen which he left parked behind his house over the weekends when he was away visiting his family. He always left on Friday evenings at 6:00 p.m. sharp.

After years of marching mindlessly around the parade ground on Wednesday afternoons, Percy, Jerry Mander, Rick O'Shea, and Toby Ornotobe thought up something more important to do. They had all started as low academically as it was possible and risen together to the lower Sixth, and here they were all lined up in a military uniform on parade in front of the visiting dignitary, Field Marshal Montgomery. The four boys had mistakenly turned and marched off to the right on Mark Time's scorching command, 'Left Turn!'

While this may have amused the boys watching, it had brought dishonour to the school in front of the visiting parents and dignitaries.

Their punishment was to march for two hours around the parade ground in full battle dress in the following afternoon's blazing summer sun.

As they marched round and round, they plotted revenge against the Sergeant-Major. Their target was his Volkswagen parked beside his house. They decided to take tools from the engineering workshop, unbolt and dismantle the car, and reassemble it in his living room during one weekend.

"It's no good running out of time with the engine sitting on his fireside rug!" sniggered Rick O'Shea.

When the appointed day arrived, they went about their work unseen, and on Sunday night at 6:00 p.m., the job was finished. The tools were returned, and Mark Time's Volkswagen was, to all intents and purposes, watching his TV in his living room. Nothing would look amiss until the Sergeant-Major returned and opened his hall door. There were bets on whether he would open the curtains for everyone to see.

When the Sergeant-Major returned on Sunday night, his hated voice was heard bellowing across Harrow Hill. Then, he was spotted quick-marching between his house and the headmaster's door.

On Monday morning, 200 boys passed his front window to get to the 9:00 a.m. assembly in the Speech Room. By the time assembly started, the whole school was sniggering with glee.

After reading the notices as if nothing were amiss, the headmaster, Dr James Dictum, removed his glasses and paused. He looked slowly around the Speech Room.

"It has been reported to me that a motor vehicle has been moved into the house of Sergeant-Major Mark Time," he announced.

The entire school immediately fell about laughing in uncontrolled hysterics while the masters around the back of the auditorium behind Dr Dictum sat sternly and unmoved in their gowns like a line of giant blackbirds.

"The culprits will stand."

The laughter died down as quickly as it had started and was replaced by a pall of silence.

"If the guilty parties come forward now, they will be punished in the normal way," Dr Dictum advised. "But if they are found later, they will be expelled from this School."

No one moved or spoke, and Dr James Dictum swept out in a swirl of the black cape and a swish of mortarboard tassel.

The four boys never said a word, and their satisfaction was complete when the headmaster was rumoured to have boasted at a cocktail party in London that it was the best prank ever.

The shooting master was Ray Gunn. He rode a Lambretta scooter around the Hill.

Six months after the Volkswagen affair, the same four boys wheeled Ray Gunn's Lambretta up to Speech Room in the middle of a Sunday night. They wound down the hooks used to hoist up the scenery in the annual Shakespearean productions and attached the Lambretta. They hoisted it twenty-five feet in the air immediately over the headmaster's table.

The school assembled as usual on Monday morning to witness the hanging of the Lambretta. The backstage key was nowhere to be found, so it was impossible to take it down before the headmaster entered.

Dr Dictum stood in his usual place immediately below. Snorting and twittering engulfed the Speech Room as his eyes upturned. He quietly asked his deputy head to take his place. He then read the notices and walked back to the door, and turned to face the school.

"Get that down!" he ordered with a straight face as the entire school gripped its sides in mirth.

*****

Percy's final year passed quickly. He excelled in the gym, and over five years, his physique had developed to a point where he could perform such stunts as somersault dismounts off the parallel bars and a perfect 'crucifix' on the rings. He was invited to Rugby to train for the Junior Olympics, where, to his dismay, the freedom and individuality that he had enjoyed in the school gym were sacrificed for a team effort. Moreover, the floor routine of somersaults and backflips had morphed into an elegant dance in line with the female programme. Percy was astounded and dismayed as he had never been a team player, and he was secretly pleased not to be in the final selection.

"How in God's name did that happen so fast and without Harrow knowing?" he asked.

The shooting on the ranges of Bisley was a perfect alternative as individual scores were simply added together, and the alternatives of individual brilliance and group effort were both recognised. Under the direction of Ray Gunn, Percy excelled at firing a .38 calibre pistol into the mouth of a cardboard human face at 50 feet. He also got good at hitting a twelve-inch black dot with a .303 service rifle at 500 yards. The cups that he won, including the prestigious King George VI Shield, were afforded space amongst the other trophies around the high shelf in the dining hall in his House at Harrow.

Percy remembered Ray Gunn, particularly for his advice in moments of stress in the search for distinction.

"Always look at something green before you pull the trigger," he used to say. "It stops any hesitation before you blow someone's brains out."

* * * * *

In the school holidays, Percy had taken up kayaking, and he investigated every waterway between Oxford and Windsor. This includes the giant ancient sewers from underneath Windsor Castle, under the royal farms and meadows, down to an open grill on the bank of the Thames at Datchet. Percy often wondered whether he should wake up the Queen from the unknown bowels of her home like a modern version of Guy Fawkes. He was quite sure that no one else had bothered to kayak up the Queen's back passage.

Percy camped beside the river in all weathers and quickly learned to fend for himself. He simply returned the gestures and waves of other water folk, and, apart from his friend Barney, he rarely took anyone in his double-seater kayak. Who needed to be splashed every ten seconds by someone sitting in the front and blocking the view?

With his first Brownie box camera, Percy started taking pictures of the river and its wildlife, and as the pictures always came out fuzzy, he joined the Harrow Photographic Club for some much-needed professional advice.

"Always prepare and envisage the result before you press the button", " advised Elova Shott from the school publicity office and the club secretary. "This will apply to most of your opportunities after you leave the protection of these walls."

The membership had an added bonus of organised trips to London galleries where, after five minutes looking at the exhibitions, Percy, Randall Crawley, and Toby Ornotobe would wander off for a few hours looking around Soho. They would snap pictures of the girls in the doorways with their bouffant hairdos. Then they would walk to Leicester Square and snap James Dean lookalikes strolling along among long-haired hippies playing guitars. It was dangerous for three boys in school uniforms with short back and sides to snigger, so they went past the weirdos with straight faces and jumped into the first café.

"We're standing out as dogs bollocks!" they agreed.

The comments from the workmen inside confirmed their worst fears.

They ignored the immediate 'Pillocks!' and 'Where's Mummy then?', but then one of a group of council workers walked up to Toby Ornotobe as he made a selection from the jukebox.

"Which zoo do you come from!" he asked.

"Actually, I escaped from the London Zoo just this morning," Toby answered in his polished aristocratic accent.

"You'd best be getting back in your cage, you baboon!" he grinned as he looked towards his mates.

Toby was one of three black boys at Harrow. Three was a big number considering how difficult it was at that time to escape from the confines of the colonies. Toby surprised everyone with his grasp of English manners.

"That girl has got breasts the size of the dome at St Paul's Cathedral!" he whispered as a young female sat on the other side of the room with a cup of tea.

"Ask her if she wants a cream bun!" whispered Percy.

"Where are you from?" Toby asked her instead, in the politest accent possible.

"Gerroff!" she replied with a sneer.

"And where is that?" asked Toby as she turned her back on him.

"A gentle male voice cruised through the air towards Toby and asked him if he wanted twenty quid?"

"Why are you wearing lipstick?" Toby asked politely.

The man sat and took out a packet of Rizlas to roll a cigarette.

One of the workmen ground his cigarette butt into a piece of charred toast.

"I think it's time to leave," Percy suggested.

"Is this what they call 'camp'?" asked Randall as they walked out, probably just in time.

They ended up on the corner of Carnaby Street and sat watching and wondering where these strangely dressed people could possibly live.

"Where are you from?" Toby suddenly asked a girl dressed in a red and green crochet blanket.

"Artlepool!" she smiled, scratching her bare left armpit.

"I read once that they called people from Hartlepool 'monkey hangers'!" piped up Randall Crawley.

"They always have a lot to say!" she answered vacantly.

"It comes from when a French frigate ran aground off Hartlepool," replied Randall in his crystal accent. "The only survivor from the storm was the ship's monkey, so you Hartlepuddlians thought he was a Frenchman and hanged him."

"Are you a Frenchie, then?" she asked as her lip turned down.

"God created the French just to get up every Englishman's nose," Randall said casually as he eyed up her colourful look and long hair. "Are you part of this Flower Power?"

"Look around you", she replied. "We're all pissed off at you lot telling us what to do!"

"Us lot?" asked Toby.

"Get up to 'Artlipool, and I'll show you the real world!" she laughed, exposing two missing teeth.

It was the first time the boys had any idea about the psychedelic movement, the peace signs, and the flared trousers. They thought this was something that was started in the United States as a reaction to the Vietnam War. What was it doing in Oxford Street, and what changes were these 'Hippies' demanding?

"It's the new world of free love and gay rights and Black Panthers!" Percy surmised. "We're out on a limb at Harrow because our parents are not about to embrace this new ideology."

* * * * *

The famous Eton versus Harrow cricket match at Lords during the half-term weekend each summer was a big highlight of the school year. Percy would phone home to remind his mother that attendance was obligatory.

"Make your own way to Lords, and we'll pick you up from school after the match", Mrs. Vere suggested.

"Oh, and enjoy the match!" she added as she struggled with the prospect of three days of Percy at home.

"How can I enjoy myself with four foreigners who can't get home?" Percy asked, but the line was dead.

"I'm rehearsing for Hamlet", Toby confirmed, but I'm game for a bit of 'flower power'."

It was on the Saturday morning of the match that Bita Fluff, the teenage German maid, came into Percy's room to clean.

"Would you like to have your photograph taken this afternoon?" Percy ventured. "You could bring your friend!"

Bita Fluff and her friend from Hamburg, Ina Rush, were the two housemaids who lived somewhere in the roof space. They normally cleaned the empty rooms during class time, and the boys were forbidden to talk to them.

"We are not allowed," she confirmed hesitatingly, batting her eyelids.

"But no one is here today," encouraged Percy, ignoring the fact that he had a cricket match to attend.

"You will be nice?" she asked.

"Alas, poor Yorick!" Toby replied.

"Forget the cricket," Randall announced. "We're all skipping the match!"

"It's a perfect plan," Percy encouraged him. "How will anyone know?"

They waited in the Photographic Club room until the girls arrived at 3:00 p.m. They hesitated in the doorway.

"This could easily be the start of you becoming models," Randall suggested as he ushered them onto one of the huge old sofas and stood back to stare at them.

Toby was standing in the background with his camera, but no one could see him.

"So, you will need photographs of yourselves", Percy suggested as he pulled Toby forward to put his camera on a tripod.

"The best way to be noticed in magazines is to take off some of your clothes," Randall announced casually.

"Where I come from, no one wears clothes", Toby confirmed as if it would make them strip off.

As the reality began to bite, Percy realised that this whole thing was not such a good idea, but it was too late. Randall had got the two maids to drape themselves together over the largest armchair, and he had undone the top buttons of their blouses.

"What do we do now?" Percy asked Randall.

"We have to cover them all over with body oil," Toby suggested, unconcerned. "It brings out the natural tone of the Scandinavian skin."

"What body oil?" asked the incredulous Percy.

"This body oil!" replied Toby, pulling a bottle of the kitchen's sunflower cooking oil out of his satchel.

After fifteen minutes, the maids had their shirts off and were giggling wildly as Toby massaged. Then, suddenly, Percy had his hands guided onto the forbidden area of a pair of breasts.

"Everything is developing splendidly!" Toby announced as he unzipped her skirt to expose her underwear.

It was the most exciting moment in the history of the Harrow School Photographic Society.

Then the door burst open, and the silhouette of Mark Myword in his mortarboard appeared.

"Now there's a picture!" he spluttered, initially seeing only Toby's white shirt.

"Too much light behind you for a decent picture!" observed Toby as he turned to block Mark's view of the girls.

Randall had ducked smartly behind the sofa, and Percy just stood there thinking he was in a dream.

"Aren't you horrible worms supposed to be watching cricket?" enquired Mark, but then his eyes adjusted to the light and he looked at what was happening on the sofa.

Then his mouth fell open.

"You horrible worms!" he repeated, but this time, it had a new and menacing vehemence. "You may not be in my class anymore, but I've got you now!"

He turned to the girls.

"We are not doing anything wrong," they stammered as they looked for their clothes.

"Get out of here!" Mark ordered.

Mark watched the maids pull up their skirts and button their tops while Percy fiddled with the camera in a vain attempt to persuade Mark that this was a genuine piece of artistic work.

"Vere! Ornotobe!" Mark concluded ominously as the girls scurried out. "You will report to me in Bradby's House in one hour."

Mark disappeared as quickly as he had arrived.

Toby was the first to try React.

"What was that bulge in his trousers?" he joked.

"Why didn't you lock the door?" asked Percy in panic.

"I thought you had!" Toby answered as he slumped in the chair. "There goes all that studying down the drain."

"I have a feeling that is the least of your problems!" Randall suggested as he emerged from his hiding place.

"The girls will say nothing happened?" Percy ventured.

"That won't help us," remarked Toby as he tried to convince himself. "You can't reason with destiny!"

* * * * *

Percy telephoned home from the call-box outside Gieves, 'Outfitters for Young Gentlemen', and reported to Commander Vere that he was probably going to be needed to pick Percy up.

"Why?" the commander asked. "Have you been expelled?"

"Not yet!" Percy replied, mortified that it was a possibility.

"Telephone me when you know," his father ordered.

"Telling your parents is always a mistake," suggested Toby.

"It's the only way I will be able to get his attention," replied Percy, realising that his father had not asked why he was even calling.

On the dot of the appointed time, the two boys knocked at Mark Myword's study door.

"Come!"

They entered into a potential end-of-life situation.

"I have thought about this carefully," Mark started.

The boys saw a chink of hope.

"I'm going to inform the headmaster on his return from Lords," he continued.

The chink disappeared.

"You may go."

Percy telephoned home again.

"I'm staying the weekend," he said. "I seem to have got myself into a bit of a jam!"

"No doubt the headmaster will contact me if there is anything I need to know, Percy," Commander Vere replied.

The following morning, both boys were summoned to the great study of Dr James Dictum. Immaculately turned out with short hair groomed and shoes shining, they stood at attention in front of the great man.

"I have decided to make an example of both of you," he said abruptly.

Dr James Dictum paused for effect, and it was obvious that there was no need for the boys to react or speak.

"Since I consider that both the girls in this sorry affair must shoulder some of the blame, I have to inform you that you will not be seeing them again. They have been dismissed. I have considered expulsion for both of you, but I feel that this would be too severe with only a year to go here at Harrow. I have therefore decided that you will clean all the windows of this House in the two weeks after your final exams and before the end of term. That is all."

The boys walked out ecstatic.

"That headmaster is a smart cookie!" Percy realised. "No public hanging and we get to sit our university exams!"

"Do you know how many windows there are in this house?" Toby asked.

"Who cares?" Percy answered. "We've just escaped everlasting damnation!"

With exams over, they had to come to grips with the fact that there must have been over a thousand windows in the building.

"Do you think he meant outside and inside?" Toby frowned. "Maybe we should get sick, and the matron will send us home?"

"At least we should make a start so he can see we have learned honour in this place?" Percy decided.

On the second day, Percy had a ladder and a bucket up the front of the Headmaster's house above the ancient carved Portland stone entrance. Dr James Dictum appeared under him on the way out. The headmaster hardly looked up.

"Love labours lost, Vere!" he pronounced dramatically before sweeping off down the street.

* * * * *

Percy was delighted to have learned that 'courting' was not holding hands. It was apparently rubbing oil on maids and touching their hidden bits, as Miles had done with Matron.

Meanwhile, a knee-jerk reaction was building not three hundred yards from the Headmaster's House.

Egor Beva, one of Percy's classmates and the son of a minister in the Czechoslovakian government, developed a relationship with Eva Orr, a Swedish maid who lived somewhere in the roof space in Newlands House. Egor was senior enough to spend five classes a week studying in his room. Sometimes this coincided with the sixteen-year-old Eva doing the hoovering around him in a short white skirt and blouse with only a loose apron. It was more than Egor Beva could stand. At first, he had bitten through his lip as she reached up over his desk to shake the dust out of the curtains, but after five times of curtain shaking, his hand slipped up between her thighs. Eva responded by dragging him down onto the bed.

It was three months later that Eva started to swell, and the truth came out with a tearful admission to the housemaster's wife.

The housemaster of Newlands at the time was the kindly and often inventive Hugh Mankind. Hugh was a teacher of literature, a devotee of Dryden and Byron, and a man who valued his contribution to the arts. He was proud to have coached a number of his pupils to literary scholarships. Egor was a talented pupil who was likely to excel. The odds were he had a better than even chance of being a leading light in the culture of Czechoslovakia. His family name was already carved in gold on the list of Harrovians on the Newlands wall.

Hugh telephoned Egor's parents and suggested a meeting to try to resolve the situation without triggering a public scandal in England and an embarrassment for the family at home.

"I have spoken to Egor, and he wants to marry the girl without further ado," Hugh opened in his soft voice at their meeting. "The school will allow no talk of abortion, so the girl can move to the village, the child will be born, and Egor will finish his studies. No one will know. The alternative is he returns home with you now."

The Egor baby was Harrow's best-kept secret.

* * * * *

The beginning of the term was always accompanied by speculation about the quality of any new cleaning staff. In the case of Newlands, they would arrive and be shown their quarters by the butler. He would then advise them of their duties and make sure they were dressed neatly in their white outfits for their first appearance in laying the place settings at assembly.

Boys would traditionally wink and snigger as they evaluated the length of the legs and the size of the breasts at first sight. However, the birth of the Egor baby had persuaded Hugh Mankind to change that hallowed tradition. He had scanned Encyclopaedia Britannica and decided the most unattractive girls by far were living in Ecuador.

"I need you to go to Quito", he told his wife. "Bring back eight females who speak basic English to replace our maids. Nothing that looks even half pretty, okay! Actually, the uglier the better, so it should be easy and make sure they don't shave their armpits!"

The first day of the new term, when the new maids appeared, there was a minute of eerie silence, a cacophony of groans as the boys surveyed eight short, dark, and sometimes hairy Ecuadorian ladies in black aprons.

Egor had just taken on board the enormity of his folly.

It was clear that Percy's virginity would not be lost at Harrow, and, as it happened, it did not have to.

Commander Vere's sight had deteriorated over the years, and three weeks into the next term, he had a car accident. The housemaster summoned Percy to let him know that his father was in hospital, and he enquired whether Percy would like a few days at home.

"That would be awfully kind," Percy agreed.

The following day, after visiting his father, who was perfectly comfortable with sandbags around his neck, Percy cycled to the local tennis courts in search of a game. Molly Cule, an athletic little server whom Percy had often noticed, was also looking for a game.

"There's no one else around today!" she had sighed.

They played all afternoon until the light was fading. Percy wanted to continue, but Molly had other ideas, and she suggested a drink at the Ferret and Beaver on the village green.

"Leave your bike inside the court. It's safe enough," she suggested. "We'll walk over."

Molly then took Percy's arm and dragged him towards the pub.

Percy had not been able to help himself staring at her each time she bent over to reach a ball, and he moved discreetly across the court for a better view.

"If you stand over there, you won't be in a good position for the backhand," she suggested.

"I'll keep myself positioned ready," Percy smiled back.

Molly bought half a pint of lemonade shandy for Percy and a large gin and tonic for herself. She then sat opposite Percy at one of the glass-topped garden tables through which she allowed Percy to snatch glances at the most powerful weapon in the universe.

"Down the hatch!" slurped Molly.

'I think you mean up the snatch!' thought Percy, blushing and looking at his feet.

"You live around here!" she asked.

"Yes."

"How old are you?"

"Seventeen."

"Mmmm."

"It's ten minutes to seven!" Percy said, jumping up. "I've got to go!"

They walked back to the courts, only to see a large padlock on the gate and Percy's bike leaning against the inside of the ten-foot-high netting.

There was no sign of the groundsman and no way to get the bike back until the morning.

"That's a bit of a pity!" Molly mused as she plucked the strings of her racquet.

"I don't suppose you'd lend me the bus fare home?" said Percy. "It's only tuppence."

"Never a borrower or a lender be! That's my motto," she answered deliberately. "But I'll drive you back to my place, and you can walk from there."

"Where's your place?"

"It's the cottage before the Esso garage on Blackberry Lane."

"That's great!" Percy lied.

"What do you do?" asked Percy as they sped off.

"I'm a laboratory technician," she confirmed as she crashed the gears.

Molly wasn't tall, but her driving seat was too far back, so she wasn't pushing hard enough on the clutch when she changed gears. Also, her tennis skirt was riding up to her waist. Percy tried not to stare at her thighs rubbing up and down against each other with her knickers in plain view. Then there was the pending uncertainty of what was to become of the stirring in his tennis shorts.

As they pulled up in front of Molly's cottage, she went straight in without glancing at Percy.

"Thanks for the lift!" Percy shouted through the open front door.

"Come in!" her voice answered.

"What for?"

"It would be rude not to!" she replied.

Percy had been disciplined to obey orders, and he walked into her space like a robot, but Molly was nowhere to be seen.

Then her voice came down the little carpeted staircase.

"Get those sweaty things off!"

Percy stood bemused in the little sitting room for at least fifteen seconds.

"There's a shower up here!"

"I should be going!"

"You'll catch a cold!" Molly answered in a silk dressing gown from the top of the staircase.

Percy stepped gingerly up the treads until she reached forward and grabbed his shirt to pull him onto the landing. She went into the bathroom and left the door half open.

Percy stood transfixed in front of an old grandfather clock while he listened to the splashing coming from a shower.

"So this is it!" he said towards the little sailing ship moving with the waves across the face of the clock.

"Great, isn't it?" Molly said, immediately behind him, in a silk dressing gown. "When I was a little girl, my grandfather would lift me up and let me wind it."

"I might just be able to do that!" Percy replied as he felt the stirring in his tennis shorts.

The warm, scented Molly was too close to him, and the stirring intensified as she pulled him up against him and positioned her lips softly against his mouth.

Percy's eyes looked urgently around for an answer.

"Maybe I'll take a cold shower," he muttered.

"I should put your tennis racquet down first!"

"That's not my tennis racquet!" he said, embarrassed.

Percy escaped into the bathroom and came back in a fresh linen dressing gown to see Molly sitting at her dressing table, her head back as she dried her hair.

"Come and lie next to me!" Molly commanded as she lay on the bed and pulled Percy down beside her in one motion.

Molly had Percy out of the dressing gown and under the covers as if she had done this before.

"Is this your first time?" she laughed.

"Don't be ridiculous!" Percy panicked as Molly dug her fingernails into his neck.

"Blimey!" said Percy in shock eight seconds later.

"I'm a laboratory technician, and I'll let you know what happens after another test," she replied.

After he was back in the safety of school, Percy received a letter from Molly. If he could get out, she could take an afternoon off work.

* * * * *

Despite this new distraction in his final year at Harrow, Percy worked hard towards his exams in mathematics and history. He excelled at maths, but he took a special interest in the history of Central Europe, which became his specialist subject.

It seems that Europe had bred the first recorded megalomaniacs, and their various power plays became something of a fascination to Percy. Modern European history focused on Adolf Hitler and his 'Final Solution', and it seemed his rise and fall fitted an age-old pattern of secret alliances. Horror was the most efficient way forward to genocide, although the word was not invented before the murder of six million Jews. Then it was expanded to anyone intent on destroying a national, racial, or religious group. Hitler was one of those people capable of generating a following of fanatics. History tells the story of these people wanting to wipe out sections of humanity. If anyone gets globalisation to take root, this will never stop.

History in school was taught under the headings 'good' and 'evil' and 'politics' – the choice of which side to blame was determined by 'historians' after the cessation of hostilities. 'Blame' was not necessarily attributed to those who had been slaughtered, but it fitted most narratives in the history books.

Generally, if the victims had no political voice, they deserved what they got, and, in historical terms, their sacrifice would be brushed under the carpet.

Schoolboy heroes immortalised in the cinema included manipulated stories of the likes of Lawrence of Arabia, who led a guerrilla warfare against the Ottoman Empire to create an independent Arab territory. The British and French betrayed the Arabs as they took control of the ports and supply routes for themselves. Same story at Rorkes Drift, where the Zulu Kingdom refused to accept the imperial dominance of Britain in Southern Africa and fought with spears and animal-skin shields. Honours were bestowed throughout history upon those who slaughtered women and children. History records the most ghastly examples across Peru and the Great Plains of North America. If an invader is determined to steal your land and everything you stood for, then they would do so with superior weaponry. So-called progress indicates that civilisation has made it possible for a lunatic to wake up and order an entire continent to be consigned to rubble with nuclear firepower.

Percy had already been aware of loosely connected groups of people with immense wealth who surfaced once in a while in history to evidence their refusal to stop at nothing to gain their ends. The real question was 'what could those ends be other than global control of the peoples on Earth!

* * * * *

'President Kennedy has been shot!'

The words flew from boy to boy as the tragedy created a poignancy previously unknown in the History classroom.

Kennedy was America's first Catholic president. This was a family so influential that they were capable of forever secreting the fact that, in 1953, Kennedy had been divorced from Drearie, his childhood sweetheart in Palm Beach. J. Edgar Hoover at the FBI and the Pope had arranged a papal annulment, so Kennedy was not technically 'divorced.' The American people could then swallow Jackie as the 'first' lady of a sex-crazed president.

Charlie Lill, head of History at Harrow, was a Catholic and one of the most conservative people in England. Harrow was not a Catholic school, but Charlie Lill had his own agenda and advocated that the Catholic Church could do no wrong.

"The Roman Catholic Church received its mandate to run the world from the Donation of Constantine," he started. "The Emperor gave the Catholic Church legal title to all the territory under the rule of the Roman Empire."

"I thought Pope Hadrian mysteriously pulled that document out of thin air in AD 774," observed Toby Ornotobe. "It was a forgery!"

The rest of the class sat up, amazed.

"And you were there, I suppose!" barked Charlie Lill.

"No, but my father was brought up in a Jesuit school in Nigeria," answered Toby. "He was told that he could be excommunicated under the 1917 Code of Catholic Canon Law if he offended the Catholic Church. Over time, he discovered that everything he had been taught by the Jesuits was a lie. He became a Freemason and aligned with the money, but he always embraced our tribal ways."

"Like swinging through the trees?" enquired Charlie Lill, restraining himself as best he could. "The Donation of Constantine, forged or not, gave the Pope ecclesiastical and secular control over all the rulers of Christendom, and anyone who disagreed with the official Papal line was instantly branded a heretic. There was no escape because the Pope had a massive network of bishops, abbots, and all kinds of clergy who had inviolate status over both religious and civil activities. They enforced a Holy Inquisition that hunted down anyone they didn't particularly like."

Charlie Lill smiled as he was just getting started.

"They used the rack and thumbscrew, put out eyes with red-hot pokers, and burnt people at the stake," he grinned. "Constantine's empire was at least Spain, France, Britain, the Netherlands, and Germany. Then, in 1493, one year after Christopher Columbus set foot in the New World, Pope Alexander VI decreed that the Donation included the rights to lands not yet discovered. So he leased the Americas to Spain and Portugal as tenants on the understanding they would convert all the inhabitants to the Catholic faith!"

"And that led to a slaughter in South America, which was unprecedented in history with 50 million dead," Toby muttered.

"They died from the flu," said Charlie Lill testily.

"You have to admit the conquistadores were fanatical", objected Toby. "They even took the Pacific Ocean."

"Oh, really?" smiled Charlie.

"Yes!" Toby insisted. "When the first priest saw there was another ocean on the other side of Mexico, he jumped into the surf shouting, 'I take possession of this water in the name of Jesus Christ.'

"And where exactly did you hear this story?" asked Charlie Lill.

"It's on page 72 of Harrap's History of Spain with a picture!" grinned Rick.

"From a camera, I suppose!" goaded Charlie Lill. "Now turn to page 67 of the Oxford European History, and who can tell me the causes of the Reformation?"

Toby's hand went up immediately.

"Pope Alexander VI was Rodrigo Borgia, father of Cesare and Lucretia," he started. "They signalled a low point in morality by stealing everything of any value from every vassal nation. The Reformation was an arrangement between the brightest minds in Europe to get rid of the authority of Rome. In England, that process was led by Henry VIII, who ransacked the priories and monasteries. In America, it brought together

Church and State as a single entity. You could say this was the beginning of what we now call 'globalisation' and to get there, more millions in their own peaceful space had to die."

The school bell rang in the distance, signalling the end of the morning classes across the Hill. It was also the signal for slamming desk lids, grabbing satchels, and scrambling for the door.

"That fat fool wouldn't last three seconds where I come from," declared the grinning Toby Ornotobe.

Percy's grandparents had both given him a grounding in history and religion and even an insight into the occult, and he was gobsmacked that Toby knew so much.

"The Niger Oil Corporation is one of the most bribed companies in history," Toby explained. "Elite forces are bent on taking over, and their first move is bribery and treachery – it's a never-ending consequence of wealth!"

* * * * *

The school curriculum included a mandatory eight hours a week sitting in the great Vaughan Library at Harrow. There was not always a specific task, but here the boys were only a few feet away from a hundred shelves, thirty feet high, full of history. It was like his grandfather's library, but this lot was catalogued and, if you chose to look, there was a financial history over centuries commanded by the same powerful families, too powerful to challenge. Their secrets were referenced way back to the medieval activities of the 'Knights Templar'.

"You should talk to Otto von Hamburger," Toby had suggested. "He's always boasting that his father is in some secret organisation that runs the world!"

Otto von Hamburger was a tall, slim boy with a ram-rod straight back who spent most of his time in the Science Labs.

"This is a secret," he replied pompously. "We Hamburgers can be traced back to the Crusaders!"

Percy started to read about these Crusaders, whose first venture into the Holy Land in 1095 was a religious quest to take Jerusalem. Then, in 1118, when they had control, they started to excavate under the 10th-century Temple of King Solomon, son of King David. They were looking for the Ark of the Covenant, which was the reason the Temple was the focus of Christian worship for the Israelites.

They apparently achieved massive wealth afterwards, and such was their prestige that Europe's youth flocked to join up. These new recruits brought, as required, all their worldly goods, including, of course, massive landholdings. The power of these Crusaders increased to such an extent that their Order became Europe's most powerful political and financial group. This definitely got right under the skin of the Catholic Church, which was being deprived of handling the largest commercial transactions between Sovereign territories, and that included the banking transactions on all sides.

By 1307, the jealous Catholic Church was anxious to subvert the influence, and they planned a Europe-wide slaughter on the night of Friday, 13th October. The greedy and unimportant French king, Philippe IV, was under instruction from Pope Clement V to kill the Knights Templar in their beds wth a symbolic coup de grâce. This was the torture of their Grandmaster, Jacques de Rotisserie. Such a torture was openly carried out over seven years in Notre Dame and sometimes over an open fire with Jacques de Rotisserie on the spit.

Some survivors of the slaughter escaped with their treasures from the Templar port of La Rochelle and scattered around the world. They regrouped in new locations in understandable secrecy under the name 'Freemasonry'. Their members became prominent in the Arts, the Sciences, and in commercial dealings, so the Catholic Church continued as their greatest enemy.

"Who do you think financed Christopher Columbus in his discovery of America?" Percy asked Otto after browsing through this ancient information. "Charlie Lill tells us it was King Ferdinand of Spain, but it says here that Ferdinand had no money and refused to help Columbus. Then it says that Columbus was financed by a secret group that had long established a military base at Chateau de Blanchefort, just across the border at Rennes, and previously a Templar stronghold. Their descendants believed the Columbus speculation of an undiscovered New World across the sea because their forebears had already been there. Columbus was himself from a Jewish family, and those who went with him were Jews hiding in Spain from the tortures and murders of the Catholic Inquisition."

"Why do you think that Columbus had a fluted red cross stitched to his mainsail?" murmured Otto. "It's the same shape as the Maltese Cross, which is black, and they changed the colour to red, the 'croix patee'. This was in reverence of their brothers in the Order who had been slaughtered by papal command."

"And the Spanish never saw the irony of Columbus signifying new hope for the Jews?" asked Percy.

"Imagine when the Catholic Church heard that a New World was really out there", Otto grinned. "He ordered Ferdinand of Spain to take it for the Church in the name of God with the justification that it was ordained under the original Donation of Constantine!"

Otto von Hamburger was being groomed as a statesman from his time at Harrow.

Charlie Lill was right about one thing with his watch phrase, 'follow the money, and you'll end up with the truth.'

* * * * *

The truth was that Europe believed the Templars had discovered a Great Secret during the Crusades, and it was described in various ways as ancient knowledge giving the Jews a mandate from a previous civilisation which had perished in a great flood. They alerted the world from the pulpits that one day they would link the positioning of the stars to reveal the existence of previously unknown inhabitants on the planet Earth.

Percy read how there was an ancient hereditary priesthood known as Rex Deus. These 'Kings of God' faithfully passed down a secret knowledge by ritual until AD70 when the Romans under Titus took Jerusalem, massacred the Jews, and destroyed the Temple.

It made sense that some of the priests of Rex Deus had escaped to Europe and had a reason to organise the Crusades to go back into Jerusalem.

"Why did they bother?" asked Percy.

"Because they needed to recover something they had left behind?" answered Otto. "It was a secret knowledge that would prove the teachings of the Catholic Church were fabricated. However, by then, Jerusalem and its Temple were under Turkish control, and it would be tricky just to walk in and scout around. It took those seven years to find what they believed was confirmation of the Bible story. Meanwhile, the Catholic Church was in overdrive to protect their version of events by rape, murder, buggery, and burning at the stake.

Percy had his own ideas that Templar symbols carved by freemasons into the stone at Roslyn Chapel outside Edinburgh were a representation of sounds, and those sounds were the possible key to the mysteries of lost technologies. It was a far cry from anything being taught or even discussed.

His Harrow days set the foundation of what Percy believed in, a period of history when Christianity started to experience a depleted audience worldwide. The Catholic Church despaired at the rise of Islam and used the threat of summary excommunication of anyone becoming a Freemason through the 1917 Code of Catholic Canon Law. So it was that Toby's father had been told that the Catholic Church would deny him entry to Heaven.

Freemasonry became a middle ground in a chain of hundreds of stunning buildings across the world as the 'United Grand Lodge'. Each represented a 'Temple' for tradesmen and professionals to group together in secrecy. Only those with political authority were able to rise above the first three levels of a 33-degree hierarchy. Those higher levels provided 'masons' with influence in law enforcement, civil regulation, politics, and banking. When the League of Nations created a State of Israel, this was to become its military stronghold.

"Jesuits made religion a big part of community life in the jungles of Africa", Toby explained. "As president of the Niger Oil Corporation, my father became a mason to group together the network of professionals he needed in oil support services like the docks, road haulage, and the building of pipelines. That was the protection he needed to stop the President and his mates from stealing the new money coming into Nigeria. That's why he was threatened with excommunication."

Otto slammed shut an ancient volume, and a mist of red and gold flecked dust ballooned into the air.

"Let's go and have a swim!" they all said together

"And a choc-ice", added Percy.

* * * * *

Percy continued his research alone to identify oligarchical family structures and their descendants with monopolistic arrangements. These had hereditary military reach into most of the Royal Courts of Europe, so it was a necessity for senior judges to be recruited into their ranks.

The structure was a mirror image of how the commercial 'families' in Venice and Genoa created the 'Great Council' in 1171 to rule financial dealings through a 'Commission'. It was this Commission that appointed the Doge in each city. By 1297, with 'family' members in place, the 'Commission' closed membership of the Great Council except by heredity. Thus, they created the first closed shop in history to prevent any takeover of their business interests. Moreover, they absolved themselves of accountability.

The 'Commission' and its Great Council were opposed only once. This was an uprising of the citizens known as the Tiepolo's Rebellion, and the rebel leaders were assassinated, their families were bankrupted, their parents were kidnapped and tortured, and all the half-decent-looking females in their families were raped in public.

The 'family' tenet of the Great Council achieved absolute control by fear and a feeling of helplessness in ordinary people. So, the 'Mafia' was born with its ruling Council forever called 'The Commission'. The word Mafia was appropriately coined by the rebel leader screaming 'Mafia' as his daughter was gang-raped on the kitchen table in front of the rest of his family.

"Lessons can always be learned from history," Charlie Lill repeatedly reminded his class. "Now we have the United Nations that will be our first step to globalisation. Harrow is teaching you about decisions that can make a difference in a changing world."

'What is this thing called the world?' read Percy from the work of the Danish philosopher Kierkegaard. 'If I am compelled to take part, where are the directors? I want to see the directors!'

* * * * *

Percy tried to find the outcome that would be relevant in his lifetime. It started in 1815, with the Congress of Vienna, when the most powerful families in Europe and their sworn enemy, the Catholic Church, agreed to use Switzerland, with perpetual neutrality, as a sacrosanct financial haven for their various fund-collecting activities. No matter how many times they would provoke wars, their money in Switzerland would be safe.

So along came World War I, and no one made any move on the Vatican, so Pope Benedict XV used all his influence to protect Emperor William II and strengthen the Vatican's links with Germany. Then the new Pope Pius X urged the Emperor Franz Joseph of Austro-Hungary to attack Serbia, which was full of Orthodox Christians. There's a pattern here. The Vatican had its own Monsignor Eugenio Pacelli appointed Apostolic Nuncio in Germany alongside the Pope's Privy Chamberlain, Franz von Papen. It was Pacelli and von Papen who devised the plan to restore the glory of the Germanic Holy Roman Empire.

They stirred up fascism and invigorated the Catholic Central Party in Germany. They voted full powers to Adolf Hitler on 26th March, 1933. Franz von Papen became Vice Chancellor of the Third Reich, second only to Hitler, and that meant the Jews, heretics, and liberals were all earmarked for extermination. The architect of genocide was Monseignor Eugenio Pacelli, who avoided Nuremberg and became Pope Pius XII.

That's why every financial group uses Switzerland to launder and store their profits from plunder, smuggling, gambling, prostitution, the arms trade, and drug distribution. Even the Triads in the East made Zurich their financial hub for the trade in heroin.

"Only one version of history is in full view," Charlie Lill agreed. "That is the history of crime because, without crime, there is no history. All the most important turning points in history are triggered by murders, acts of violence, robberies, wars, rebellions, massacres, tortures, and executions. This is the history that is visible because history is what history attributes to itself."

Charlie Lill has provided the last piece of the jigsaw before Percy and his friends would join the rest of the world to find what part they might play in it.

* * * * *

That world was forging a future dictated by economic influence created by such bodies as the Institute of Economic Affairs, founded in 1955, the Council on Foreign Affairs, the Tavistock Institute, the Committee of Liberation Theology, the Centre for Financial Innovation, the Adam Smith Institute, the Club of Rome, the World Economic Forum, and the Pinus Inner Circle. They linked to promote their alternative philosophy with the world's leading financial and raw-material institutions. It all started at the Hotel du Parc in a tiny hamlet in Switzerland."

At first, they were 38 real smart-arses with Catholic-only membership under the economics guru Professor Milton Friedman. There were no funny handshakes, and their objective was simply to defeat socialism in all its forms. Milton Friedman became a Nobel laureate with a mission to set up local think tanks to spread the word. The first 'word' was a reunification of Germany to become the hub of European policy that would take control of every aspect of society. The counter philosophy was a society that puts equality before freedom.

It seemed that the Vatican's objective of domination across the globe never changed. A Catholic Germany was their natural springboard, led by their new chancellor, Konrad Adenauer.

Percy was reminded that Charlie Lill had a sealed glass bottle of formaldehyde on his desk containing Napoleon Bonaparte's genitalia.

* * * * *

Percy and his prep-school friend, Miles Long, with scholarships in mathematics, would reunite at Cambridge.

In his last week at Harrow, Percy met Sir Winston Churchill. After a formal address of thanks to an Old Harrovian, the prefects were invited to drinks in the Headmaster's house.

Percy made sure that he was able to speak to Sir Winston amongst the chatter.

'You are a great author, and I believe you are a master of paraprosdokians, ' Percy ventured.

'Ah!' he replied. 'Figures of speech in which the latter part of a sentence is surprising. What is your favourite?'

'Since light travels faster than sound, some people appear bright until you hear them speak', Percy answered. 'And may I ask your own favourite, Sir?'

'That's easy', Sir Winston replied. 'Knowledge is knowing a tomato is a fruit. Wisdom is not putting it in a fruit salad.'

* * * * *

"I'm not cut out for this mathematics," Percy was quick to complain. "I've requested a change to the law."

There followed various areas of constitutional law, law of contract, a history of law, tort, and property law. The so-called families were part of an Establishment that protected itself through the laws of land ownership.

"Look how it's moved on and is shaping up internationally", Percy noted to Miles. "This guy Han Shandi, recently arrived from the Punjab, is going to court to open a new door of liberalisation. He's a Muslim arguing his democratic rights in the UK for breach of contract against his landlord, Mr Christian Temple."

"That's because the British took over control of the whole subcontinent, and he wants revenge", answered Miles. "It started with the East India Company in 1857, looting as much of the wealth as they could carry back to the UK over two hundred years. Indians were excluded from any government in their own country, and this fucker Shandi probably wants his stuff back."

"But we built a massive rail system for them to create trade?"

"That was to access every part of the land famously known as the 'Silk Road,'" Miles sneered. "The main reason for the trains was to connect the areas fortified by the British so their East India Company could loot from everywhere under their protection. They were the Establishment supported by Parliament in a series of Government of India Acts. That meant the British could carry away everything that wasn't nailed down, and it was duty-free!"

Irrespective of the UK bias against the immigrant usurper, the head of the university law faculty, Professor Courtley Shyster, doubted whether Percy was going to stay the course.

"Shyster just called me inferior and is threatening to send me down," exclaimed Percy on a Saturday afternoon by the river. "I've got to get out of here!"

"So, ruin your life," replied Miles casually as he lay back on the lawn and rested his head on a book to allow the sun to warm his face.

"But I've got this burning feeling that I'm not inferior?" Percy ventured.

Miles was soaking in the sun, but he managed to reply dreamily 'It was Eleanor Roosevelt who said, 'No one can make you inferior without your permission!'"

"Nevertheless, it's time to move on," Percy decided as he pulled the cork out of the second bottle of Château Neuf du Tap. "Remember your Keats?

'Stop and consider! Life is but a day;
A fragile dew-drop on its perilous way,
From a tree's summit;
Life is the rose's hope while yet unblown...'

"For God's sake, shut up," replied Miles. "And don't think some stupid poem is going to help you when your parents find out you've ended your best chance of becoming anything!"

"They're also worried that I won't be tested in a war!" Percy answered as he filled two beakers.

Percy had made law a little more tolerable by collecting some courtroom moments out of the mass of papers he was expected to read. He pulled a sheet of paper out of his leather folder.

"Look at this transcript, Miles," he suggested. "This puts a new international slant on court proceedings:

Barrister: Can you describe the individual?
Witness: He was about medium height and had a beard.
Barrister: Was this a male or a female?
Witness: Guess.
Barrister: Do you recall the time that you examined the body?
Witness: The autopsy started around 8:30 p.m.
Barrister: And the subject was dead at the time?
Witness: No, he was wondering why I was doing the autopsy.

"So, you're making Shyster into a joke, and that's your mistake", Miles pronounced. "So, maybe you should treat him more seriously?"

Percy raised his glass in the air.

"He who lives without stupidity is not as wise as he thinks," he answered.

Miles paused.

"Life is like a minefield", he concluded. "Some people can walk through a minefield and not tread on a single mine. You're treading on the first mine you come across, and it may kill you. Life is a matter of chance, so the only way forward is to be careful where you tread and have as much sex as you can!"

Miles raised himself on one elbow.

"Public school has taught us how to survive without sex with a woman", he advised. "What else did it tell us except there is nothing better than staying free and, of course, having a relationship with a big pair of tits. Therefore, respect that you are free to find your own way!"

"You're right," Percy agreed, pulling a sheet of paper out of his folder and handing it to Miles:

The United Nations has just issued an urgent warning about BARS (Beer & Alcohol Requirement Syndrome), a newly identified problem that has spread rapidly throughout the world. The disease affects people in different ways.
Believed to have started in Ireland in 1500 BC, BARS seems to affect people who congregate in Taverns or who just congregate. It is not known how the disease is transmitted, but approximately three billion people worldwide are affected, with thousands of new cases appearing every day. Early symptoms of the disease include an uncontrollable urge at 5:00 pm to consume alcohol. This urge is most keenly felt on Fridays. More advanced symptoms of the disease include talking in riddles, singing off-key, heightened sexual attraction towards unattractive women, and unprovoked arguing. In the final stages of the disease, victims often vomit and lose their balance, and loss of their virginity can occur. Sometimes accidents follow from shouting, 'Hey Fred, bet you can't do this!" Side effects include bruising, broken limbs, lost property, killer headaches, and the ruination of any relationship.

"We're trapped in a system where control is everything and sex has to be earned unless you've been trained to bend over properly," Miles replied in obvious exasperation.

Miles sat up, slugged back his wine, and picked up his things.

"There's a fine line in fishing between watching from the riverbank looking like an idiot!" he shouted as he was headed towards the boathouse.

"Bye, Miles," Percy muttered prophetically. "See you in another life."

* * * * *

Percy didn't mention to his parents that he had decided to change course, and he had no idea what he was going to do. He had a camera, and after his inglorious experience at the Harrow School photographic club, he had taken a mountain of photographs of his everyday time at Harrow and in the holidays. He flicked through them and thought of sending a selection to Red Alert, the boss at Reel Life International. Three days later, he telephoned the Reel Life office, and Red Alert's secretary made an appointment. He was amazed at how easy it had been.

When the day came, Percy dressed smartly and took the train to London. He had a nasty feeling that his approach was ridiculous.

"Did Mr Alert like my pictures?" Percy ventured to the receptionist.

"And what pictures would they be?" asked the girl as she filed her nails and answered the phone at the same time.

There was a pause as she picked up another line.

"Red Alert will see you now," she answered casually without looking up from her half-manicured left thumb. "Go through that door, and his secretary will meet you at the end of the corridor."

"I've been reading about the ancient ruins of the Khmer Empire at Angkor," Percy enthused before the handshake was complete. "It would be a perfect subject to present to Reel Life readers."

"Cambodia's very pleasant at this time of year," Alert replied casually, as if he was thinking of something else. "The dry season is from December to May, so you should go around now. I suggest you keep away from the Vietnamese border areas, and when you get back, we'll look at the pictures."

There was a small silence as Red looked down at the unopened packet of Percy's pictures.

"Are you using a proper camera?" he asked.

"The small problem is I don't have any money at the moment!" Percy ventured.

Red Alert looked up at a calendar on his wall. It was December 10th, 1969.

"You can have a return air ticket and £100," he suggested. "My secretary, Daisy Chain, will pass you on to Art Farty, who handles features."

Percy walked out as if on a cloud. He stopped in Berkeley Square and sat on a bench under the trees. Then he felt a folded piece of paper in his pocket. It must have come from Miles when he last wore this suit. He opened it up:

THE PERFECT DAY FOR HER

9:15	Breakfast in bed
10:15	Soothing hot bubble bath
10:00	Manicure and make-up
12:00	Lunch with best friend
12:45	Catch sight of the overweight husband's secretary.
2:00	Unlimited shopping
3:00	Nap
4:00	Three dozen red roses delivered with no name
4:45	Massage - personal trainer says body is perfect
5:30	Choose an outfit from the designer's wardrobe.
7:30	Candlelit dinner for two at the Café de Paris
10:00	Carried onto freshly ironed, crisp linen sheets
11:00	Pillow talk, light touching
11:30	Fall asleep in his strong arms.

THE PERFECT DAY FOR HIM

6:00	Alarm
6:15	Blow job
6:30	Massive shit while reading sports news
7:00	Full on breakfast – cooked by a naked wench who bends over a lot, showing her growler
7:30	Car arrives
7:45	Several beers on the way to the airport
9:15	Flight in a personal jet
9:30	Car to Mirage Resort Golf Club (blow job en route)
10:00	Play the front nine in 2 under par.
12:15	Blow job
12:45	Lunch – steak and lobster with a bottle of Dom Perignon
3:00	Play back nine in 4 under par.
4:30	Car back to the airport (several bourbons)
5:30	Fly to Scotland

6:30 Early evening fishing with all-female gillies, all nude, who also bend over a lot, showing growlers

7:30 Land a world record salmon on light tackle.

9:00 Fly home with a massage and hand job by Marilyn Monroe, bending over, showing her growler.

11:00 Watch the news of the assassination of singer Cliff Rich-Nerd.

11:30 Dom Perignon (1953), big juicy fillet steak followed by ice cream served on a big pair of tits.

11:45 Napoleon Brandy and a Habanos cigar in front of the afternoon's European Cup replay with three naked women masseuses, all with lesbian tendencies

01:30 Nightcap blow job from all three.

02:50 In bed alone

02:59 A twenty-two-second fart that changes note four times and forces the dog to leave the room

Was this the minefield Miles was talking about?

* * * * *

Browns was the hot nightclub in London, around the corner from Berkeley Square. VIP guests were segregated from a massive heaving dance floor by way of a glass staircase and walkway, and famous personalities, eager to be seen, ran the gauntlet for the privilege of sitting up there in the Gods with their own. Most of them were out of their brains on different kinds of stimulants supplied by the richest man in the club, the resident drugs dealer.

Percy didn't know any better and walked right up there into a private party without being stopped by the two large gentlemen at the bottom of the steps.

'Hey, Mick, that 'orse ya tipped me last time cost me a monkey', someone was complaining to the lead singer of the world's most famous band.

Mick Jagger put them straight.

'A horse is a four-legged animal which sometimes wins', he grinned with lips big enough to French kiss a medium-sized Canadian moose.

That evening progressed into a sort of oblivion where these people lived in a different world where a rare life-form congregated. These get-togethers would find their way into the glossies, so their eccentricities became some kind of folklore.

Percy spotted the king of short stories, Truman Capote, of Breakfast at Tiffany's fame and, more appropriately, In Cold Blood. Capote held his masked black and white ball in New York in 1966, and anyone who wasn't invited had to leave the city so they wouldn't be seen and lose face.

Percy then saw Goria von Botox, whose party for her husband's 60th was famous for her two-foot-high pink wig. Then there was Vivien Duffer, daughter of the property legend Charles Claw, last pictured in the specially redecorated Savoy for her birthday party. Vivien was overshadowed by her husband, Joystick Stevens, head of English Heritage. Joystick hosted a jewellery ball in Gstaad, where the tables were decorated with diamonds, emeralds, and sapphires. His guest of honour had been His Perfectness, the Aga Khan, a direct descendant of the Prophet Mohammed. HRH was married in Paris at a reception attended by 2,000 guests. The stars of that show were the stuffed animals with real gems as eyes. Of course, it all made sense now. This was all about being seen to be in control and about sex with the young ladies aspiring to be models hanging on like a sprinkling of hundreds and thousands.

He received a very large vodka, which he buttoned onto the order at the table he was standing next to.

"This is the life!" he muttered as he watched the drug dealer trading openly in the men's room.

"Thank you!" he quipped directly to the last customer who was laying out a line on the tiled basin surround.

"Be my guest", he replied, laying out a second line.

"Thanks!" Percy replied as he was joined by three others, presumably friends.

He emptied the entire contents onto the same space and cut it all into lines. Fifteen seconds later, it was all gone.

Percy went back to the bar to sit next to Goria von Botox and a German midfielder.

"I only like two types of men, domestic and foreign," Goria was saying as she smoothed back her blonde hair.

"That's because men are superior to women," the midfielder replied into a sort of vacuum.

"How is that?" Goria retorted.

Percy couldn't help himself.

"For one thing, men can urinate from a speeding car", he answered as he felt his eyes burning and his head starting to ache.

The Germans' look made it clear Percy was not welcome, so he moved towards the good-looking woman sitting behind him. An hour passed in ten minutes as they drank and chatted and even went down the stairs for an energetic dance.

"Have you ever tried a sportsman's double?" she asked suddenly.

"What's that?" Percy asked, thinking it was a boxer and a tennis player.

"It's a mother and daughter threesome," she replied.

"No, I haven't," blushed Percy as he wondered how good-looking her daughter might be.

Then she said it was Percy's lucky night, and she asked if he would like to come back to her house in Cheyne Walk.

Lost in the haze of opportunity, he agreed. After a twenty-minute drive in the back of her car, her driver pulled up outside an impressive white house with a garden at the front. She opened the front door and turned on the hall light.

Percy closed the door. This was going to be special.

Then she shouted upstairs, "Mother! Are you awake?"

* * * * *

Percy had two weeks before he was leaving for Cambodia, and he had no money, so he thought it useful to ask around to see what he could do.

Percy first met Philip Wayward when he was running a nightclub in the backwaters of Windsor. Unknown bands were paid £5 and a meal to perform. The building was an abandoned stable, which he named the Ricki Tik. Some of the acts he hosted were the young Strolling Bones, Eric Clapton, and a homeless, blind person who called himself Stevie Wonder. The music was incredibly loud, and the sound alone attracted the young from the whole of Windsor and beyond. It was inevitable that the police and local authorities were alerted to witness a phenomenon of people throwing themselves about to ear-splitting guitar riffs. There was even a complaint from an important resident in nearby Windsor Castle, and suddenly Philip was instructed to shut the place down. Philip ignored the notice pinned on the stable door and carried on for six months. During that time, he was arrested five times, and there was Press coverage of clashes with the police, with thousands of crazed fans behaving illegally in acts of public disorder. Curiously, the bands moved to astronomical worldwide acclaim.

Philip Wayward discovered an alternative venue in a roadside shack called Pantiles, isolated in Bagshot, where no one lived close enough to complain. Pantiles had struggled for years to make a profit out of selling cream teas to passing motorists. Business was sporadic and had not improved even when one of their customers, the legless fighter-pilot Douglas Bader, had married the waitress Thelma and he had become a legend in his own lifetime.

Bader was shot down in 1941 and had escaped death because he stood out, so to speak. In the interrogations, he met David Miles Lubbock, a Fleet Air Arm officer and they planned escape using Bader's hollow legs to disperse the soil from digging a tunnel. After the '*Great Escape*' from Stalag Luft Drei on the Polish border at Zagari, Bader's legs were confiscated and Lubbock would carry Bader on his back. Percy's favourite book, which he read at least five times, was *The Great Escape* and what it failed to mention was the weather. Percy had made a field trip visiting both labour camps and death camps in the area and for three months of the year, it was a steady ten degrees below zero with an additional minus ten degrees from the wind factor over vast flat open ground. Starved in these conditions for four years until their release in April 2045, was a monumental feat and a lesson in hardship.

The Douglas Bader card was played to the full by Philip by pretending to the community, particularly the parents, that his new music venue was still serving sandwiches and scones to their precious offspring, especially in the evenings when there was nothing to do. The truth was that, once inside, there was a curtain hiding double doors into a massive barn with side rooms where the young found a new way of life. Teenage beauties got permission from their parents to go with their friends for a Coca-Cola and an evening get-together while Pantiles built a huge stage, a fully stocked bar, a private movie club, a dimly-lit dance emporium, and a pleasure palace. The ever-hospitable Philip made himself seen supervising teas and cakes in the front as if nothing had changed.

The stalls for horses on the sides were lined with mattresses for fondling and groping. So popular did Pantiles become with young girls that it attracted men from as far afield as London to try their luck.

Percy and Philip were amazing friends, not least because Philip was blessed as one of the world's naturally funny people. He could charm the birds out of the trees, and it fuelled a meteoric success with money enough to acquire a very nice house on the Wentworth Golf Course.

At that time, Wentworth was a local meeting place for the ladies and for some celebrity golfers who lived in the exceptional houses on the estate around the course. No one would have thought it would become one of the most famous PGA Tour courses worldwide.

Percy and Philip often played golf. In the summers, after Pantiles had closed at two in the morning, the boys would take girls back to the Wentworth swimming pool for a nocturnal dip.

That part of it ended one sultry night at 3:00 a.m. when some unknown hand turned on the outside floodlights. Percy was safe with a fifteen-year-old in the shallow end, but Philip was on top of some young thing on the diving board.

"Smile, we're on camera!" he shouted to Percy.

Unfortunately, Philip had parked his large Rover 3 litre car at the front of the clubhouse entrance and, although they escaped with the girls through the rhododendrons, the two boys were identified by the caretaker.

"I left my car there the day before!" Philip protested at the committee hearing.

"You are a resident here", they conceded, "so please take care in the future."

Percy was not as fortunate.

"I want the names of the girls," insisted the president of Wentworth, who also happened to be the president of Pan American Airways.

"I don't know what you're talking about," argued Percy.

"You are banned from here for life, and I never want to see your face again!" shouted the club secretary, the predictable Chip Shott.

"You're a disgrace!" added the president.

"Can you imagine the publicity if they thought it was me?" asked Philip Wayward.

Philip was let off because his golfing buddies included Jimmy Tarbuck, Sean Connery, and Bruce Forsyth, and Bruce's wife, Willina Mercedes, the 1975 Miss World.

They made up a fourball, and losing Philip would be suicide for Chip Shot when his re-election loomed.

Percy had a lot of fun at Pantiles, and he didn't have to pay. It was such a release from the nonsense at Browns, and it was a joy to say 'hello' to the occasional celebrity who would answer as a human being with an 'are you enjoying yourself' or 'how was your swing today?'

These exchanges were proof enough that this was the way to go.

* * * * *

When Philip Wayward was invited to play a celebrity round of golf with Jimmy Tarbuck in Spain, he asked Percy if he would stay at his house as a sitter until he returned. It happened to be convenient as Percy was waiting for his ticket from Reel Life to fly to Cambodia. Philip asked him to cut up some logs and clear the gutter while he was away.

"And please could you check out the car?" he asked as he handed over the keys. "There's something wrong with the gearbox!"

It was a week before Philip was due to return, and Percy turned to his friend Aard Dijk, the son of the UK chairman of Philips, the Dutch electronics giant.

"I'm going to need some help with a car repair," Percy admitted.

"I'm right handy with cars," Aard Dijk confirmed as he threw the butt of a spliff in the hedge. "I'll move in with you for a few days."

Before Percy could think, Aard had arrived at Philip's house with a suitcase and his latest squeeze, Thelma House, the estate agent in Virginia Water.

Aard immediately had his tongue down Thelma's throat as he backed her onto the sofa.

"Can you kiss in private after we've fixed the car?" asked Percy. "Philip thinks it's the gearbox."

"I don't think Aard knows anything about that kind of gearbox!" Thelma spluttered. "But I have a friend, Jack Hammer, who rebuilds the Jaguars he gets from the cinema car park in Staines. He changes the colour and switches the seats around and sells them at a bargain price, and he's right handy!"

The following day, Jack arrived to look at the car, and he explained what was needed.

"To get the gearbox out for repair, the manual says you take out the passenger seat and get it out through the floor", he pronounced. "I can make it quicker by cutting out a section of the chassis and dropping the fucker out the bottom!"

"Are you sure about this?" asked Percy.

"The handbook is wrong", Jack confirmed as he opened his car boot and took out an industrial blow-torch and an oxyacetylene bottle.

As Jack got to work, Percy went for a round of golf, but he developed a sinking feeling. By the 11th hole, he also developed a slice and was losing his grip, so he abandoned the round. He arrived back at Philip's house just as a three-foot-long piece of steel chassis clonked onto Philip's driveway. Fifteen minutes later, the gearbox was out, and Jack started to open it up.

Two hours later, he bolted the gearbox back in place and welded the three feet of chassis back in place, and the job was finished. The car looked great and, more importantly, it drove like new.

"That Thelma is great in the sack!" Jack said casually as he wiped his greasy hands on a rag.

"Since Aard Dijk is banging her five times a day on the other side of that wall, you're probably right!" Percy answered.

Jack didn't look fussed.

"Come round in a few days to collect your money from the guy who owns the car," Percy concluded.

When Philip returned, he was delighted that his car was repaired.

"It's nearly lunchtime," he noted. "We'll take her for a spin down to the Rose and Crown of Thorns."

"I've got to get ready for my new job", Percy replied.

"After we see how she runs," said Philip as he opened the passenger door and pushed Percy inside.

Philip was accelerating halfway down Egham Hill when there was a loud crack, and the car broke in half.

"What was that?" enquired Philip, clutching the steering wheel as the driver's seat hit the tarmac and the prop shaft tore up 100 feet of the road before catapulting the back half of the car into the hedgerow.

"The pub's just round the corner," Percy ventured. "Perhaps we should have a drink?"

"You know who Ronnie Kray is?" asked Philip, still looking straight ahead and holding the steering wheel.

"Yes."

"When he's upset, he'll hold an arm in the fire until it starts to burn!"

"That's incredibly brave of him."

"It would be if it were his own arm," replied Philip.

That evening, the phone rang at Philip's house.

"I'm coming round for my money," Jack Hammer merrily advised Philip.

"You can come over and talk to my accountant," Philip replied. "You can't miss him. He's the one with the close-cropped hair and the fishhooks sewn into the back of his tie!"

"Fish hooks?" asked Jack, perplexed.

"He likes to know who's hanging on, you bungling moron!" Philip whispered.

Chapter Five
ASSIGNMENT CAMBODIA

Key Witnesses:

ORSON CART	*American War Correspondent*
MAJOR ACHILLES HEEL	*U.S. Special Forces – Saigon*
GENERAL WILLIS JEEP III	*Head of the US Joint Chiefs of Staff*
AUSTIN VAN AERIAL	*Dutch War Correspondent*
MUN CHING	*Khmer Dancer – Cambodian National Ballet*
DONG HUNG	*Choreographer – Cambodian National Ballet*
POL POTTY	*Head of the Khmer Rouge*
VET ING	*Press Secretary to Princess Bumpha Sihanouk*
PHUC WIT	*Prime Minister of Cambodia*
SHIVA NAKED	*Receptionist – Old Grand Hotel - Siem Reap*
LI LO	*Vietnamese Professor of Philosophy*
HANG YU	*Ropemaker and Blacksmith*
HI YU	*Sales and Service – AK47 Kalashnikov*
GENERAL PACO PUNCH	*American Field Commander – Vietnam*
PHUC OPH	*Owner – King Kong Bar - Phnom Penh*
HOP ON	*Singer – King Kong Bar*
HO LEE SHIT	*President of North Vietnam*
BAT PIS	*Boatman – Mekong River*

In 1923, Somerset Maugham wrote, *"I have never seen anything in the world more beautiful than the temples of Angkor in Cambodia, but I do not know how on earth I am going to set down in black and white such an account of them as will give more than a shadowy impression of their grandeur."*

The most sensible way to reach Angkor, some 300 kilometres north of Phnom Penh, was by light aircraft. As Percy arrived during the Christmas holidays, he decided to stay a few days in the capital before travelling on. He would enjoy the traditional New Year's Eve festivities before his assignment to photograph and capture the magnificence of Angkor.

On the plane from London, Percy had sat next to Orson Cart, an American journalist whose every story ended with, 'I nearly got my arse shot off there!' Orson had been in Biafra, Angola, and Vietnam, and this was his second stint in Cambodia after a trip home to New York to recover from an infected gunshot wound to his backside. This had gone septic and apparently nearly killed him.

"You can't amputate an arse!" he confirmed.

Restored by a month in a real hospital, he was eager to resume work and, equally urgently, to get back into a dancer at the National Ballet.

"You must be some kind of pussy going up to Angkor!" Orson declared mid-flight. "Come with me to where the action is on the eastern border!"

"But isn't that where a war is going on?" Percy replied politely.

Phnom Penh, with its French colonial architecture and tree-lined boulevards, exuded a relaxed, timeless calm. Flowers spilt from balcony window boxes; neighbours chatted beneath them. Conversation everywhere revolved around American troops and the daily struggle to contain the spread of communism. Even so, shoppers moved with unhurried grace, acknowledging those resting in pavement cafés. The cyclo-pousse drivers pedalled without haste.

The Monorom Hotel, with polished wooden floors and slatted shutters, not only had the best rooms in town but also one of Phnom Penh's finest restaurants. Christmas and New Year brought families out in style, and the hotel buzzed with activity. While Percy discovered the room prices were beyond his reach, Orson telephoned his dancer and arranged to meet her at the Café Centrale later that evening.

"I've got you fixed up with her friend!" he announced.

"We're either sharing your room, or I need to find another place," Percy reminded him.

"You're only here a few days, and there are two beds in my room, so you can stay with me," Orson replied shamelessly.

Percy doubted he would have offered the same courtesy in reverse.

Orson led him upstairs to a back room. He tossed his bag on the floor, kicked the twin beds apart, and watched Percy tuck a folded pair of pyjamas under his pillow.

"Let's go!" Orson sighed theatrically.

They began at the bar of the White House Hotel on Achar Mean Boulevard, well known as the gathering place for journalists and photographers. Correspondents from all major American agencies were there, many fresh from the carnage in Vietnam. Now stationed in Phnom Penh, they were trying to uncover whether the war was spilling into Cambodia and whether anyone had witnessed secret B-52 strikes on North Vietnamese positions along the border.

Orson was greeted immediately. After everyone confirmed that his arse was indeed "back in working order," he was soon immersed in updates on who was in charge of what, how the situation had shifted, and what people in the Pentagon were thinking.

"This is my friend Percy," Orson said as they squeezed into a crowded corner. "He folds his fucking pyjamas!"

From then on, Percy received little attention except when ordering beers.

"Your call!" they chorused.

Orson took notes as people talked. General Waugh Torn had assumed control of covert operations in Vietnam and held his 'five o'clock follies' briefings on the veranda of the Rex Hotel in Saigon. He had reportedly authorised night raids to eliminate village headmen. His chief enforcer was Major Achilles Heel, hated by protesters back in America for allegedly wiping entire villages off the map.

There was consensus that the CIA had helped fuel the narrative that communism was at America's doorstep, and that General Willis Jeep III, head of the Joint Chiefs of Staff, was tasked with keeping the 'red tide' from polluting the 'free world.'

"Vietnam keeps everyone's eye off the Israeli ball," observed Austin van Aerial of the *Amsterdam Post.* "No one's paying attention to the hardware flowing into Israel - hardware the Israelis then pass to Iran to fight Iraq."

"At the same time, the Brits are giving Iraq everything it needs to start a real war - nuclear included," added Sam Bucca of the *New York Post.* "Keep this up, and they'll kill each other off. Your call, Percy!"

"Don't mind, Sam," Orson said as Percy ordered more beers. "He still thinks the Kennedy boys were shot by assassins hired by the Secret Service!"

"Don't start me off," Sam growled.

"Lee Harvey Oswald was a Marxist. He loved Castro. He spent time in Moscow. So he must have killed Kennedy, right?" Orson goaded.

"The Kennedy brothers were killed, yes - but Oswald didn't kill JFK, and Sirhan didn't kill Bobby," Sam shot back.

"So who killed JFK, genius?" Orson demanded. "You're the only man alive who knows, after a thousand hours of research!"

The beers arrived as Sam launched into his explanation.

"The CIA, Mossad, and Lyndon Johnson murdered President Kennedy," he started. "Two reasons - JFK demanded Israeli Prime Minister David Ben-Gurion allow inspections of the Dimona nuclear weapons and Israel refused and, second, Kennedy demanded transparency from AIPAC - the American Israel Public Affairs Committee – to disclose payments to members of Congress to vote through $ billions of military aid to Israel. JFK was ready to block the bribes and even the payments!"

Orson cut in.

"And JFK was going to terminate the Federal Reserve's control over the printing of U.S. currency," he insisted. "The Fed's a private company printing our dollars for seventy years with compounding interest accumulating as forever debt. It was too valuable a stranglehold on the U.S. economy to let it go!"

Percy looked around as if he had an opinion.

"Orson's still into that 'second gunman' rubbish," Austin whispered. "There's a film - hidden for obvious reasons and it shows JFK being shot in the neck and Jacqueline reacting. Then the driver, William Greer, turns with a pistol in his left hand, fires over his right shoulder, and shoots Kennedy in the head. It was a special CIA pneumatic pistol with the bullet carrying a deadly shellfish toxin which would have killed him if the bullet didn't. That's why his brain was switched between Parkland Hospital and Bethesda Naval Hospital. Any autopsy of his own brain would have blown the truth wide open."

"Variations will keep coming until the missing film is public information," Sam concluded.

"So Sirhan didn't kill Bobby?" Percy ventured.

"Where'd you find this one, Cart?" Sam slurred, swivelling so his eyes were level with Percy.

"You ever hear of Castro's 'Fair Play for Cuba Committee'?" Sam demanded.

"No."

"Or Santo Trafficante, the Cuban Mafia boss?"

"No."

"The FBI - when they were honest - admitted the Cubans and Mossad were shaping world events for their own ends."

"For God's sake, Sam - enough," Austin pleaded.

"I'm finishing," Sam declared. "Sirhan was a Palestinian. Bobby supported Israel. And he's dead - killed by four shots to the back. Those shots came from the pantry or the refrigerator, not from Sirhan standing on the other side of him!"

He slammed his Zippo lighter on the table.

"And since you're here, Percy - this whole war began because that rabid anti-communist Robert McNamara lied to Johnson in '61. He made up the story about U.S. warships being attacked in the Gulf of Tonkin. Johnson believed him and sent in the troops - and now 58,000 young Amcricans arc dcad."

"Marilyn Monroe knew everything," someone else chimed in. "Jack and Bobby told her when they were banging her senseless!"

"The CIA and Israel needed the war to continue," Sam insisted, lighting another cigarette. He blew a perfect smoke ring into Percy's face. "Marilyn Monroe must have told Bobby she was sick of being pronged daily and planned to spill the beans. Bobby destroyed the Beverly Hills Hotel guest register and injected her with a lethal dose where no one would check."

"And don't forget Project Artichoke!" another voice shouted.

"Artichoke?" Percy asked.

"It was a hypno-programming operation run by William Bryan," Sam explained. "The CIA had an established program for assassins to lose their memory after a job."

Orson began to laugh.
"Oh, really!" he burped.
"Yes, really!" Sam answered deliberately. "It goes all the way back to Rockefeller and Carnegie, initiating the possibilities of delusion and then the Security Education Act of 1934. That was to legitimise influencing behaviour in the education syllabus. It started as 'social engineering' to lead people to think what you wanted, and it developed into a CIA program of intense behavioural manipulation."
"I'm out of here!" Orson announced, standing up straight.
"You're so full of shit, Cart!" Sam muttered. "It's no wonder the VC shoots you in the arse!"
Percy burst out laughing at the whole exchange, spraying beer across the table. He picked up Sam's Zippo to dry it and noticed the slogan etched into the metal: *Ours not to do or die. Ours to smoke and stay high!*
"So you guys write the history out here," he said.
"None of us believes we can change anything," Orson replied. "We risk our lives to uncover the truth, but politics and the media decide what goes on here!"
"We're all living with a Jewish rod up our arse!" Sam mumbled before his head dropped onto the table.
"Remember," Austin added, "the Jews invented guilt - and the Catholics turned it into an art form."
"Watch your arse, Cart!" someone called as Orson headed for the door.

* * * * *

Mun Ching, Orson's girlfriend, and her friend Lilly Pad were waiting in the shaded courtyard of the Café Centrale with a man who stood politely as they approached. He introduced himself, in a polished English accent, as Dong Hung, a choreographer at the National Ballet. Orson introduced Percy, then ordered three beers and two Cokes without asking.
"Dong Hung's the pimp," Orson muttered to Percy.
The girls looked as though they had just left school, dressed in regulation white shirts and black skirts. They giggled as Orson launched into the story of how he'd been wounded at Lộc Ninh, a Vietnamese village just across the border, when it was overrun by the "gooks," as he

insisted on calling the North Vietnamese. He had run, lost a shoe, bent over to retrieve it, and been shot in the backside.

"A rather large target - hard to miss," observed Dong Hung in his immaculate accent.

The National Ballet, the pride of the Head of State, Prince Neardoom Sihanouk, was performing on New Year's Eve - unknowingly for the last time - and Dong Hung offered to get tickets.

"Dancing's not really my thing," Orson shrugged.

Dong Hung looked crestfallen.

"I'd love to go," Percy offered.

After twenty minutes, Orson grew restless.

"We should head back to the Monorom and get something to eat," he announced, winking as he tossed some dollars on the table.

The girls giggled again, as if he'd said something charming rather than crude.

On the walk back, Mun Ching and Lilly Pad hooked themselves onto Orson, while Dong Hung chatted about how their Buddhist God-King, Neardoom Sihanouk, was working his way methodically through the ballet chorus - and that no one dared refuse him. It was a far cry from the original purpose of the Cambodian Royal Ballet, created centuries before to help the King communicate with the ancient spirits.

"The songs were prayers for fertility," Dong Hung explained.

"Now the singers are being fertilised," Orson laughed.

"Neardoom Sihanouk fuck everything," Mun Ching added meaningfully.

Percy was beginning to understand when Orson removed all doubt.

"Haven't you got something else to do, Dung?" he asked as they reached the hotel steps.

"It's Dong, not Dung."

"Well, Dong or Dung - whatever. Get lost."

Percy winced as Dong Hung stiffened, turned sharply, and walked away.

"Fairy," Orson scoffed.

"So speaks a man with two holes in his bottom," Percy said.

Orson ordered dinner without looking at the menu and ate most of it himself. He then suggested a private viewing of his scar upstairs.

He practically dragged Mun Ching up the stairs, leaving Lilly Pad and Percy alone.

"Him, huge!" Lilly announced, as if evaluating him.

"Shall we sit outside?" Percy suggested, eager to escape any such inspection.

For two weeks, while the girls rehearsed for the New Year's celebration, Orson showed Percy around Phnom Penh. In the late afternoons, they met the dancers between performances. On New Year's Eve, Dong Hung presented Percy and Orson with tickets.

The grace and poise of Khmer traditional dance wasn't quite Percy's cup of tea, yet it was impossible not to be captivated by the ornate costumes embroidered with gold thread and jewels, the headdresses and masks representing gods and goddesses, and the music of xylophones and bells. It was unthinkable that the coming war and genocide could tear such cultural heritage from a nation as easily as the throat from a goat.

* * * * *

With surprising help from Dong Hung, Percy arranged a photographic session with Princess Bumpha Sihanouk, daughter of Prince Neardoom Sihanouk and his half-Italian wife, Monique. Princess Bumpha, a dancer and Dong's partner in choreography at the training school, granted Percy a half-hour audience. Her private apartments overflowed with ancient silk tapestries and silver treasures of the old Khmer Empire.

Seated on a carved chair that resembled a throne, she explained how, during the Second World War, the Japanese had placed her father on the Cambodian throne. After the war, he emerged as the nation's undisputed political force.

Percy suspected the Vichy French had more to do with that appointment, but said nothing.

"In those early years, my father's reign was known as the *Temps de Splendeur*," she said in perfect English. "He persuaded the French to release Cambodia from colonial status in 1952 without a shot being fired. He kept Cambodia neutral by maintaining good relations with China and therefore with the North Vietnamese."

"I understand the issue," Percy said as he set up the lighting. "Those good relations allowed the North Vietnamese to build major bases along the length of Cambodia. They send weapons and supplies down the Mekong from there."

Orson had already explained that the Prince later courted the Americans by allowing the bombing of those same bases. Every shift in policy was accepted because people viewed the ruler as semi-divine. Orson had even met the Prince and liked him - largely because he was an accomplished jazz saxophonist.

Percy knew he needed to tread carefully.

"Nixon and Kissinger have only one objective," the Princess insisted. "Pacification of the North is impossible. The goal must be a negotiated independence for South Vietnam without drawing China or the Soviet Union into war. As you say - sausage in a roll!"

"I think you mean 'fly in the ointment,'" Percy said. "Your father keeps allowing the North further into Cambodia. That has upset the Americans."

"They are threatening to cut off aid."

"Did you know Henry Kissinger was a Harvard professor?" Percy added. "When *Dr Strangelove* was being made, Kubrick asked to meet the expert on the bomb. They sent him to Kissinger - and he was so horrified he named the film after him!"

"Strangelove," she repeated slowly.

Percy mentioned his upcoming trip to Angkor.

"My only advice is to hire a personal guide," she said. "Angkor once had over six hundred monuments, surrounded by walls twelve kilometres long, housing one million people. It was swallowed by the jungle for five centuries. The French 'discovered' it in 1860 and claimed it as part of their own empire. Even now, experts uncover new structures. The layout follows Mount Meru, the mythic home of the Gods. Without a guide, you will see only stones tangled in roots."

Princess Bumpha stood elegantly and posed for half an hour.

"Send the photographs to Vet Ing, my private secretary, for approval!" she commanded

"It has been an honour," Percy began after she had swept out of the room.

*****

Back at the Monorom, Percy found a note from Orson tucked in a history book. He had left for Saigon and could be contacted at the Kum Inn.

Percy packed up and flew to Angkor, crossing the vast Tonlé Sap, the largest freshwater lake in the Far East. During the flight, he read about how, in the 9th century, King Yasovarman had built the first city of

Angkor and harnessed the lake's natural hydraulic power to create reservoirs, dams, and canals linking towns so trade ships could travel up the Mekong before transferring their cargo to smaller barques.

This control of water and transport had enabled Angkor's kings to expand their influence and build successive temple mountains using slave labour from conquered lands.

In the 12th century, King Suryavarman II constructed Angkor Wat - a monumental sandstone temple of self-glorification rising 130 feet, enclosed by a mile-square courtyard and a vast moat. The three tiers held galleries of carved Hindu deities and stone Buddhas.

In the 13th century, King Jayavarman VII built Angkor Thom, over ten square kilometres, a last grand attempt to preserve the empire. The city represented a celestial paradise; moats symbolised seas, and the causeways mirrored mythological paths to divine realms.

By the 14th century, the empire collapsed. Canals clogged with weeds, trade died, and the Chams - enslaved centuries earlier - sacked Angkor Wat. The Siamese followed, stripping the holy mountains bare.

Percy's flight landed in Siem Reap just as Prime Minister Phuc Wit declared war on North Vietnam. With the U.S. withdrawing aid, Sihanouk had changed course, ordering the Vietnamese out - publicly at least.

At the airfield, a crowd shouted in panic.

"You're crazy!" they cried as Percy passed. "We get out now!"

He drove north alone against a tide of fleeing carts and bicycles and reached Siem Reap's only decent lodging, the Old Grand Hotel.

"Is it safe here?" he asked the young receptionist, Shiva Naked.

"You may choose any room," she said brightly.

That evening, Percy weighed his options: continue his assignment, return to Phnom Penh, or head east toward the fighting. The last idea - fuelled by the fantasy of photographing the American arrival - seemed both foolish and attractive.

The staff moved about as if nothing unusual was happening. Shiva assured him this was just another variation on a Sihanouk theme. Percy, irrationally reassured, decided to stay — one day at a time.

* * * * *

The next morning was chilly. Percy, in a U.S. Army surplus shirt, jeans, and sunglasses, stepped onto the veranda.

"You believe in God?"

Percy turned and saw an expressionless man behind him.

"I'm an atheist," Percy replied. "It's the way God made me."

"You need Li Lo as a guide," the man said, pointing to himself. "Otherwise, you get very lost."

Remembering the Princess's advice, Percy agreed to hire him.

Dressed in black bell-bottom trousers, a frayed white shirt, and broken sandals, Li Lo knew everything - history, politics, and mythology. He proved an ideal companion.

"Angkor is impossible to visit briefly," he said.

Percy suspected this was because he'd agreed to pay by the day, but Li Lo's knowledge soon proved indispensable. The ruins were far larger and more complex than Percy expected.

Li Lo told him how his entire family had been killed near the Vietnamese border two years earlier. He described lying conscious as shrapnel tore open his leg, the bone moving in and out of the wound like a piston.

"Children gathered to watch the leg perform," he said without emotion.

After months of isolation and recovery, he returned to the forest where his family died and lived for a time in the grotto system of Hang Son Doong — the vast limestone cave hidden for centuries, 150 metres high and six kilometres long.

"There are stories of reptilian creatures living in Inner Earth," he added softly. "American troops see them. Some never return. Others speak of horrific lizard men."

"That matches the Aztec legends," Percy said, "and the Mayan tomb of Pakal - serpent deity."

"How do you know?"

"I spent eight years in places of learning with fine libraries," Percy said. "Not the Vatican, but close."

* * * * *

In the evenings, they sat by Tonlé Sap, talking like old friends.

"Proteins in water sustain many fish," Li Lo mused. "When the water is low, fish flop across land to find a lake. Gills adapt. Fish live out of water for hours."

As if on cue, an elephant fish flopped through the mud toward the lake.

"He is very tasty," Li Lo smiled, pointing to a truck near some huts. "Goes to Hong Kong. Put alive in a tank. People eat - nyum nyum."

The war felt remote. Percy followed Li Lo through Angkor's vast sprawl: the Bayon, with its 54 towers carved with 216 faces of Jayavarman VII, each staring serenely in every direction.

"You see, Khmer trick," Li Lo explained. "The third eye on the forehead shows Jayavarman, the first Hindu god. Later knocked off - changed to Lokesvara, Buddha Lord of World."

Occasionally, the ping of a machete echoed. Two men dangled from ropes, hacking off one of the better-preserved heads.

"Do something!" Percy cried.

"Too late," Li Lo said as the head fell into a sling.

The thieves staggered into the undergrowth.

"Impossible stop. Everyone helps themselves."

Malraux had once stolen more than a ton of carvings; major museums still bought looted pieces. Percy photographed the mutilated plinths.

"Real birthright hidden from view," Li Lo said. "Stones show celestial movements - code of planets. Our temples hold a catalogue of civilisations before us."

* * * * *

Angkor Wat - the so-called *Temple of the Universe* - embodied a self-contained universe built to honour Vishnu. Percy and Li Lo walked for days between balustrades carved as cosmic serpents, through mile-long galleries of bas-reliefs showing celestial maidens, demons, flowers, and the tales of the *Ramayana*.

Percy spent a full week studying '*The Days of Judgement*', the 32 hells of Brahminism — rape, choking, burning alive, tears, and his favourite, the hell of sharp-thorned trees - each overseen by Yama, judge of the dead.

Then he focused on '*The myth of Abhimanyu*' - the churning of the Sea of Milk, and various battles to record the mysterious history of Angkor. Percy had thirty rolls of film, but would anyone want to know?

At the temple's centre stood a giant *linga*.

"Did you say 'thing' or 'ling'?" Percy asked, staring at the massive stone phallus.

"Ling contains the soul of God-King," Li Lo whispered, bowing.

Percy thought of his grandmother's stories of astral travel and reincarnation. Perhaps, he mused, she had been onto something.

"Secrets of the zodiac and planets in Angkor, the biggest temple on Earth," Li Lo continued. "Far larger than the Great Pyramid in Egypt, which only covers thirteen acres with six million tons of stone, but it is aligned to true North with perfect precision. Same as Teotihuacan in Mexico. Civilisations before us left messages, and Angkor is a very organised, symmetrical plan with causeways, moats, and towers with the same geometry as a modern RFID chip that is used in every credit card. It does not need power, but coupled with an antenna, it sends a signal. Angkor used the sun as part of a worldwide system to create a free energy power grid. The only difference between Angkor and the RFID chip is the scale!"

Percy felt as though he were walking among people from another reality - people he couldn't quite see.

"Our civilisation can barely imagine the universe," Percy said. "The Milky Way is 120,000 light-years across with 300 billion stars. We see only 2,500. There must have been ancient civilisations with cosmic genius. Nothing we know explains what they left."

Each evening, Shiva Naked sometimes joined them on the porch.

"I went to school in Paris," she said once. "I returned to teach, but my father died. I took this job to care for my mother. This war has no good end - it is a battle of ideologies; neither side will lose."

Signs of war grew clearer.

Li Lo urged Percy to leave.

"You have taken thirty rolls," he said. "Enough."

"You made this so much more than I expected," Percy told him. "At first, I saw only tangled roots and stones. Now I have a story."

"You have not paid me yet," Li Lo reminded him.

"You've been a great guide," Percy said as the sun dipped below the trees.

"These stars are messages of our ancestors," Li Lo murmured as a shooting star streaked across the sky. "But outsiders have no eyes to see."

"I've run out of film," Percy admitted.

"The miracle continues for you," Shiva said. "No tourists – so we have a cupboard full. You take."

Percy spent evenings writing Li Lo's stories as expected for his assignment at *Reel Life,* describing a people guided by the seasons, and seasons ordered by the stars, with myths handed down as lessons for the future.

A bell rang in the distance.

Li Lo craned his head and closed his eyes.

"What is that sound?" asked Percy.

"It is our connection to the ancient world", he answered quietly as the ringing tone faded. "The sound of a bell has a healing and protective effect. It aligns worshippers with sacred rhythms, and in the Hindu and Buddhist faiths, it is considered a bridge between human and divine realms because the low-frequency vibrations can be felt physically. The largest bells were made out of carefully tuned bronze alloy that gives up a harmonic richness that can create a sense of timelessness. It helps the process of both grieving and joy because it is the interaction of sound, belief, body, and community - a form of what you call holistic healing long before the term existed.

"I am learning myself on a more basic level," Percy agreed, recalling an old Irish blessing:

> *May there always be work for your hands to do;*
> *May your purse always hold a coin or two.*
> *May the sun always shine on your window pane;*
> *May a rainbow always follow the rain;*
> *May the hand of a friend always be near you;*
> *May God fill your heart with gladness to cheer you*

Percy knew it was time to leave, and Li Lo suggested he join him on a three-day walk to Puok, where friends could help Percy cross into Thailand. Percy agreed; he needed to avoid the North Vietnamese Army in the countryside.

Early the next morning, they set off with knapsacks along a dusty track into a green, hazy void.

"You go back to a world of determined and ruthless leaders," Li Lo said as they walked. "Your world is full of luxury and extravagance. Your people make war for greed because they have no soul. When leaders interfere, the soul cannot be free outside, so the soul must be free inside. West thinks Cambodia can only survive if neighbours allow freedom, so we wait for terror and repression to pass."

They walked on in silence, drowsy in the warm, heavy air.

"You see, Angkor was built with flat stones," Li Lo continued gently. "No arches because the Khmer do not think of a keystone. If there is no keystone, the roof is not strong. If the roof is not strong, the building falls. The keystone of a person is the heart. A person is no good if they have no heart. A state is no good if there is no religion. Religion is no good if there is no universe. Secrets of planets and stars are key to all things. That is why I help you."

They made good progress until the sun was high. Percy dropped his knapsack under the shade of tall palms and lay back in the grass.

"This is a beautiful country," he sighed.

"Terror is coming," Li Lo whispered.

Two days later, they hitched a lift to Puok in a jolting wooden ox cart. The village stood above the river, surrounded by land cleared by slash-and-burn through generations. A ring of thinly thatched huts with open windows framed a central compound. All around were small plots of rice, sugar cane, aubergines, melons, cotton, and tobacco, each with a bamboo lean-to for the watcher who scared away birds and animals. Pigs and buffalo, used for ploughing, were kept in pens; long-legged chickens and goats wandered freely.

Over the next few days, Percy watched the women doing most of the work: hitching oxen to carts, hauling crops, drawing water from ancient wells. The men went hunting wild boar. Children played near a pond covered in mauve water hyacinths. Everything felt centuries old.

The old man of Puok, elected to oversee communal affairs, sat each late afternoon under trees beside a long wooden platform. His silver hair was slicked back beneath a grandak, the straw hat that hung down behind his head. Percy resisted wearing one; he felt ridiculous with a lampshade on his skull.

The old man's every gesture was slow and precise, his sinewy arms tracing shapes in the air.

From the first moment, Percy was treated as an honoured guest, which embarrassed him. In the evenings, after fieldwork, the women prepared barbecued fish dipped in fragrant sauces, or pork stewed in coconut oil, spiced with garlic and chilli, then wrapped in rice paper or lettuce leaves.

"In England, we have a famous cook called Fanny Haddock," Percy smiled. "She should come here for lessons."

He knew that if these people did not tend their fields, they would starve, so he took only small portions.

On the third night, Li Lo introduced Percy to a young woman who seemed to appear from nowhere: Hi Yu. She wore the traditional vict: trousers beneath a long skirt split to the hip on both sides, and a non la, the straw conical hat. She was delicate, almost shy, but her black, bewitching eyes showed a strength as resilient as bamboo in a storm. It was three more days before Percy spoke to her alone.

Hi, Yu had grown up in Hong Ngu, the northernmost Cambodian town on the Mekong in Kien Phong province, only a few kilometres from the Vietnamese border, where most of the contraband trade passed. She had been a runner from the age of six until her father, Hang Yu, a blacksmith and rope maker, moved on from forging ploughshares to repairing AK-47s, the standard Communist rifle. Her grandfather was the headman of Puok.

Hi Yu's news had been discussed gravely in the village. On 10 March 1970, Cambodia's God-King had gone abroad for treatment of a skin condition at a spa on the French Riviera. Many believed he had actually gone to Beijing to persuade the Chinese to force the North Vietnamese out. In his absence, Prime Minister Phuc Wit encouraged protests against the North Vietnamese presence on Cambodian soil. It was Phuc Wit who deposed Neardoom Sihanouk in a popular coup.

The Russian premier, Alexei Kosygin, regarded the coup as American-inspired and urged Sihanouk to realign with the communists. It was too little and too late to prevent the Khmer Rouge from emerging as a new, brutal force.

Meanwhile, General Paco Punch, commander of the American 1st Division, had already ordered the secret bombing of North Vietnamese inside Cambodia: 1,045 B-52 sorties dropping 108,823 tons of bombs on border regions.

"I won't have these slitties making a fool of me!" Paco raged, adding napalm to his shopping list.

Operations with names like Igloo White, Steel Tiger, and Tiger Hound targeted the trails used by the North Vietnamese and their leader, Ho Lee Shit, who was already pushing ground forces south through tunnels in preparation for an offensive.

Paco ordered another million tons of ordnance dropped along those trails, including a new breed of anti-personnel weapons designed to maim rather than kill. Sixty-nine million aerial mines fell on villages and jungle alike, many contained in cluster bombs that released hundreds of steel "tennis balls." About thirty per cent failed to detonate and would lie hidden for decades as shiny toys, waiting mostly for children.

Nixon's policy stated that no American personnel could be involved in de-mining or even be in areas where de-mining took place. There would be no systematic attempt or even a passing thought to prevent decades of child mutilation.

* * * * *

Percy was growing increasingly uneasy at being hosted by these kindly villagers, and he already had his message for Reel life readers. So he decided to take the best-known route out of Cambodia to Thailand.

He pulled out his airline ticket for the first time, only to realise it was non-refundable and valid only from Phnom Penh, a long way south, and his only viable way out.

In preparation, Percy bought an old bicycle for three dollars, thinking it would help in any direction.

"Everyone on the radio is talking about Vietnam and expanding conflict," Li Lo warned.

Percy reflected how this war was nothing like the old days of hand-to-hand battles. Nebuchadnezzar had faced his enemies on a level playing field, but this new American model was encrusted with vice, excess, pride, folly, and arrogance, fuelling such ferocity and firepower against villagers like these? How sad the progress of mankind!

* * * * *

Babylon had boasted two of the Seven Wonders of the World - the Hanging Gardens and the Tower of Babel. Rembrandt had shown its splendour at Belshazzar's feast, echoing the writing on the wall. The Bible, in the book of Daniel and Revelation, and Dürer in his engravings, had cast Babylon as a city of madness and sin:

Then the angel carried me away into a desert where I saw a woman sitting on a scarlet beast covered in blasphemous names, with seven heads and seven horns. The woman was dressed in purple and scarlet and glittered with gold, precious stones, and pearls. She held a golden cup filled with abominations and the filth of her adulteries. Written on her head was: "the mother of all prostitutes."

The Americans regarded communism as a similar blasphemy, a threat deserving of building a fleet of monster aircraft carriers and thousands of bombers to eliminate their 'enemies' from the air. Their President promised there would be no bombing in Cambodia or Laos, but Percy had become a witness to that lie. How many others thought they were safe?

Percy stayed in Puok for two more days as tension rose. Something had shifted. It was Hi Yu who finally made it clear.

"You should not be here!" she shouted by the well as three fighter jets passed low in formation overhead.

Hi, Yu had heard that Phuc Wit's brother had been captured and roasted on a spit by Cambodian communists. North Vietnamese units were pushing south. B-52s were following them, now dropping napalm on suspected depots. Entire villages were evaporating even when locals neither supported the North nor supplied them.

Worst of all, the North Vietnamese Army had moved into the area around Angkor. Local guerrillas sympathetic to them had joined in, building bases with anti-aircraft guns among the temples. Monks who refused to leave were hacked to pieces where they prayed.

At night, Percy watched men of the village gather under kerosene lamps. Li Lo told him, in fragments, what was happening, and said Percy must go.

"I am going to Svay Rieng," Li Lo announced between distant flashes and dull thuds. "We can go together around the lake to Phnom Penh. If you stay, you die with us."

* * * * *

Svay Rieng was a thumb of Cambodian territory jutting deep into South Vietnam, a key ground for both sides. The Viet Cong used it as an approach route to Saigon; it was an area any sane person would avoid.

"Why Svay Rieng?" Percy asked.

"I am a professor of philosophy," Li Lo said quietly. "American master's degree in Oriental Studies. I chose to collaborate with America. That is my life."

He drew a finger across his throat.

"There must be somewhere safe you can go," Percy insisted.

"No run anymore," Li Lo replied. "I go to Svay Rieng. You get out of Cambodia and tell the story of the Cambodian people."

Percy added to his notes:

'Victor Charlie (no pun intended), you have already beaten the US military by digging deep.

The best efforts of Nixon's finest, Generals Achilles Heel, General Willis Jeep III, and General Paco Punch have dropped more ordnance on you than the entire amount in World War II, and you prevailed with tunnel-vision.'

Even Percy knew a Westerner cycling alone the length of Cambodia to Phnom Penh was madness. If Li Lo really was an American asset, travelling with him might be just as dangerous.

"You sure fooled me," Percy said in stark awareness that anyone going to Svay Rieng, at the hinge of the conflict, had to be insane.

"We leave in the morning," Li Lo said, walking away.

"Why not?" Percy called after him. "I'm not exactly busy!"

Percy couldn't sleep. Was he a coward? What did it feel like to step on a landmine? What would his grandfather have done?

"Remember Mark Antony," his grandfather had once said. "When you die, it's possible you will have died without ever having lived."

But this wasn't Percy's country. He had to get out.

Percy was up before dawn, ready, afraid of being left behind.

"Life here is like a taxi ride," he told Li Lo as they set off. "The meter starts slowly. Then you join the traffic. Then suddenly you're in the fast lane and the years blur, and one birthday is the same as another. And then - departure lounge!"

In the event, the journey was uneventful. No patrols, no air strikes, just miles of road along the edge of Tonlé Sap. They rode through the morning mist and soft colours netted across the fields, while locals quietly went about their lives.

Closer to Phnom Penh, that changed. There was army activity, barricades, and shouting.

"I leave you now," Li Lo said.

Percy rolled into a mass of checkpoints and frantic soldiers shoving people to the ground. Every attempt to ask a question drew only screams and pushes. There was no way through.

"Wait for me!" he yelled, but Li Lo was gone.

* * * * *

Army trucks choked the streets. Percy slipped in among the crowd. Three helicopters full of troops dropped into a cleared space; people screamed and backed away. Percy fell with his bicycle, hitting his mouth on the ground, when a teenage girl tugged at his trouser leg. He almost leapt away from her.

She pointed down a tree-lined street.

"Friend!" she cried.

He picked up his bike and followed her direction until he reached a bar with chairs on the pavement: King Kong.

"Friend," the girl insisted, pointing inside. "Your friend!"

King Kong was crowded with military and hangers-on, all drinking hard. An old radio blared rasping Western pop from a shelf. Men taunted the bar girls, who squealed and dodged groping hands.

"Friend there!" the girl repeated, pointing to the far end of the bar where Li Lo sat talking to the bloated barman, chewing a cigar stump and imposing rough order whenever a soldier grabbed a girl.

Li Lo smiled.

"This is my friend Phuc Off," he said. "He has been here thirty years."

Phuc Off slid a beer towards Percy.

"You will find many girls," he said. "Not because you're good-looking - they want a Strolling Bones tee-shirt."

"You know Strolling Bones?" asked the nearest girl, who introduced herself as Hop On, the bar's resident singer.

"Give me satisfaction," Percy replied.

Li Lo and Phuc Off conferred, clearly agitated, then explained: there was no way Percy could get a flight out of Phnom Penh. It was too dangerous for him to be alone. He would stay in a room at the back of King Kong, and they would work something out in the morning.

The next day, Li Lo took Percy to the river. At the crowded docks, boats were moored three deep, stacked with animals and vegetables. Percy raised his camera to capture the confusion. A man on one of the boats called to Li Lo.

Minutes later, Percy found himself sitting on a crate of chickens, surrounded by baskets of produce, as a heavy boat with an oar at each end threaded downstream through the traffic. No one seemed remotely interested in him. He took more pictures, satisfied that these were at least something he could take home.

"We now leave the area controlled by Phuc Wit's forces," the boatman shouted as they passed a landing. He kicked a cage of chickens for emphasis. "Last chance to vacate the coup!"

Percy glanced at the riverbank, forbidding and strange. Li Lo sat quietly with his own demons. Percy stayed put as, with a single practised stroke, the boatman steered them effortlessly into the current.

They moved into faster water towards the far bank, where boats were tied to poles and swayed together.

The two boatmen were Ding Bat and Lo Fat, and, after a nod of acknowledgement, they fell into low, serious conversation with Li Lo. This was clearly no chance encounter. Realising he was the only one not in on the plan, Percy quietly shifted under the bamboo awning that served as the cabin and dozed.

"Percy, you get down quick!"

He jerked awake and pulled on a grandak, then flattened himself on the floor, peering out through the bamboo slats. A heavily armed boat churned past, combat troops lined on the roof, staring down at them. Their own boat rocked in the wake, but no one stopped them.

Dusk fell. Lo Fat said it was too dangerous to be on the river at night, so they moored under overhanging trees. In the distance, thunder rolled, and sporadic orange flashes glowed over the tree line. No one spoke.

At first light, they pushed on towards Svay Rieng. Ding Bat explained to Li Lo that American and South Vietnamese troops were moving into Cambodia to relieve pressure on Phuc Wit's forces. The tactics were simple: B-52s saturated any suspected Viet Cong village. C-130 gunships followed, spraying the ground with 40mm Bofors shells and 20mm Vulcan rounds at 2,500 per minute. Then came the Huey helicopters, bristling with machine guns, rockets, and grenades. Only after that did the infantry arrive to blow the tunnels. The Americans had no way of identifying the Viet Cong; this was their way of fighting with minimal risk to themselves.

It was obvious that Ding Bat and Lo Fat were more than boatmen, but still no one told Percy anything. They left the main river for a narrower channel. The water turned greenish-yellow, and the banks grew dense with overhanging trees.

"Dangerous here now," Ding Bat said after an hour. "Now you see how we supply our own people."

"Don't worry," Percy joked weakly. "My passport commands the rulers of every nation to look after me."

"Maybe not in Svay Rieng," Ding Bat said.

They landed in a village like any other: dogs roaming, children playing, radios blaring, mopeds puttering. Phuc Wit's teenage soldiers stood in truck beds, shouting and waving rifles at peasants who looked as though nothing had changed for a hundred years. Everyone talked about the Khmer communists who would come and "save" them.

Lo Fat reported that Sihanouk was now living in Peking, giving the Viet Cong the chance to recruit Khmer Rouge sympathisers in villages along the way. These recruits reported troop movements and the state of food and ammunition. Local guerrilla militias, led by "Political Commissars," were supposed to protect villagers and wield absolute authority. Confused by rumours and abandoned by their ruler, the peasants were tempted to support Ho Lee Shit's forces.

Ding Bat laughed that even portraits on public walls were in dispute.

In the two months before Percy's arrival, 100,000 Cambodians had died. The void had opened for zealots under Pol Pot to breed a fanatical communism that aimed to thrust Cambodia back into a medieval agrarian model.

Li Lo recognised how clever the Khmer Rouge were. They courted peasants - the providers of food, the base of trade. Through that policy, their "Political Commissars" would, he predicted, crush all other communist factions. They were already stealing Viet Cong food. The Viet Cong retaliated by wiping out entire Cambodian villages in ambushes, while Pol Pot quietly persuaded Vietnamese-aligned guerrillas to join him.

"This whole area is full of North Vietnamese and Khmer communists," Li Lo told Percy, "Villagers will die whichever side they choose."

* * * * *

The Americans hit Lộc Ninh first, then villages along the Vietnamese border. Jets dived in threes and obliterated anything that looked like a target. The dull thuds of bomb blasts rolled across the land; B-52s opened their bellies, dumping more destruction onto the forest. Reports of horror followed the orange flashes and black smoke.

Li Lo finally laid out his relationship with the Americans when he introduced Percy to Bat Pis.

"If anything happens to me, Bat Pis get you out," he said.

Bat Pis, like Li Lo, had been recruited by the CIA. Both seemed calm and fearless. When Bat suggested Percy become a "proper journalist" and come with them to a key village in the American supply chain, Percy agreed.

That night, they celebrated, of sorts, with Li Lo, Bat Pis, Ding Bat, and Lo Fat all together at Mon Sewer, a grubby bar with a back room that used to be a restaurant. They ate what food they could find, drank potent rice wine, and breathed in the smoke from the fire pit. Whoever distilled that liquor had sensibly left his name off the bottle.

Emotions simmered close to the surface. Fuelled by alcohol, Ding Bat finally cracked, emptying his revolver into the ceiling and crashing through a flimsy table. No one moved until a woman clutching a sheet tumbled through a trapdoor from above, shrieking. There was a moment's silence; then the room erupted in laughter, and the stories flowed again, near misses, comradeship, madness. It was obvious, as obvious as "dog's balls," that this was a dangerously thin edge of life.

Everyone knew the truth: nobody on the ground or in the chain of command could or would stop the bombing. Life went on until a shell arrived with your name on it.

The next morning, after a welcome wash in the river, Li Lo, Bat Pis, and Percy set out on mopeds. An hour later, they reached the remains of a village in hell. It had once been called Dang Me.

Bodies with limbs missing lay in the dirt, fought over by stray dogs. Percy retched, then forced himself to take photographs, searching, in horror, for the "right" images.

"I've left my lucky Strolling Bones tee-shirt," he gasped, and threw up again.

They moved to what had once been a school, children's drawings still pinned to the walls and strewn on the floor. It was now a makeshift hospital.

Tear gas had been dropped with the bombs, and everyone inside — mothers, babies, old men — must have run outside and straight into the advancing infantry. The green, happy village had been turned into an abattoir floor, with blood, feathers, bodies, and rubble mixed into one obscene carpet.

Percy discovered a new depth to the word "revulsion".

These were conquerors who claimed to bring civilisation, but their soldiers raped village girls and shot them afterwards. Little wonder that Cambodians were turning to their own Khmer Rouge.

History, Percy reflected bitterly, showed that every invading power left its mark: the Greeks their philosophy, the Indians their mysticism, the Arabs their faith, the Jews their financial acuity, the Japanese their manners, and the Americans their ruthless superiority.

Nothing Percy did would change anything. He was a spectator in acts of insanity. Death and torture were part of life here; history would forget what the Americans thought they were achieving. The population had grown used to waves of colonial mayhem. Bat Pis reminded him that Michelin, the French tyre company, had starved a quarter of its 48,000 plantation workers to death. Public outrage over American soldiers returning in body bags was, he said, the only thing that might stop this war.

It was no different, Percy thought, from when Cortés beheaded the Aztecs and destroyed their culture as casually as flicking a flower's head. Columbus had once written to the Queen of Spain that European civilisation would "bring light" to the natives - and yield gold for the Crown.

"So what's new?" Percy murmured, recalling Frankie Bacon, hailed as the father of "new learning," who warned that science and technology would be used to subdue man and, finally, nature itself.

"There were no flies on Frankie Bacon," Percy muttered, looking at the blackened bodies in the undergrowth.

Pol Pot would now use his command of the Khmer Rouge to "start again" from year zero. Percy had no idea what was coming.

* * * * *

Dang Me had once been a cluster of thatched huts. Percy thought nothing living remained until Bat Pis came running, pointing to the jungle.

"VC here!" he shouted, as if that needed saying.

Percy's heart hammered as sharp cries and bursts of gunfire echoed nearby. A young man ran out of the trees, apparently unhurt. He told Li Lo they were close to an ammunition dump. In a sudden burst of madness, Li Lo insisted he had to see it and followed the boy down a narrow path. Percy, unable to find Bat Pis, followed.

Under a tarpaulin lay sack upon sack of grain, all clearly stamped:

GIFT FROM THE AMERICAN PEOPLE TO THE PEOPLE OF SOUTH VIETNAM.

"Americans feeding the North Vietnamese army!" the boy explained.

He then pulled back another corner to reveal a tunnel entrance. Below, in a hidden space, were piles of American combat rations, flak vests, morphine syrettes, M79 grenade launchers, and racks of AK-47s with their ammunition - an arsenal for a small army.

Percy wanted to be anywhere else.

"I've got a bad feeling," he muttered as they climbed out, spotting planes high in the sky, heading their way.

"Let's go!" he shouted. They jumped on their mopeds.

Percy strapped his camera to the handlebars. Li Lo checked the petrol.

"Enough to get some distance," he said. "Then pedal."

There was still no sign of Bat Pis when they set off, passing a cloud of flies buzzing around a blood-smeared torso. Percy stopped long enough to untie his camera and take one grim, iconic picture.

The air was unnervingly still as he caught up with Li Lo. In the fading light, there was no mistaking the intent of the approaching planes. The young man darted away as Percy photographed bombs spilling from their bellies. Then he pedalled, frantic, away from the dump across open fields - until his front wheel hit an irrigation ditch and hurled him over the handlebars.

He hit the ground, rolled, and ended up on his back, staring at the falling bombs not much further than a football pitch away. He scrambled into the ditch, burying his face in the mud. Breathing ceased to matter.

The chain of explosions was deafening. Percy gulped a mouthful of dirt and choked. The ditch was barely two feet deep; he could still feel the furnace blast and the earth shuddering. He vomited and tried to gasp at the same time.

When the bombing stopped as suddenly as if someone had closed a tap, he lay coughing, scraping mud from his throat. His ears rang; his eyes stung, though he had kept them shut. He was more afraid of choking than of anything outside.

Eventually, he lifted his head. Beyond the ditch's edge, a wall of smoke and fire boiled into the sky. A sharp pain stabbed his side, but his moped lay miraculously jammed in the ditch, only a few metres away. He dragged himself to it and pulled himself upright.

"Di di mau! Di di mau!"

It was Li Lo, riding towards him through smoke and debris.

Percy wondered if he was hallucinating.

"Gunships come now!" Li Lo yelled, helping him heave the moped out. "We move quickly!"

The thump of helicopter blades vibrated the air. Percy stumbled.

"You dead, Percy, if you no come quick!" Li Lo cried.

The rotor noise grew louder.

Percy mounted his moped, pedalling hard until the engine coughed into life. It carried him across the field at full throttle, dodging wreckage, then into the trees.

Gunships swept in behind them, guns blazing. More explosions shook what remained of the village.

"Jesus Christ! Jesus Christ!" Percy cried. "The Americans are blowing up the villagers and their own supplies!"

"We go this way!" Li Lo shouted, turning onto a side path.

The roar of gunfire receded, becoming something distant and unreal, as if it belonged to a different world.

Li Lo finally stopped beside a pond.

"What happened to Bat Pis?" Percy asked.

"Bat goes to see his mother," Li Lo said softly, lowering his head.

The pond's surface quivered like a sheet of glass.

"You're lucky," he added, as Percy slid into the water, rinsed the dirt from his mouth, and cleared his throat, splashing until his eyes stopped burning.

"That was fucking close," Percy whispered.

"Not half as close as Li Lo next to ammunition," he replied, wading in and revealing a body covered in scars and tattoos.

"Fuck me," Percy blurted. "Were you in a war film?"

Li Lo splashed water across his chest, sending ripples across the pond.

"You take a moped in the morning," he said, pointing toward the rising sun. "Go to the river at Banam. My people find you and help you. Otherwise, you rely on God to take you home."

"God has no place here," Percy said.

"God does not show himself," Li Lo answered. "It would spoil the end of the movie."

* * * * *

The word 'movie' jolted Percy into remembering his camera. The rolls of film were in the knapsack strapped to the moped. The camera itself was still tied to the handlebars. There was nothing to be done; he had to move if he ever wanted to get home.

Li Lo was not coming with him. Their parting was brutally matter-of-fact.

"You take care. I'll see you soon," Li Lo said, as if they were meeting for lunch in a few days.

As Percy rode off alone, panic seeped in, and he fought it by repeating lines he'd memorised at school:

"Let him learn the prudence of a higher strain.
Let him learn that everything in Nature,
including the dust and feathers, goes by law
and that what he sows, he reaps…"

Or was it what he reaps, he sows?

"Law?" thought Percy. "What law?"

Less than an hour later, the moped died. Percy, bruised and aching, pointed down the track and mouthed "Banam" to cyclists passing by, but they pedalled faster away from him. Six hours on foot brought him at last to the Mekong and its bustling boats.

The film, he decided, had to end well, and it did. Six days after the bombing, Percy was on a plane from Phnom Penh to Bangkok. As it rose from the runway, relief washed through him. He had seen the slaughter of simple people ordered by politicians in armchairs. Whoever claimed to be "saving" these villagers had guaranteed their destruction.

"It's every man for himself out there," drawled an older Australian in the next seat.

The woman beside him calmly painted her fingernails.

"You know something?" she said to her husband. "In twenty years, half the American population won't know where Vietnam is on a map. Names like Saigon, the Mekong Delta, Svay Rieng, the DMZ, Huế - they'll be just film titles. The Americans will forget their veterans. Their new leaders won't even admit they were here."

Percy saw no reason to respond.

She pulled a half-knitted jumper from her bag.

"Could I have it without sleeves?" Percy asked.

The Australian turned out to be a doctor, a senior psychologist who had volunteered his decades of learning to “do something useful” with the American forces.

“And what have you learned?” Percy asked.

“The agony of war doesn’t stop at the battlefield,” the doctor said. “People die in territorial nonsense all over the world. The stronger or better-equipped side usually wins. Death and mutilation are accepted as the price of duty. My work is stopping officers from killing themselves when they return without their men. They meet widows with young children. That’s when the real suffering begins.”

Percy pressed the call button for drinks.

“These tours of duty,” the doctor went on, “have become normalised. People at home watch sanitised newsreels with dinner. But the men out there - they know what they’ve done. They get used to battle, maybe. What they don’t get used to is living with the memories: their own men’s guts on the ground, their legs blown off. That’s bad enough. But the real wound is in the heart. That pain goes into the soul. It never heals.”

Thomas Jefferson had once said: *“The care of human life and happiness is the first and only legitimate object of good government.”*

Richard Nixon had said, *“Kissinger, my boy, if you can’t wipe out these little yellow bastards on the ground, flush them out with the bombers.”*

Percy was a student of history. History was supposed to prevent the same mistakes. Yet once again, bullets and napalm were the preferred strategy.

Kissinger, a historian, should have known better. The Romans had defeated Carthage in the Third Punic War not with grand charges but by cutting supply lines, breaking morale, and waiting for collapse. The same principle applied in the Soviet winter offensive of 1942, designed not to smash Nazi Germany in one blow but to stretch it to breaking point. These were wars of attrition, not conquest.

And in this latest war of attrition, the Americans did indeed lose 58,000 young men — for nothing.

Chapter Six
HERITAGE

Key Witnesses:

MARTINI BIANCO	*Medical Student – Santiago*
DIEGO VERESI	*Hotel Management Student Santiago*
MANUEL LABOUR	*Engineering Student – Santiago*
BAMBI GASCOIGNE	*TV Presenter*
GONZALES BIAS	*Chilean Chargé d'Affaires – Peru*
DOM ESTOS	*Barman*
HARTY MEAL	*Amazon Botanist*

"Next time, do what you're told!" shouted Red Alert. "You've got a thousand pictures of some peasant girl and some body parts?"

"The pictures of Angkor aren't so bad," suggested Percy as he tried not to move where the pain was coming from.

"Get out of my sight!" Red replied.

"Is he always like that?" Percy asked Daisy Chain on the way out.

"Always," she answered immediately. "Don't worry. Arty Farty is planning some features on some other ancient ruins, and I think he's sending you to Peru. He's in his office if you want to have a word."

"Don't take any notice of Red Alert," Arty Farty advised. "He's only the boss!"

As Percy walked out into Berkeley Square, he appreciated that his pictures weren't as good as he had thought.

He sat on a bench and, flicking through his work, he decided that he had really failed to capture the urgency of the moment. Even the pictures of what Red Alert had referred to as 'body parts' seemed to lack that certain immediacy that other photographers had achieved in moments of horror.

It was only later that Percy had understood why Red Alert was annoyed. The Americans had been forced out of Vietnam with dramatic coverage of the escape of diplomatic staff from Saigon. In their place, the Khmer Rouge had started to sweep up every poet, teacher, businessman, and engineer to exact a massacre and reduce the entire country to an agrarian society. There was a system of brutality that was hard to imagine or believe. Torture was to be graded in length of time up to six months, depending on how influential you would have been.

When death came, it was by a blow with a bamboo or iron bar to crack the skull because bullets cost money. Children were killed by having their heads smashed against a tree. The dead were consigned to pits, each holding up to 400 bodies. The whole country was rounded up for slaughter. Percy's photographs were at best irrelevant and at worst useless.

* * * * *

Six weeks later, Percy was on his way to Peru and, in the circumstances, grateful for a new assignment. He was to investigate the origins or remains of Machu Picchu, the centre of a civilisation so remote that parts high in the Andes were never found by the Spanish conquistadores in their plunder of the Inca Empire. The ancient structures had been preserved until 1911, when a youthful explorer happened upon what he thought was a temple. Unlike Angkor, where the origins were not in question, here was a location remote and uncontaminated, where a massive structure defied any modern building capability.

Percy was thrilled to see these massive lumps of stone weighing up to 200 tons. Here was something to investigate, and Arty Farty had given him another chance.

Once in Lima, Percy stayed first for two days at the Crillon Hotel, reading up on the local history, and then he made his way up to Sacsayhuaman, just to the north of Cuzco. The ancient ruins there provided a convincing argument that a great civilisation existed prior to anything acknowledged by contemporary historians. Here was a geometric jig-saw of angles without space in between. Man could not have moved these mammoth chunks from any quarry, let alone carve them into polygonal blocks and lift them perfectly into position high above the ground. It followed that there had to be some connection between how these structures came into being in Peru and on the Giza Plateau.

The world was fortunate that Napoleon's troops in 1799 had found a fragment of a pillar in Rosetta, an Egyptian village. This *Rosetts Stone* bore the same inscriptions in three different scripts, including ancient Greek and this duplication allowed **Jean-François Champollion** in 1822 to be the first to decipher the Egyptian hieroglyph system and open up their forgotten.

'We can only be a witness' Percy noted. 'It does not prove the existence of previous civilisations'.

Percy wandered high up in the Andes amongst the jig-saw of exact monumental boulders and hundreds of geometric shapes on the ground. These were created by the Nazca peoples long forgotten by removing topsoil to reveal kilometres-long shapes by exposing the lighter-coloured rock underneath. These looked like landing stations or greetings cards for arriving extra-terrestrials.

Since no one could ever know the meaning of this vast-scale archaeological site, Percy thought it pointless to give his opinion to readers of Reel Life.

* * * * *

That night, on a bus that looked like it had been borrowed from a junkyard, Percy went to Cuzco, a town up in the Andes that was frozen in its own time warp. It was there, in a tiny bar amongst groups of Indians in a variety of ponchos and colourful woollen hats, that Percy Vere met three students on holiday from the Catholic University in Santiago. They had secured $3,000 of American sponsorship to go down the Amazon and study the hallucinogenic effects of tropical roots, bark, and sap.

Bambi Gascoigne, the BBC university quizmaster, would have introduced them as follows:

'And from the University of Santiago, we have Martini Bianco, studying medicine. He is the captain of their team and something of an expert in drug abuse. On his right, we have Diego Veresi, studying hotel management. He is their cook. And the third member of their team is Manuel Labour, studying engineering. Manuel can fix anything.'

"You want to come with us?" Manuel asked.

Percy thought he was joking.

"The fact is one of our team decided not to come at the last minute, and we would not have to change anything," Martini added. "You have enough time, and you are healthy are the only two questions we need to ask."

Their 'starter for ten' in the University Challenge might be what was arranged, and the answer was that Manuel had confirmed a meeting with Gonzales Bias, a Chilean ambassador in Iquitos. Iquitos was the first commercially navigable waterway from the various sources of the Amazon. Their first objective was Mazan, where the river divided, but either fork would round a massive island, and they would rejoin the mainstream on the other side. Then they would head to Tamaniqua, where they could rest and resupply. After that, there was the long haul to Manacapuru before the final leg to Manaus.

Percy was assured that they had researched this trip carefully. There was no doubt that along the way, there were huge dangers. They could be swept down the wrong channel after a fork in the mainstream and then be unable to return because of the strength of the water's flow. At Manacapuru, if they got that far, there were several options, and it would be vital to avoid losing the mainstream as the river widens after that, and they would be lost with no one to help. Moreover, they would not be able to see the two banks to know where they were. Then there were all kinds of dangerous animals in the water, and many capable of either eating you or just killing you.

Gonzales was indeed organising supplies under the direction of their university and, more importantly, he had sourced a bongo, a huge hollowed-out and shaped tree trunk to carry them in all kinds of weather and rainstorms into a void.

"We need to be authentic!" Manuel reminded everyone. "We need to stay alive, but we must be authentic."

"How far is Manaus?" Percy asked.

"That's the fourth time you've asked," Manuel replied testily. "We've been planning this for over twelve months, and everything is set. You paddle, and you arrive is all you need to know."

"You can come with us," Diego joked.

"Yeah!" Manuel laughed. "We can be on the front page of Reel Life!"

"He wouldn't last a week," said Martini as he drew heavily on a spliff.

"When you went to university, presumably, you were being tested," Percy surmised. "Is this part of the syllabus arranged by the university?"

Diego looked back at him vacantly.

"We are here for four more days," Manuel confirmed as he grabbed another round of beers from the bar. "If you decide to come, you can leave a note with Dom Estos. He's the owner of this shit-house."

Dom Estos waved four tobacco-stained stumps that were his fingers as if he were being paid a compliment.

The following morning, Percy decided he had enough time for the 100-mile train journey to Machu Picchu. He started as the sun lit up the mountain tops around Cuzco with the train carriages zigging and zagging across a lush valley. There were tiny houses scattered for the Indians who tended the cattle and grew the crops. Then the ground rose up into a green hillside, which became a mountain, and then an even higher range of black mountains jagged and topped with snow. The train clawed its way up through the impenetrable jungle during the morning until gravity-defying progress. The few passengers changed to a bus that struggled up the remaining impossible way to Machu Picchu.

'No wonder the Spanish didn't bother with this,' thought Percy as he got his first glance of the moss-covered piles of wet rocks.

As the day unfolded, the mystery of the ancient Inca city enveloped Percy through his lens. A higher culture had designed this place. It wasn't only the jigsaw of granite boulders, it was the sheer inaccessibility of the place.

Some of these immense blocks of stone at Machu Picchu were polished flat. They interlocked perfectly with their partners on each side, and there, overlooking the mountains and valleys below, was the 'Intihuatana,' or, exactly translated, the 'post where the sun would tie up.' It was clear that this massive single piece of granite, cut into a geometrical base with an upright centre, did not come up the mountainside by itself. It materialised in some ancient engineering trick that was lost to modern man.

The idea that a primitive people had decided to protect themselves from earthquakes by fitting together massive stones meshed together was not the immediate explanation.

The sense of solemnity and importance at Machu Picchu was probably because of its known astrological alignments. Percy would not allow himself to leave that night, and he made an effort to celebrate the moment of magic by climbing Wayna Picchu, the secondary highest adjoining peak that poked out of the jungle complex like an upturned thumb.

It had taken some time to feel his way up the slippery stone steps, which were rarely trodden by tourists, and although he had seen only small insects, he was aware of rustles in amongst the roots and undergrowth as he grappled and slid to get to the top. Percy took his time because it was impossible to find any sure foothold. At the summit, and not referred to on any guide map, was a massive polished granite slab some six feet long, five feet across, and something over five feet deep. It was quite unlike the structure of the rock at its base, and it was precisely positioned. It must have weighed 50 tons.

If any proof of some unknown power was needed, getting this lump of granite onto the peak of this mountain was the answer that had eluded mankind.

The light started to fail, and there was no option but to stay for the night, even though the darkness threw up ghostly images. Percy had not told anyone how to contact him and he looked up 360 metres above Machu Picchu to Huayna Picchu accessible only by slippery stones known as the 'stairs of death' but on the top was a remarkable ceremonial slab. Percy made himself as comfortable a sacrifice as possible as he looked out like a god over the whole expanse of the Urubamba Valley.

From this perch in the heavens, it was easy to be intoxicated by the view of the cosmos with Mother Earth below.

Percy remembered Martini muttering about how drug crazies went up to the top of Machu Picchu and were overcome with a compelling sensation to fly. A number had flown, for a short time at least.

In the early hours, it became deathly cold even though Percy was wearing everything he had in his bag. To make matters more intense, the stillness of the night was occasionally split by peculiar noises, and Percy had no way of knowing what any of them could mean.

Martini Bianco, who had been fascinated with the Amazon since he was a boy, had mentioned that the Indians call all unidentifiable sounds in the night 'Curupira', which is the word they use for the 'spirit' of the Amazon forest.

'Very helpful,' Percy thought as he wondered what was slipping through the grass five feet below his head.

Percy was aware that the stone had retained some of the warmth it had gathered during the day, but after a while neither Percy nor the stone was sharing.

He looked sideways over the sombre silhouette of the jungle below. It was February. Within six weeks, the rains would come and lift the level of the Amazon by twelve metres into a torrent of water rushing from an unknown number of tributaries. Should he stay and do his job or go on this crazy trip down an animal-infested river with three drug dealers?

Percy fell into a fitful, shivering sleep, amused at the same thoughts that had crossed his mind in Cambodia only a few months before.

"What the fuck!" he muttered at the crystal-clear carpet of millions of stars looking down at him.

*****

Dawn sprang crimson and orange in a sudden flash as the world turned to reveal the sun. The majesty of that moment over the jungle canopy prompted whatever confirmation Percy needed that he couldn't miss such an opportunity.

He sat up cross-legged as the sun started to warm Mother Earth. He pulled open his canvas bag. The contents spilt onto the slab. Percy took his razor-sharp hunting knife out of its sheath and unscrewed the hilt. Out of the handle fell a fishing line, lead weights, two hooks, a small plastic float, a scalpel blade, and the nugget of amethyst which he had found as a boy at Cudgel Manor. He held it up to the light and smiled as he remembered how he kept on losing it at school, but it always turned up.

'If you're a lucky charm,' he thought, 'you'd better wake up.'

Percy coiled the fishing line around his fingers and inserted it back into the handle with the other bits and pieces. He screwed on the cap and held the nine-inch blade up against the sky. The jagged steel teeth along the top edge glinted threateningly. Percy folded his groundsheet and mosquito net and put them back in the bottom of the bag with his cameras wrapped in T-shirts on top.

In front of him lay the rest of his survival kit. There were about 40 rolls of film, a plastic mug, a bar of soap, a compass, a sponge, a needle and thread, a roll of bandage, quinine tablets, diamorphine, two syringes, a cure-all magnesium sulphate paste, and the most versatile and valuable tool of the jungle traveller, a pair of nail clippers.

Percy scooped it all into his bag, stuck his knife down the side, adjusted the laces on his leather boots, and looked down at the undergrowth. He could sense slithery things waiting for him to leave their sunbed.

Dropping the stone onto the long grass, he stepped carefully to the edge and looked down where the dew-soaked stone footholds led back down to the lost Inca city.

The way down was almost vertical, and the stones were so slippery that Percy had to turn, facing the slope, moving his feet carefully backwards to find footholds. With his face so close to the ground, he could smell the earth and hear the tiny rustles of something going about their business. On both sides of his face, spiders were very much in evidence, with their bulbous bodies and crooked, hairy legs moving inquisitively to check their dew-beaded webs for breakfast.

An hour later, Percy was safely back in Machu Picchu amongst the stone ruins high up in the Andes. He was changing a lens when Martini, Diego, and Manuel appeared from nowhere.

"What are you doing up here?" Percy asked.

"This irrigation system is incredible!" Manuel was saying as Percy looked up and took a picture of the three of them against the massive backcloth of the impenetrable jungle below.

Martini Bianco was tallish and well-built, Diego Varese was short and fat, and Manuel Labour looked like a stick insect.

"Great picture!" smiled Percy.

Percy moved forward and slapped a mosquito on Diego's arm.

"So, you come with us?" Diego asked.

"Maybe," replied Percy, feeling a stab of excitement.

Percy worked furiously that day to capture the images of a civilisation lost in time and to understand some revelation from these extraordinary groups of stones. He knew that he wasn't getting anything new and certainly not what Arty Farty wanted.

"I'd be better off taking pictures on the river," he persuaded himself.

"Are you coming?"

Martini Bianco was standing on a great slab of stone, looking up. He gestured to Percy and pointed towards the track that led down the mountain. Then Percy was suddenly with them in a truck with no bonnet and an engine that sounded like a hundred wounded animals on the way back down the death-defying road to Cuzco.

The next morning, they were at the tiny airfield where a light aircraft was waiting to give them a white-knuckle ride to a landing strip cut between the trees in a dot of a place called Iquitos.

The plane stopped for only enough time for them to get out. They were beside a small shed with a concrete floor and a corrugated iron roof boiled red-hot by the sun.

"Where is everyone?" asked Percy.

A man appeared from between the remains of two pick-up trucks that were sitting in the shadows. He smiled as they approached, and an acrid smell from his infected gums escaped into the air. There were obvious gaps where numerous teeth had rotted and dropped out.

"We want to find Gonzales Bias," Manuel asked.

There was a short response.

"What did he say?" asked Percy.

"He said we had to pay $10."

Miraculously, it was $5 that secured their ride to the door of the house of Gonzales Bias, and after three minutes of knocking, the man who was Chile's chargé d'affaires opened the door. He was clutching a sheet to cover himself.

Gonzales looked totally bewildered as Martini spoke to him for some time on the doorstep. Then, there was a reluctant spark of recognition, and he let them in.

The inside of Gonzales's house was a pigsty. Everything was filthy, and when he put some glasses and a bottle on the table to offer them all a drink, Percy first cleaned his dark glasses with his shirt.

By his own admission, Gonzales was less of a diplomat than an entrepreneur. This was not his official residence because his business was having as many of the local women as possible, alongside taking bribes to cheat the new oil exploration companies.

They were finishing the bottle and feeling the effects of whatever spirit was in it when a young woman appeared out of what must have been the bedroom. She was wearing a white smock and carrying a doll with one eye missing. Percy recoiled as Gonzales kissed her. She looked at them all with a vacant stare over their heads.

Gonzales looked for a second as if he might offer her some food, but instead he pushed her back into the bedroom and shut the door.

"Politics is derived from two words," Gonzales ventured as he smacked his arm. "Poly meaning many, and tics meaning a lot of blood-sucking."

Then, the alcohol kicked in, and he went back into the bedroom.

* * * * *

There was a pile of maps and some tourist guides to the Amazon on the table, with a shopping list that looked like their catalogue of supplies. Scanning the list, it was comforting to think that Gonzales must have done this before.

With Gonzales snoring away in the bedroom, there was no alternative to arranging the sofas into beds and sharing out the blankets in a pile in the corner, and Percy fell into a deep sleep. It was a lot different from the night on the slab.

The next morning, as they were driven through the town to the dock, their supposed mentor and provider did nothing but complain that it was a chore to help them.

"Getting the supplies has been very difficult," he kept on saying. "It was much more expensive than I had thought."

Manuel reminded Gonzales that his father was an electrical engineer with government contracts back in Santiago.

"What's that got to do with it?" Percy had to ask.

"These electrical contracts are to supply the prison service with all they need, and you won't be surprised to know that the shopping list includes metal bed frames and transformers," Diego explained. "One day, Gonzales may want to go back home!"

Gonzales changed the subject.

"Iquitos is isolated by the jungle," he went on. "It is the capital city of the Amazon because it is the highest point on the river where big boats can come."

At that moment, they turned a corner, and the great river was in front of them.

Percy had been used to the River Thames at Maidenhead, and it was difficult to take in the scope of such an expanse of water. This river was miles wide.

"What you see over there is not the far bank," Gonzales said as if he were mind-reading. "That's an island in the middle of the river. It's thirty miles long, a mile wide, and the river continues on the other side."

On it were all kinds of floating craft carrying pigs, cows, chickens, and huge loads of oranges, coconuts, and fruits. Here was the meeting point for commercial craft from downriver to collect goods from the interior and for the jungle traders to make their deals. Here also was the greatest body of water on the planet and a rainforest with an abundance of treasures that had inspired conquerors, nations, and businessmen to rape and plunder in an orgy of greed. The gold and rubber had made the intruders rich and enslaved the indigenous peoples.

The Indians had died in tens of thousands from the abuse, from their suffering in defending their Mother, the forest. She was their Mother from the time they were born, and it would be her who would trigger an international movement for the survival of the entire planet Earth.

The forest people had indeed performed one of the most miraculous achievements of all time. They had stopped the middlemen and their henchmen from cutting and burning millions more acres of rainforest. They had prevailed against the suitcases of payments to the politicians who used the police and the judges to remove their legal rights. They had won against the profit motive to cater to the unending demand for hamburgers. However, they had not won the war, and oblivion was still on the cards, fed by overwhelming greed.

Percy climbed down the wooden steps to where two Indians stood up to their waists in the muddy water. They were cleaning fish on the cross spars of a bongo, a hollowed-out tree trunk about twelve feet long, which was to be both their vehicle and their home.

"You can't be serious!" Percy blurted out as he looked around at all the other boats.

A ramshackle motorised barge lashed to two smaller barges laden high with tons of sacks of Brazil nuts was trying to reach the pontoon, and the sound of the engine drowned out anything Percy had to say. Someone looking like Long John Silver's brother with one gold front tooth and a pirate's hat threw a rope at Gonzales and started screaming at him.

As Gonzales got involved in a shouting match, the boys surveyed and panicked.

"This looks more like a coffin!" Diego groaned.

"This is a big mistake," agreed Manuel.

A closer look revealed that this was a sturdy type of canoe made from hardwood. It was at least four feet wide in the middle with plenty of room for the four of them, one in the bow, one in the stern, and two on the cross-spars in the middle. This had been a massive tree, and it must have weighed more than the four of them could possibly lift.

Percy was trying to think of a way out.

"It's going to be impossible to steer!" he reasoned. "Once we get going and it turns sideways, we're definitely fucked!"

Percy was looking beside him on the dock at four long-bladed paddles for punting along Indian style and a 25-horsepower engine with four 5-gallon fuel cans.

"Everything you need is here," Gonzales said as he waved his hand over the stacks of supplies.

Manuel picked up a paddle and put it in the bow, and a second under the spars in the middle.

"This is ridiculous!" Percy almost cried as he took the paddles back. "These have to be tied to the spars, and we use two to steer."

"So you're coming with us?" asked Martini.

"I cannot walk away and leave you to do this alone because you'll all drown," Percy replied.

Percy took out his knife and cut two lengths of rope from a coil on top of some boxes. He then tied the two paddles under the middle cross spars.

Manuel just stared.

"If we turn over, you'll thank me," Percy muttered.

"If this thing turns over, the last thing you'll be worried about is a paddle," retorted Gonzales. "However, if you look, you will see that this bongo is not a tree anymore because it has a flat bottom like my little chaquita; she is difficult to turn over!"

"Chaquita?" Percy asked.

"The little one he left in the bedroom!" answered Diego.

Manuel then shouted.

"Look at the size of that log!"

As if in foretelling the future, a giant log was passing them sideways in the swirling water.

As if a light had turned on, Percy knew the retreating Gonzales was on another planet because he was looking up at the sky and shouting, 'Where?'

The Indians stashed the supplies neatly in the ends and under the seats of the bongo. There was room enough for everything, which included a box of local limes, two baskets of papayas, a sack of pineapples and platanos, three cases of assorted tins, some dented and some even rusted, a huge bag of rice, and a mixture of fishing tackle and machetes. These were being packed along with sleeping bags and groundsheets. There was also a selection of pots and pans and cooking stuff with an iron grill, five bottles of gas, and a plastic bag full of matches. Then there was a satchel full of medicines.

Diego opened the satchel and picked among the contents. There was lip salve, bandages, malaria tablets, and various jungle medicines.

"That is Sangre de grado," Martini noted as Diego held up a brown bottle. "It is a resin extract from the grado tree, which congeals over a wound like a skin and protects it from infection. This we will need."

"Your confidence is overwhelming," Percy frowned.

The two Indians climbed onto the dock and left the four of them holding the bongo back on the ropes that were stopping the whole lot from being swept away by the current. Gonzales was still on the dockside chatting to two Indian girls under a canvas awning as the four boys started to feel the heat of the rising sun.

Gonzalcs gavc a final wavc as hc took thc girls into thc shcd bchind them.

"He seems glad to end this intrusion into his private routine," Percy suggested.

* * * * *

The four boys had some initial difficulty getting into the bongo and casting off without tipping it all over. There was a lot of shouting that they were too heavy as they got in, arranged themselves, and pushed off to be taken immediately by the current. Percy was dismayed to notice an impromptu farewell party on the jetty. Amongst the shouting and laughing, he heard the word 'loco' several times and assumed it meant they were only making a local trip.

* * * * *

Percy had taken the precaution of taking the paddle and sitting in the seat at the back. He was sure that all his kayaking up and around the rivers and drains around Windsor Castle was about to come in useful.

The banks of the inhabited Amazon River town of Iquitos quickly gave way to wooden shacks and then to swamp ground with several unhappy-looking farmers sloshing about in waterlogged fields. Then the jungle took over completely as if someone had cut off civilisation with a knife.

The bongo was pulled along by the water and sometimes dragged sideways by some unseen underwater hand, and Percy had to paddle hard to manoeuvre through. Once they were in a straight line, it was plain sailing, but there was a point where losing direction was serious, as the whole bongo would want to self-propel then sideways. Then getting straight again was very difficult and even dangerous.

Derelict large half-sunk boats littered the banks, seemingly trapped in the undergrowth. Occasionally, they needed to give way to avoid larger boats, rafts, and other craft plying the local trade.

The awesome pull of the waters of the Amazon was scary for each of the intrepid four in the bongo. Martini gave them a running commentary when he felt it was needed to keep them attentive to staying alive.

"The river is called the 'Maramon' on this part of Peru," he educated them. "Then later along the Brazilian border, they call it 'Solimoes'."

"So we need to know that for our epitaph," Percy replied as he was getting familiar with the steering and telling Manuel in the middle when he needed additional help paddling with all his strength on one side or the other to get the bongo straightened up.

The force of the water was formidable, and getting out of control needed only a short lack of attention. It was better to stay at the side of the river and go with the flow rather than move further out into the swirls and churning eddies.

"We are like a leaf in the water," Diego smiled.

Percy was using the paddle as a rudder at the back to keep them straight, and then there was no need for any of the others to join in, and Percy was keen to be the one in charge of the steering. He was scared to death at the idea of any of the others getting control, but he was sane enough to know that they each had to take turns learning the tricks of the water if they were to be safe.

Percy asserted that this was his work in exchange for the pleasure of being invited along.

Percy kept them on track within a few hundred yards of the bank, occasionally paddling further out where the current was weaker until Martini insisted, quite casually, that they should get into mid-stream if they were to avoid getting lost up some tributary. He was the first to recognise that massive forks in the river made the mainstream indistinguishable from getting trapped in some massive swamp. The problem was that the river was so wide that they might not know if they had gone the wrong way.

"Especially when we travel at night," added Manuel casually.

"Travel at night?" Diego burst out, incredulous.

All four of them knew that the danger was not from the piranha or the rarely seen anaconda, but from sickness. Martini told the story of how an English botanist, Harty Meal, was travelling in the province of Goias, close to the Araguaia River, and his horse went missing in the night. The next day, after a lengthy search, one of the Indians found the 40-foot-long body of a bloated snake stuck in the fork of a tree. They used six horses to drag it onto open ground, and then Harty cut it open with a machete. His horse was half-digested inside.

Percy quivered as he looked into the swirling water. The anaconda was too bulky to chase them, but there was a realistic chance that it was somewhere undetected.

"There was this picture in a magazine, only a few months ago," Diego added. "There was the shape of some bloke inside an anaconda, and he was punching or maybe just kicking from the inside."

"Shut up!" ordered the others in chorus.

They had agreed in principle to make the best of the early mornings between 6:00 a.m. and 8:00 a.m. They would then stop for a leisurely breakfast and paddle for another two hours or so before resting in the shade during the worst of the blazing heat. They'd go on at 4:00 p.m. and make camp around 7:00 p.m.

The schedule was immediately shattered because, in spite of protestations from Diego that he was starving, there was nowhere even vaguely possible to beach the bongo for their first midday stop. The bank was a marshy swamp overhung by an impenetrable tree line.

It was not until after 3:00 p.m., when all four of them were fainting from the heat and bitten to pieces, that they found a suitable clearing on the bank.

Percy steered them into the mud, and they pulled the bow out of the water and tied it to two trees with two lines.

Diego and Manuel optimistically swept the forest litter off an area of dried mud while Percy used his knife to cut four stakes from the undergrowth. He jammed them in the ground as uprights for the largest ground-sheet to be a roof tied to the trees on either side for some shade.

Martini stood looking out over the water, his shoulders lobster red from the sun.

"You ought to put a shirt on!" exclaimed Diego.

"I never burn. I tan," replied Martini optimistically.

They agreed that it was important to stick to a plan, and so they pushed back into the water only an hour later. No one seemed to object to Percy continuing his position in the back.

They paddled under forest trees, which rose at irregular intervals towards the sky. Sometimes, their tops were locked together, and, leaning over the water, they provided welcome shade close to the shore. Massive roots, exposed by the long dry season, rose like giant serpents out of the water onto the land. They resembled great fluted arches in a church. Sometimes, the forest canopy high above them was a massive entwined embrace of magnificent acacias, garlic trees, cashews, balsa, rosewood, and the immense mahoganies and hardwoods. The dead trees amongst them leaned against their neighbours, their trunks rotting and playing host to a mass of unknown creepy-crawlies. New generations of moss, vines, and creepers fought each other for the dappled light.

Martini knew a lot about plants.

From time to time, Percy rested by dangling the paddle over the side of the bongo with the water dribbling off the blade as they drifted with the current in this incredible flood downstream.

In the calm of that late afternoon, they listened to the occasional slapping of fish breaking the water's surface amongst startling bird calls and the screams of unseen howler monkeys ripping the air. Even Martini, normally not at a loss for words, was silenced by the raw tranquillity around them.

"I think I'll have a paddle," Diego announced as he stood up.

After a dangerous moment changing places, Diego settled down in Percy's seat. His only problem was that the top of his thighs and his nose had burnt medium-rare, and, after only an hour of holding the paddle, even though it was late in the afternoon, the backs of his hands had become painfully pink.

By 8:00 p.m., the heat, although abating, had sapped all their strength, and they were more than anxious to find a suitable gap between the water and the wall of vegetation to spend the night.

They swept past two opportunities as Diego paddled furiously against the current, but to no avail, and it was not until past 9:00 p.m. that he managed to punch the bow of the bongo into the bank.

Having struggled in the jungle and swearing heavily, Manuel took the bow rope up into the trees and tied it to an overhanging root. Then, the others got out and dragged the front half of the bongo as far as their strength would allow onto the bank.

Manuel cleared a space between the tree roots using broad banana leaves as a broom, and the four of them erected the awning in the middle. Percy then unscrewed the handle of his knife and put out two fishing lines with caterpillars impaled on the hooks as bait. He watched the floats for some twenty minutes before checking to find that the bait was missing.

"Cheeky bastards!" he swore.

"Maybe they don't like caterpillars," suggested Diego as Percy was finding more bait.

Then, after ten minutes, Percy had a bite.

"Oh, ye of no fucking faith!" he shouted as he reeled it in.

And there it was, twisting and jerking in the air. It was silver, it was armoured, and it was more than a foot long. It looked better shaved of its fins, gutted, headless, and roasted for twenty minutes over the fire.

"Madre!" smiled Martini as he sliced it into two halves and then into four pieces of white meat off the bone.

"I've never caught anything before," admitted Percy proudly.

"Apart from the pox," said Manuel as he served the four pieces onto plates,

"That is seriously delicious," laughed Percy. "It's like I never tasted my food properly in my life!"

With a mosquito net fixed over him and comforted by the crackling of the campfire, Percy fell asleep snugly in his sleeping bag. The last thing he heard was Martini swearing about his sunburn over the bickering of the night monkeys, the occasional howling, and perhaps the cry of a stray jaguar.

It was miraculous to be in this place and still alive.

* * * * *

It must have been a whole troupe of howler monkeys that heralded the dawn with ear-splitting screams. Then, a group of uakari monkeys with their crimson faces started chattering in the trees directly above. They were shelling seeds from the overhead creepers for their breakfast and dropping the empty pods on the camp below.

"Fuck off!" screamed Diego as some shell landed in his hair.

Percy sat up under the awning and listened as various animals announced the arrival of a new day.

"Let's break camp," suggested Martini.

"You mean pack up our stuff?" Percy laughed.

They each grabbed some fruit and loaded the bongo as neatly as possible and then struggled to get in. Diego was last with the ropes, but the bongo wanted to leave him behind. It seemed to have a mind of its own, trying to escape their clutches, but they won the fight and were on their way. The night mist had cleared, and the sun was rising fast as the current swept them downstream along the north bank. Soon, the sun had moved directly overhead and was glaring down, causing reflected heat off the surface. Clouds of pium flies hovered annoyingly around the bongo, and Percy would keep on smacking his arms. They all ended up splattering themselves with their own blood.

Then, there was an obvious place to moor against the bank with tree roots convenient for tying up.

"I feel like staying here for the rest of the day," suggested Martini.

"Yeah, what's the rush?" agreed Manuel.

Percy took a long slug of lime juice, planted a ground sheet where it looked safe, and dozed off under a shirt spread over him. He looked out sideways at ants energetically trekking across a bed of moss.

"Let's go!" shouted Martini.

Percy was in a deep sleep, dreaming that he was back at university, enjoying those precious moments of leisure. He found himself smiling as he remembered his law curriculum:

> Barrister: The youngest son, the twenty-one-year-old, how old is he?
> Witness: He's twenty-one.

Barrister: Were you present when your picture was taken?
Witness: No! I was nine thousand miles away on holiday.
Barrister: She had three children, right?
Witness: Yes.
Barrister: How many were boys?
Witness: None.
Barrister: Were there any girls?

Percy opened his eyes and stopped smiling. He was looking at Manuel making coffee over a few embers against the backdrop of the most dangerous swirling stretch of water on the planet.

"Our ride looks as if it could break free?!" shouted Percy as he saw the bongo jerking against the rope.

"I always make coffee," announced Diego accusingly. "I tell my girlfriend not to make coffee. It's written in the bible that men make the coffee."

"And how are you going to make coffee if our fucking boat gets away?" Percy asked as he jumped up to the water's edge.

"It was the Hebrews," Diego grinned.

"Really?!" laughed Percy as he paused and got the joke. "He brews!"

Percy collapsed with laughter, made worse by the underlying fear of what lay ahead.

"He brews while this current is enough to leave us stranded. Help me!"

That afternoon, they made steady progress further into nowhere-land. Then it was time to find a place to land for the night, and rather than wait for the right spot, Diego thought he'd ram the bongo into the bank of undergrowth.

Grabbing the plants, he jumped out and was dragging the bongo into the mud when he slipped and lost the rope. The bongo was now going backwards with Percy paddling furiously to get back against the bank.

"Diego!" screamed Manuel. "Can you hear me?"

"Diego!" screamed Martini.

They heard a faint reply, then nothing.

"Shit!" Manuel moaned.

"We wait!" Percy said. "We tie up here, quick!"

Manuel struggled into the undergrowth with the rope and secured the bongo.

It would have been impossible for Diego to get to the bank where they were.

"Diego, swim! We are here!" Percy screamed. "Diego!"

Then they were all screaming.

Only a minute passed, and it was in agony.

* * * * *

"Ola!"

It was Diego with his arm outstretched, grabbing onto the side of the bongo.

Manuel was crying, and Martini had sat slumped with his face in his hands as Percy helped Diego swing his leg up to get back into the bongo.

"Fuck this," was all he could muster as Martini grabbed him around the waist and slowly pulled him back in.

Half an hour later, they found a gap in the wall of vegetation and a sensible piece of dry land. They quickly erected the awning and lay down on groundsheets underneath the mosquito nets to nurse their sunburn and to try and escape the hum and buzzing of anything hungry.

After an hour of thanking God for the life of their friend amongst the chattering and screaming of the fruit-eating monkeys overhead, they all started to laugh, and they carried on until their sides were aching. There were intermittent shrieks of others above them, celebrating their life.

They were beached in a clearing, and Percy walked to the water's edge and took an orange out of the box. He sat looking out at pure Mother Nature while, in practised style, he quartered the orange with his knife, sucked it dry, and threw the skin into the undergrowth. In that time, he had been bitten at least five times.

"Fuck this!" he shouted as he slapped his own face, but missed whatever was sinking its fangs into the orange pith around his mouth.

Percy moved back under the mosquito net at the thought of the millions of ants, spiders, frogs, lizards, and snakes just waiting for him to venture out again. Then, he noticed his orange peel being devoured by a moving mob of ants or something worse.

"People come here for a family holiday?" he asked. "There are people who pay to cruise up here?"

Martini was asleep but woke a few minutes later with a shout. He slapped his leg and picked off a squashed insect that was the size of his thumbnail and full of his blood. He flicked it at the sleeping Manuel, stood up, grabbed the machete, and disappeared into the vegetation.

"Don't go too far!" yelled Percy, not a little frightened as the slashing noises became more distant.

"I'm buggered if I'm going to lie out here and be stripped to the bone!" came the faint reply.

Less than twenty minutes later, a hitherto unfamiliar scream cut through the air and woke even the deep-sleeping Manuel. They all held their breath and listened to what could only have been Martini crashing through the undergrowth.

"Mother of Jesus!" he was shouting as he arrived out of the trees, manically slapping hundreds of ants off his legs with his free hand and waving his machete like a windmill with the other.

"You know you're supposed to tap an ant's nest and they stay inside," suggested a revived Diego. "You tap again so they sense danger and come out and spray you with formic acid."

"That's true?" asked Percy.

"It's a natural mosquito repellent," perked up Manuel.

"Fuck off!" Martini screamed as he swiped at his legs.

Once he had calmed down, Martini explained that he had been trying to reach what looked like fruit halfway up a cecropia tree, but it was hollow and occupied by a tribe of Amazon fire ants. The stings he had received were not just on his legs because he had fallen backwards, and the ants burst out of the branch all over him. He bit right through his lip against the pain.

Suddenly, a large and very ugly rodent nipped out of the tangle of roots behind Manuel and grabbed one of the insect-covered quarters of Percy's orange skin.

"Jesus!" screamed Manuel. "What the fuck was that?"

"It looked like a giant rat," said Percy as Manuel jumped up.

"Let's go back to Iquitos," Martini shouted as he managed a good impression of the hornpipe.

They all knew going back was impossible.

"I got lost after the first fifty feet!" Diego shouted.

"Not much of an explorer, are we?" Percy said to Martini.

"My shoulders are burnt to a crisp," Manuel screamed.

Percy looked into the medicine bag and handed Manuel some ointment.

"I'm being eaten alive!" screamed Martini, continuing to slap his legs.

"Calm down!" Percy shouted back.

"Fuck you!" exploded Martini as he kicked his foot viciously, just missing Percy's knee.

"Some fucking leader," grimaced Diego.

Martini lifted his machete in the air and swiped it down against the upright to their shelter. The whole thing collapsed on Diego and Manuel.

"We're going back to Iquitos!" Martini announced even more angrily as Manuel fought his way out of the tangle of mosquito nets.

"How about a vote?" piped up Percy.

"I vote that this is fucking pathetic," interjected Diego as he emerged from under the collapsed awning. "We've only been here one fucking day."

"Do you think that little engine will be any good against the current?" Percy asked as he looked across the swirling water.

"We'll throw out all the food to lighten the boat," suggested Manuel. "We won't be needing it if we go back, will we?"

"Brain of bloody Chile," mumbled Percy as he changed the camera lens and snapped Martini tangled in the guy ropes.

"Vote!" ordered Martini, jumping towards the bongo and spearing a tin of spam out of the box.

"You can't be serious?" Diego retorted.

Percy sat still as Manuel put up his hand.

"I say we go back," he confirmed. "We could disappear here, and no one would ever know."

"Let's toss a coin," said Percy helpfully.

"Fuck the coin, we're going back," said Martini as he stabbed the air in front of Percy's face with the speared tin. "I'm in charge of this expedition. I arranged everything, and as far as I'm concerned, you've got no fucking vote, and stop pointing that camera at me unless you want a picture from inside your arsehole!"

* * * * *

"Okay, okay!" Percy quickly agreed.

Manuel had walked the length of the bongo and was pulling the engine out onto the bank.

"Diego, give me a hand with this fucking engine," he asked.

The two of them stood in the water as they attached the 25-horsepower engine to the back end of the bongo. Then they tried to start it.

"Don't flood it," said Manuel as Diego kept pulling the little ripcord with the choke full-out.

A howler monkey screamed unseen in the canopy above.

"That sounded like 'arsehole,'" said Percy as he adjusted the lens to snap a picture of Manuel dropping the plug spanner into the water.

"Jesus!" cried Manuel as he reached down into the muddy water, "I've lost it."

"Call yourself a fucking engineer?" shouted Martini.

"Arsehole!" screamed the howler monkey again.

Percy snapped, Manuel, being dragged off balance by the current.

Martini stopped hopping from leg to leg and jumped into the water. He grabbed Manuel by the arm.

"You've flooded the engine, so go get that fucking spanner so we can dry the plug!" he ordered as Manuel tried to pull his feet free from the mud.

"Leave it to me; I've got the magic touch," Diego confirmed as he started pulling the starter cord.

On his second pull of the cord, it broke, and he opened his hand, and the wooden grip fell into the water.

"Oh shit!" he said quietly.

Manuel took over and knotted the new end of the cord around a tent peg as the new handle.

"I think it's still flooded," suggested Percy, trying to be helpful.

"You don't have to tell me my job, okay?" shouted Manuel.

"Anyone want some spam?" enquired Percy as he picked up the pronged tin.

Percy dropped it immediately as the tin was hot enough to burn his fingers.

He rephrased the question.

"Anyone want some cooked spam?"

After 45 minutes of trying to turn the engine over, it had failed to start, and whatever the merits of a return to Iquitos, the opportunity was lost. Manuel checked what tools he had left and laid the engine down in the hull where he could work on it as they went along.

"That poxy paedophile, Gonzales," muttered Martini as he kicked the bongo. "He's fucking lucky he's not here."

Percy started folding the groundsheets, ignoring him.

Martini kicked some leaves and struck a big root.

"Now I've stubbed my fucking toe!" he howled.

"Let's get organised and let's get going," Diego suggested practically. "The more distance we can make today, the happier everyone will be. Anyone who wants to go home can get out if we stop at the next village."

As the bongo was loaded, Martini suddenly grabbed the paddle.

"Right!" he ordered. "Percy, you get in the front and take the fucking pictures. I'm in the back from now on!"

Percy stood in the mud, holding the bow. He then pushed the bongo off into the swirling water and hauled himself in at the last minute.

Martini was busy back-paddling away from the bank, and then he had to turn the bongo as they were speeding along backwards, but the wind had come up, and the water was now choppy. The current was already starting to spin them downstream.

"Steady eddy!" shouted Percy over the side.

"Paddle!" shouted Manuel as they turned sideways, and Percy grabbed a paddle.

"Madonna! We're too heavy!" screamed Diego as choppy waves slopped over the edge into the bongo.

"Fuck this for a game of soldiers!" shouted Manuel.

"You mean sailors!" Diego corrected him.

"Martini, for God's sake, paddle!" shouted Percy as he jammed his camera into a plastic bag and knotted the neck.

Percy then turned round and grabbed the engine.

"What the fuck are you doing?" shouted Martini.

"We're getting rid of this piece of shit," replied Percy. "Unless you want to swim home."

Diego helped lift out the engine and drop it over the side, but it made little difference as they were still travelling broadside at some pace with water sloshing in.

"Now, throw the fuel out!" Percy shouted to Manuel as he pulled the nearest steel jerry can from under the pile of groundsheets.

"We need the fuel!" shouted Martini.

"What for?" Percy reasoned as he threw the can over the side and grabbed the second one.

With all three cans gone, the bongo had lifted just enough to stop the waves coming over the sides and maybe sinking them.

"We've gained a good six inches!" shouted Diego.

"You wish!" muttered Manuel as he continued to bail furiously with the saucepan.

"That was really fucking close," observed Martini as he failed to prevent a wave of water swinging them round again.

"Is this some new method of paddling that only you know about?" asked Percy.

"All right, you do it," agreed Martini as he clutched the side of the bongo and moved forward.

The waves were getting higher.

"I'd rather starve than drown!" shouted Manuel as he started pulling tins out of the largest box and throwing them over the side.

"Get rid of the lot!" encouraged Martini as he took Percy's seat. "God knows what's in them."

"I'm too fat anyway," admitted Diego as a sheet of spray soaked him.

While the bongo was discernibly more buoyant without the extra weight, the waves were high.

"Waterfall!" screamed Diego, looking urgently at the river in front of them.

"Don't fuck with me!" argued Manuel, stopping scooping water out of the hull to look up.

As soon as Diego had shouted, Percy attacked the water to get to the bank.

"Joke!" grinned Diego. "It was a joke!"

No one spoke as Percy straightened the bow.

"There is nothing in spoken language that can describe what you have just done," said Manuel quietly to the sniggering Diego. "You are no longer my friend, and I shit on the grave of your mother!"

They were now moving along at a ripping pace and without sight of either riverbank as the sky clouded over.

It was two hours later that the wind calmed, but they had made several miles safely.

Percy steered them accurately as confidence returned, and they even started to enjoy the light dancing on the water against the jungle backcloth of lush greens, silvers, and blues.

"That was scary," said Percy into the silence.

"Don't fucking talk to me," snapped Martini. "My legs look like I've got the pox, and Diego gives me a heart attack!"

"And your sunburn went white," laughed Percy.

No one mentioned that they might have tipped over.

"What is that scar on your side?" Percy asked Diego.

It was about five inches long and about a quarter of an inch wide in the middle.

"I got into a spot of bother in a club back home," Diego admitted. "As the situation got ugly, I said I was the brother of the ringleader of these thugs because I knew he was really secretive and not many people even knew what he looked like. I expected them to ask if there was anything I needed and maybe buy me a beer. Anyway, when they finished laughing, the three of them took my watch and my boots and stabbed me in the guts for good measure."

"You should learn the art of pragmaticism."

"What?"

"The art of the reply in any awkward situation."

"Like?"

"Like if you fart accidentally in a lift with an Irishman and his woman is facing you and a nasty smell of fish rises up."

"And?"

"And the Irishman says, 'You've gone and farted in front of my wife.'"

"So, what do you say?"

"Something like, 'I'm sorry. I didn't know it was her turn!'"

* * * * *

The day progressed with a vulture soaring in the thermal winds high above, and alongside them, fish were biting, and the occasional water snake wriggled by.

"That splash was the swish of the tail of a black caiman, the largest alligator on the Amazon," commented Diego lazily as he looked over the bow.

"Shut up," said Percy.

"I'm being serious, and they're very good to eat," Diego continued, adjusting his hat to shade his burnt face. "That is, of course, if you're ever in a situation where your friends have thrown away all the food!"

Even though it wasn't funny, everyone collapsed in hysterics.

That night, as they found a place to land and make camp, no one said very much. Percy dried and cleaned his camera and hoped that he wasn't going to die.

The next morning was much more relaxing, even though they started off at 7:00 a.m. Diego was on the paddle, and by 11:00 a.m., they had reached the mouth of the Napo. This was the place where the Spanish rapists and killers arrived from Ecuador. The power of the water pushed them further away from the bank, even though Diego paddled frantically; he was unable to land when they wanted to. They were forced to drift helplessly past a small village, its children waving as if they were on a holiday cruise.

From one of Gonzales's maps or the map he had brought with him from Chile, Martini admitted that the Napo River was not marked by name, but he estimated that they had come at least 200 miles.

"How old is that map?" enquired Percy.

They continued to drift out from the bank, looking for a suitable landing point, but there was nothing. Then the river was split by what looked like a large island, and Diego chose the channel nearest the shore.

"This will be the dry land," he explained reasonably.

Manuel said the islands were originally created by something being caught up on the riverbed.

"The tree branches sometimes get stuck and collect debris, and that becomes vegetation and then an island," he concluded.

As the channel narrowed from what seemed like a whole river to hundreds of yards, the water flowed faster, and Diego was unable to do anything with the paddle to slow them down.

In the glare of the water, the horizon in all directions was a continuous reflection of images.

"At least we know the water only goes one way," Manuel ventured.

"There are no rapids down here," said Martini casually.

Suddenly, there was an opening where the trees on the bank had fallen in a colossal entanglement into the water.

"Paddle into the trees!" shouted Percy.

Diego steered right into the entanglement of foliage and branches. They had no choice but to get out and pull the bow of the bongo up onto a mound of mud on the shore. The clearing was large enough for them to make camp, empty the bongo onto the land, and hang everything out to dry.

Percy went back into the water up to his waist to cool off. He splashed himself gaily.

"This isn't so bad," he remarked to Diego, who was dangling two fishing lines from a root over the water.

Ten minutes later, they had caught two fish, which, unfortunately, were not edible. Percy's piece was a mess of scales and bones, and

Manuel, after trying one mouthful, threw his into the swampy vegetation and spent fifteen minutes trying to loosen a bone stuck between his teeth.

"Where's the flesh on this fucking thing!" shouted Martini, putting his plate on the ground.

Within seconds, something splashed through the undergrowth and carried off his supper.

Manuel picked the eye out of the fish head on his plate.

"I'm taking up microsurgery," he announced.

"A steak and chips would be nice," Diego mused out loud.

"I'm off to sleep," said Percy.

That night, thousands upon thousands of Sauba ants ran all over their chosen site, investigating where the food could be. They found the remaining fruit, and millions of their comrades arrived to carry it off. The woven wicker baskets that contained the bananas and pineapples were cut open to a sound like maracas in the distance, but the team was far too tired to take any notice. By morning, all the fruit was gone.

"I guess it's fish and more fish," Percy grimaced.

"That assumes we catch anything worth eating," frowned Manuel.

"We are not paying attention!" Martini said firmly. "This channel of water is not the way forward, and it certainly isn't the main river."

To go back was the only safe option because it was possible that they could end up, after miles, at an impassable swamp, and they would all die there.

It took hours of exhausting pushing and pulling all day to make any headway against the current, and no one could say for sure how far it would be to rejoin the main river. Then, before the light faded, they saw the other side of the Amazon again.

"That's called progress!" smiled Diego.

"We're not making any more of that kind of progress!" Martini shouted at him. "Next time, stop and think before we make another mistake like that."

"Fucking idiot!" he added. "It's the responsibility of whoever is steering to pay attention and not just sit there asleep."

* * * * *

During their spells on land over the next few days, Percy took delight in watching the varieties of insects and spiders, some the size of his hand, with their hairy legs appearing out of crevices in the tree trunks and hollow fallen branches. Their intricate sticky webs would catch a myriad of flying creatures unawares, and for those spiders that had a talent for imitating the appearance of flowers, they caught all manner of insects looking for pollen. Their prey was seized and eaten alive without so much as a "pardon me."

Then there were the cicadas, clicking constantly in the background like a jungle orchestra. On close examination, they could be seen simply rubbing the edges of their wings together. All around, there were varieties of berries and beautiful flowers, including the Saffron Spike, which looked like a beautiful golden feather duster.

As they grew into the situation, they started to look the part. Martini's burns became a tan with scabs; he was sporting a beard, and he continuously scratched his crotch. Percy had his knife hanging from the belt of his shorts and a bandanna tied around his forehead. Diego, in his army shorts and a purple string vest, had lost his corpulent look and said he was fitter than he had ever been. Manuel was in his element, making fires, untangling the tackle, fixing things, and telling jokes. He had even started hanging the spare fish on a string soaked in insect repellent at night.

Martini had not forgotten Diego's supposed joke about the waterfall.

"Be careful!" he warned Diego each time his friend ventured to wash in knee-deep water. "The anacondas keep down the alligator population by swallowing them whole, and electric eels carry 240 volts. Oh my God! What's that coming up behind you?"

"Fuck off!" Diego replied.

That was the last time Diego went into the water past his knees, even to do his business.

"I'd rather see what is going on under my bum," he explained as he washed and cleaned his teeth in a bucket.

They all continued to drink the river water without boiling it, thinking a mix of concentrated lime juice was an overall antibiotic.

"I've got a big pain in my stomach," Martini complained.

"That's better than being a big pain in the arse," retorted Manuel.

* * * * *

The early mornings on the water were the best times, with the trusty bongo stable and speeding through the various eddies, whirlpools, and currents. During the heat of the day, to get cool, Martini and Percy would hang onto the bongo with one hand and drift downstream in the water alongside. After getting used to the idea, there was nothing to it.

On the fifth day, the reluctant Diego got the message that he was being jibed and took his turn in the water. It just happened that a hairy rodent with a square head, about the size of a pig, popped up in the water next to him.

"Madonna!" screamed Diego as he almost pole-vaulted back into the bongo. "What does he want?"

"Don't worry," replied Manuel as Martini doubled up with laughter. "It's a harmless capybara."

It ranked amongst the ugliest things that any of them had seen, with its nose positioned on top rather than in front, but it turned out to be very friendly. Martini nicknamed it "Pedro the Pig" and suggested that they kill it and roast it.

"Why don't you fuck it as well?" asked Manuel.

"If he fucks it, I'm not eating it!" Diego insisted. "I'll stick with the fish."

Pedro the Pig stayed just out of reach and followed them, and when he eventually swam away, they waved farewell.

"Adios!" said Percy.

"Come again," said Manuel.

"There goes your date for tonight," snapped Diego towards Martini.

"Then I may have to fuck you, Diego," Martini replied.

The four had been absorbed in conversation with Pedro, and they had not noticed they were once again between an island and the bank. Soon, it was shallower, too, because they could see the pebbles on the riverbed. Then, suddenly, their passage was blocked by a carpet of vegetation, branches, leaves, froth, and flower blossoms, and it was impossible to go any further.

"Not again!" screamed Martini.

"All this water must be going somewhere," Manuel observed.

"Not again!" repeated Martini.

"The only expedition ever to lose the Amazon River," confirmed Percy in something of a panic.

To stop the bongo from being forced deeper into the vegetation, the four of them climbed waist-deep into the water and just managed to turn the bongo around. Then they held it steady with the bow upstream as the water and debris rushed by.

"We've got to go back right now!" yelled Percy as he felt himself being pinned back by the water.

The forest at that point was impenetrable, with thick, forbidding undergrowth. Overhead, twisting and looping vines and lianas thick enough to swing between the trees, Tarzan-style, were hosting a canopy of orchids and other sprays of colour.

"Jesus Christ!" screamed Manuel, leaping out of the water and trying to pull himself back into the bongo.

Manuel still had his legs dangling in the water as two eel-like snakes about four feet long wriggled past him like synchronised swimmers.

"Don't shock me like that!" Martini shouted at them.

A group of large yellow-striped frogs in the swamp, not five feet away, started to croak.

"Those are poison-arrow frogs," Martini informed them. "They carry the most lethal toxins known to mankind."

"I assume you're trying to be funny," moaned Percy as he continued to strain against the rushing water.

Then, as they neared the bank, Diego pointed to a long brown tree boa-constrictor hiding and pretty much camouflaged like bark in the crook of a branch above them. The snake was half-dangled over the next limb of the tree, some four feet away. Its front end started moving slowly and deliberately around the wood as if positioning itself.

Then Manuel pointed to another snake with translucent blue scales, easing itself effortlessly out of a patch of undergrowth into the water.

"It's a rainbow boa," he announced as a macaw screeched unseen.

"Who gives a shit?" Percy whispered as he continued to struggle forward.

"AAAHGH!" screamed Diego. "I've been bitten."

"Don't be stupid!" shouted Martini. "You're ten feet away from it."

Manuel was already helping the screaming Diego back into the bongo.

Diego had not been bitten, but as he had pushed the canoe forward, his fat foot had been impaled on a thorn or a splinter of wood. It now protruded through his foot above his second toe. He looked at it in disbelief as his fingers gripped the sides of the bongo.

"What the fuck do we do now?" enquired Manuel.

"Get in and paddle!" shouted Martini, who had been keeping the bongo from going backwards.

Manuel scrambled into the middle of the bongo and took hold of Diego's impaled foot.

"Christ Almighty," he grimaced. "It's gone right through."

"We can hardly get it out now!" spat Martini. "So, paddle!"

It was obvious from watching the trees on the bank that they were making pitiful progress against the current. A sloth pretending to be a large leaf, hanging upside down from a branch not twenty feet above them, looked down at them inquiringly.

"Do you think we look stupid or something?" gasped Manuel as he frantically plunged the paddle into the water.

"How the fuck are we going to get out of this?" Diego asked.

"Just paddle!" retorted Martini, pushing forward.

It became too deep for Percy and Martini to wade, and they both climbed back into the bongo, taking over the two spare paddles and going to work with a fury.

"The Indians do this all the time, even when they're blind drunk," Percy tried to reason as he nursed his aching arm muscles. "It's a doddle."

"What's a doddle?" asked Martini.

"Who gives a shit what is a doddle!" shouted Diego. "Just get me to a doctor."

"Isn't Martini a doctor?" asked Percy.

"You want me to die?" replied Diego, his gaze fixed on the spike through his foot.

Percy tasted the fear in his stomach moving up into his throat, and he wondered if it could choke him.

"We're not moving very far," gasped Martini as they continued to struggle against the current.

Percy looked up.

"And if it rains, we're fucked in spades," he added helpfully as the breeze freshened and rustled the top branches of the trees. New creaking noises started, with a variety of moaning sounds.

"Who are you calling a spade?" Martini demanded as a large fruit fell from an amazing height and caused a loud plop into the water beside him.

As if on cue, a group of tamarin monkeys, with their distinctive white moustaches, stopped their playing and chattering high above. In a moment, they had all disappeared.

Just as quickly, the sunlight was replaced by swirling steel-grey clouds and, less than a minute later, the sky blackened. Then the heavens opened.

The rain was so heavy that they could barely see each other, and there was nothing for it but to paddle into the undergrowth, get out of the bongo, and then hold onto it whilst knee-deep in debris.

Diego stayed put, grimacing with pain as he used the saucepan to throw out the water.

They stood fighting the swirling water in silence, each with their own fear, until the squall cleared as suddenly as it had come, and the sky brightened.

"What the fuck was that about?" said Martini.

"That's what happens when you say the word 'spade'!" answered Manuel, as he grabbed the saucepan and started to scoop water out of the bongo.

Diego shifted position and looked straight at Percy.

"The next time you say it's going to rain, I'm going to smash you in the face," he warned.

They emptied out the water, reorganised their drenched belongings, and took turns in panic paddling. In an eerie silence for over three hours, they ignored torn shoulder and stomach muscles and the relentless biting insects until, exhausted, they came upon a clear space on the bank. The channel had widened to 1,000 yards, but it was impossible to know how much further they had to go.

"I've got to lie down," said Percy.

"And we've got nothing to eat," Martini observed.

"That should be the last thing on your mind," said Diego.

"And what do you mean by that?" shouted Martini, who had got out and climbed onto the bank to pull the end of the bongo out of the water.

"I mean, precisely, that!" screamed Diego. "We've got nothing to eat, and we haven't the faintest idea where we are!"

"I'm all you've got, amigo, so button your fucking lip!" Martini screamed back right in his face.

Percy determined that keeping silent was best. He turned away and started brushing a clearing between two massive roots to make sure there were no snakes.

"All we need now is a fucking fer-de-lance to finish us off," he mumbled as he poked around in the undergrowth.

"Worse would be a bushmaster," Manuel muttered as he and Percy laid out a groundsheet. "It's the most feared snake in South America, and once it decides to get you, you're doomed. It can't see, so it tastes the air to find you, and then it'll either chase you through the trees or drop on you. It strikes by jumping at your face and ripping your skin open with its fangs. The poison makes your veins explode in about an hour."

Percy closed his ears. He then closed his eyes, but a picture of a bushmaster eating Diego in great gulps invaded his brain, and he had to open his eyes to see reality.

They lifted Diego onto his sleeping bag, and Martini then lifted his leg up to examine the splinter of wood. It was like a shard of glass, about half an inch wide at the base and tapering off as it went through.

"We've got to get it out, amigo," Martini said in as conciliatory a manner as he could muster.

"We've got plenty of aspirin," Manuel tried to joke. "Great cure for open wounds, snake bites, and amputations!"

They took a length of rope from the bongo and tied Diego's ankle to the tree root.

"It'll go numb in the air," reasoned Martini, who then rummaged through Manuel's tools, coming back with a pair of pliers.

"You can't be serious!" Diego winced.

Percy folded his bandanna and offered it to Diego.

"Bite on this," he suggested. "The famous Doctor Martini Bianco is ready to operate."

Percy jammed the bandanna in Diego's mouth before he could say anything and then held his arms down. Manuel held his foot, and Martini pulled out the splinter in one swift movement.

There was a muffled, blood-curdling scream from Diego.

"That was pretty easy," Martini concluded.

Blood poured out of the hole as they moved Diego to make him comfortable. Manuel boiled some water and, with the cleanest piece of cloth he could find, he bathed Diego's foot with disinfectant. Percy then administered some of his magnesium sulphate paste, and Martini smeared some Sangre de grado over the whole thing. They then bound Diego's foot with Manuel's spare underpants.

"Keep that clean, Diego," muttered Percy as if he were a hospital intern.

Percy rinsed his bandanna in the river and tied it back around his neck.

"I think I've died and been reborn in a Japanese death camp," moaned Diego.

Manuel had found a dry, dead branch and chopped it up with the machete, and that evening, they had a welcome fire.

"God forgive you all your sins, Manuel," said Percy later as the chill of the night was kept at bay.

"If we don't get back up this channel, I'll be speaking to Him personally," Manuel whispered back.

* * * * *

At first light, Percy rigged two fishing lines from a branch overhanging the water, and after he had finished, he stepped back and raised his arms in the air.

"And what are you doing?" asked Martini without getting up.

"Praying for breakfast," Percy replied.

Percy sat and watched the world wake. It was frightening to think that all this worked so fluently if man was not around.

"Is Diego okay?" he asked Martini, who was brushing a square of earth to smooth out the soaking wet map.

"I think his foot is already infected," Martini acknowledged. "It's bright red up to his ankle."

"Have you any idea where we are?" Percy followed up.

"I can't tell where we are because this fucking river looks the same all the way until we get much further down," Martini admitted.

"I thought you worked it out so this shit didn't happen," came the voice of urgency from Diego.

"If you start on me this morning, you won't have to worry about your foot because I'll cut your cock off," Martini snapped back.

"I'm completely useless," said Percy, looking at the meaningless map. "In England, in moments like this, we just call the AA."

"My father went to Alcoholics Anonymous," volunteered Manuel as he stopped boiling some water and stuck his hand in his duffel bag for his bottle of cachaca. He unscrewed the cap and took a large slug of the raw cane spirit.

The others looked at him open-mouthed.

"As Alcoholics Anonymous would say," Manuel gasped. "One day at a time."

"Very helpful," said Percy. "Give me the bottle."

Percy took a large gulp. It burnt its way down his throat and exploded in his stomach.

"Give some to that poor bastard," Martini ordered, nodding towards Diego.

It took no time until the bottle was empty, and they were all light-headed.

"We can't miss Leticia," laughed Manuel. "It's a border post."

Everyone collapsed with laughter.

Percy had put his compass on the map.

"The river's flowing north-west," he said as if it was a great surprise. "According to this map, the only place that it goes north-west is past Leticia, so maybe we missed it."

They collapsed in hysterics, although it was so unfunny.

Martini gasped as he rolled on the ground.

"How can I go back to Santiago and say we drifted right past the drug capital of the world?" he shouted.

There were no fish for breakfast.

Paddling against the upstream current was exhausting, with the only highlight being the fish Diego caught. It weighed at least six pounds even without its head.

There was no break in the wall of vegetation to beach the bongo until a gap appeared in a space they could clear.

"Magnificent!" said Manuel as he took the fish out of the bongo and looked up at the dappled light. "Now we can eat!"

"It would be nice if we knew where we were," gasped Diego, using a paddle as a crutch.

"A technicality," said Martini as he turned the fish above the fire.

"Let's wait until tomorrow to go on?" Percy suggested as he collapsed back against a tree trunk. "I can't paddle another stroke, and we might not find another spot like this."

No one had the energy to object as their magnificent fish sizzled gently on the fire.

"So, we rest and tomorrow, maybe we get back to where we went wrong," added Manuel.

"I think someone should say the Grace," suggested Diego as he opened the fish, took out the backbone, and split the two sides easily in half.

Percy ate his food slowly.

"That was the best!" he said. "But next time, Diego, we need to catch something a little larger."

"I'm going for a hike - anyone want to come?" asked Martini, grabbing his shoulder bag and starting off between the trees on a way never before trodden by humans.

Miraculously, Martini returned before the sun disappeared, and the others were dozing.

"Look what I've got!" he announced proudly.

Martini had collected a dozen samples of root, bark, and leaves. He had also collected a host of ticks with their puffed-up little bodies stuck on his legs. He casually pulled a stick out of the fire and sizzled them off. Then he pulled their bodies and extracted the bite.

"How did you get on?" asked Percy lazily.

Martini held a piece of root in the air to show them.

"This one's barbasco," he replied. "The juice from the sap is so strong that the Indians use it as bait to paralyse the fish in the water. The fish simply float to the surface and get collected in a basket. The women also take it for an instant abortion. Tomorrow, Diego, you're not pregnant, but you'll have no pain."

Diego frowned as Martini held up the next piece of root.

"This one's for us now," he said, cutting it into thin strips and massaging the inside of his thighs with a sappy sliver.

"Thanks, but no thanks," Diego replied.

"I think I'll pass!" added Percy as Martini pulled another length of root out of his bag and sat cross-legged, crushing it between two stones.

"I think this one is ayahuasca," he continued. "Its liquid is called diame, and one taste of it sends you to Heaven. This is the stuff the Indians give to their kids in tiny doses, so they get used to it. The Spanish name it 'de la muerte' because it makes you see your own death. This is the world's most powerful hallucinogen. You see yourself dying, and you can even work out the time and place it's going to happen. It makes you into a great warrior because you fight like crazy if you know you're not going to die."

"Give me some," exclaimed Percy. "I want to see if we're going to make it out of here."

As Martini and Percy lay back to dream, Diego turned to his friend.

"Well, it's you and me, Manuel. These two are gone."

Manuel didn't reply. He just yelped and waved away a bug that had bitten his eyelid.

That night, Percy lay in and out of consciousness in his sleeping bag under the giant trees and a diamond-studded sky. Streaks of cloud moved across a full moon while the cold river breeze fanned the fire. It emitted a mystical herbal smell.

"Tomorrow is the day of truth," muttered Diego to himself as he tossed in pain.

"You wouldn't know the truth if it bit you on the arse," Manuel ventured.

"The truth of the matter is that we'll still be in this shit tomorrow," Percy slurred.

"I thought you'd gone to another planet," replied Diego.

"I'm on my way," said Percy. "But Martini's gone for good."

Percy fell into a deep sleep alone in space, an atom in a void, until the drug took a firm hold and a wondrous feeling of comfort and warmth.

The chuckles, wheezing, ticking, whining, wooing, hooting, screaming, shrieking, and chirpings of the day had been replaced by the nocturnal chorus of crickets, bats, and a battery of ever-oppressive biting insects.

"I'm starving again," said Diego in the early hours. "Did anyone put the hooks out?"

"You won't be needing food if we don't get out of this place," argued Manuel, slapping at the fiftieth bite. "You'll be the food."

At 6:00 a.m., Percy found himself shivering in a cold sweat to see Manuel trying to raise Martini.

It was not until 11:00 a.m. that they were back on the water and paddling frantically for five hours in the searing heat to make any meaningful progress, and suddenly, the river widened dramatically, and they were surely at the point where they had gone wrong.

"No way!" Diego shouted back. "We stick to the bank."

"But that's an island," Manuel reasoned. "We've got to cross over to the mainstream."

It was all guesswork when informed judgment was needed, and the current was demanding that they make a decision. Percy wanted to stop and pull the bongo up onto the bank between the trees. They could ready themselves for a final effort to cross the distance to the mainstream without being pulled back into the same channel where they were swept along.

Martini was awake but saying nothing. He was stroking his crotch and wondering what had caused a vicious rash around his genitals.

"My balls are on fire," he announced.

"Don't think for a moment that anyone here is going to help in that department," fumed Manuel.

It was 6:00 p.m. when they all agreed they were ready to push the bongo back and paddle across to the fork in the river and back to the mainstream.

"We can't do this again," Diego moaned. "I definitely won't survive it, and where are all the people, for God's sake? There's no one living here!"

Percy sat in the back with the solid backrest, and Manuel was in the front with the stronger Martini in the middle, his heels against the ribbing on the floor. Percy started out directing them at an angle upstream to get across to what must be the flow of the main river.

It was easy to see how they had gone wrong. The island that divided the river was easily mistaken for the opposite bank of the mainstream.

"Strangers in the night," sang Martini.

Halfway across, it was a battle until they crossed the critical point where the current took them effortlessly downstream once again.

Diego started to sob with relief.

Straight away, they chose a place to push the bongo high up into the undergrowth on the island to take a positive break and eat whatever they had left or could catch.

"It's a good thing we're too tired to eat," said Manuel, drinking a mug of boiled Amazon water.

"Have a yucca root!" suggested Martini as he looked at the space where their supplies should have been.

"Well, guess who threw all the food away?" asked Diego.

"Be grateful there's plenty of water," dribbled Martini.

No onc laughcd.

Percy baited his two fish hooks with fat insects and tossed them into the river attached to the back of the bongo.

Martini rubbed more roots into the general area of his dick, hoping for any kind of numbing sensation.

"You're going to make that worse," argued Diego. "Isn't one soon-to-be-dead person enough for you?"

"I hope you're making medical notes," observed Percy. "The rest of the world needs to know how you're killing yourself."

Diego took the bandage off his foot and washed the area of red in boiling water at the same time as Manuel complained of a terrible pain in his stomach. He had swollen and distorted eyelids from bites.

"Can you see out to enjoy the experience?!" Percy asked.

Martini put a wet cloth over his eyes while he again sang 'Strangers in the Night.'

They slept until Manuel was woken by the movement of something in the thick vegetation. It was a lizard about two feet long with grey and black striped, chequered armour. He eyed it hungrily.

Martini then stirred and took his handkerchief out of his bag. He opened it to reveal two remaining strips of bark.

"Man, this stuff is fucking great!" he smiled.

"You look like shit," expounded Diego.

Martini stood up, swayed, and stepped into the shallow water, and he got stuck in the mud as he splashed his face into life.

"Just fucking great!" he repeated as he slurped back through the mud and picked up his bits of bark. "Last chance, anyone?"

He picked up both slivers and dangled them in front of Diego's face.

"You must be out of your mind if you think I'm rubbing myself with that stuff!" exploded Diego. "Look at the state of you!"

"He's always had this death wish thing," muttered Manuel.

Percy shrieked. There was a fish caught on one of his hooks. He took great care to avoid losing it before chopping off the head. Even though it must have been dead, it was flapping about.

"Is that fresh or what?" laughed Manuel.

"That was brilliant," Diego agreed as they rearranged the fire to cook their prize.

"I think we might need to amputate your foot," Martini was saying as he looked at the spreading red area past the bandage.

* * * * *

During the next two days, they stayed in the middle of the river to make the most speed and to keep sight of the northern shore for any sign of life. The great river had turned to the east, and Percy had relieved Martini of the map in exchange for the magnesium sulphate paste to save his manhood. Percy was guessing, but confident he knew where they were.

The high point of their menu over those days was a barbecued green iguana, which had been stalking along the bank, minding its own business, until Manuel's machete slashed off its head.

"That's saved us from all that yucca acid and poison," Diego managed to say.

They grilled the iguana over the fire, and it was quite a moment. It tasted just like rabbit.

"This is an unbelievable place," said Martini, joyfully sucking the main iguana bone. "Apart from the rash around my balls, I feel normal."

Martini's eyes were glazed and piercing.

"You look like someone who's just been smashed on the head with a rock," Percy exclaimed.

"You know," Martini mused as if he was talking to God, "It's a great privilege to be here in the backyard of the great Inca civilisation. The jungles of South America, all the way up to the United States, supported millions of people without cutting down the trees."

"He's off," warned Diego.

"You mean, off his rocker?" added Percy.

"Now he's going to tell us about his favourite subject, the Lacandon Maya," butted in Manuel. "They grew over seventy different crops on one-hectare plots on the forest floor, isn't that right, Martini?"

"How do you know that?" asked Martini, rubbing his head.

"Because you've been repeating yourself twenty times during the night," Manuel yawned.

"And just in case you didn't know, it's called 'multi-layered forestry,'" mimicked Diego.

"Smart-arse!" rebuked Martini. "Anyway, it's all over—with the roads and the ranchers and the loggers and the gold-diggers. That's why I had to make this trip. A quarter of the world's medicines come from rainforest plants, and we're cutting down 138 square kilometres of them each year. The Amazon jungle supports over half of the world's animal species. If no one stops the fast-food companies from cutting down the trees for grazing, it'll all be gone."

"That was a very coherent statement," observed Percy as Martini fell back and passed out.

Diego had continuously bathed and redressed his wounded foot, and he had it covered with the Sangre de grado for the lack of anything else that might help. He kept it as dry as possible during their time in the boat, but he was complaining about pains in the back of his knee and in his groin.

"You're fucked," mumbled Martini the next day as they got ready for the next phase downstream.

"Well, you're a great help," moaned Diego. "This expedition was your idea, and look at you; you're out to lunch!"

"I wish I were," Martini answered for all of them.

The heat in the middle of the day had become overpowering, but they were in good spirits as they were sure to reach a religious group at any moment. That comforting thought was lost when Manuel spotted a black triangle cutting through the water behind them.

"If I didn't know better, I'd say that was a shark," Percy's voice whistled through his teeth as he stopped paddling and grabbed his knife.

"And what do you think you're going to do with that?" asked Manuel with as much scorn as he could muster.

"I think it was a shark," Diego agreed as the fin disappeared.

They all sat motionless in the boat for a full minute, scanning the water, and then whatever it was broke the surface not fifty feet away.

"It is a fucking shark!" screamed Diego, grabbing onto Manuel.

They all sat stunned as the fin passed effortlessly across the river behind them, and it was a full two minutes before anyone spoke.

"Let's get out of here!" squeaked Diego.

"At least onto the land!" agreed Percy.

"I can't stand much more of this, amigo," Manuel announced towards Martini. "I'm getting sick."

"Sick!" exclaimed Diego, slapping Manuel's arm with the back of his hand. "What about my leg? I can almost smell gangrene! Where the fuck is everyone?"

"Sharks never attack unless they swim round you first," observed Martini helpfully after the fin suddenly reappeared on the same side.

"Are you sure the shark knows that?" groaned Manuel as he clasped his face in his hands.

"Take me now, Jesus!" Diego screamed at the top of his voice.

The shark disappeared.

"Now you've frightened off that nice shark," said Percy.

That evening, they hardly spoke to each other, and no one could sleep in their various states of pain, hunger, and exhaustion. Percy wondered if anything worse could happen before they reached a ranch, a town, a village, a boat, or anyone.

The next morning, while he was washing at the water's edge, Martini let out an almighty scream and plunged forward into the water. Percy pulled his knife out of the earth beside him and jumped forward to pull Martini's head out of the water. Manuel helped drag their screaming leader onto the bank. The only thing unusual was that Martini's shorts were down by his ankles, and he had both hands buried between his buttocks.

"Something's up my arse!" he screamed.

"Thank God something's woken you up," moaned Diego without even lifting his head as he had no intention of looking up Martini's back passage.

Martini's body contorted as he screamed again.

"It's going up inside me. For fuck's sake, get it out!"

Manuel and Percy dragged him over to the bongo and bent him face down over the bow. Manuel pulled Martini's fingers away from tearing at his own bottom and opened his buttocks. Sure enough, right there in his anus was jammed a fish with spines extended in every direction.

"I think you've got a candiru," explained Manuel, trying not to look too closely. "And if we pull it out, the spines are going to take your whole arsehole with it."

"Do something!" screamed Martini.

"That's a big problem, Martini," answered Diego sarcastically and without looking up. "Why do you think Amazon Indians wear bark guards over their private parts? To decorate their willies? No! It's because they know that those voracious little candiru just love piss and shit!"

"Fuck off!" Percy shouted at him.

"Shut up, Percy, and hold his buttocks open," instructed Manuel.

"Do you do this often, Manuel?" enquired Percy as he enabled Manuel to get the pliers into position and clamp them on the rear end of the fish.

Manuel then yanked at it, and Martini's whole body convulsed as he screamed in agony.

They examined the pliers.

"We got the tail," Manuel declared calmly.

Martini continued to scream uncontrollably.

"Hang on," said Percy, "we've got some morphine."

Percy went and grabbed the diamorphine and a syringe. He came back and handed it to Manuel.

"You do it!"

"You must be kidding!"

Martini was clearly in terrible pain, so Percy shot the lot into his left buttock.

"We've got to try and get it out, otherwise he's going to get infected," continued Percy as he rummaged in his bag.

Martini stopped shouting.

"We've all fucking had it," Diego moaned.

"For fuck's sake, shut up!" remonstrated Percy. "It's not your arse."

Percy found his nail clippers and handed them to Manuel.

"Try these!"

"I think you should take a picture," Diego suggested as Percy pulled Martini's buttocks apart.

"Don't move," ordered Manuel as the morphine seemed to have taken the edge off the pain, and he fished around with the nail clippers, pulling out bits of the candiru and then its spines one by one. Then they bathed his bottom with boiled water.

"Anyone for breakfast?" asked Percy.

* * * * *

"I'll take another shot of that morphine," grimaced Martini.

"If you give that spaced-out bastard the rest of our medicine, I swear I'll cut your fucking throat while you sleep!" Diego piped up.

Percy filled the remaining syringe. He held it up and squeezed the plunger until a drop appeared at the tip of the needle, just as they did in the movies.

"Fair's fair," he said to Martini and injected it into Diego's leg.

Martini was still lying over the bongo as if in anticipation of something else happening.

"I think you can do this yourself," said Percy as he spread some antiseptic cream on his bandanna and folded it between Martini's buttocks.

As Martini pulled up his shorts and tightened his belt, Percy made a mental note never to put his bandanna around his head again.

"We need to get moving!" Percy was insisting as he swallowed his last two secret quinine tablets and helped Diego back into the bongo.

"Why do you have to tie up the paddles every fucking time we stop!" shouted Manuel.

"Because we would look pretty stupid if we lost them," replied Percy, undoing the knots.

"Remember what Gonzales Bias said about the border and about the Colombians running the drugs," said Martini as they pushed off. "We should move over to the other side to avoid being shot."

"If we're still on the Colombian side, we can't have reached the Brazilian border, right or wrong?" asked Diego.

"That has to be right," Manuel agreed.

"Can't we tell from the sun? Diego asked as they drifted with the current.

The truth was that none of them knew where they were, and the plan was that they would paddle across this great expanse of water and along the opposite bank until they found people.

"We stay a good distance from the bank so we get the current and we can make contact with any other boat we see!" Percy suggested it as a reasonable strategy.

"Where the fuck is everyone?" Manuel was asking as they paddled diagonally downstream.

It was an awesome ambition, looking over the massive surface of the river all around them.

"This is truly weird," Percy commented as they seemed to be making no progress. "What's happened to the normal people who live here with boats to go fishing, for God's sake?"

They reached the other side as it was getting dark and stuck the bongo into a clump of roots and tied up.

That night, Diego started crying in his sleep, and by the morning, he had become delirious with a fever and unable to move his swollen leg.

Martini lay face down with his legs apart.

"I'm not feeling very well!" announced Manuel, clutching his stomach.

"The weather's great, and pray this is our last day," Percy said unconvincingly.

They got going as quickly as possible, with Percy steering from the back. The river took them along without paddling, steering to keep straight.

Percy had diarrhoea and stomach pains himself, and he was continuously leaning over the side to retch. This was a painful affair since his stomach was contracted and empty besides sips of river water.

That night, no one had the strength to drag the bongo onto the bank, and to make matters worse, the sky had darkened and become streaked with varying shades of slate grey and black. They had given up cutting stakes for an awning and simply tied the bow line of the bongo around a tree. That evening, Manuel ignored a large yellow snake that had dropped out of the tree, not three feet from him. They looked at each other, and the snake slithered past him back into the undergrowth.

"He obviously didn't find you attractive," Martini managed to laugh.

"There's not enough of me left for a meal," Manuel replied without a hint of humour.

There was no moon that night, only a still, unnatural silence under a heavy dark sky, broken suddenly by a drum roll and a savage roar as the clouds burst and discharged millions of gallons of water that fell like a trillion arrows. The four simply put their ground sheets over their heads while an incredible storm enveloped the forest. Single lightning bolts ripped out of the sky to find the earth. The ghostly magnesium flashes whitened the river as far as they could see while the black billowing banks of cumulo-nimbus thundered with artillery barrages that vibrated the ground and deafened even the "curupira."

Percy and Manuel were doubled up in pain with their knees against their chests while Martini continued to lie face down. Diego moaned in distress, his leg purple and blotchy.

The storm was not stopping, and the level of the water had risen to a point where the water-logged bongo tied to a root was in danger of being swept away. Percy and Martini struggled in the undergrowth to tie the bowline double and stop the current pulling them downstream.

"Get back on the bank!" Martini screamed towards Manuel, who was holding onto Diego and pulling him back from the rising torrent of water.

Manuel no longer cared, and Percy had to pull him back while they both hung onto Diego.

They watched helplessly as their ground sheets and sleeping bags disappeared in the flood, and they no longer swatted the insects that were feasting on them from the air and even below the water.

"If we lose the bongo, we lose our lives," stuttered Percy as he hung onto the side of the bow to stop the ropes from letting go.

No one answered.

* * * * *

The storm raged on until five in the morning. Then, as if the Gods had turned off a giant tap, the water stopped falling and left a new and earthy smell, with the river still crashing through the forest floor around them. Only then could Martini and Percy see Manuel and Diego locked together between the trunks of two trees.

The bongo was saved with the ropes looped around a group of sturdy roots.

Both Martini and Percy looked like they had been lashed with a cat-o'-nine-tails from the scratches they received all over in the struggle.

"Stay where you are!" Martini shouted up the bank as he moved position to stand with his back against the bongo, holding it steady. "Find the saucepan to empty the boat."

The bongo was at least half-filled with water, and they took what seemed like thirty minutes to empty it with the one saucepan they could find. Then they struggled to get Diego back in. Manuel got into the bow, and Percy clambered into the stern as Martini pushed them out of the undergrowth and tried to untie the ropes. There was no way to untie the knots, and Percy simply cut the lines, knowing too late that they needed the whole length to keep the bongo during the stopovers.

Martini hauled himself back in, and Percy guided them back away from the bank.

The new torrent of water carried with it branches, roots, and vegetation of all kinds. It was like a wild obstacle race, and there was a good chance of the current turning them round and the debris flipping them over.

Brilliant sunshine ensued, with new sprays of tropical flowers opening high above them all along the bank, but this was no time to appreciate them. It took all Percy's strength to hold the paddle in the water as a rudder and for Manuel to stop Diego, in his delirium, from trying to get out into the river.

It was only about an hour after they had started that they rounded a slow bend, and Manuel lifted his arm, pointing.

They all stared at five alligators with only their gold-flecked eyes and blunt snouts breaking the surface of the protected shallows. Manuel slipped down lower into the hull, clutching his stomach.

"Vai te foder!" he shouted into the air.

"My Portuguese vocabulary improves by leaps and bounds," smiled an incredulous Percy as he started hitting the side of the bongo with the paddle.

Martini bashed the side with the saucepan.

The alligators disappeared in an eddy, but Martini and Percy continued to bang away, knowing that they were close by and maybe even underneath them.

"I'd wrestle the four of them for a dry sheet of bog paper," Percy said seriously as an explosion of parakeets burst out of the jungle canopy.

Percy looked up at the screeching and screaming to see them flapping like a mass of red and green flags in a stiff breeze.

"My arse is in great trouble," Martini announced suddenly.

He need not have mentioned it because he had been shifting position and contorting to find any way to sit without putting weight on his back passage.

"It's time to think of getting a proper job," said Percy out loud as his stomach contorted into a spasm of pain and an uncontrolled release into his shorts.

They drifted until midday, when the sky started to darken again, and a wind came up out of nowhere. It whipped up the waves and then, in a moment of distraction and pain, Percy let his paddle be wrenched out of his hand.

He stared at it, being carried away in disbelief.

It was a full minute before he groped forward and untied the other paddle.

"I apologise for anything I said about tying them up," Manuel smiled as the lost paddle gathered pace.

Percy cut off a length of rope and attached the spare paddle to his wrist so he could have his spasms without losing it. He straightened the bow and moved into the fastest water as his stomach repeated a contorted movement that felt like a knife cutting through his insides.

That afternoon, the rains came again, suddenly blocking their vision and filling the bongo with water. It was impossible to see where they were heading or how far they were from either bank, so all they could do was bail and keep the bongo straight.

As suddenly as it had begun, the rain stopped again, and the wind cleared the clouds. Then they stared in disbelief at the ranches that had replaced the jungle, with jetties and powerboats at the water's edge. Even if they thought it was safe to approach drug boats, Percy had no strength to paddle towards them.

At this sight of civilisation, Manuel smiled as if he had seen God, Martini cried in pain as he shifted position to get a better look, and Diego was no longer interested.

Gonzales had mentioned the Peruvian military presence at the border at Puerto Alegria and the Brazilian border and other missionary encampments and all between the drug dealer pontoons, but they had not seen anything, so they must have passed it all. Now, no one had the strength to do anything but drift where the current dictated.

Percy tried to speak to Martini, but no words would come out.

"I'm not moving from this position again until I get some medicine for my arse," was all Martini could say.

Then they heard the shouting of a group of Indian children playing on the shoreline, not a hundred yards away.

As Percy focused, he took in the surreal sight of children in cast-off Western clothes and a variety of T-shirts. The one closest to him announced in red letters: PEOPLE WHO LIVE IN ITALY ARE CALLED STALLIONS.

Pigs and chickens were on the shore in a backdrop of open-sided shacks on stilts joined together by duckboards.

Percy suddenly found his voice and started screaming for help as hard as he could in Portuguese, "Ajuda! Ajuda! Ajuda!"

Manuel looked up and smiled faintly as the children started to wave.

Percy steered towards the landing stage, now whispering, "Ajuda, Ajuda."

Within less than a minute, the locals had gathered at the water's edge to lift the unconscious Diego Veresi out of the bongo. Martini was next, holding his legs wide open, and then Manuel and Percy both extricated themselves from their own mess.

Percy sobbed uncontrollably.

The four of them transferred to a primitive infirmary that had some twelve patients in a row of mattresses on basic bed frames. There was a series of what looked like medical cabinets and some equipment plugged into the wall. They all ended up together at the end, separated by a curtain but privy to the individual sighs and chats of the other patients.

"Time to open your legs, Martini," Manuel teased. "The large gay nurse is here!"

The nurse was associated with the Belgian charity Sang Froid.

"That is such a disaster in your rear end," he started. "Those spines are all inside, and there will have to be an operation, but first I'm going to give you some antibiotics."

The nurse smiled as he pulled on the medical gloves and opened a pot of cream. He scooped some out of a jar, and his forearm disappeared up between Martini's legs.

"We will operate tomorrow," he advised, "but you should know, the next time, how to get a candiru out of your bottom. You must blow cigarette smoke up your arse, then the spines will retract, and the fish will pop out."

"I think Martini has a new friend!" Percy observed.

* * * * *

Percy was the first to recover his strength and think about his own situation. They would stay together for a few days and decide how to move on, and never see each other again.

It was not immediately obvious that this collection of buildings thatched with stalks and leaves was any part of Manaus, where they thought they had landed. Manaus was the three-centuries-old capital city of Amazonia, founded by the Portuguese Jesuits. The indigenous groups had been subjugated over time by epidemics and atrocious persecution that forced a containment of communities to serve their masters as a pool of labour and as a brothel.

Over the days of recovery, Percy learned that the "civilizados" were the Portuguese who had replaced the centuries-old traditions of hunting, fishing, and gathering in the forest with expanses of vast commercial farms, cutting wood, and prospecting for minerals. Their agents, the regatões, would arrive, rape the women, and take everything away by boat. These people who were left stayed on to look after the sick and injured. The fact was that the majority over the years were buried in areas they call the roças.

The local people had been reduced to selling woven hats and handbags to tourists, but there were still tribal leaders who made sure that their ancient culture was not entirely lost. At intervals, the villagers would still gather round a central fire pit used for cooking and keeping the chill away at night. In the days, they used the river to bathe, wash their clothes, and secure their canoes. The men went on daily food-gathering expeditions to collect pumpkins, yams, and sweet potatoes from the limited guaraná fields allocated to each village by their commercial bosses. If they wanted to gather nuts, berries, and roots, they had to go on expeditions further away, where anyone else would be lost and unable to find any way home.

Percy was curious that they had a cosmology represented in a heavy carved walking stick called a porantim. These were carved with figures painted in white representing their spirits. These spirits had magical properties of intuition to solve the political, judicial, religious, and mythical questions in their traditional tribal way.

Percy learnt that a spectacular rite involved the sting of the bullet ant, where the ants are first rendered unconscious by submerging them in a natural sedative. Then hundreds of them are woven into a large glove made out of leaves with their stingers facing inward. When the ants regain consciousness, a boy would enter manhood by slipping on the glove and keeping it on until he is paralysed by the ant venom. Meanwhile, the whole village starts a spiritual dance in a rhythm with all their porantims beating in unison on the ground.

"This is part of the reality of every person, animal, and plant being in one living community," the head man explained to Percy in broken English. "After a period of shaking uncontrollably, the boy regains consciousness as a man."

Percy returned to the area of the dispensary cordoned off for his three friends.

"I've got a solution for us," he shouted. "There's a party tonight, and we are going to connect with the spirits and rejoin the world as men!"

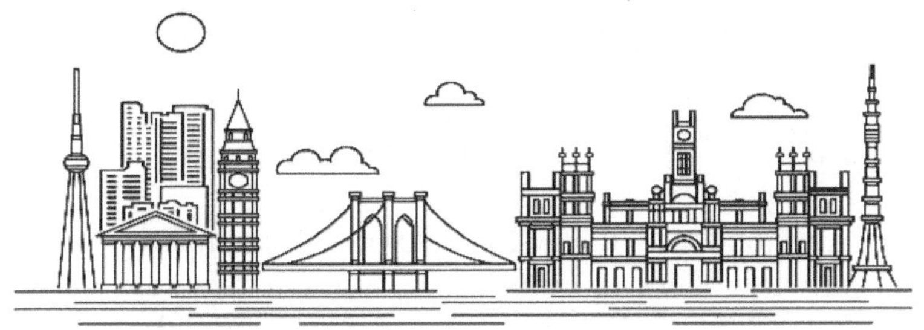

Chapter Seven
WELCOME TO WORK

Key Witnesses:

HARDY BREED	*Bank of England Trainee*
SEYMOUR CLEARLY	*Salesman – Golden Products*
DALY GRIND	*Designer - Pyramid Sales*
HAL ETOSIS	*Greek Shipping Clerk*
DAWN RAID	*Trust Beneficiary*
ZORBA PINT	*Greek Barman*
EURIPEDES JENES	*Minister of Consumer Affairs*
APHRAIM WINDOWS	*Glazier*
FAWCET BLOCK	*Apprentice Plumber*
LOU PLUNGER	*Plumber*
ALFRED D. NEEDLE	*Jamaican Tailor*
JESS LAPSED	*Sales Director – Golden Life Assurance*
SHEPERD SPY	*Chairman – Golden Life Assurance*
NORMA SNOCKERS	*Research Assistant*

"Always be proud of being English," muttered Percy Vere's friend, Hardy Breed, a trainee in the Bank of England's currency exchange operation.

They were walking out of San Lorenzo's restaurant and up Beauchamp Place on Saturday afternoon.

"I agree their food is awful, and who knows what kind of cock is in the chicken béarnaise," Percy murmured.

"You really should work in the City," Hardy suggested. "You need the learning curve, and it's vital to have some decent names at the start of your résumé. You'll make contacts easily and move from firm to firm as you learn the ropes. Forget what you do - just get the names of sensible firms at the beginning – they'll stand you in good stead for all time."

Hardy offered Percy a lift, and someone had left a calling card under the windscreen wiper of his nearly new green Triumph Stag. Percy plucked up the card and handed it over.

"This is for you!" he said wryly.

Hardy wasn't interested so Percy read it out anyway:

**IF YOU WANT TO BE RICH AND FAMOUS,
RING SEYMOUR CLEARLY ON: 888 1244**

"It's a scam!" Hardy said immediately. "Ring it and find out for yourself!"

That evening, Percy dialled the number.

"Seymour, clearly speaking," came the abrupt answer in a heavy Australian drawl.

"I've got one of your cards in front of me."

"Okay, mate!" said the drawl. "I represent an international company in twenty countries with everyday consumer products. We start people like you in business. If you want to know more, you'd better get yourself to the Diamond Suite at the London Hilton at 7:00 p.m. on Monday night - and don't forget your chequebook, mate."

The phone went dead, leaving Percy excited somehow that this was an opportunity, even with an Australian accent. He didn't stop to think that he was one of a hundred calls Seymour had received that day.

On Monday evening, all the available parking spaces around the front of the Hilton were jammed with Maseratis, Ferraris, and Porsches. Some were parked in the taxi rank, causing terrible congestion. There was similar congestion outside the Diamond Suite alongside a large sign announcing 'Golden Products' - with an arrow pointing through the double doors. Inside, there was another hubbub of activity, with probably a hundred people milling around in front of a packed stage. The hosts were presumably those with the fixed smiles and immaculate suits dotted amongst the gaggle of visitors.

Percy noticed that the suits of the people who looked like hosts each had a lapel pin studded with one or more tiny rubies or diamonds. Seymour Clearly introduced himself. He had four diamonds in his pin.

At exactly 7:15 p.m., Seymour commanded his group of invitees to sit down around him, and suddenly there was silence as a speaker appeared on centre stage.

Percy peered at the commanding figure with a microphone. He was in his mid-forties, tall and sturdy but not overweight. He looked silently over his audience.

"That's Daly Grind, the architect of pyramid selling and president of Golden Products," whispered Seymour. "Pyramid selling provides anyone with the tools to start their own business!"

"Who wants to be successful?" Daly suddenly screamed over speakers round the hall.

"Me, me!" the company representatives shouted back.

"I didn't hear you!" Daly screamed again, like an American cattle auctioneer.

"Success does not fall into your lap," he beamed more quietly, slicking back a stray hair. "It only comes as a result of planning, setting goals, and hard work. Golden Products is an opportunity for anyone who is serious-minded to start a business of their own and be on track to respectability and a fortune. All that's required is an unshakeable belief in yourself and absolute commitment to hard work!"

Daly Grind spoke for half an hour, explaining the benefits of joining a 'multi-level marketing' structure. This was a phenomenon of ordinary people in a pyramid of recruitment and sales, so each individual becomes the top dog, earning commission from those below.

Seymour explained in his own way.

"Each of you recruits two agents, and each of them recruits two more. Imagine if you recruit fifty salesmen in a year and they recruit, say, ten each, and they, in turn, recruit ten more. You are going to end up with a sales organisation as big as ICI!"

"Look at Amway as an example," he recited. "Amway sells cosmetics you ladies use every day! Amway is based in Michigan, America, and it's here in the UK with their agents earning thousands every month. Look at Herbal Life selling nutrition; everyone needs to drink healthy instead of these fizzy drinks that rot your guts. Here is Golden Products with cleaning products, soap, shampoo, dishwasher liquid, oven cleaner, window cleaner, and car wash – everyone's a buyer. You choose your own community as your buyers – how simple is that?"

Then came the punch line.

"The products sell themselves because they're biodegradable," he beamed. "They don't pollute the environment. That puts us at the lead in protecting the future of our planet!"

* * * * *

Daly Grind's voice was tempered and skilled with practice. The content was almost unimportant, such was his confidence. His audience had been reduced to a sea of sponges, even though not one person there would have admitted it.

"Before I hand you over to your individual distributors," Daly summarised as if it were the law, "I would like to identify our achievers for last month."

"**FIRST, SEYMOUR CLEARLY**!" he screamed.

"**WITH EARNINGS OF**," he screamed.

"£10,300!" he screamed.

"**AND THE FIFTH DIAMOND FOR HIS PIN**!"

The Diamond Suite erupted in a frenzy of applause. There were gasps from some of the invitees. Percy was riveted as he watched the permanently grinning Seymour return from the stage with his cheque and a tiny diamond to stick in the remaining hole in his pin. Ten others received amounts over £7,000 for a month's work.

Then it was the turn of the recruiters.

"Right!" Seymour announced to his new flock. "All you have to do is bring people to meetings like this, and you get paid £500 for every one that signs up. Do you all know two people who want to make money?"

Seymour stared straight at Hal Etosis, a teenage Greek shipping clerk.

"Everyone I know wants to make money," Hal admitted, as his right hand grabbed his left hand, which had started to vibrate.

"In that case, all you have to do is become a distributor working in my team and bring two people to the next meeting," Seymour demanded. "I'll do the selling until you get the hang of it. You'll earn £500 for each of them, so you've got your £1,000 back. Before you know it, you'll be earning £10,000 a month. It's like clockwork. Did you all remember your chequebooks?"

"Yes!" some answered, albeit hesitantly.

"Well, let's get them out and write a cheque for £1,000," ordered Seymour.

"I haven't got £1,000 in my account," confessed a now frightened Hal.

One of Seymour's colleagues pushed Hal back into his seat, and Seymour put his hand on Hal's shoulder.

"Then I suggest you write out a cheque, mate, post-date it for four days, and you borrow the money because this is an opportunity which will never come again."

Seymour's colleague joined in.

"You can start tonight as soon as we're finished here," he added. "You've got at least four days before your cheque's presented. Then you're in business!"

"It's a marvellous way to start being your own boss!" Seymour grinned.

Percy fearfully wrote out his cheque for £1,000. It was as if he had been hypnotised.

"Are you stupid, or are you stupid?" he heard himself repeating as he went down the back stairs of the Hilton in embarrassment.

"This requires a good drowning in alcohol," he muttered, turning down into Curzon Street.

* * * * *

Half an hour after the meeting, Percy was on his third vodka and grapefruit and trying to win over a young secretary at the bar in Mortons, the in-place run by the ebullient Simon Drummond Brady, or 'DB' as he was known. Percy realised straight away that this was no place to speak about going door to door and selling soap - the money was all about recruiting.

Notwithstanding his fury at his own misjudgement, Percy would not bring himself to cancel his cheque. He owned £1,000 of soap and not much else to do, so he visited the cobbler he had known as a child. The original sign offering a myriad of odds and sods at a few pennies was still in the window. Nothing had changed after all those years.

"Please put some of these household products in your window," Percy asked as a ridiculous greeting, "and everyone who comes in will buy something!"

Percy brought in his boxes of product, a stack of brochures, and the price list. The cobbler was standing quietly as he stacked the boxes in front of his counter.

"Thank you so much!" he said sheepishly as he walked backwards out of the door, thinking he would never see the soap again or any money.

Weeks later, Percy happened to be passing his boyhood village, so he decided to pop in to his cobbler. He looked in the window and saw no sign of any of his product, so he went in dismayed.

"Have you thrown it all away?" he asked, slightly annoyed.

"It's all sold," the cobbler laughed. "Can I get any more?"

Percy took a step back before he grasped the chance.

"Expect a call!" he smiled in apology. "This is a continuing business!"

Percy was emboldened with a new intent on finding just one recruit. Battersea seemed a sensible place to start because he knew no one there would recognise him. As luck would have it, the second girl he approached at the bus stop agreed to join him for a drink in the café in Battersea Park.

"I can only stay for a few minutes!" she warned him.

"That will be enough," Percy nodded.

Jan Boree was a down-to-earth receptionist in the garage in one of the railway arches next to the RSPCA pound. She was willing to know about this opportunity after Percy explained the product wouldn't harm the environment. She agreed to attend the Diamond Suite on the following Monday as long as she could bring her friend, Dawn Raid.

That following Monday, Jan signed up and went home, and Dawn, looking every bit composed and sensible, went with Percy for a drink at Mortons.

"Jan will do well for you," she surmised. "The garage is always busy, and it's right next to a flower shop with a constant stream of customers."

Dawn was friendly and attractive, already running her own business as a designer of blinds for every kind of window imaginable. Percy enjoyed being with her, and an hour slipped by.

"I need to be in Upper Grosvenor Street," she told him, glancing at her watch.

"I'll take a taxi and drop you off," Percy agreed straight away.

By the first set of lights, Dawn was explaining how her father had stolen her trust fund and taken to the bottle. He apparently lived in the apartment directly above her and often popped in during the early hours to beat up her boyfriends and, as often as not, smash up her flat in the process.

"I live four houses down on the left!" she announced to the cabbie.

"You mean where that man with the beard is waving a fire axe out of the second-floor window?" the driver asked.

Percy looked up from her legs and then further up at the lunatic leaning out of the window.

"Come in for a cup of tea?" she asked.

"I'll come in for a few minutes just to make sure you're safe," Percy agreed.

"Shut up, daddy!" Dawn shouted without even looking up at the snarling figure above.

Dawn ransacked her bag for her door key while the screaming continued from above.

"Are you sure he's your father?" Percy grimaced.

"He'll be down here in a jiffy," she replied, opening her door on the first floor. "So we'll make this quick!"

As he closed the door behind them, Percy couldn't help noticing unmistakable axe marks in the door and frame, but Dawn acted as if this was part of her normal life, just like she was putting on the kettle. Percy looked around to see where there was a quick exit.

"The only way out is through the back window and down the fire ladder!" Dawn confirmed casually as Percy decided to drink his boiling tea as quickly as possible.

That evening was the beginning of a wonderful, if spasmodic, relationship whenever Percy visited - or even dropped Dawn off. He always had one ear open for the raving maniac above.

Three weeks later, there came the inevitable screaming that Dawn had anticipated, followed by the sound of the front door splintering.

"It's you he's after!" Dawn clarified. "I'll be fine!"

Percy wasted no time in opening the rear window and jumping out onto the balcony and down the fire escape. He went straight round to Mortons. DB commented that he looked pale.

"You're quivering, Percy," he noticed.

"Nothing that a triple vodka won't cure," Percy replied.

* * * * *

Jan Boree made an astonishing start to her business with Golden Products. Within a month, she invited Percy to join her again in the Diamond Suite, so with nothing else to do, Percy showed up.

Percy was astonished when he heard that Dawn had signed over fifty ladies in Battersea. He was even more astonished that he was credited with an override of £1,780.

"How did you manage that?" he asked.

"I had a leaflet printed and gave them out to all the customers at the garage and the flower shop!" she admitted. "There's been a steady stream of ladies signing up, and customers at the garage and the flower shop are all buying one or two bottles of something. In Jan's third month, she received a cheque for £7,000."

Percy saw Hal Etosis at the meeting and waved to him. Hal thought Percy was right on the ball as he introduced his Greek friend, Zorba Pint, a barman who had been the first of his own distributors.

"It's bio-degradable," Zorba was telling his own guests before he told Percy he had dumped his entire load of product over his fence for his neighbour to do whatever he wanted with it.

"What's the point?" he confirmed. "I've signed up seventy-four Greek nationals, and I'm lining up the Albanians and Czechs next. They're great buyers because cleaning is a new way of life for them."

It was on a Tuesday evening, whilst Percy was visiting Seymour in his suite at the Grosvenor House Hotel, that there was a polite knock on the door. It was the first real sign of trouble.

"Mr Clearly, we would like to speak to you about pyramid selling," a voice requested.

"I'm not in, mate," Seymour replied through the closed door.

"Mr Clearly, we insist on speaking to you," the voice demanded. "We've had many complaints that you have taken money under false pretences."

Seymour jammed a heavy dining chair under the door handle.

"Look, mate, bugger off!" he shouted at the inside of the door. "I've got nothing to say to you!"

Seymour lifted the phone for hotel security.

Twenty minutes later, Percy opened the door and stuck his head around the corner. The coast was clear, and it was definitely time to go.

That same week, the investigative team at the TV programme *Despatches* confirmed that thousands of people had borrowed £1,000 against their homes, from their families, and from friends. Seven out of ten had given up and complained to various authorities that they'd been robbed in an effort to recover their money.

'They could always sell the product,' thought Percy as he poured himself a vodka and grapefruit in his kitchen.

Curiously, it was the authorities who didn't want to give multi-level marketing a chance. They were intent only on protecting household brands and the High Street. They called it 'pyramid selling' and a dishonest way to do business.

Percy was getting over-ride commission, and he read that the American authorities had just embraced Amway and proved a point when the value of the company soared to $3 billion – on their UK side, 70 recruits had become millionaires. Herbal life had also proved the same point, as girls who started with nothing had thousands in their sales pyramid, and Percy met several who were earning thousands a week. These were the entrepreneurs grasping the nettle, and unfortunately, there was no creative mind in the UK Government to create an acceptable regulatory framework to support that initiative.

* * * * *

Jan Boree went on to earn an average of £13,000 a month and became a member of Mortons and DB's lover.

They watched *Despatches* together in the lower-ground-floor screening room at Mortons.

"The shampoo's not bad!" DB admitted. "I've been washing the car with it!"

Percy caught only the end of the programme:

'The Secretary of State for Trade and Industry, Euripides Jeynes, speaking in the House of Commons today about multi-level marketing, has promised a Parliamentary enquiry to set the stage for prosecutions.'

As the credits rolled, with a background of a huge pile of boxes of Golden product at the Hammersmith refuse tip, Percy's phone rang.

"No worries, mate!" Seymour burbled with excitement. "The Establishment's after us, so I'm already looking at 'timeshare'. They're cutting up industrial buildings in Spain into flats and selling a week a year to retired people in the UK. It's 50% commission, and you own an apartment on the Costa del Crime after ten sales, mate!"

Seymour had booked that same Diamond Suite at the Hilton for 'Time Abroad,' and it took only three weeks for *Despatches* to be on the case.

"They must be following Seymour around," Percy said to Penny Sworth, a girl with long legs and a short skirt he had met in Waitrose.

Percy turned up the volume:

'Following our exposé of pyramid-selling, we continue tonight to report on the hard-selling techniques of the same salesmen in Spanish 'time-share'.

The program then started to film Mr Ephraim Windows.

'Ephraim was on a glazing job when he was approached by someone at the bottom of his ladder. He was given a card saying he had won a boat in a competition, and all he had to do was collect it from the Hilton Hotel in London. Even though he hadn't entered any competition, Mr Windows rented a trailer and drove with his wife and five children from Birmingham. On arrival at the meeting in London, he found he had in fact won a blow-up children's toy in a cardboard box and an opportunity to buy a week each year in a one-bedroomed apartment in Spain. Mr Windows claimed he was locked in a hotel room with his wife and family until he signed the application for finance, and by the time he got out, his car and trailer had been clamped.'

Percy dialled Seymour's number.

"Turn on the TV. They're after you big time!" he said as the programme continued:

'And here is Mr Clay Potts, a hardware shopkeeper from Sheffield. Mr Potts was one of 400 happy recipients of a card inviting him to pick up a new Volkswagen he had won in a timeshare lottery. Mr and Mrs Potts were delighted. They arranged insurance cover and, just in case no one had thought of it, they took along a gallon can of petrol.'

Percy could hardly stand the strain of what was to come:

'When Mr Potts was presented with a Volkswagen Dinky Toy, he lost his temper and demanded the real thing. The salesman from Spain, Costa Lott, started to laugh at him, so Mr Potts unscrewed the cap of his petrol can, splashed Mr Lott with petrol, and flicked open his Zippo lighter. The police were called, and Mr Potts is now in custody, charged with attempted murder.'

Percy's phone rang.

"Hey, mate," said the exuberant Seymour. "These Dinky Toys are a ripper of a draw to the meetings. We're getting free publicity, mate!"

"It's time for a few days' holiday to think," said Percy.

* * * * *

Four days later, Percy was lying on a beach in Montego Bay, about a mile from his own hotel, when a sudden, tearing pain gripped his side. He doubled over on the sand, unable to move. Late afternoon light stretched long shadows across the beach, and only a few people were in the distance.

Suddenly, something large and dark swung a baseball bat, blocking out the last of the day's sun. Percy squinted upward to see a mess of plaited hair spilling from a multi-coloured woollen hat.

"You need help, man," said a deep, smooth local voice.

Before Percy could respond, the figure leaned down and then casually walked away, flipping what looked like a wallet onto the sand. Percy scrambled to check under his towel - and sure enough, his lizard-skin wallet was gone.

"Hey! That's mine!" he shouted, the pain tearing through him.

"Bastard!" he muttered as the stranger casually gave him what Percy understood as 'the finger.'

Barely able to move, Percy gathered his things and crawled up the beach. Twenty minutes later, a tourist jogging along the water's edge spotted him.

"You alright, buddy?" gasped Jim Shoes from Texas.

"I think I'm sick," Percy groaned, trying to stand.

"You come up to the house," said Jim kindly. "You can't stay here."

"Thanks," gasped Percy.

Jim Shoes was athletic and helped Percy up the long flight of steps to his holiday house overlooking the bay.

"I'm going to get a doctor," he insisted as he led Percy to his bedroom and laid him down.

Two hours later, the doctor arrived. After some painful prodding, he wrote a prescription and handed it to Jim.

"I'm staying at the Riu Ocho Rios Motel," Percy said weakly. "If I could get back there, I'd be okay."

An hour later, Jim returned with Percy's suitcase and a bag of medicine from the motel.

"I've paid your bill at the hotel," he smiled.

"You've what?" Percy exclaimed, horrified.

Percy swallowed a double dose of medicine, but an hour later, the pain hadn't eased. Panic set in at being in a strange place, completely reliant on strangers.

Dragging himself off the bed using a chair, he walked unsteadily toward the living room, suitcase in tow.

"Forget it, man, the guy's really sick," Serge, Jim's companion, said from the veranda.

Percy flinched as he saw Jim lean over and kiss Serge full on the mouth.

"I have to go," Percy announced through the door. "You've been wonderful, but please tell me how much money you've spent—I need to pay you back."

"That's pretty insulting," Serge frowned.

"I didn't mean it like that," Percy countered. "You've been generous, but I want to pay my own way. I hope one day someone helps me out, as you did."

Jim got up and put his arms around Percy, who recoiled instantly. It was a terrible moment.

That night, back at the hotel, as Percy retrieved his surviving American Express card from his sponge bag, the pain intensified. Collapsing onto the bathroom floor, he passed a kidney stone onto the red-and-green striped tiles.

Sometime in the night, Percy regained consciousness and dialled reception.

"Please get me a doctor," he croaked.

No doctor came. A maid arrived as the sun rose to check the mini-bar. Percy decided he had to get home, irrespective of the pain.

"I lost my money, and I can't tip you!" he said, embarrassed.

"What's new?" she replied automatically. "When I got married, money ceased to exist."

"Very droll," Percy muttered, deciding he would rest two days by the pool and fake good health through the airport.

On the second day, lying by the pool, Jim and Serge reappeared on either side of him.

"Feeling better?" asked Serge.

"Come up to the house this evening," invited Jim.

"I really don't want to impose," Percy replied, squinting into the sun.

"Maybe we'll stay here for dinner," mused Serge as Jim ordered three rum cocktails, then spent fifteen minutes staring at Percy's crotch.

"What are three two-letter words to describe the groom's shock on honeymoon?" Serge asked into the air.

"I've no idea," Percy answered.

"IS IT IN!" screamed Jim in a well-practised joke.

"I'm going to have a quiet evening," Percy announced.

"Then we'll see you at 8:00 p.m. for a quiet one," Serge confirmed, placing a hand on Percy's thigh to stop him from getting up.

Percy went across to reception, ignoring the pain.

"When is the first plane out of here?" he asked.

"Mexico City at 6:00 p.m.," the receptionist replied without checking.

"Perfect," Percy said. "Can I put a taxi to the airport on my card?"

* * * * *

There were only a handful of passengers on the flight, and Percy felt a sense of normality returning - not just because the stewardess seemed to be flirting with him, though that helped. She had the legs of a dancer, although the top half would have been a problem in a ballet technique. Percy couldn't get his eyes to look at anything else.

"We have a layover at the President Hotel in Mexico City tonight, then I go on to Acapulco tomorrow," she eventually volunteered.

"I could stay at the President," Percy decided on the spot. "It'll be late when we arrive, so maybe we can go to a club for a drink?"

Percy checked his luggage with the concierge without booking a room, and they met an hour later in the lobby to go across the square to the Cha Cha.

"You never asked my name?" she frowned. "It's Wanda Lust!"

"Wanda, I'm Percy," he replied. "What can I get you to drink?"

"The English are so polite," she commented. "I'll have a Paloma, gracias."

Percy looked bewildered.

"It's tequila with grapefruit soda and lime juice," she explained.

"Dos, gracias," Percy ordered in his best Spanish.

After three of those each and two half-hearted samba dances when Percy was forced to reckon with her leaning forward and swinging round, Wanda said she needed to sleep. Percy took a last glance at her silkiness as they walked back to the hotel.

"My room is 310," she said casually, as if commenting on the colour of the carpet.

Percy calculated the timing: twenty minutes for Wanda to get ready, half an hour to fall asleep. Twenty-one minutes later, he knocked gently on her door.

No reply. He used his shoe to knock again.

"Madonna! Not so loud," she whispered as the door clicked open against the chain.

There she was in a man's shirt, most of her legs visible, longer than he remembered.

"I expect you wonder why I'm here," he asked.

"It won't be a mystery for long," she laughed.

* * * * *

At 7:00 a.m., Percy woke with a start. There was no sign of Wanda, but she had left behind an image of tousled hair and a mischievous sparkle in her eyes.

Percy had woken from a dream of the owner of Bootlegger's nightclub in London, driving his Rolls-Royce on the M4, when a scaffold pole fell from a bridge. The twelve-foot-long pole turned slowly in the air and pierced the roof of his car like a spear. Involuntarily, Percy sat bolt upright as if the spear had struck him instead.

"Call it divine intervention," he muttered, reaching for the phone to order coffee and toast, assuming the airline would cover it.

His eyes fell on a book on the side table by the phone - *Don't Cry for Me* – clearly about Eva Peron, the adored first lady of Argentina.

With the window open, Percy could hear Mexico City coming alive. He flicked through the pages and read how Eva Peron's husband became President in May 1946. From that day, Eva allegedly welcomed prominent Nazis to Argentina, facilitating their travel by sending blank passports to the Vatican to help leading Nazis escape Nuremberg. By 1947, the worst murderers of the medical experimentation in the Holocaust had fled the sanctuary of Catholic abbeys and seminaries and set sail via the so-called 'rat line'.

Eva had also provided Swiss bank accounts in Geneva, Berne, Neuchâtel, and Lucerne to hide hundreds of millions of dollars, along with cash, jewellery, and art, for safekeeping.

Percy was no longer surprised that history portrayed Eva as a traitor and criminal rather than a hero of the poor and oppressed in her own country.

He paused at one passage that struck him into full consciousness:

"To see poverty and misery, it is not sufficient to draw near and gaze on it. Poverty and misery do not let themselves be seen in all the magnitude of their suffering because, even in his saddest need, man has the courage to mask his condition, at least a little. The rich are wont to say, 'the destitute do not cry when their children die,' but they do not realise that they, the rich who have everything, have taken away from the poor even the right to cry, except that it is out of gratefulness."

* * * * *

Percy cringed, unable to think of any selfless act he had ever performed.

His thoughts wandered to a time long before, when he had been riding through the woods with his school friend, the recently ennobled Duke of Rutland. They came across a farm worker painting a gate.

"What on earth are you doing?" Rutland enquired from on high.

"I'm painting this gate, m'lud," the man stammered politely, grabbing his cap. "This is a pot of paint, and this is a brush."

"How many hands have you got?" asked Rutland.

"Just the two, m'lud," the man answered, somewhat confused.

"Well, get another brush!" Rutland instructed before riding off.

It was a moment when Percy had been prodded to contemplate how the simple, pragmatic approach to life could be so corrupted by complexities, and here he was in another of those moments.

Percy let his ears wake him up as he stretched and glanced out over the sprawling city below. Mexico City hummed with life, its streets pulsing with early morning energy. He had mixed feelings of awe, guilt, and an odd relief at being far from the chaos he had left behind in London with Amway and the nightmare in Montego Bay.

A faint knock on the door announced the arrival of his coffee. He drank it on the balcony, feeling something approaching excitement - little did he know that was temporary.

* * * * *

Percy needed to leave Wanda's room before the 12:00 check-out time, so, as he felt the heat of the sun permeating the haze, he showered, collected his thoughts, and went down to the concierge to pick up his knapsack.

Free of any plan, Percy wandered across the square through the traffic to see great architecture as a façade to a compromise with urban poverty. The numbers in the streets were unsustainable, and only yards from the main shopping centre was a crisis of filth, open drainage, hunger, and crime.

Destitute children huddled in the doorways, women in rags stared into empty space, and a sense of abandonment suffocated any other expression.

The horror opened eventually into a market where hundreds jostled between stalls of brightly coloured vegetables and fruit. There were also cheap clothes and shoes amid pots and pans and kitchen utensils next to sacks of grain and rice. In the confusion, dirty banknotes and carefully counted coins made their way into grasping hands from every side. This was a hell of hardship and misery.

* * * * *

If Percy was confused about the state of his life and what he was going to do, this trip clarified nothing. He was looking at the world unfolding and people with no chance of seeing their children grow up with any dignity. That didn't seem to stop any breeding. Creating children gave an immediate relief with a bonus that maybe some of their seed would survive to look after their parents when they had nothing left.

Percy took a bus to the airport, ignoring the obvious question. He said out loud, "Why the rush?"

Then the Qantas sales desk advised him that his ticket to London had expired.

'It is better to be lucky than skilful!' his grandfather had told him, and it was suddenly true as he spotted Wanda Lust across the hall. It looked as if her crew was checking in to her flight to Acapulco. Percy thought it better to hold off approaching her, as it would look too deliberate, so he went instead to the sales desk, wondering why she got up so early.

The flight to Acapulco had one seat left. Percy thought that was also lucky, until he was jammed in between a large Mexican lady and an even larger man, pressing him into a sandwich.

"These seats are a little small," he observed loudly as the man wiped beads of sweat from his forehead and both his cheeks with his shirt sleeve.

"You've clearly not visited before!" he muttered in broken English. "You'll like Acapulco. Very friendly!"

Percy ignored what he thought was something between sarcasm and a forecast of doom as the coffee trolley arrived, and he had to smile broadly at his recent conquest.

"You are lovely," he whispered.

"Si?"

She moved on, and the man clearly wanted to talk. His English wasn't perfect, but Percy understood he was asking if Percy was familiar with the culture of Mexico.

"Not at all," Percy replied politely.

"Did you hear the one about the three businessmen at a reception given by the mayor of Acapulco, where you are going?" he seemed to be asking.

"I guess I'm going to hear it now," Percy sighed.

* * * * *

"Three guys in a beach bar are talking about their children," he started. "They each have a son, and the first man says, 'I was worried that my son was a loser because he started out washing cars. Then he became a car salesman, and he sold so many cars that he bought the dealership. In fact, he's so successful now that he gave his best friend a new Mercedes for his birthday.'

The second man then says, 'I was worried about my son too because he started out raking leaves. Then he also became a commission salesman and sold so many houses that he bought the real estate firm. In fact, he's so successful that he just gave his best friend a new house for his birthday.'

The third guy says, 'My son started out sweeping floors in a brokerage firm. Now he's a broker, and he's so rich that he just gave his best friend $1 million in stock for his birthday.'

At that point, the mayor joins them, and they tell him how successful all their sons are. He replies, 'Well, I have to admit that my son is a major disappointment because he started out as a hairdresser in Acapulco. He's still a hairdresser after 15 years. Now I've found out he's gay, and he must be doing something right because he just had a birthday, and he got a new Mercedes, a house, and $1 million in stock.'"

"So, you like boys?" asked Percy.

"Let me put it like this," he replied. "The last time I was inside a woman was when I visited the Statue of Liberty."

"Don't you feel you're missing something?"

"Hell no," he replied immediately. "Women pay no attention to you until it's time to read the will!"

Percy looked around desperately to see whether he could catch Wanda's attention, but she was up the aisle.

Percy was only able to speak to Wanda when they disembarked. Then she pressed a scrap of paper into his hand. He opened it as he walked across the tarmac:

'Villa Vera Racquet Club.'

Young boys lined the central reservation of the highway from the airport into Acapulco, with American tourists in taxis jockeying for position at the kerbside to pick up their choices.

"This is the playground of California," the slimy-looking taxi driver confirmed.

"Are you speaking to me?" asked Percy.

* * * * *

Without knowing that the Villa Vera Racquet Club was the hotel of choice for the wealthy, Percy had asked the driver to take him there.

"You've lost my reservation?" he exclaimed to the beleaguered lady receptionist with long stick-on fingernails. "Do you seriously think I have flown halfway across the world without reserving a suitable room?"

Percy ended up with a 'superior' room for the same price as a 'standard.'

Half an hour later, he came back to the reception desk.

"Wanda Lust?" he enquired. "Is my friend Wanda Lust registered?"

Wanda insisted on taking Percy to the obligatory tourist dinner with cliff-divers dropping past the window, waving on their way down.

"I can't imagine what they would look like if they misjudge the incoming wave!" he muttered.

After dinner, Percy was keen to show off his superior room, as it had a private plunge pool and a bar full of miniatures.

They drank and splashed about and joked under a twinkling sky, and even one or two shooting stars made their way across the firmament. Then they collapsed together as if there were no care in the world.

Sometime in the stillness, Wanda Lust wandered off on her merry way without a word and probably without any recollection of who he was.

'That girl does like to get up early!' Percy reminded himself.

* * * * *

Percy spent the day sleeping by the pool, anticipating venturing into anything other than young boys in the evening hustle that was Acapulco. He asked the same receptionist to recommend a lively bar, and she immediately replied, *Amando's*.

The space was full of jostling Americans slugging back beers and talking football, so he moved a short distance to the *Dome*, which had an entrance down steps into a dark space. The club was not yet full, but the first guests blocked the way to the bar. Percy should have noticed that he was the only white person there. He got a large vodka and grapefruit whilst squashed by some wrestlers, and was trying to make his way back to the seating area, when he was being pushed by Sonny Liston look-alikes. Percy felt critically out of place and turned to leave, but unintentionally bumped into a black girl passing in front of him.

"You clumsy motherfucker!" she screamed.

"Smile so I can see you," replied Percy as he tried to make room.

Before he reached the exit, Percy was flanked by two large men who accused him of messing with their 'sister.'

"She's really lucky to have such a big family," Percy started to say as he tried to move out of their way.

Then he was lifted off the ground like a toothpick.

"See you for a dance later," Percy smiled at the girl.

"In your dreams, arsehole," she answered ominously.

Percy was totally unprepared for what happened next. His new friends opened the double front doors, and he was thrown up the steps onto the pavement. Then he was kicked in the balls and punched in the stomach, followed by a crashing blow to the face from a practised knee. Percy felt his nose shatter, and his head hit the pavement. The kicking all over that followed didn't really hurt, but he knew he was in serious trouble.

It ended with a cursory kick to the back of the head and a heel stamped on his left wrist and his back. Percy could hear the gathering crowd of tourists through the explosions of blows.

"Look, Mabel, they're going to kill the guy!"

"Stand back, Ethel, you'll get blood on you!"

The two men strolled back down the steps into the club as casually as lions after a meal.

Percy was not unconscious, and he tried to take stock, only to realise he couldn't move. His own blood had splattered three feet across the pavement, coming, he thought, from his head. The doorman threw a bucket of water over him and the pavement.

* * * * *

Percy woke to the sound of birds twittering outside a white-painted room. He checked each limb tentatively to check which bits hurt, but they all hurt. He felt bandages on his chest and head, his left arm in plaster, and his genital area as if in a vice.

Tentatively, and with excruciating pain, he tried to move his legs over the side of the bed, but his ribs screamed back. He held on with his good hand and moved slowly so he could see himself in the mirror above a basin. Every movement sent razor blades of pain through his limbs and organs.

"Gordon Bennett!" he spluttered, seeing his left eye purple and the area around it swollen like a bloody tennis ball. Splints were sticking out of his nostrils, his lips were split and swollen like inner-tube tyres. He could feel with his tongue that he had no front teeth, and blood was seeping through over his left ear out of the bandage around his head.

Percy inched over to the window and, out of his right eye, he saw a serene garden and the bright blue bay beyond, dotted with yachts.

The door opened without a knock, and a white-coated brown girl entered.

"Get back into bed," she ordered.

"Where am I?" hissed Percy.

"You're at Gil Turner's villa," she replied.

"Who's Gil Turner?" Percy whispered as she helped him back onto the bed and lifted his legs onto the covers.

"He's the man," she confirmed. "Now, be quiet and get some rest."

Two days later, Gil Turner appeared while Percy sipped clear soup through a straw.

"My car was pulled up in the traffic outside the Dome," he said with a grimace. "It sure looked like you needed some help, bud."

"Where am I?" asked Percy.

"The hospital wouldn't take you," Gil replied.

"I mean, why are you doing this for me?" Percy croaked.

"I'm the good guy," he answered. "Anyway, what's done is done, and I've got a weak stomach, so it's best I don't look at you."

* * * * *

Gil Turner was a renowned wine merchant with a chain of liquor stores along Sunset Boulevard in LA. He was staying alone as usual for a holiday in his rented Acapulco villa. The sounds from his next-door bedroom attested to why he chose Acapulco.

Three days later, after the doctor pronounced Percy would need months in recovery, Gil burst into his room.

"There's a bunch of guys with flame torches coming down from the hills," he shouted. "Get up!"

"What do you mean, get up?" Percy gasped slowly through his split lips. "And do what precisely?"

Percy staggered behind Gil through the living room and onto the sun-deck. Sure enough, men wearing red bandannas and carrying flame torches moved through the trees. Gil pulled Percy back inside, locking the French windows. The telephone rang; it was Gil's brother, screaming that he had been attacked in Gil's house in Los Angeles. Gil slammed down the receiver.

"Don't you think we should ring the police?" Percy hissed.

The brown nurse shouted that the police were coming as two gunshots rang out. Percy saw a black boy out of the corner of his right eye, leaving Gil's bedroom and heading to the back door. Then the blue flashing lights of the police arrived. Three officers knocked on the sliding glass window and came into the villa with their weapons drawn.'

"Bandits come out of the hills, Senor", the officer reported, touching his cap and obviously bemused at the wreck of Percy. "They rob the tourists, it's normal!"

"This is a very bad here, senor" one of the other officers confirmed.

"They never put that in the brochure?" Gil stammered. "We need to get back into town."

"As you wish, Senor," replied the officer as Gil reached into his pocket and pushed a wad of dollars into his waiting hand.

They were driven straight to the Villa Vera Racquet Club and, after some more cash, they were allocated the three-bedroom chalet vacated the night before by the Mayor of Los Angeles, Dustin Pann.

"He's my friend!" Gil added to the reception manager as he was slipping him some cash. "I want armed guards and dogs twenty-four hours a day, you understand me!"

Gil looked at Percy.

"And a wheelchair!" he added.

* * * * *

"Are you staying with me?" Percy asked the nurse.

"He's paying!" she replied as Gil took hold of Percy's plastered arm and told the receptionist to get someone to push Percy.

The nurse helped Percy into bed and collected some water from the fridge. She checked his bandages, drew the curtains over the window, and muttered, 'Sleep!'

Percy stayed in bed for three days with her continuing visits. Gil was nowhere to be seen. He apparently refused to leave his bedroom. There were, however, noises evidencing visitations in the night.

On the fifth day, a doctor arrived and took the splints out of his nose. Percy asked if there were X-rays.

"Si."

"I'm having terrible headaches."

"Si."

"Should I be in a hospital?"

"Si."

"What should I do?"

"Si."

The nurse came in, and Percy asked her what was happening. She said there were no medical facilities for foreigners in Acapulco hospitals.

"Are there any X-rays?"

"There are no X-rays," she answered.

"You mean my arm was broken, and my ribs cracked, and they patched me up without any X-ray?" Percy asked.

"Si," answered the doctor, snapping shut his bag and leaving with an envelope.

That evening, Gil appeared looking like there was nothing wrong.

"It's time to go," he announced.

"You're not leaving me here?" Percy panicked as the consequences of his benefactor disappearing bit him like a rabid dog.

In this intolerable situation, Gil had already been advised that Percy had lost too much blood to fly, so he had arranged a private medical evacuation to Cedars Sinai in Los Angeles.

Two hours later, with a police escort to the airport, and another fistful of money changing hands to the police and the duty manager in the private jet park at Aeropuerto de Acapulco, they were in a medical jet with a proper doctor on the way to the world-famous Cedars Sinai Neuro Unit in Los Angeles.

In the pressurised cabin, Percy's headache became unbearable, and he started retching with a stomach cramp. A dysenteric explosion to end all dysenteric explosions followed and flushed him through in one movement.

On arrival and after scans, the team at Cedars Sinai confirmed seven skull fractures amongst Percy's other injuries.

* * * * *

Two months later, Gil arranged and paid for Percy's transfer in a Dutch air ambulance to London.

"Please don't be offended when I say I'd like to pay you back when I can," Percy sobbed as the tears rolled freely down his cheeks. "Just don't die on me before I'm back in the money!"

"I'll hang on, bud!" Gil retorted.

"And if you can think of anything I can ever do for you," asked Percy. "Please just call!"

"It so happens there is one little thing," Gil replied quietly. "I would like some French wine bottles, the empty throw-aways from the great restaurants and nightclubs in London!"

"I don't understand?" Percy asked, perplexed.

"I need the labels, not the bottles or the wine," he explained. "I supply the stars here in Los Angeles, so soak off the labels, iron them flat when they're still wet, and bundle them up fifty at a time and send me a parcel once a month. No one here knows the difference!"

"Consider it done," confirmed Percy as he took hold of Gil's hand. "You know you saved my life!"

"Well," Gil smiled. "It's not every day that I have that privilege."

* * * * *

On his arrival in London, Percy was admitted to the Chelsea and Westminster Hospital courtesy of the system of free care in England. They started procedures to check the Cedars Sinai repairs to his smashed nose, the temporary teeth, and the MRI scans in the neuro unit as his skull continued to heal. His arm had already been rebroken and set.

It was impossible for Percy to forget Gil Turner, and at the first opportunity, he called Thelma House, the estate agent in Virginia Water. He remembered she was the girlfriend of his mate Aard Dijk, who would do anything for money.

"I have a little job for your friends," he started. "Luckily, it takes no brainpower!"

Percy asked her to arrange for some students to collect empty wine bottles from the dustbins behind the top West End hotels, restaurants, and clubs when they close at night.

"I want only the best vintages that start with the word 'Chateau,'" he explained.

Percy told her the way to fill a bathtub with hot water.

"The labels soak off by themselves!" he assured her. "Then iron them flat, bundle up fifty at a time with elastic bands.

Percy reminded Thelma House that her friend Jack Hammer had destroyed Philip Wayward's car!

"That wasn't my fault," Thelma objected.

"This will make it right!" Percy insisted.

After three months, Gil received 600 ironed-flat labels of selected fine vintages valued at anything up to two hundred pounds a bottle glued on his own Napa Valley grapes.

Gil Turner's liquor store on Sunset Boulevard at Doheny Drive flourished, and he sent Percy an advance account statement:

Received with thanks – 5,000 units Chateau Percy.
Signed: Gil Turner

* * * * *

In Percy's ward at Chelsea and Westminster, every cough, splutter, and fart gave rise to detailed public speculation.

"Take cover, he's going to blow!" warned the ever-vigilant Fawcett Block from the bed opposite.

A number of other patients were in bad shape, to the extent that Percy considered himself lucky. At the foot of each bed hung a chart that named the doctor and a description of the ailments and injuries.

All eighteen stone, Fawcett Block, an apprentice plumber, was propped up by a mountain of pillows. He had walked out of a laundry with clothes piled up to his chin and been hit by a truck as he crossed the road. The stack of clothes had protected his chest, but his hips had been crushed and his intestines mangled. His hydraulic bed was the only one in the ward, and Fawcett adjusted his position to any angle at the touch of a button.

The hum of the hydraulics would be accompanied by cries of pain. This was worst when he wanted to sit up before his mother was expected and his bleeding insides were repositioning to greet her.

"Hello, Mum," he grimaced.

"I've brought you some of that nice Perrier water from France," she would reply.

This was the highlight of Fawcett's day, as his only other sustenance was from the tap.

"Lou Plunger called; he's very upset you're not at work," his mother continued.

"I'm not surprised, Mum, it's bloody slave labour," Fawcett complained. "I didn't finish at Mrs Crackpipe's until gone 9:00 p.m. I did all the work while Lou stared at Mrs Crackpipe's cleavage over twenty cups of tea."

"Now, there's no need for that kind of talk, even if you are a bit poorly," she chastised him.

"Is this what you call a *bit bloody poorly*?" Fawcett agonised.

He didn't finish what he wanted to say.

Fawcett had tried to lean up and jarred his fractured pelvis. His face contorted, and he collapsed back in a sweaty heap.

"He can stick his job!" Fawcett moaned before sliding into semi-consciousness.

"Hey, brother, you can open your eyes now. She's gone," said Alfred from the next bed.

Alfred D. Needle, formerly from Jamaica, was a tailor in East Ham. He had been in the same bed for two months and made everyone his friend. As in all hospital wards, there was one comic, and Alfred D. Needle had assumed that role. Under his bed was an inflatable black sheep from his closet.

"Just as good as the real thing," Alfred used to mutter in the middle of the night as he thrashed around under the sheet.

Alfred D Needle's groaning and relieving himself in the sheep broke the night silence, and Percy whispered to Fawcett.

"You should ask to borrow the sheep?"

"I've got a girlfriend!" he replied proudly. "She works in waste management."

Alfred was across the ward opposite Fawcett. He was a big man, but he'd been severely beaten by three drunks outside the Black Horse pub in Putney. He was run over as he lay in the road. The surgeon had cut off his left leg below the knee.

"If you're black, you've got to be careful after dark," he explained generously.

"Why's that?" asked Fawcett.

"Because the white boys can't see you," Alfred explained.

Alfred recalled the state of race relations in the East End of London, where he was constantly a target of abuse. Just weeks before his assault, he had been in his own car picking up some bolts of new cloth, and a man towing a caravan pulled up behind him at some traffic lights and didn't stop in time. He came to Alfred drunk, carrying a baseball bat.

"I told him to stay home if he couldn't afford a hotel!" Alfred admitted.

"And?" asked Percy.

"The guy started whacking me, and I fell over in the road," Alfred recalled. "Then he walked away and left me semi-conscious."

"And?"

"There were two women in the caravan who got out to see what was happening, and he drove off without them!" he carried on. "They were screaming all kinds of stuff about me, and they started kicking me!"

"Is this normal?" asked Percy.

"We all came from Jamaica to fight with the Brits," he frowned. "Now we wish we had stayed home on the beach smoking a bit of weed!"

Alfred's voice was a constant comfort to Fawcett because no one else was interested in speaking to him."

"Nurse! Nurse!" Fawcett moaned.

"Are you okay, Fawcett?" Alfred asked immediately as he heard the hum of the motor.

Fawcett was gripping the control knob instead of the nurses' call button.

As the top of the bed lifted sideways, Fawcett started to panic.

"He's going for a somersault," shouted Wilfred Last from the last bed by the swing doors.

Fawcett's bed had reached the full extent of the tilt, and the nurse arrived just as Fawcett was tipped onto the floor.

Wilfred Last, at 48, was also good-humoured in spite of falling twenty feet off scaffolding and cracking three vertebrae in his spine. He was separated from his wife and looked after his two children and his mother as best he could.

Wilfred had received no compensation from his employers for his accident, and the only protection that his family had was a £3 a month insurance policy that he had bought from a man on the knocker.

"It's useless!" he complained in a serious moment. "The insurance is designed to stop me ever getting any money. If I have an accident, I can't afford to keep the premium going, so then the insurance is cancelled. If I cash it in, I lose all the money in surrender penalties."

"We could all have used a sensible insurance policy," replied Percy. "And who better to design one than we who have cheated death?"

* * * * *

Percy spent his last three days in the hospital going round the patients and compiling notes on insurance cover. Only 3 in over 60 cases had collected on insurance protection, and the other 57 had their claims stalled or rejected.

Percy had gathered his thoughts, and his first telephone call was to Seymour.

"Where on earth have you been, mate?" he asked immediately. "This time-share's a beaut. We're cleaning up."

"I'm going to wake you up, Seymour," Percy replied. "We've been going about this all wrong. You've got to sell a product where the Establishment can't attack you, and the reason *they* won't let you get away with your direct selling soap or time-share is that *they* have no mechanism to enter the space! Apart from that, it smells criminal!"

"Bollocks, mate," said Seymour. "We can sell any way we want!"

"You know, Seymour," said Percy in exasperation. "If your brain exploded, it wouldn't even mess up your hair."

* * * * *

As soon as he was out of the hospital, Percy started his homework towards a business platform. The opportunity was that there was no future in time-share because the property boys in that game were organised crime and their funding was from drug dealing. As for the pyramid selling, the Establishment was hitting all the direct sales operations to stop any comparison with their own pyramid commission structuring.

Percy checked that £7 billion a year was being paid in shareholder dividends, and it all came from insurance products from working people.

Percy's model was based on the direct sales structures of Golden Products, Herbal Life, and, of course, the US phenomenon Amway.

How could the UK regulators condemn their own industry structure of selling and creating commissions as a fraud? Anyway, pyramid structuring was far too attractive to ignore, and there was an amazing bonus - Seymour had over 200 top salesmen on his Rolodex, and he could get them all together fast.

Multi-level marketing was potentially rocket propelled, and it would be unchallenged in a new insurance product, as it was the core strategy of the financial power base for centuries.

"There's a reason I've called you, Seymour," Percy said calmly. "How do you think insurance companies run? They invented pyramid selling. The top man is the sales director, who has a team of regional managers, each with a team of branch managers who, in turn, have unit managers who run hundreds of local salesmen who run around trying to get customers. Each level has more people than the one above. That's why they call it a pyramid and, officially, only *they* are allowed to use it!"

"Look, mate," Seymour objected. "We've got everything organised here, and you want to see some of the girls who are coming from the country. They've got nowhere to stay, mate!"

"Read my lips, Seymour," Percy insisted. "I think I've got a product here that everyone will be tripping over themselves to buy, and the Establishment won't be able to say boo, and Seymour?"

"What now, mate?"

"You get commission up front and then every year afterwards from the same sale until they die!" Percy insisted. "And Seymour, guess what the commission is?"

"Tell me."

"100% of what they put in."

"You're pulling my cock, mate."

"What a disgusting thought," Percy answered. "Seriously, Seymour, it's even better than that!"

"How, mate?"

"The client pays the first month, and you get commission up front for the whole year!"

"You're lying, mate!"

"When can you get all the boys together?" asked Percy.

"As soon as you want!"

* * * * *

Seymour was as good as his word, and Percy found himself presenting to over 100 of the deadliest salesmen ever assembled in direct sales. They were interested because they were reading that the barrow-boys from the East End were being recruited on big starting salaries in all the banks. Seymour had spread the word, and the meeting was packed.

"We're all aware of pyramid selling," Percy opened. "We're also here because we want to get into the money world, and we're all inquisitive. Your proven sales talent is begging for a commission job in the City!"

There was more than a spark of interest.

"No one is enthusiastic about getting out of bed to buy insurance," Percy continued as he could see the eagerness building. "So I am going to show you how to make fortunes where there is nothing bad anyone can say about the product or the way we're going to sell it."

Percy explained that insurance customers normally have to die to receive anything back from years of putting in hard-earned money.

"Imagine saying to the wife, 'I've arranged money for you, my love, but I have to die for you to get it!" Percy suggested.

"My wife needs no further encouragement," came a shout.

"So, we insure them and then kill them?" suggested the voice of Lee Otard, who had recruited over 100 ladies into Herbal Life from his daily exercise classes at the Chelsea Harbour Club.

"There's a concept developed by a man called Mark Night-Hood at a company called Shabby Life Assurance," Percy continued. "The product they're selling is basically a savings plan where you can save a little money each month into their investment funds. The savings plan is sold with life insurance to get tax relief, and guess what? Shabby Life takes all the money to pay the commission up front."

"So why does anyone buy this stuff?" came a voice.

"Because they're selling it as a 'savings plan' with insurance for free," Percy answered.

"The opportunity for us is that his savings plan doesn't break even for 7 years, and the average life of a plan is 7 years, so the insurance companies are taking all the money in commissions and fees!"

"That Mark Night-Hood's a smart boy," observed Lee Otard.

"The point is that he's gained acceptance in the Establishment for this massive rip-off," continued Percy. "All we have to do is create a better deal for the saver, and off we go! We're not threatening the High Street or any Establishment brand!"

There was a ripple of applause.

"We have the key!" Percy shouted. "The Government can't risk letting the cat out of the bag if it brings attention to centuries of pyramid scamming!"

"So what's next, mate?" asked Seymour.

"We're going to join in with a better contract, and they can't say boo!"

"How do we do that. mate?" asked Seymour.

"I've found this tiny insurance outfit which is perfect for us," Percy announced. "It's a subsidiary of the mighty United Dominions Trust known as UDT. UDT has centuries of history. The insurance division has three employees and sells almost no product door to door, but it has a great name: **Golden Life Assurance**!"

"Where are they?" came a shout.

"Here in London, in a basement of UDT," Percy beamed. "That doesn't matter because I've got an option on the entire 57,000 square feet of space on the ground floor on the City side of Southwark Bridge, and I've designed a new savings product for them. It will be easy to sell, and we get paid the same level of commissions as Shabby Life. That's over 100% of whatever the punters invest in the first year paid up front!"

"How do they pay out more than they get in?" asked another voice.

"Because the savings plan is designed for thirty years, and insurance companies value themselves on the basis that everyone keeps on paying for that length of time," Percy explained. "It's called 'embedded value,' and it's a fraud, and it keeps their Stock Market values artificially in the stratosphere. We don't care because they can't challenge us without exposing themselves, so we are protected by their own system!"

"That's ridiculous!" came a voice.

Percy waited for it to sink in.

"We are going to provide a public service and get paid ridiculous money for doing it!" Percy concluded as he pointed to a pile of Golden Life applications and a jam jar of biros.

"If we work in an office, then how do we meet potential customers?" came a voice of reason.

There're going to be lining up at the doors, mate!" Percy shouted towards Seymour.

* * * * *

Percy had already started on recruiting girls for 'market research'. They would collect thousands of customer names and phone numbers from the five million commuters pouring into London every day through the London Underground system. All these commuters had jobs, so they had income.

Now he had to get the girls to get the names and phone numbers, and Percy had a way to do that because he had tested it himself.

* * * * *

"Did you get that job?"

Percy's voice carried out of the open car window as he pulled up at the bus stop alongside a young, long-legged creature in a mini-skirt. She looked bewildered but leaned forward out of the queue to see if the comment really could have been addressed to her.

"What job?" she exclaimed, pointing at herself.

"You're perfect!" Percy beamed. "The job in market research. Didn't I see you in reception yesterday?"

The words rolled off Percy's tongue.

The girl hesitated for only a second and then looked immediately as if she had missed out.

"You have to come for an interview," Percy insisted. "I'm sure I can get you in, and we're only around the corner."

"You mean round the bend!" said another voice in the bus queue.

Percy opened the passenger door so she could slip in.

It worked every time.

* * * * *

So, Rosa Villas's life as a supermarket cashier ended when Percy introduced her to their new venture.

Simultaneously, all over central London, beside every bus stop, Maseratis, Ferraris, and Porsches of super-salesmen with the gift of the gab were recruiting girls. Only Seymour seemed to find it difficult to find the right words.

"Did you get that job?" he started.

"What job?" came the guaranteed reply.

"The blow job!" answered Seymour by mistake.

Percy's recruitment campaign of getting the names and daytime phone numbers of tube train travellers went ballistic from the start. In the history of street surveys, never before were men waiting in line to answer questions. They self-qualified by being clean-shaven with a glint in their eye. The girls made sure to get their coordinates by a smile and the top two buttons of their blouse or shirt undone. Some went further, and the incremental value of their success could be measured in buttons.

They followed up from the office.

'It's me from the station,' they would start. 'Would you like to come over to see the new UDT Wealth Plan?'

The resulting flow of appointments for these skilled salesmen resulted in a massive inflow of cash from strangers in the new land of plenty.

* * * * *

All the top salesmen from the time-share project had joined and grabbed a desk in their vast open-plan space secured on a short lease. It was cheap because the building was scheduled for demolition.

It was the lure of going 'legitimate' in the City of London that was the magnet for all salespeople, and it didn't hurt that they were getting laid beyond their wildest dreams with the throughput of their market researchers.

Rosa Villas had recruited five girls, including her younger sister, Mimosa Villas. Mimosa was straight out of college in Brentford and perfect for standing at the entrance of a tube station on the London Underground.

Then came the magic day when Percy took Rosa and Mimosa back to his flat for supper. He had arranged the candles and two bottles of champagne with a bottle of decent red in reserve. After the first champagne cork hit the window pane, the ice was broken, and after the second, it was all downhill.

Percy finished the sprouts from the Chinese takeaway and suggested they retire to his enormous couch to watch a film. It wasn't long before they were all entangled in cushions and covered by a large duvet.

Rosa had her arm around Percy.

"Don't you dare touch my sister," she warned.

"Where?"

"You know exactly where, you sick bastard!"

"Just because we work together, you can't tell me what to do," muttered Mimosa as she snuggled up.

"I agree," confirmed Percy.

"This is like the Kosha Nostra," muttered Rosa as her sister came up for air.

"I think you mean the Kama Sutra," Mimosa corrected her.

"The Kosha Nostra is the Jewish Mafia," said Percy to clarify the matter.

* * * * *

The next day, Percy rang Seymour.

"We're ready for our first full meeting of the boys and the girls," he announced.

"Where shall we have it, mate?"

"In our new offices, of course!" Percy beamed.

The meeting was an eye-opener as the boys were a mix originally from the world of double-glazing, computer reps, petrol-pump attendants, musicians, boiler repair men, brush salesmen, and window cleaners. More recently, all of them had retrained in soap, cosmetics, or health drinks. Then there were thirty young girls all dressed to kill, and everyone had ended up in one place for the first time.

"This is how we will work," Percy started. "From Monday, and for the first three months, our girls will get the names and telephone numbers from sensible-looking men with clean shoes at the Underground stations."

Seymour then handed out folders with instructions on how they should dress, their kerbside manner, and the questionnaires for the clipboards.

Mimosa smiled as she read out the street survey.

'*Excuse me, would you mind answering a few questions on saving and inflation?*' Percy read out.

"It's a yes or a no," she suggested.

'*Do you think the rate of inflation will go up or down?"*

"The question is simple enough - it looks like another market survey," she confirmed.

'Do you save money on a regular basis in a bank or Building Society?'

'If you saw a method of saving that was guaranteed against loss and designed to beat inflation, would you be interested in learning about it?'

"This is the trick question," perked up Rosa Villas. "They will say, 'Well, yes, I suppose so,' and we answer, 'In that case, may I have your name and daytime phone number?'

Mimosa glowed as she addressed *her* girls.

"Everyone a coconut!" she screamed, adjusting the neckline of her blouse down by two more buttons to make sure everyone knew the potential.

Both Rosa and Mimosa were looking pretty as a picture in short, flowery skirts and white blouses with a revealing light grey jacket. Percy has asked them all to wear an alluring combination of revealing skirts and flimsy tops.

Next, they each had to pick the name of an Underground station out of a hat.

"You'll say you're doing 'market research,', Rosa confirmed as she claimed the status of commander of the team.

The girls all started to scream in delight.

"You will each be teamed with two boys and, if asked, you will call them 'investment advisors at UDT'.

"There is a separate area upstairs for the girls we are calling the 'phone room,'" Percy added. "Their phones are already connected. Boys are not allowed up there, or up anywhere, for obvious reasons. The girls are starting tomorrow to get names and make appointments for the boys who will start presentations next Monday."

There were some gasps.

"We are creating an in-house system, and it's a new world in this insurance industry," Percy grinned, addressing the boys. "First of all, unless you're wearing a dark suit and a sober coloured tie, you can't work here - no exception."

Percy looked around. This was major.

"As you already have seen from the plugs in the floor and the boxes of handsets, the phone lines are in, and there are enough desks and chairs for you all."

Percy's last instruction was to the girls to hand out to the boys a carefully contrived script for them to introduce the Wealth Plan. It ended with their bank details.

"You will all learn this script exactly until you can say it in your sleep!" Percy commanded. "Later, you will find your own style that works best for you."

The girls were starting at the stations the next day to fuel the pump for the boys to kick Percy's ball into play.

"No time for sex, then!" shouted a chancer from Herbal Life.

"Well, not with someone looking like you!" Mimosa shrieked.

* * * * *

This was a new dawn for commuters, and the girls started notching up names and numbers as fast as they could read the survey. They would return to the office to make the appointments and share in the boys' commission on every sale.

After three months, Rosa had risen to become a top salesperson herself, and she was replaced as 'recruitment commander' by the explosive Dinah Mite, a former sales manager at Vernon's Football Pools.

Dinah was from Braintree in Essex, and she recruited a hub of Essex girls who caused a litany of home truths that spread far and wide – like their legs in a way:

Why do Essex girls only have half an hour for lunch?
So, they won't have to be retrained.

How does an Essex girl turn the light off after sex?
She shuts the car door.

How does an Essex girl heat up the lunch?
She slides down the bannisters.

"You Essex girls are the best!" Dinah encouraged them to keep up the pace, and if it slowed, she would remind them in their own language: 'if you want to keep on fucking breathing, I would think seriously about putting a fucking sock in it, okay?'"

* * * * *

Golden Life Assurance had been selected because UDT was a respectable name in the marketplace, and they were failing to break into the savings market. The directors and shareholders would say nothing as commission on the clients' savings started to flow automatically up the pyramid structure to the directors and eventually as dividends to the shareholders.

The huge, open-plan office buzzed with excitement as the 'in-house' concept accelerated, with the best performers signing up to eight new insurance plans a day.

It took six months before Percy received a call from Jess Lapsed, the sales director - now considered a rising star by his colleagues.

"This is important, Percy!" he started.

Percy was keenly aware that the company had become more than visible and the directors needed information to protect their 'embedded value'. If the Press got its teeth into this massive new, obvious multi-level marketing phenomenon under the UDT umbrella, it would be a disaster.

For every policy sold, Jess received a £1 override, and that had reached over £11,000 a month on top of his salary. He couldn't help himself, moving to a six-bedroom new-build in Weybridge and part-exchanging his Ford for a top-of-the-range Mercedes. He also kept an E-Type in the garage, and he moved his children to private schools. As for his wife, Cynthia, she acquired a maid and two-carat diamond earrings. She tapped her ears in all the shops in the village, even when she bought nothing.

Jess seemed agitated.

"You need to keep a low profile," he ordered.

"How?" Percy asked. "Should I cancel the 5,000 new brochures for the Wealth Plan?"

"It's the girls stirring up the Press," Jess hissed. "They're half-naked across the country, and when it rains, they're in T-shirts with no underwear!"

"If you ever came to look - between all your golfing - you'd see a proper business and reception overflowing," Percy replied. "People passing by see the commotion and can't resist coming in to see what's happening. If they get lucky, they end up with a Wealth Plan!"

"I'm not asking you to go back to selling door to door!" Jess reasoned. "I'm not asking you to sell funeral plans, I'm just asking if the girls can stop short of getting their tits out!"

"It'll will come as a shock!" Percy answered.

"Why's that?"

"Because all I've ever said to them is to get them out!"

* * * * *

Roland Rock was a guitarist of sorts who had been a star performer selling cosmetics at Amway. Now he was destined to become one of the great life insurance agents of his day, and no one could say that Roland didn't look the part. He had the Savile Row tailor Wynne Colla make him a morning suit with permanently pressed pin-stripe trousers.

"Wynne told me he could sew in the creases!" he explained proudly.

Roland was in a starched white shirt with the ensemble complete with a Hermes grey silk tie and a pearl pin.

"Even at seven plans a day, Roland earned £40,320 last month," commented Mimosa. "Where does he think he's working in that gear?" Mimosa asked.

"Coots Bank?" her sister answered. "Just don't tell him!"

"They can't bear to sign when I'm in this outfit," Roland grinned as he flicked back his tails and sat to open a dented tin of Old Holborn. He lit the butt of a spliff and took a drag.

"Go outside with that!" Percy ordered. "This whole operation depends on it!"

"And what amount of money will I have accumulated after putting in twenty pounds a month over thirty years?" asked one of his prospective clients.

"How much would you like?" Roland answered.

* * * * *

Two of the most successful salesmen were Mal Function and Lou Natic, who were both introduced to Golden Life by Seymour Clearly. They were each signing as many as a record 10 new clients in a day with larger-than-average premiums. Their lives became a constant celebration of clocking up these enormous monthly commissions and spending the money.

The power of the salesmen had never been better targeted. They each developed their own style, but every prospective client was trapped by a meticulously orchestrated presentation.

"I want to discuss this with my wife!" a nervous bank clerk would plead.

"Does your wife ask you every time she has to get a new toaster?" argued Mal.

"I want to think about it!" an uncertain youth would beg.

"Now what exactly do you want to think about?" Lou would reply. "Let me list 1 to 10 on this blank sheet of paper. Now, what's the first thing you want to think about? Let's write it down and then, if I can satisfy you on each point, there won't be anything to think about!"

"I can't afford it!" a young man, recently a father of twins, would argue.

"You can't afford to afford it, mate," Seymour would insist. "If money's tight now, how much tighter will it be if you were to be ill or die. What would your family live on? I assume you love your new babies and want to protect them?"

"I haven't got a cheque book!" a smart guest would smile, sure of his escape.

"Right," Seymour would confirm as he opened a drawer and whipped out a book of blank cheques. "Just sign this house cheque, and it'll go through your bank in the normal way."

After twelve months from a standing start on the new Golden Life platform, with 100 salesmen, the company was coughing up over £500,000 a month in commission.

"There's a trick in here somewhere?" ventured even Seymour. "They must have a screw loose."

"It's the actuaries and the regulators who design these things, and you're right, mate, it's madness," concluded Percy.

"Well, the 'embedded' part suits me," Seymore agreed. "I've got two of the girls living in my new flat in Kensington, mate, and there's only one bed."

Percy recognised the value of competition, and each month the salesmen would compete on a giant performance table on the wall with the name of every salesman for all to see. Every sale was recognised by a coloured plastic chip, and these ran across the wall. At the end of the month, there was a big celebration acknowledging the leaders. Then the board was cleaned, and it all started again. The chart was an exceptional incentive to strive to avoid ridicule.

The end-of-the-month meetings were held at London's finest hotels. There were prizes for the top performers handed out on the spot. Cases of liquor, concert tickets, boxes of cigars, airline tickets, weekends to beaches abroad, and even cars. The salesman would run up to receive their prizes, and it seemed there was no greater motivation.

At Christmas, there would be turkeys and Fortnum and Mason hampers for everyone, with the choice of a Concorde to New York return or a box at a leading European opera house for the three top producers. Naturally, the December meeting would be held as close to Christmas Day as possible, so the top performers would work themselves to the bone on the last lap so as not to be pipped at the post.

As they worked furiously, they also played in a world of individual achievement, over-consumption, and a special form of camaraderie. They roared down the motorways in convoy to take over the floors of country hotels and Scottish castles for weekends. Elderly people eating their cucumber sandwiches on a hotel terrace would stare in horror as ten Ferraris, five Maseratis, and a host of Porsches burst into the car park.

Any damages were always paid for in cash, and many a pale hotel manager would thank them for their custom and breathe a huge sigh of relief when they left. It was not unusual to see chambermaids peeking out of windows as the cars left with a shower of driveway chippings and a cloud of blue exhaust. Repeat bookings were rare.

* * * * *

The board of directors of Golden Life was mesmerised by the exponential growth of their company, with the share price hitting an all-time high and more than doubling in the twelve months since launch.

"Fuck me!" jerked Jess Lapsed as his over-ride commission of £27,400 hit his bank account for the month of March.

Jess's only official reaction was at the following quarterly board meeting when he thought of referring to his success, albeit obliquely.

"Should we be worried that our salesmen are accumulating direct debits and standing orders like petrol tokens?" he suggested without an alert that they had a tiger by the tail.

As the sales director, Jess Lapsed had chosen his words carefully. During his golfing, he sometimes thought about how his whole sales team could get poached by an industry major. He was aware that the giant Illegally General had run a slide rule over the extraordinary numbers. That alone caused his golfing swing to deliver a slice into the woods.

He dared not interfere as there was the miracle of the director-exclusive share option scheme, which was far more valuable than the cash. It had been devised in a deliberate lapse of morality and kept secret from both the salesmen and shareholders.

"How does their spending affect us?" asked the Golden Life chairman, Shepherd Spy. "The more they spend, the more they have to sell! All we need to do is nothing, and nothing also means no conversations with the regulators!"

The sales machine was already out of control with competition extending to whose apartment was best located, who had the more expensive art, whose girlfriend had the biggest tits, and, most obviously, who had the most important timepiece – Patek or Rolex. They had all latched onto unheard-of lines of credit available with their commission history, with no worry about repayment schedules, because there was no fear in keeping up interest payments, as payments were automatic.

Excess was success.

* * * * *

The commitment and verve required to participate in this game were inherently a part of the character of the players. Golden Life simply gave salesmen the opportunity for expression. Obstacles and dangers, seen in isolation, might never be entertained, but in a group where winning was everything, they were simply challenges to be overcome.

Why else would Seymour, on a visit with ten Golden Life salesmen to Australia's Gold Coast, agree to accept $1,000 in bets to be towed naked at midnight across Sydney Harbour?

"What are the chances of a shark getting him?" his mother asked as she was the guest of honour.

"Don't worry, Mrs Clearly," replied Seymour's school friend Muff Diver. "We've tied his hands to the rope in case he falls off."

"Pity the shark," remarked Lou.

Equally ridiculous to outsiders was Percy jumping from the bow of the ferry between Madeira and Lisbon after a feisty Golden Life weekend.

Will Power and Yul Dye, both prolific in seduction and gambling, led a drinking party on the stern deck. They flung a large coil of mooring rope over the back; it trailed in the wash behind the ferry at around seventeen knots.

"Five hundred quid says you can't jump off the bow and catch this rope at the back," they challenged Percy as he downed his fifth lager and a vodka shot.

Percy looked at the seventy-five feet of rope snaking behind the propellers.

"I've got another fifty that says you won't do it, mate," Seymour added.

"I've got £100 that says we'll never see him again," shouted Roland.

"Oh no, you bloody well won't do this," shouted Dinah, grabbing Percy's arm. "He's not going anywhere!"

"He's chicken!" jibed Will, taking more bets. "If I wasn't so pissed, I'd do it myself!"

"It doesn't look difficult to me," slurred Rhoda Mann, Will Power's girlfriend. "Why don't you just get on top of it?"

Rhoda Mann, a former Hickstead champion rider, who now ran her father's stables, had the physique of someone used to hard work. No one knew what Will saw in her.

"Well, you do it, Rhoda, if it's so fucking easy," Dinah snapped.

"No one bet me!" Rhoda replied.

Percy stripped to his Ralph Lauren boxers and walked to the bow. He looked over the edge and felt the same fright he remembered from the high diving board at St. Abra.

Everyone was leaning over the rail in anticipation; he had to jump.

From twenty feet up on a seventy-five-foot vessel, Percy hit the water like a knife. Before he had taken a stroke, turbulence from the propellers clawed at him. Seven seconds later, after three strokes, Percy broke the surface and lunged for the rope. It felt as if the skin was being ripped from his hand, then he got a second hand to it and hung on and bounced along the surface. The whole thing took less than twenty seconds.

There was a roar of applause, whistles, and hoots from the stern.

Unaware, Percy had been three feet from the end of the rope. All those hours climbing at St. Abra and gym sessions at Harrow paid off. His team had screamed for the crew to cut the engines, so he was able to get back onto the narrow steel platform above the propellers. The ferry had slowed, and his boys hauled him up. He knelt in exhausted relief, unable to move until willing hands helped him stand up again.

Dinah wrapped a towel around him.

Percy turned to Rhoda Mann, who looked demonstrably upset that he hadn't drowned.

"You know why women don't fart?" Percy grinned. "Because their mouths are open so much of the time, they can't build up pressure!"

"My ability to fart is not the issue," she retorted. "You need a psychiatrist!"

"You could at least have done some barefoot skiing!" cheered Will.

"Yup! All the way to Lisbon," Dinah retorted.

Mal handed Percy a beer.

"That was fucking something!" he said. "You scared the life out of me!"

Percy felt indestructible. Little did he know that, apart from the lease at Southwark Bridge ending, Golden Life's option scheme would be the smoking gun.

* * * * *

Percy had built the ready-made sales team at Golden Life, and he had kept on selling himself to sophisticated savers and older businessmen. His girls filtered them by instinct out of the hundreds as they made the appointments. It was so successful that Percy decided to create an elite squad of top producers to develop the Golden Life pension and money management business.

It quickly became everyone's goal to aspire to this group because investors who needed more than a Wealth Plan were candidates to part with huge premiums into tax-planning schemes and corporate arrangements. These high-net-worth individuals had never shied away from responding to the girls in the street, and they started to arrive in increasing numbers. The commission income of the more professional salesmen skyrocketed as the company lapped up that new business.

Percy needed a product co-ordinator to make sure that advice was at hand in any complex circumstances, including tax planning, trust arrangements, and eligibility for grants and benefits. He interviewed three candidates, and the one who stood out was Norma Snockers, the product development director at Illegally General.

"I want this to be an entirely professional relationship!" Percy briefed her at their second meeting. "You need to be available for all kinds of positions as 'technical director'."

"That's a curious way to say what you really want!" Norma replied, taking Percy's hand off her knee.

* * * * *

The salesmen who joined this group had become educated and were justified in calling themselves 'financial consultants'. They had progressed into explaining all manner of insurance and investment products, including mortgages, pensions, group life cover, and key man insurance. Then they started looking at gemstones, coins, and direct investment in shares. Golden Life knew nothing about all this, and Percy asked Norma to coordinate arrangements with other companies offering such services and products so commissions could be paid in an orderly fashion. This had to be arranged to avoid a repeat scene of Seymour Clearly ringing the accounts department at the embryonic mortgage broker, John Cauldwell, demanding his commission.

“Pay up, mate!” was not what Caldwell wanted to hear.

These other insurance and investment companies were surprised to receive signed application forms and cheques from the clients of a competitor. After all, it was Golden Life who was paying all the overheads. However, once they had been assured that the directors of Golden Life were turning a blind eye to their becoming a brokerage, they ran a courier service for exchanges of documents. The directors of Golden Life were too greedy to kill the goose that was laying them golden eggs.

* * * * *

The principles of winning were recorded and distributed on cassette for home and car. Fierce domestic arguments and broken marriages followed the relentless pressure to sell and make money. No one was allowed to weaken, however damaging the side effects.

The girls all got a copy. Joy Stick, Roland Rock’s market-survey girl, had her tape looped and played it softly under her pillow. All her suitors had to listen to it during advances.

Joy would switch it on as she entered the bedroom, and the messages were carefully spaced out to coincide with her preferred pace of seduction.

‘A winner makes mistakes and says ‘I’m sorry’; a loser says ‘It wasn’t my fault.’

‘A winner credits good luck for winning, even though it wasn’t luck; a loser blames bad luck for failing.’

At this point, if her date was still there, Joy would allow herself to be pulled down on the bed.

‘A winner works harder than a loser and has more time; a loser is always too busy staying a failure.’

‘A winner goes through a problem; a loser goes around it.’’

‘A winner knows what to fight for and when to compromise; a loser compromises when he should fight on.’’

'A winner respects those who are superior and tries to learn from them; a loser resents those who are smart.'

'A winner is responsible for more than his job; a loser says 'I only work here'

Then the climax would be brought on with:

'A winner says 'I'm good but not as good as I ought to be; a loser says 'I'm not as bad as some.'

Afterwards, Joy lit a cigarette as the tape finished:

'A winner shows he's sorry and makes up for it; a loser says 'I'm sorry' and does the same thing next time."

"What the fuck was that about?" a rare successful date would ask.

"Here's another one," Joy added. "When you get what you're after, don't complain!"

* * * * *

Lou Natic and Mal Function paused work to take flying lessons. They bought a Piper Cherokee and a parking spot on the turf at Biggin Hill. Their plan was to get two girls in the back and fly off for a few days to every ace spot within reach.

"No more sniffing about in nightclubs!" Lou grinned.

After passing their exams, they invited Seymour and Percy to the Isle of Wight for Cowes Week. It seemed like a lovely idea.

Lou took off from Biggin Hill with Mal in the co-pilot's seat. Seymour, sitting behind Lou, with fingernails digging into the headrest. Seymour went pale from the start as they climbed through a thousand feet. The plane bumped viciously through the cloud base, and Seymour's face drained like bath water.

Without warning, the Cherokee dropped and bounced on heavy air over the Channel, and Seymour projectile-vomited. It spattered as far as the instrument panel, obliterating the altimeter and the tiny plastic aeroplane on the artificial horizon.

Lou pitched forward. The nose dipped while Mal's jaw dropped in horror at the dual controls.

"For fuck's sake, pull yourself together!" Percy pleaded from the back.

Mal held a handkerchief to his nose as the engine screamed and the altimeter unwound. Percy felt his stomach lurch.

"How did either of you bastards get a licence?" Seymour spluttered, crossing himself and wiping his mouth.

"You complete arsehole!" Mal shouted as he got hold of the joystick and lifted the nose. He wiped the instruments with his handkerchief and levelled out at 200 feet.

"Something's wrong!" Lou murmured.

"Who'd have guessed it!" Percy remarked.

"We can't be at 200 feet and still be in the clouds," Lou shouted.

"Jesus Christ, there's the fucking sea!" Mal cried out as the plane punched into a gap in the fog.

The water looked only a few feet away; then it was gone, obscured by the wet fog hugging the windscreen.

"This is Golf Alpha Romeo Charlie, come in," Lou stuttered.

Seymour was as white as a sheet.

"Golf Alpha Romeo Charlie, Gatwick Control," the radio replied. "What is your height and heading?"

"Gatwick Control, this is Golf Alpha Romeo Charlie. Our height is 200 feet, heading one seven zero."

"Romeo Charlie, repeat?" the controller said in undisguised horror.

"Gatwick Control, 200 feet," Lou confirmed.

"Romeo Charlie, climb to 3,000 feet. Maintain heading one seven zero. How many on board and destination?"

"Gatwick Control, Golf Alpha Romeo Charlie, destination Newport — two pilots and two passengers out of Biggin Hill."

"Romeo Charlie, what is your height again, please?"

"1,000 feet and climbing, Gatwick Control."

"Why the fuck did you tell them we had two pilots? Now you've put us both in it," Mal said, wiping vegetables off the instruments. "Come on, baby - climb!"

The plane buffeted higher, and Lou confirmed reaching 3,000 feet.

"If we had passports, we could drop in on Paris?" Percy joked. "We must be nearly there."

"Romeo Charlie, maintain 3,000 feet," Gatwick answered. "Turn right heading two six zero. Call Newport on one two six decimal four. They're expecting you. Good luck."

"That sounded ominous," Percy said as Mal drew two lines on the chart and realised they had somehow turned left and were halfway across the Channel.

Mal pushed Percy's face away from the small open window to get some air.

After fifteen minutes, they were back on track and positioned to land.

"What do you think a flight plan is for?" the Newport officer asked Lou sternly as they taxied.

Once out and at the car hire, they all burst out laughing.

"That really wasn't funny," Percy said.

Avis rented them a Ford, but only Seymour had a driving licence.

"You've scared me shitless, mate," Seymour told Lou. "Now it's my turn!"

Seymour was a dreadful driver. On the way to the pub at the mouth of the River Yar, he drove down a footpath and hit a rock. The car landed sideways with the driver's door against a boulder. Seymour climbed out of the smashed window on the passenger side and started down the road.

"And where precisely do you think you're going?" Mal shouted.

"To hire a boat, mate," he replied calmly. "We'll call Avis later."

They checked into a pub for one night. The rooms were fine and, after a couple of beers, they went to meet the tender from the boat hire company. They chose the most powerful speedboat with twin 100-horsepower Yamahas.

"Here's the £1,000 deposit," Mal agreed.

After the basic instruction, Percy took the wheel, and they thundered along towards the races at Cowes Week. Girls in snappy boating outfits filled boats, and Percy throttled back as Mal offered 'the trip' - a ride round the Royal Yacht Britannia and back to the hotel for a grope.

"Jolly nice of you," purred a recently released convent girl.

"Would one like to give one one?" Mal asked in what he thought was a posh accent.

"I'm so sorry, I didn't quite catch that," Kristal Glass twittered, slugging vodka back.

Then the girls were waving at someone in white with four stripes on his shoulder beside a silk-scarf-clad lady and her corgi on the Royal Yacht.

Kristal and three school friends were staying on Daddy's boat. After entertaining them with more alcohol than they'd ever drunk, Seymour took the wheel and turned the speedboat toward their own hotel instead of returning them to mummy and daddy. They tied up at the hotel dock.

"Are we stopping here, yar?" Kristal slurred.

"Yar, yar!" answered Mal.

"Will we be all right?" her friends asked.

"Yar, yar," Lou echoed.

They ordered champagne and beers and stumbled up to occupy four bedrooms on the first floor.

"I want to see if Minnie's all right," Kristal demanded as Mal pulled her into a bedroom doorway.

Minnie Buss, a sixth-form friend, was not all right. She was groggy and stumbling in the passageway, clutching a bath towel, saying, 'Seymore, take your hands off me!"

"Who were you just with?" Lou asked.

"The one with the funny accent who called me 'mate,'" she moaned. "I was having a shower, and he came in naked, but I escaped."

"Come here, you poor thing," Lou said, pulling her onto the bed and tossing the towel aside.

* * * * *

The trip back to Biggin Hill was almost as bad. Despite a £150 commercial clean, the cockpit still reeked.

"I think I'll take the train," Percy hesitated.

"It's only a few minutes in the air, so hold your breath," Lou persuaded him.

They were late; Biggin Hill had turned off runway lights and refused landing permission.

"We close at 6:00 p.m. Try Gatwick," the controller said.

"Fuck you, Biggin Hill - our cars are down there!" Lou snapped after the radio went dead.

"You fucking moron," Mal muttered into the microphone, forgetting their plane's home was there.

The tiny plane was buffeted by wind and rain as Lou climbed.

"Gatwick Control, this is Golf Alpha Romeo Charlie, come in," Lou called.

"Romeo Charlie, Gatwick approach. Radar contact. Turn right heading two four zero, descend to 2,000 feet," came the crisp reply.

"Jesus, it's the same bloke," Mal muttered.

They heard a Pan American jumbo roaring overhead as it passed like a flying aircraft carrier.

"You're out of your fucking mind going into Gatwick in the dark in this weather!" Percy protested.

"Let me out, mate," Seymour groaned. "I've had enough!"

Seymour chewed his nails as the Cherokee nearly flipped.

"Gatwick Control, this is being Air India 610 coming from Bombay - are you reading me - namaste?"

"Why is Air India called Gatwick 'nasty'?" Seymour asked.

"It's a greeting of respect," Mal replied. "It's when you put your hands together, pointing to the sky. "Now let Lou concentrate!"

"Romeo Charlie, you are cleared to land runway two six right. Try to land at the far end and follow green lights onto the taxiway. Acknowledge."

"Romeo Charlie, steering two four zero, height 1,000 feet," Lou replied, pushing the stick forward.

They saw a bank of lights through the rain and aimed for the runway.

"I see the runway!" Lou confirmed as he dropped the plane just past the threshold.

They bounced and nearly flipped before coming to a halt. Lou throttled forward, and he steered the Cherokee between tarmac lights.

"Get off the fucking runway," Mal screamed as their plane pulled to the right with the Air India jumbo passing overhead, blasting them sideways in its wake.

A film of sweat covered Lou's face as he turned onto the grass.

"The tarmac is over there," Percy said helpfully.

Seymour had lost all colour. He leaned forward.

"We are supposed to have faith that these situations end well," Lou breathed. "Isn't that what you always say, Percy?"

"The trick is to think of the life you've lived as over, Seymour," Mal said. "Then think of the years ahead as a bonus."

* * * * *

Without knowing it, their last trip was to celebrate Percy's birthday with his best friend Aard Dijk, the blonde son of Hugh Dijk, chairman of Philips Industries UK. Aard lived in a fully staffed country house and was always on permanent holiday. Percy felt welcome by the parents as he would be likely to curb some of Aard's more outrageous behaviour.

Aard favoured pub crawls, drinking until he spotted likely girls. The further north he went, the easier the pickings. He had spectacular success with Lilly White, a postman's daughter from Northamptonshire.

Lilly and a friend sat at the Dog and Bone pub.

"And where are you girls from?" Aard asked, standing in front of Lilly.

"Barrow-in-Furness," she answered. "We're at uni."

"And where would you like to be kissed?" Aard asked, eyeing her.

"On the continent," she replied, looking at her empty glass. "Two port and lemon, thanks."

"Have you been abroad?" Aard asked.

"Yer what?" she said.

"I mean - have you got a passport?"

Lilly didn't need a passport; the furthest Aard took her was round the corner into the car park.

"Now there's an idea," Aard mused to Percy later. "We could have your birthday on the continent."

"Maybe Paris?" Percy said. "We could ask a few friends and drive?"

Percy called Dinah to invite some of the girls for a weekend in Paris.

After a few days, Dinah had done well. Will Power and Yul Dye planned to drive their matching Ferrari 308 convertibles, and Seymour paired with Roland Rock in his Ferrari Daytona. Lou Natic with Mal Function would fly their Cherokee. Aard Dijk was persuaded to borrow the Philips jet as long as it was just for himself and Percy.

Percy asked Dinah to make sure Norma Snockers was included.

Dinah coordinated that they'd all meet at the Bristol Hotel in Paris on Friday evening, where she reserved the ten available rooms, including the honeymoon two-bed suite for Percy, with a deposit for all of it on Percy's AMEX card.

Lilly had applied for a passport, but it wouldn't arrive in time.

Dinah arranged a big birthday dinner for Saturday evening at the Coq d'Or and afterwards at the Moulin Rouge.

"I think I'll go without a girl," Percy made it known. "I fancy a bit of French."

"You speak French?" Mal asked.

"Moi êtes français!" Percy replied.

The Ferraris and the Cherokee and the Philips jet all arrived without incident, and they grouped as arranged at the Bristol Hotel. Dinner was at 8:00 p.m. at La Vieille Russie on the Left Bank. Everything was fine until La Vieille Russie presented a wine that tasted like lighter fluid.

"Vous êtes champagne!" Yul pronounced, waving the bottle and ordering a litre of vodka and two magnums of Cristal.

A group of Swedish girls in their twenties at the next table looked like fun, so Mal ordered two bottles of the lighter fluid for them.

Dinah has booked a table for fourteen for after-dinner at a new nightclub, Le Croque de Shit. She had in mind that the boys without girls could get lucky. However, the Swedes were there, and Lou suggested they join them at the Croque.

There was a look of disdain at the least, and they said they were already discussing their next stop, Anastasia's. This happened to be the most popular and expensive nightclub in Europe, and the bill could easily be six figures, but they insisted. Anita Ekberg was probably going to be there. Anita Ekberg was the Swedish sex symbol and star of the iconic La Dolce Vita, and the boys thought she was making it up.

"There are too many!" Percy reasoned, and we have a reservation at Le Croque.

They went their separate ways, with the girls leaving the lighter fluid on the table while the cream of Golden Life moved on to Le Croque.

"Did you know this was a pole-dancing club?" Percy asked Dinah as Seymour and Lou went immediately into booths with two of the topless girls on the stage.

"That was lucky!" Percy said as they went off. "Now we can have a drink and enjoy the show without being thrown out!"

Roland was missing, and Percy presumed he had gone with the Swedes as he was immaculately dressed as usual and wearing a difficult-to-miss hand-embroidered waistcoat by Wynne Colla.

"Don't panic!" Percy surmised. "When they give him the bill, he'll be back!"

They didn't have to wait long as Roland appeared an hour later, unusually shaken.

"The girl who seemed to be in charge was ushered with her friends into Anastasia's roped-off VIP area, and she waved at me to join them," he reported. "She had two bottles of Chopin Polmos vodka on the table, which is the most expensive drink made in Sweden. She asked me what I wanted, so I said 'Coca-Cola'. Then the waiter handed me the bill, and it looked like two digits and three noughts on the end, so I said I was waiting for you guys and I excused myself and escaped to the bar. Then the stunning Anita Ekberg was escorted in with some sophisticated guys and, of course, they got to sit with the Swedes in the VIP area."

"No way!" Aard questioned.

"The barman said she was Crown Princess Victoria of Sweden, daughter of Carl Gustaf," Roland continued. "She was about my age and blonde and stunning, and that explains the vodka and the waiter giving me the bill. I was the only man at the table!"

A topless pole-dancer was standing in front of Roland, and he stuffed some notes into the top of her string that was masquerading as knickers.

"You would like something?" she asked quietly.

"What have you in mind?" Roland replied.

"You know… the white something," she answered.

"That's a great idea!" Roland chirped up. "I'll have a gram of coke, you in a booth, and a bottle of vodka in that order, merci!"

Roland turned to Percy.

"It's going to haunt me that I fucked up my chance of becoming King of Sweden!" he said wistfully.

"So she didn't come over and jump you?" Percy laughed.

"Fuck off!" he replied.

"I'll sort you out!" Aard butted in as he produced a lump of something he announced as 'Turkish Gold.'

Aard torched it with his Zippo, crumbled it, and pulled out Rizla papers.

"This will take the edge off the pain!" he muttered.

"For fuck's sake, be discreet," Percy slurred. "It'll stink the place out."

"Save it for later," said a French-accented girl in a miniskirt. "We could party at your place, oui?"

"Yeah, let's have a party at your place," her friend screeched.

Norma Snockers was her usual chatty self, but this time on steroids. She seemed to be button-holing one of the topless dancers. She looked round at Percy and broke off to whisper in his ear.

"What are you thinking when you could have these!"

* * * * *

An hour later, looking like the drunken rabble they were, they were in a crude attempt to sneak past the tapestries and colonnades into the Bristol without being seen.

"I don't think so!" challenged the night porter, holding up his hand like a policeman.

Percy took out some money, and he looked at it dismissively.

"That will not keep you out of trouble here, monsieur!" he said firmly.

With Mal standing at over two metres tall, ready to smash him in the head, Percy forked out three thousand francs to avoid a police incident and a safe passage for them all up to Percy's double suite.

Percy phoned for room service and ordered champagne, vodka, a bucket of ice, and a whole chicken with salad and plates.

"Don't forget the glasses," Seymour added, "and the mixers, mate!"

"I am Marie Uana, and my friend is Sal de Bain," the extra girl from Le Croque announced as she planted herself on Aard's knee. "We are students at the Beaux-Arts de Paris."

Aard pulled out his lump of Turkish and popped a pill, and he theatrically started to lick the Riza papers to hold his crumbled hash and tobacco mix.

Lou and Mal arrived separately, grinning like cats that got the cream.

"I thought we'd lost you!" Lou smiled as Dinah handed them miniatures from the fridge.

Aard Dijk produced his masterpiece joint in the shape of an ice cream cone and lit it.

"Someone open a window!" Roland shouted.

The waiters arrived with all the booze and the chicken, and obviously noticed the change in air quality.

"It's a special birthday party," Will winked as he fired the first cork into the ceiling.

"It's funny how these frogs like francs," Roland said, waving a 500 franc note at the waiter for his loyalty.

You are my menu!" Roland smirked at Sal de Bain.

"Later, Cherie!" Sal replied, taking the joint from Aard and taking a long drag.

Seymour took it next. His eyes widened as he gazed up at a portrait of a girl about to be burned at the stake.

"Zat was a heroine!" Marie Uana slurred.

Seymour thought Joan of Arc was Noah's sister, so he missed the point.

“For God’s sake, Seymour,” Yul observed from inside a cloud of blue smoke. “Get a grip!”

“They broke the mould after they made me, mate,” Seymour replied proudly.

The chicken and a platter of salad had been placed on the dining table in the study area, and Aard had moved across and taken a plate. He was gazing into space.

“I’m going to complain,” he announced, picking up the phone on the desk and tapping the speaker button. “This chicken has no legs!”

“That’s impossible, monsieur. All our chickens have legs,” a voice replied.

“Not this one,” Aard insisted, stabbing the bird.

“Are you sure no one else has eaten the legs?” the kitchen asked.

Aard pushed the chicken around.

“I’m looking straight at it,” he argued.

“I don’t think you can look straight at anything,” Percy said, going to the table and apologising to the kitchen. “The chicken is upside down!”

Roland had remembered the folded packet from the club, and he laid out sixteen neat lines on the dining table. He rolled up a note as the phone rang, and Seymour answered it.

“There’s no one here!” Seymour declared.

By the time Percy had turned round, all sixteen lines were gone.

“That was for all of us,” he observed, realising this was out of control.

Percy noted that Norma Snockers had sneaked out with Sal de Bain.

It was suddenly 4:30 a.m., and they had Percy’s birthday party to attend that same evening, so Percy announced they should all go to their own rooms or move upstairs to Bristol’s rooftop pool and lounge.

Within half an hour, the pool area was chaos with most of them naked in and out of the water with glasses and bottles strewn everywhere. Mal lay on a lounger with a girl astride him, and Will and Yul were in the shallow end with two naked girls sitting on their shoulders. Then two security guards walked in.

Everything froze as if a film had jammed in the projector. Roland was holding what looked like an Indonesian root vegetable in the middle of the exercise area. There was a silence that said everyone knew the game was up.

“Out! Get out, you English!” the guards shouted.

“I’m Dutch, and I’ve come for a quiet swim,” slurred Aard.

"We do not care if you are the Queen of Egypt, monsieur," the guard replied in perfect English.

Everyone was still. Then the double doors opened onto Seymour, standing naked, holding the wooden headboard from his bed under one arm.

"Surf's up!" he announced.

* * * * *

The hotel staff were joined by several gendarmes to supervise getting their things together and leaving with double and triple vision. They left the cars at the Bristol and took taxis to the George V, where cash for two nights saved them from sleeping rough.

* * * * *

Dinah Mite was in Percy's new suite at the George V, and she gave him his birthday present when they woke up at noon, but it took until 6:00 p,m. for everyone to be regrouped in the George V bar, ready for instruction. Roland was the last to arrive as he ushered Marie and Sal into the street.

"Everyone puts in five hundred francs for a competition!" Dinah declared to the boys. "Pair up. Whoever comes into the Coq d'Or on the Champs-Élysées at 9:00 tonight for Percy's birthday dinner wins the pot! The girls will have a quiet drink and get dressed. I think we can forget the Moulin Rouge afterwards.

"Why have I put in five hundred francs?" Seymour protested.

"Are you deaf?" Dinah snapped.

"If I want a souvenir, I can buy one," Seymour continued.

"Shut up, Seymour!" four voices cut in.

"Fat chance," Dinah said, pairing them off.

"Seymour – go get yourself a gendarme's hat and gun!" Will suggested with a laugh.

Seymour suddenly brightened. "Oh, that kind of souvenir!"

"This is madness!" Percy admitted to Dinah. "We're asking for more trouble."

* * * * *

Regulars at the Coq d'Or noted eight pretty girls giggling in eight of sixteen seats around a table sectioned off for a celebration.

However, the restrained ambience of the Paris elite dining evaporated when the boys arrived with their souvenirs. Yul and Roland carried a nameboard from a Bateau-Mouche. Aard and Mal arrived, waving a flag they'd swiped from the Dutch Ambassador's residence, and Seymour appeared, dragging in a large Persian rug with Will supporting the middle and Lou assisting at the other end.

"Oh God!" Percy cried as muffled shouting came from the rug.

The locals craned forward.

"I give you the doorman of the Bristol Hotel!" Seymour announced to the stunned diners.

The doorman was helped out of the rug, and he bowed. Dinah and Norma Snockers leapt up and held up their arms in victory, and the room erupted in clapping.

"I think you should have this," Dinah said, handing the doorman the winnings.

"I've already paid him!" Seymour complained.

"Calm down, Seymour," Norma said, hugging him. "It's only money!"

"Well, at least I've still got the carpet," Seymour smiled. "I threw it out my window at the Bristol before I left."

"You're all insane," Holly Bush, Yul Dye's new conquest, exclaimed. "I want an early flight home."

"You know the difference between an Essex girl and a Boeing 737?" Lou asked her. "The 737 stops whining at the end of the day!"

"Once you get mixed up with these lunatics, it's for life," Dinah warned as the doorman downed a cognac and the party got underway.

* * * * *

Sunday was a day of recovery, at least until the afternoon. A few visited the Louvre to see the newly installed Mona Lisa, and some took a boat round Notre Dame. Percy visited the Paris Motor Show.

"Oui, Monsieur," the stunning salesgirl pouted as she lay back across the bonnet of a blue limited edition Maserati. "We've got this one available in red or blue, but only with the wheel on the left."

"Marvellous!" Percy observed as she moved her legs.

"We are not producing many of this one, so you will have to be quick!"

"I'm faster than you know," Percy replied. "Only pleasure slows the pace!"

"So you will have it in blue?"

Percy pulled out his cheque book.

"I will have the car in blue and collect it on the Friday after the show is over, if you will come with the delivery for dinner?" Percy asked as if it were normal.

Percy held his pen in the air.

"Just zee dinner?"

"But of course!"

* * * * *

Dinah had come to Paris in the Philips jet with Percy and Aard Dijk and, as a surprise for Norma Snockers, Percy checked that she could fly back with them. She could stay with him overnight, and they would drive together to the office in the morning.

It was only when they arrived at work that Percy found out that the Ferraris hadn't arrived. The Calais ferry crossing had been a horror story, and they had all been drinking, so no one was fit to drive home, let alone well over the alcohol limit and in the dark.

Roland arranged for them all stay at his brother's house near Tunbridge Wells.

There was a sign by the gates of the house:

POT PLANTS FOR SALE

Nobody thought much of it - until they saw the massive greenhouse in the back garden.

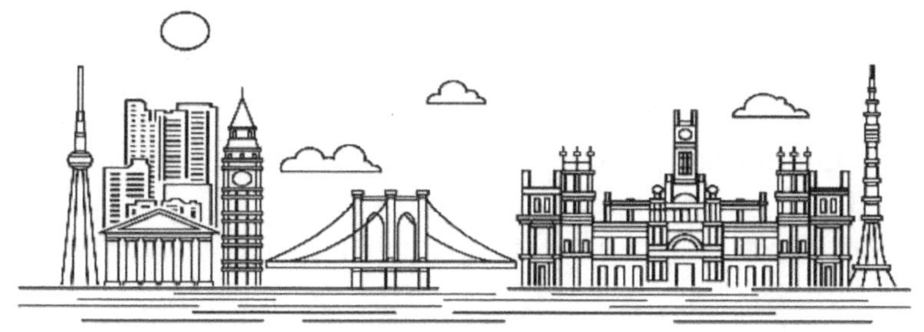

Chapter Eight
WELCOME TO THE CITY

Key Witnesses:

BOOBI TRAPP	*Maserati Sales – Paris Motor Show*
BILL CLINTORIS	*Governor of Arkansas*
SIR PURE SCAMMER	*Head of the Crown Prosecution Service*
JIMMY SALIVATE	*Child Molester*
COUNTESS MONA LOTT	*Human Rights Activist*
THE RT. HON. PAUL BEARER	*Minister of Education*
MAX DOSAGE	*Heir to DOS Pharmaceuticals*
URINA TRAPP	*Golf Club Masseuse*
SIR DAVY LAMP	*Chairman – Golden Life Assurance*
SHERIDAN COX	*World's Leading Fraudster*
OLIVE PIP	*Percy's Girlfriend*
CASE CLOSED	*Partner – Spicer and Oppenheim*
JOHN GUNN	*Director – British and Common Cents Bank*
EWAN CRY	*Parliamentary Journalist*
KIEL DOVER	*Managing Director – Soundalarm*
LINO FIRE	*Stockbroker – Target Resources*
MARK NIGHT-HOOD	*Founder – Shabby Life Insurance*
DET. INSPECTOR BOKHARA	*Head of the Rug Squad*
DR. BUCK TREND	*Salesman – Golden Life Assurance*

Percy's new Maserati was delivered in Paris as requested to the Montalembert Hotel on the appointed day – with the girl who had sold it to him. Percy remembered her decorating the bonnet at the Paris Motor Show, but she got her name from her business card that had come with the invoice - Boobi Trapp, and she was from Latvia.

Percy came down to reception to greet her and to gloat over his acquisition.

"The food here is fantastic," he smiled.

"Remember what you promised?" Boobi said immediately. "Just dinner!"

Boobi was with Metro Models, a top-of-the-line management company with international clients. The Paris Motor Show had hired no fewer than forty-five of their girls, and Boobi has sold eight cars.

Percy had dinner arranged in his suite with the temperature slightly higher than usual, and it was past midnight when she asked to go home.

"I'll drive you", Percy offered too gently.

They woke up at eleven, and Boobi's last words to Percy were 'You are a big liar'.

"But every time I drive the car, I will remember the pleasure of our time together," Percy replied.

Percy drove back to London without insurance and without incident apart from some alarming moments when he approached roundabouts with the left-hand drive.

"Fuck!" he shouted several times, lorries blaring their anger as they braked to let him regain his orientation. It was almost as bad in England, with the reverse way round.

The first thing he did was flick through the available number plates until he spotted **1 KUM**. It had to be bought, and he had the plates made up before the Department of Vehicles could get into gear. That means he was still driving uninsured, which meant he had to delay his planned weekend away with Hattie Tude.

By the following weekend, the car was insured and plated, so all he needed was to confirm Hattie.

Hattie was a career model he had met at the nightclub Dial 9, and she agreed to spend a weekend with him in the Cotswolds. She had explained that she was very upset and needed some time off work.

Percy picked her up in the new car on the following Friday and, as they headed down the M4, she explained why she was disoriented. She had returned from a three-week shoot in China for American Express.

The leading society magazine *Avant Merde* had arranged its front page as part of a six-page feature on the new autumn collection of the Chinese fashion house Li Ning, a brand that led the Chinese fashion move from manufacture to design. The photographers were the acclaimed brothers from Amsterdam, Dik and Prik van Gerkin.

"Like every photographer on a foreign shoot, they want to sleep with the models," she said, pulling the latest copy of *Avant Merde* from her bag. "They cut my face in half!"

Percy was incredulous. The front cover showed exactly half of Hattie's face.

"And why would they do that?"

"Because I wouldn't suck Prik's dick. It's not fair!"

"I suppose it goes with the territory," Percy replied.

There was a silence.

"I mean, how horrible that must have been," he corrected himself.

"It was awful," Hattie cried. "He was standing on the Great Wall of China with his penis sticking out of his trousers! What's more, he wanted his brother to take the picture!"

"More to the point, you don't have to do anything like that this weekend," Percy said. "We're visiting my old school friend Jerry Mander. His parents live in a fuck-off pad in Gloucestershire. It should be fun."

"It's good to get out of London," Hattie agreed. "By the way, is this your car?"

"Yes!"

"Then can you slow down?"

Percy called Jerry to check everything was in order for their stay.

"I'm in High Wycombe!" he replied.

"We're on junction 7 of the M4, so we'll be there before you!" Percy said anxiously.

"I doubt that!" Jerry replied. "I'm leaving now, and I have my own runway on the estate."

Percy had forgotten that Jerry had his on the plane.

"See you there!" Percy confirmed remembering when Jerry attempted to take off across the lawn at his family estate. He had been too low over the first field and collected half the harvest in the undercarriage. It was the only aircraft in the Mandrax Aviation fleet, and his paying passenger spent four days in a private clinic receiving treatment for shock.

Percy and Hattie had a stop after they came off the motorway and arrived after ten o'clock. Percy pulled neatly into one of the garages off the enclosed cobbled courtyard.

Jerry's mother, Lady Mander, must have heard the throaty burst of the engine because she greeted them at the door, clearly annoyed.

"You're very late!" she shrieked, marching them upstairs.

"Hattie, my dear, you will sleep in here," she commanded, opening the first bedroom on the fourth floor. She then seized Percy's arm and dragged him down the corridor. "And Percy, you are in here."

She disappeared, switching off the lights.

Jerry appeared in pyjamas, wearing a Japanese Second World War leather flying helmet with goggles.

"Don't worry," he stammered, adjusting the woollen ear flaps. "I told Mum you weren't coming till after dinner. Anyway, see you in the morning. Maybe we'll go flying."

Percy groped his way back down the corridor and found a giggling Hattie.

"How's your room?" he enquired as he went in.

After a quiet Saturday, a long walk, and an early night, they woke at ten on Sunday morning. They went into the bathroom together. Hattie filled the huge iron bath to the brim, poured in bubble bath, and thrashed it into foam. Percy had no option but to jump in.

Half an hour later, shrieks rose from the courtyard below, shattering the moment. Then came a hammering on the door.

"Percy Vere, of all Jerry's friends, you are the most revolting!" shrieked Lady Mander.

"Oh God!" Percy muttered, stepping out of the bath. "What now?"

As the water level dropped and the suds subsided slightly, he noticed the four-inch overflow pipe and glanced out of the arrow-slit window. They were forty feet above the courtyard.

"Jesus Christ," he whispered.

"What's the matter?" asked Hattie, giggling in the bubbles.

"We've pumped soap all over the local hunt," Percy gasped. "They're all down there in their little red jackets, on horseback, having a sherry - and they're covered in suds."

Hattie shrieked with laughter.

"I think we'll skip lunch," Percy suggested.

When they eventually came downstairs, Lady Mander had disappeared, but Jerry was still wearing his flying helmet and goggles in the drawing room.

"Let's go for a walk," he insisted, putting down his flight log. "We'll sneak out the back way to avoid the enemy!"

They selected Wellington boots from the chaotic pile by the door and set off through the garden. Jerry pushed his goggles up onto his forehead.

"I think we'll take a spin in the old rowing boat," he announced as they walked towards the lake.

Percy rowed them out to the small island in the middle, and apart from Jerry punctuating the conversation with aeroplane noises, it was idyllic.

"Hattie, you have stolen my boots!" came a sudden shrill cry from the bank.

"I just borrowed them," Hattie shouted back, then muttered, "You old bat!"

"What?" came the reply.

"Can't hear you," Percy shouted cheerfully.

As Percy rowed back, the hunt returned past the lake on its way back to the courtyard.

"Time for a spot of lunch," Jerry said, spinning round with his arms out.

Twenty-four guests sat around a substantial dining table as the butler served soup.

"The manners of youth today are appalling," Lady Mander said loudly to Pam Flett, the local Conservative agent. "They even steal your boots!"

"Why don't you go and get yourself stuffed?" Hattie burst out, throwing her napkin down.

"I think we're leaving, Jerry," Percy said into the stunned silence.

Sir Jerry Mander, diminutive at the head of the table, did not move. Percy assumed the reason was long-term partner abuse.

"Is that what you call a quiet weekend in the country?" Hattie giggled as they roared down the lane.

"If I get a move on, we can catch some oysters at Scott's," Percy said, pushing the car towards 140 mph.

"Percy?"

"What?"

"What am I going to do with my life?"

"How can I tell you what to do with your life, my baby, when I haven't a clue what to do with my own?"

"But yours is a natural progression in the City", she replied. "I'm going to be out of work when I lose my looks because there's nothing in my head but a mess of useless information."

"That's true!" Percy agreed. "Give me an example of useless information and let me see if it's of any use?"

"Like the similarity between John F. Kennedy and Abraham Lincoln - apart from the fact they were both assassinated?"

"So, tell me, my little harbour of useless information."

"Well, Lincoln was elected to Congress in 1846, and Kennedy was elected to Congress in 1946. Lincoln was elected President in 1860, and Kennedy was elected President in 1960. The names Lincoln and Kennedy each have seven letters. Both Presidents were shot on a Friday. Both were shot in the head. Lincoln's secretary was named Kennedy, and Kennedy's secretary was named Lincoln. Both were assassinated by Southerners, and both were succeeded by Southerners. Both successors were named Johnson. Andrew Johnson, who succeeded Lincoln, was born in 1808. Lyndon Johnson, who succeeded Kennedy, was born in 1908. John Wilkes Booth, who shot Lincoln, was born in 1839. Lee Harvey Oswald, who shot Kennedy, was born in 1939. Both assassins were known by three names. Both names contain fifteen letters. Booth ran from a theatre and was caught in a warehouse. Oswald ran from a warehouse and was caught in a theatre. Both Booth and Oswald were assassinated before their trials.

Now comes the best: a week before Lincoln was shot, he was in Monroe, Maryland, and a week before Kennedy was shot, he was in Marilyn Monroe!"

"I wouldn't say that was useless!" Percy suggested.

* * * * *

The kitchen at Scott's was already closed, so Percy dropped Hattie off to continue her career assessment. He then drove out of London to visit his friend Aard Dijk, who seemed to be in great form. Aard had arrived back from Percy's birthday party in Paris and gone to the RSPCA to see if there was a dog that needed a home. He had a special dog in mind.

'I'm looking for a retired police dog?' he enquired politely. "Do you have one of those that needs a good home?"

That same day, Aard went home with his new pet, a retired police sniffer dog. He arrived at the Philips home at around three in the afternoon, and the dog went into each room sniffing like he was back at work.

"This is saving me a fortune," Aard beamed to Percy as the dog was sitting bolt upright in the library in front of the bookcase.

"Watch this!" Aard said excitedly, pulling out a few books and shaking them until a packet fell out onto the carpet. "He's found stuff in my medicine cabinet, the toolbox in the kitchen, with the box of balls in the snooker room and under the Persian rugs. It's about ten grams of coke and three kilos of weed, and now he's been congratulated, all he wants to do is lie in front of the fire!"

"I'm sorry to say he's not what I wanted," Aard explained as he returned the dog to the RSPCA. "All he does is sleep!"

* * * * *

Aard Dijk had bonded with Roland Rock in Paris at Percy's birthday weekend, and they had a mutual interest. Roland's brother had a flourishing cannabis business, and Aard had mentioned Philip's Industries country pile with a massive area under glass. The greenhouse was empty except for a bench in the corner used by Aard's mother to grow a few orchids for the house. It was her original intention to make a business selling orchids, and Philips had installed controlled temperature to suit the orchids and an overhead mist-generating watering system.

Roland's overnight stay with his brother on the way back from Paris had alerted him to the world of cannabis germination and harvesting, so he was keen to talk to Aard. What if Aard could grow a forest of weed in that space so perfectly suited for a cannabis business?

Roland always thought big, and he asked his brother for a few seeds.

“Take what you want, bro!” was permission enough to remove two jars each holding thousands of seeds marked ‘female’.

“I’m coming to your house in the country when your parents are next away!” Roland informed Aard. “I’m bringing something amazing to show you!”

Roland was no gardener, but he knew enough to buy 3,000 tiny propagating pots- he estimated one for each seed - a few bags of potting compound to start them off in life, and some large trays to position them under the automatic mist of warm water twice a day.

After Aard called to confirm the coast was clear, Roland loaded up his Range Rover. If cannabis needed the same growing conditions as orchids, here was £250,000 of free greenhouse space - purpose-built!

Aard explained that his mother required Philips to ensure she could simply flip a switch and leave the orchids to flourish on their own. That meant that Roland had no need to go into the greenhouse until the growing plants needed pots for the next size up.

“This is huge!” Roland blurted out immediately as he looked towards the far end of the glass emporium.

Aard helped him lay out the trays of 3,000 tiny pots on a small island in the middle of this monstrous space.

“My mum won’t even notice these tiny plants”, Aard presumed as he turned on the heat and the automatic watering system.

“What about her getting a clue if she breathes in?” asked Roland.

“I hadn’t thought of that”, Aard confessed. “Maybe she’ll just get stoned!”

Aard repeated that the night lights and heating were after Philips had received expert opinion for Mrs Dijk for what they thought was orchid city!

“We’ll have to learn how to do this properly!” Roland insisted. “These seeds were marked ‘female’ on the jars so clearly that’s for a reason.”

They went into the house, ordered a takeaway, and Roland called his brother to get some guidance.

“Why are these seeds marked ‘female’?” he started.

"They're the ones that yield the resinous buds with a shorter cultivation time to the flowering stage", he answered. "The ones you took have a high germination rate, and they're not the medical strain; they're for recreational use. You're a beginner, so you'll have to get some help if you want a decent result."

Roland's brother went on to explain that at the pre-flowering stage, the cannabis plants start showing their sex, and it's a critical window for weeding out any males, leaving only female resin-rich buds.

"It's a good thing this greenhouse is well hidden and behind all these trees", Aard laughed. "With the lights on at night, it looks like a spaceship has landed!"

* * * * *

Weeks later, Roland assumed everything was in order, and he had the local garden centre deliver 3,000 three-litre pots and 20 sacks of some special horticultural compost.

"Leave them by the entrance gate!" he instructed, "and I'm giving you cash."

Aard then asked his loyal and discreet Philips gardener to go about the repotting.

The next stage was to organise a party to celebrate the first crop. In preparation, they rolled 50 joints from the dried and shredded buds, and they invited Percy to join them.

"Should we try a little now?" Aard suggested.

"Can't do any harm!" agreed Roland as they all lit up.

"Shit!" Aard started a few seconds after two long drags. "We've got to collect the booze before the shops shut."

"I can't stand up, let alone drive!" Roland said first, so Percy and Aard set off in Aard Hillman Imp and loaded up the booze.

Aard was turning the corner by the chicken farm of Dandy Lyon, their friendly neighbour, when Aard suddenly hit the brakes, and the car bumped to a halt with the boxes of booze jumping forward on top of them.

"Look at that!" Aard shouted wide-eyed as he looked over the field.

"Look at what?" Percy asked, squinting.

"It's a giant lampshade!" Aard replied as he got out of the car.

Percy could only watch as Aard tipped the circular aluminium chicken-feeder onto its side, spilling the corn on the ground amongst hundreds of frightened chickens. He then started rolling it like a giant yo-yo towards the car.

"Give me a hand to get this on the roof!" he called.

The two boys lifted the empty nine-foot-wide feeder onto the roof of the Hillman Imp, and with the boxes of booze jumbled up inside the car, Aard started off round the corner towards the house. It was as they were nearing the gate that a blue flashing light came up behind them.

"Hello, hello, what do we have here?" the officer enquired as Aard wound down the window.

"It's a lampshade, officer," he replied with his eyes bulging.

"It looks more like Dandy Lyon's chicken-feeder to me, Sir," the officer reasoned. "Please would you turn off the ignition and step out of the car, as we will need you to accompany us back to the station."

Dandy Lyon received the call, and rather than press charges, he collapsed in hysterics. The police were obliged to let the two boys go.

"That was a bit close!" commented Percy as they walked down the steps to freedom.

"Why is that?" asked Aard as a matter of fact.

"Because we have all those joints rolled up on the coffee table in the hall and half the world arriving tonight to sample the crop!"

"No shit, Percy!" Aard said with a straight face and a crooked jaw.

* * * * *

Guests began arriving in the early evening, and by ten o'clock the house was full. By midnight - after consuming the equivalent of six entire cannabis plants - everyone was unconscious. Aard ignored the sprawl of bodies and collapsed comatose on his bed. His final conscious act was to press a switch, lowering a bank of Philips Industries sunlamps from the ceiling.

At four in the morning, Percy woke on the study floor to the smell of something between burning and cooking. He stepped carefully over the inert forms scattered through the house and made his way upstairs to Aard's room. Aard was about medium-rare, and, unable to rouse him, Percy had no choice but to call an ambulance.

Half an hour later, Aard lay strapped to a stretcher, carried gingerly over the bodies lining the hall.

"We'll need more than one ambulance!" the crew advised.

"These are all just asleep after the marathon today!" Percy answered. "This is the only burnt one!"

The following morning, at eleven, Percy answered the phone. He was expecting the police, alerted by the hospital, but it was the hospital itself.

"Your friend has regained consciousness," the doctor said dryly, "but we have a situation. He called for a nurse and ripped her uniform blouse open while she was trying to take his temperature. If he's well enough to attack the staff, he's well enough to go home. Keep him warm. If further treatment is required, contact his own doctor."

"Are you sending him back in an ambulance?" Percy asked.

"No. We don't provide transport," came the reply. "Perhaps you could order him a taxi."

Percy surveyed the unconscious sea of friends still in the house. He cleared a space in front of the fireplace by dragging two moaning bodies by their ankles and replacing them with a mattress from the downstairs bedroom. He reckoned it would be safer to keep Aard warm where he could be seen. Percy lit the fire before the taxi arrived.

The driver was helpful in unloading his passenger and even in guiding Aard through the bodies onto the mattress. Aard was glowing in the light from the fire like a peeled beetroot.

"You look awful," Percy ventured.

"The doctor asked if my regular intake of liquids was more than fifty units at a time," Aard muttered.

"And what did you say?"

"I said it depended on the kind of day I was having."

"And?"

"He asked whether three bottles of alcohol were a weekly or monthly amount," Aard said. "I didn't dare tell him it was a daily average."

* * * * *

Later that day, the guests began to stir, and no one seemed inclined to leave. Their first instinct was to raid the fridge for a fry-up and, locust-like, they devoured the contents of the larder and continued drinking from the bar.

It happened to be the afternoon of the Brazilian Grand Prix. Some watched it on the giant Philips television, others lounged on the terrace, and between them, they finished every drop of alcohol in the house.

The afternoon unfolded in a haze of spliffs rolled from the mountain of prepared material on the coffee table with Rizla and filters. The roar of the Formula One race blended with Bob Dylan pleading for peace from hidden futuristic speakers. Some attempted snooker, endangering the felt with aggressive cueing, while others queued to phone friends around the world.

By early evening, a fresh wave of guests, mostly girls, arrived. That prompted a raid on the garage freezer. By eight o'clock on Sunday night, a new and energetic party was in full swing. Someone came back from the garage and prepared a new pile of weed, and no one seemed particularly interested that their host lay naked on the floor in front of the fire.

"Where's the booze, mate?" Seymour asked, kicking the unconscious Aard in the ribs.

Without attempting to cover himself, Aard stood and wandered naked through the haze of smoke. He reached a small door at the end of the hall and shook the handle only to discover it was locked.

"Well, that's it then," said Fran Tick, the neighbour's daughter, sucking on the neck of an empty cognac bottle.

“Don’t be ridiculous,” Aard replied, still naked, as he climbed the stairs. He paused to glance at his Dutch friend Rawl Plugge, sprawled across his parents’ four-poster bed. He seemed to be on top of a semi-conscious Norma Snockers, but without the energy to plug her.

“Watch the antique lace bedspread,” Aard remarked, opening a cupboard.

He removed one of his father’s shotguns, loaded a single cartridge, and walked calmly back downstairs. With one blast, still naked, he blew the lock clean out of the wine cellar door.

“Shit!” Percy observed. “Now you’ve done it!”

“Give me a hand,” said Aard, setting the gun aside and dragging two cases of red wine into the hall.

It was a fine year, 1952. Bottles were opened, and Aard brought a stack of tumblers out of the glass-fronted cupboard behind the bar. He handed one to Percy, slapped him on the back, and returned to find the least painful position naked on a single sheet on his mattress. Percy covered him with a rug.

“Thank God for that,” four guests moaned in unison.

Percy returned to the snooker room, where some version of strip poker was unfolding in front of the Adam fireplace.

At around one-thirty on Monday morning, Aard’s elder brother, Butch Dijk, arrived unannounced. A disciplined merchant seaman, he froze in shock at the front door. Spotting Aard, he began shouting in Dutch. Aard glanced up, shrugged, and lay back down.

Butch charged upstairs two steps at a time and returned moments later with a .410 shotgun, which he promptly aimed at Seymour standing in the snooker-room doorway.

“No need for that, mate,” Seymour said calmly. “I should tell you - I hate guns!”

He stepped forward, grabbed the barrel, wrenched it from Butch’s hands, and smashed it against the wall. Miraculously, it didn’t fire, but a chunk of plaster fell out of the wall, and he handed the gun back to Butch.

Butch stared at him, then at the barrel, now bent like a boomerang. He dropped it and fled upstairs.

"You've done it now!" Percy muttered.

"All right, mate, calm down!" Seymour replied just as Butch reappeared brandishing a kukri, a large curved Malay jungle knife.

"Get out! All of you - get out!" he raved.

"Fuck you," Seymour replied. "It's not your party!"

Butch hurled the knife at head height. It flew like a curving wave through the air inches above Seymour's head and embedded itself in the snooker-room door. Seymour straightened, lunged forward, grabbed Butch by the shirt, and headbutted him unconscious.

He carried the body upstairs and dumped it onto the principal bed beside the naked Norma Snockers. Then he returned downstairs and poured himself another tumbler of the 1952.

Twenty minutes later, Aard stirred, walked to the kitchen and emerged wearing only a kitchen apron. He was carrying a silver tray with a full decanter of vodka and an array of shot glasses.

He poured six brimming shots, handed them to the nearest guests, chugged his back with a loud '*nostrovia*' and hurled the empty glass into the fireplace.

"Nostrovia!" he shouted again as the room echoed back

"nostrovia!"

"Nostrovia!" came the guests in turn.

"Nostrovia!"

"Nostrovia!"

"Nostrovia!"

That was six glasses gone, and Aard poured the remaining vodka into new glasses. The ritual continued until all twenty-four glasses lay shattered in the hearth. Aard drained the final drops from the decanter and threw it into the fire, followed by the stopper.

"Nostrovia!"

The party surged on. Numbers swelled when Yeung Stud - the eccentric son of Taiwan's microchip king - arrived with a gaggle of village girls and a bag of pills. His father had recently bought a sixty-room hotel on the Thames, and Yeung planned to turn it into a brothel.

“This acid is great, man!” Yeung announced, colliding with a plate-glass window and sliding to the floor.

“Ignore him!” said two of the girls together. “He’s been like this since Thursday.”

“Which Thursday?” Percy asked. “I’ve known him like this since the day we met.”

By five in the afternoon, a few guests managed to leave, with the rest asleep where they were sitting or unconscious throughout the house. Every light burned in every room, and no one had noticed the hi-fi needle stuck in one groove of *Doing the Locomotion* by Little Eva.

* * * * *

As the drugs took hold of the new arrivals in the study, the girls abandoned what little inhibition remained.

“My mother should see me now!” shrieked Dawn Chorus, inviting Abe Solution to massage hand cream over her upper body.

“Come on - it’s my turn!” Yeung interrupted, recovering enough to slice a tab with a razor blade on the desk.

“It’s beautiful!” Dawn moaned as someone else’s hands took over.

Underwear littered the study floor while Little Eva sang, " *You’ll really get to like it if you give it a chance* for the millionth time.

* * * * *

Around the house later in the day, the guests started to stir, and their first move was to raid the fridge for a fry-up. It seemed that no one planned to leave, and like an onslaught of locusts, they worked through the food in the larder and continued with the booze from the bar.

It so happened that this was the afternoon of the Brazilian Grand Prix, and whilst some were watching it on the giant Philips television and some were relaxing on the terrace, they finished every drop of alcohol in the house.

That afternoon was liberally interspaced by spliffs rolled from the mountain of material prepared with the Rizla and filters ready for smoking on the coffee table, with the noise of the FI race in the background and Bob Dylan pleading peace from some hidden futuristic speakers. Some were trying to play snooker, endangering the felt cloth with manic stabbing of the cue, while others joined the queue to telephone friends around the world.

* * * * *

Unbeknownst to anyone, the Philips Industries jet, with its chairman, Hugh Dijk, was touching down at Heathrow.

Hugh had been through one of his worst weekends with boardroom opposition to his expansionist plans. He had come back to England from Holland two days early for further discussions about European integration and was deep in thought as his car sped towards his country retreat. He planned a few days of peace to finalise a boardroom reshuffle.

The Philips chauffeur opened the front door so Mrs Dijk could step over the mat, announcing 'Welcome'. The chauffeur paused to get instructions from his boss.

At first, Mrs Dijk seemed to be frozen in the doorway. Then she screamed, with her eyeballs prancing around the devastation. She focused on the body of her younger son on the floor with the cheeks of his arse poking out of her favourite apron. She stormed over and kicked the unconscious Aard in the guts with a high-heeled shoe.

Aard Dijk remained motionless on the mattress with his mouth open as his mother then smashed her handbag into the face of the first person within reach.

Those who were capable of movement shook each other awake and headed for the exits. In most cases, this was the French windows except for Seymour, who got the idea quite quickly that everyone was leaving in a hurry. He launched himself towards the kitchen door. In his haste, he forgot it was made of toughened glass, and he knocked himself out cold.

Mrs Dijk stopped screaming for a second and then uttered an ear-splitting shriek as she noticed what used to be a George II decanter and 24 matching stipple-engraved glasses in the fireplace. These were her prized possessions, a wedding present from her Dutch cousin, Queen Julia.

Hugh Dijk had paused to give his chauffeur orders for the next day, and he couldn't understand the screaming until he came up to the door. He stooped to pick up two empty bottles of 1952 Chateau Lafite. He recognised them as part of a personal gift from the Chancellor of Oxford University to celebrate the endowment of a Philips Industries scholarship.

"You are a disappointment that is difficult to tolerate," he said sternly towards his younger son.

It was a week before the Dijk household had calmed down and decided to send Aard on his merry way. They agreed that Aard was unable to recognise the chaos he caused, and he offered to move out. He could pack his things and move to the staff flat over the garage until he had arranged where he was going and booked a flight.

"I'll pay as long as it's not Holland!" his father ordered. The truth was, Aard needed to be near the greenhouse to close shop."

"Thanks for the flat over the garage!" he said calmly as he picked up the remains of the bent .410. "I'll use the workbench to fix this."

Aard took it into the garage and sawed off the barrel so it was left with the remaining straight part of the nine-inch barrel. Then he went outside and tested it as a flame-thrower on two weeds at the side of the driveway.

"I think you should move out now and get a job in South Africa, where there is a big contingent of Dutch-speaking Boers," Percy argued as Aard blasted a large dandelion nestling against the gatepost.

"Got you, you bastard!" was all he said to the disappeared little yellow flower.

Percy offered to pay Mrs Dijk towards the damage to the house.

"And you think that makes it better?" she replied. "How do you think my husband feels about his 24 bottles of Lafite, not to mention how I might feel about my George II decanter and glasses from the Queen?"

"I can't see what else I can do."

"You think money is the answer?" Mrs Dijk groaned in despair. "We welcomed you into our home because my husband thought you might be some kind of solution for Aard. Now look at this disaster. You bring in friends with drugs, and you smash everything!"

With that, Mrs Dijk started to sob. She put down the apron which she had grabbed from her son, and her whole body was shaking on her way to the kitchen.

"I think you'd better leave," Hugh Dijk remarked.

"I'm very sorry," Percy said before he went round to the garage.

The mighty boss at Philips turned on his son.

"Aard, your mother is seriously upset," he said as if he were making a speech. "What can we do with you?"

"She'll get over it," Aard replied with an air of disinterest.

The following weekend, Percy drove to see if anything had calmed and to check on the greenhouse. He was amazed that it was still virtually untouched as a forest of six-foot-high cannabis plants, and the smell was overwhelming.

Then, unfortunately, Mrs Dijk was striding towards him.

"Yes?" she said, stopping right in his face.

Percy was definitely not welcome.

"Is Aard here?" he asked hesitantly.

"No!" Mrs Dijk almost snarled as Percy guided her round to retreat away from the greenhouse. "And look at my orchids, the whole greenhouse is full of weeds!"

"Yes!" Percy agreed. "Weeds are taking over!"

Percy spotted Aard dodging across to the garage with three big plants under his arm. Percy followed to find out the score.

"I've got myself chucked out, even of the garage!" he admitted, "but I've sold fifty plants so far at a hundred quid each! Only two thousand to go!"

After the greenhouse had been raided over the following weeks, Percy saw Aard for a beer, and he said he had made enough from the sales to go on holiday.

"I'll see you when I see you," he waved to Percy as they came out of the pub into the darkness.

Percy spotted four tennis rackets and golf clubs on the back seat of the Hillman Imp as Aard drove off.

Percy never saw Aard again, but reports surfaced about how he was a gun for hire in South Africa before he ended up in the USA, where he continued his interest in the drugs business. Aard became part of an operation bringing in shipments of cocaine from South America into Arkansas with drug drops protected by the CIA. It was the CIA that picked Bill Clintoris, the State Governor, as their distributor to fund the wars against the communists in Nicaragua. They hadn't factored in that Bill was a prolific sex maniac, but Hilary Clintoris came to their rescue by tracking the girls. They fell off balconies, they drowned in bathtubs, and they walked in front of speeding cars. Conveniently, Bill enlisted the coroner, Fahmy Malik, to adjust the causes of death. His favourites were 'choking on a chicken bone' instead of strangulation and 'tripping' off a bridge onto a train track. Bill Clintoris showed he was above the law by having his brother, Roger Clintoris, found guilty of drug trafficking. Aard's body was never found, and Percy was scared to even speak about his information.

"He was completely out of control" was the judgment of his friends. "He crossed the line and never made it back!"

"And we were no different?" cried Rosa Villas.

Crazy or not, Percy missed his longstanding friend because he was never in judgment.

Then a letter arrived stamped in Little Rock, the State Capitol of Arkansas:

'I never knew love in my life. My parents were too important to have any time for me. Neither my father nor my mother ever took me to the park or to see a film or anywhere else, for that matter. My life was

meaningless, and I couldn't get through it without the booze and the drugs.

So when death finds me, it will find nothing to take, only a body that once pretended to live. My soul rotted long ago, eaten away by my own despair. My time is close by, and when it comes, death will pity me in that final moment. There will be no cry – just the cruel truth that I had already been dead while life demanded I breathe.'

* * * * *

When Percy returned to the office to announce the sad news of the death of Aard Dijk and the marijuana project, he had never been so pleased to see the familiar faces. It was a revelation in the context of his team working together. He gave them details of a memorial service he had arranged to be held at St Luke's in Sydney Street in Chelsea - a huge cathedral of a building for those who wanted to pay their respects.

Percy was waiting for the printers to finalise the photographs of Aard Dijk in his few minutes of happiness, always making faces at the camera. There was a choice of appropriate hymns, readings and two tributes. One was to be from Butch, Aard's brother, and the other from Percy. Butch had arranged a trumpeter to sound his farewell at the end of the service.

The Dijk parents were not interested in attending, but Golden Life made up for it with their own brand of respect, and Percy read his own message to his friend:

> *'Not every battle matters. If you argue or push back against every single thing that bothers you, then you'll lose the strength to win what actually matters. Not everything in life deserves a fight; some things are not yours to fix. Now we have learned that lesson from you, so go now, troubled Aard, and find your peace.'*

As the trumpet sounded from the steps at the end of the service, there were six red Ferraris in a row outside St Luke's courtyard with Aard's Hillman Imp in the middle.

Norma Snockers gripped Percy's arm, sobbing.

"I'm a mess!" she whimpered.

"Don't worry", Percy answered, holding back his own tears. "I'll fix that situation later this evening!"

"They look good even in black!" Roland smiled.

Percy pushed some money into the hand of the gardener who had tended the crop and brought Aard's car up to London.

"Don't worry, I managed to sell a few plants when Mrs Dijk told me to clear the weeds", he said softly, pocketing the money. "I took a few plants back home, and my wife showed signs of life after twenty years. She even started coffee mornings for the ladies in our village!"

After the Hillman Imp drove away, the seven Ferraris drove in convoy to the private room at Mortons. On the way, they all accelerated one after the other down Curzon Street past the police guarding the new Saudi Embassy. The glorious sound of seven V12 engines accelerating reverberated and then echoed between the high granite walls on either side. It was a fitting end to the life of a friend lost in anguish.

* * * * *

One of the joys of being part of the team was impressed on them that day, but there was no lessening in a desire to show off – in fact, there was an enhanced sense of invincibility.

The Ferraris still accelerated off the ramp out of the office garage in a haze of burning rubber back onto the public road at the end of the working day. You weren't trying very hard unless you reached 80 mph up to Mansion House. There was just enough distance for the V12 to reach the incomparable screaming point.

Manley Deeds was an uncompromising achiever. He had three Ferraris of his own, and nothing was as sweet to him as flooring his very special F40.

The keen young policeman in the Panda turned on his blue flashing light as the F40 screamed past him, doing 130 mph along the sometimes clear part of The Mall. Manley was obliged to pull up with a tyre-screeching halt at the traffic lights. The policeman arrived a full half minute later and didn't say a word as Manley slowly levered himself out of the car.

"The joy of this particular model is that it sounds like you're doing 130 mph when you're actually doing 30 mph," Manley started.

"Don't worry, sir," the officer replied. "Just open the bonnet as I have always wanted to have a look at the V12 engine!"

"In that case, I'll open the boot!" Manly corrected him. "I think they made that change a while ago!"

Manley Deeds was famous for talking his way out of a multitude of traffic violations with every policeman in London. Even on the route to his house along the M3, he knew so many police that on occasion they waved a greeting as if he had police protection! Even when he was caught drink-driving, he somehow avoided prosecution.

"Why else have a car like this?" he would smirk.

Manley was with his mate Sheridan Bureau, a manager over at Shabby Life Assurance, when they were zooming through the Surrey countryside to reach the Four Horseshoes for another pint before closing on a Saturday afternoon.

"Let's see what a Ferrari can do on country roads," Manley suggested as Sheridan rolled the last of the Thai grass into a Rizla paper.

With hedgerows on either side, Manley floored the F40 down the straight lane before the humpback bridge over the stream, before the Four Horseshoes. He must have been doing 150 mph.

By chance, on the other side of the bridge, the police had set up a speed radar trap, and they had pounced on the village butcher who had been doing 33 mph in his delivery van. The butcher was protesting his innocence as the Ferrari hit the front slope of the bridge and took off with a tar-meets-metallic grinding crash. It flew past the police four feet in the air like a jet aircraft.

It took Manley 500 yards to stop and miraculously not crash into either hedgerow as he skilfully landed, slid, ploughed up the roadside grass, straightened and braked to a stop.

Sheridan was white and one level below being terrified.

If Manley could have escaped, he would have driven across a field in the four minutes it took the police to arrive.

"We heard you coming from two miles away," the officer claimed, breathless with his nose running as the smell of the Thai grass wafted out of the window. "But you went right over the radar!"

"Over the radar, did you say?" smirked Manley. "We're all right then!"

A starry-eyed Manley spun the car round and roared off, throwing up mud until he disappeared sideways round the next corner.

"I need that drink," a pallid Sheridan frowned as Manley pulled up at the pub.

"I think I hit a pipe," Manley replied, looking at a stream of liquid pouring onto the ground.

"You've also bent the wing when you went too close to the hedge, and it's going to need a respray", Sheridan remarked as he looked at the scratches down the side.

* * * * *

Manley had a younger brother, Garish Deeds, known as Gary.

"Don't mention that I said so," Manley advised his little brother in a rare moment of sanity. "If you come into this finance business, you should buy yourself a house before you get a Ferrari."

Gary Deeds joined Golden Life a week after he left school, and exactly three months later, he bought a house and furnished it. Admittedly, the contents amounted initially to a fridge, a deck chair, a sofa and a stereo, but he went on to buy a Ferrari. The month after that, he drove it to watch the Monaco Grand Prix.

It didn't occur to Gary to book a hotel room. It was as if the Ferrari was a key to open any door because there were no limits to what he could achieve. An indication of what Golden Life was doing to him was evidenced by his going into Harrods and buying a custom-made tee shirt and having it printed in six-inch capitals FUCK OFF.

The alarm bells were ringing, and Gary was told that his attitude would cause him self-destruction.

'Just because you're a big earner doesn't mean you are a better person!' was Percy's message. "Don't let me ever see you wearing that shirt, and if you wear it in Monaco, I know you will lose the freedom to wear it at all!"

After hammering down the N7 and getting the finger from English and French onlookers in their Ford Cortinas and Volkswagen convertibles, Gary slept in the car in Monte Carlo on the eve of the race. He woke up to a tapping on the window.

"Allez! Allez!" shouted the gendarme through the glass and tipping his hat in that Monaco way. "You are on the racetrack, monsieur."

Gary moved the Ferrari forty feet forward but was then trapped inside metal barriers opposite the massive Olympic pool complex – the Rainier Water Sports Stadium. The gendarmerie was about to have the busiest World View Day in the Monaco calendar, and Gary was trapped with no possibility of the gendarmes letting him go anywhere except off the track. That was only possible on the quayside next to the most expensive yachts on the planet.

Gary had no option. He turned to the left and parked, waiting for guidance from some official. He waited some more and got out of the car, only to fully appreciate that the whole of Monaco was heaving with a million visitors. He looked up and around and was aware that he alone was parked behind nine superyachts in the prime viewing position next to the track. These visitors had shelled out a minimum of $100 million for the pleasure of showing off their extraordinary wealth. Most of their guests were similarly endowed from inherited money or receiving monster salaries for their good looks or screen presence.

Gary walked along, soaking up clutches of ladies dressed to kill for the superlative party weekend. Gary paused to admire two girls on the gangplank and another three on the after-deck of the eighty metre '*No*

Apologetics' designed by Pietro Gutsi. One of the girls shouted down, 'You're late! We were expecting you last night!'

Gary found himself on board with all the chrome and glass and neatly dressed stewardesses offering him the finest champagne. He blagged himself into conversation without revealing that he was 24 hours away from wearing a shirt that told them where to go!

Gary found out only that the owner had invited his son-in-law and his best mate from Harvard to join them for the race, and his name wasn't Gary. It was Harry, so with the son-in-law being a no-show, Gary answered as Harry for the next 48 hours. He was therefore not only blessed with a view of the race which no money could buy but with a cabin of his own and a bird that cost someone else 5,000 francs and the comment 'be happy and enjoy a last throw of the dice!'

* * * * *

The number of verbal and written complaints about the various exploits of Percy's sales force had escalated over the year. They all landed on one desk only - Jess Lapsed, the Golden Life sales supremo. Percy had to report to Jess so as to avoid the guaranteed disaster of any direct enquiry by any regulators.

"Percy, what's this nonsense about Mal Function?" Jess complained. "Countess Mona Lott, the human rights activist. She's written that Mal had attended her daughter's birthday dinner party uninvited."

The complaint simply said, 'Somehow your man Mal sat down at our table in the private dining room at the Savoy, and I tried to find out who he was.'

Mal had been subjected to an inquisition by the Countess at the table.

'Malcolm, do you play tennis?' she asked.

'No, I'm afraid not, Countess. I never took it up.'

'Well, Malcolm, do you play golf?' she continued poignantly.

'Sorry, I don't, Countess.'

'Malcolm, did you go to University?'

'No, Countess, I didn't.'

'Do you sail?'

'Unfortunately, not, Countess. I'm not keen on water sports.'

Afterwards, over coffee, Mal had moved seats next to her daughter and stuck his hand in her lap. The countess launched into him again.

'Malcolm,' she said sternly. 'Do you shoot?'

'No, Countess, I'm not into killing …. yet!'

'I suppose that means you don't fish?'

'Correct, Countess!'

'But Malcolm, you must at least ride?'

'I'm planning a decent canter this evening, Countess!' he replied, looking straight at the birthday girl.

All other conversations had stopped by this time, and the guests were listening intently to the exchange.

'Malcolm, you will leave my table!' she blurted out.

'But this table belongs to the Savoy, Countess!' Mal argued.

The intimidating Countess Mona Lott was married to the vice chairman of the Bank of England, and she had written to Golden Life. She had entreated Jess Lapsed to consider seriously whether these were the kind of manners which should be entertained in a responsible financial organisation.

"She's got so many carrots up her arse that she doesn't know which one to pull out first!" said Mal in his defence.

Percy translated.

"Malcolm has apologised and says it will never happen again," Percy reported to Jess.

A week later, Percy was with Lou Natic at a private reception at the St. James Club hosted by Max Dosage, heir to the giant DOS Pharmaceuticals headquartered in Milan. It was more than noticeable that the food consisted of a few slices of quiche and only one sausage roll between every five guests.

"In future, please be able to afford the party before you give it," suggested Lou to Max Dosage as another guest snatched a slice of quiche and a gherkin off his plate.

And still, the sons and daughters of prominent politicians and businessmen invited them to their homes.

The Rt Hon. Paul Bearer, Minister of Education, lost his young daughter to a drug overdose. His wife had been unable to contain her grief, and Paul thought a party would be appropriate to get his other children back to normal. They invited fifty young business people, most of whom he had never met, to his London home. Percy's school friend, Miles Long, was a guest after being appointed chief executive at Banque Longchamps in Switzerland. Miles had also become the 20% shareholder, and he suggested that Percy go and celebrate with him.

As usual, Jamie Wriggle invited himself because he heard that Lady Helen Melons would be there. Helen was his pin-up and as near royalty as he would ever get without pole-vaulting into Buckingham Palace.

Wriggle was a noble family of sheep farmers who lived surrounded by private meadows in the Isle of Man, and Jamie was as dark a sheep as ever got accepted into any flock.

"A large scotch and soda, thanks," Jamie instructed the Bearer butler as he entered through a huge black door.

The man was the hired security, and he explained that the reception was upstairs, followed by a buffet lunch in the dining room.

There was no shortage of drinks available and no lack of illegal substances going around the guests. There were queues of couples waiting outside the three bathrooms.

"Have the civility not to do it in front of the grieving host," muttered Lisa Wake as she sold Jamie a one-gram packet of cocaine.

Paul Bearer was talking not yards away about the former prime minister.

"The rarest thing in British politics is an unsigned copy of Edward Sheath's autobiography," he jested.

Any casual observer would have confirmed that the desired effect of the party had been achieved. Everyone except the parents had forgotten the tragedy.

The butler called for silence for the Minister to address the guests.

"We all know why we are here today," he started.

"Any excuse for a party!" Jamie answered.

The speeches avoided mentioning the deceased's boyfriend, who had supplied the fatal overdose. The family had no idea that their seventeen-year-old 'gorgeous girl', who was supposed to be studying at university, had been introduced to drugs. They accepted she was 'out of their sight' but never thought she could be 'out of her mind.'

The fact was that they were too busy to notice.

After the buffet had been demolished, Miles found Percy among the rowdier group.

"Your friend Jamie Wriggle is making a bit of a spectacle of himself," he whispered.

Miles pushed Percy through the guests to where Jamie was standing, his pupils fully dilated, with his hand in a large bowl of salad. That was not all he was holding. Swaying backwards and forwards, he had his fly open with his manhood held upright in his other hand. Jamie was picking out the onion rings from the lettuce and tomatoes and hula-hooping them onto his dick. The guests closest to Jamie were chanting, 'four, five, six' in unison.

"Situation normal," Percy confirmed as he checked that the Minister was nowhere close.

"Why are his eyes so wide and watering?" asked Zizi Zani, daughter of the Greek Ambassador in Zimbabwe.

"It's the onions!" Percy suggested as he guided her away from the spectacle.

Percy followed her upstairs and grabbed the moment to ask her for dinner later that week.

"Any time you are passing over central Africa, you have an open invitation to drop in," she invited. "As for dinner here, I'm busy!"

"You've got no chance!" sneered Miles as he reappeared out of the cloakroom. "An affair needs two people to participate!"

"What do you call an affair with only one person involved?" asked Percy.

"That's called a shag!" Miles confirmed.

* * * * *

The weekend parties held by the Golden Life salesmen became increasingly outrageous as escorts infiltrated the guest list.

"Why do you think they prefer to perform with each other rather than with us?" Lou asked.

"That should be obvious, even to you!" answered Percy, looking at his state of alcoholic paralysis.

The fact was that the girls did whatever was required of them for money and occasional jewellery, and that prompted continuing invitations both at home and abroad.

Jess Lapsed revelled in the financial success that had been thrust upon him as overlord at Golden Life. It was through that success that he ran out of things to buy, and it was a natural sequence that he decided to get rid of his boring and no-longer-sexually-arousing wife.

It didn't occur to him that he was monosyllabic and had no conversation except for how his golf swing was the problem. It was at his golf club that he met Urina Trapp from Ukraine, working as a masseuse in the men's locker room. In the beginning, he was face-up naked with a towel over his business as Urina focused on relaxing his muscles. The change was when Urina started brushing her naturally full and pert tits gently back and forth across his chest. It would have been better if she bothered to wear a bra or had done up the buttons on her blouse.

"Don't you think you should wear hospital scrubs?" Jess suggested that he lost control.

"We are trained not to wear these things in Kiev", she answered, adding a little weight to speed the inevitable result.

The club secretary heard an unusual noise in the massage room and didn't need to open the men's locker room door. Urina had screamed as Jess was finishing her off. He remembered that kind of scream from his own wife on the first night of their honeymoon thirty years before.

The golf club secretary had the good grace to wait for her to leave that evening before telling her she was fired. He later often wished in his bed at night that he had banged her himself and allowed her to stay.

"In leaving, Urina jumped out of the shadows and started bashing on Jess's car door.

"You 'ave got me the sack!" she screamed with a slight Ukrainian accent. "You 'ave to take me 'ome as I have no money!'

When Jess returned to his own home at 2:00 a.m. and looked at his wife in a wool jumper, snoring with her mouth and legs open, it was enough to push him into a divorce. The thought of a new life with Urina was compelling. He decided to make it easy by giving up the marital home, both cars and his £260,000 savings.

The boys were impressed with Urina.

"They're larger than Norma Snockers!" was the frequent comment of the Golden Life elite. "Jess doesn't deserve those, especially on a plate!" Mal insisted as the spokesman whenever Urina was spotted.

Jess Lapsed made the serious mistake of taking Urina to Seymour Clearly's 30th birthday party out of London on the river by Windsor. The mistake became fatal when Jess left to get some petrol before the garage closed.

"The needle is in the red zone!" he observed.

"That's not all that's going into the red zone!" Seymour spluttered as Jess went out the door.

In those vital forty-five minutes for Jess to find a garage open, Urina unveiled her secret habit of drinking. She got paralytic and staggered backwards against the wall for support.

"What do you think you're doing?" she managed faintly as a drunk and stoned Seymore moved her back against the snooker table.

"That's a nice ring," Seymour complimented her on the three-carat engagement ring while he undid her blouse.

To a roar of encouragement, Seymour pushed his face in between her bare breasts and pulled up her skirt.

"For Christ's sake, Seymour!" Mal shouted as she leaned back.

"I'm just potting the pink, mate!" Seymour replied.

Seymour looked at all his mates as if he had won the lottery.

"Seymour, you animal," Manley observed as he finished the last of the Eton Mess trifle from the buffet. "Don't you know who that is?"

"Great dessert, mate," Seymour replied.

* * * * *

This little episode occurred at the start of the longest obscenity trial in English history. The issue at stake was a 16th-century legal precedent about 'arousing and implanting in people's minds lustful and perverted desires.'

"The court has to separate promiscuity from sexual abuse", Miles noted for the benefit of his closest friends. "This trial will decide what sex is with and without consent."

"I definitely saw Urina nod her head!" confirmed Seymour.

"How come?" asked two voices.

"Because I examined her nod!" Seymour concluded.

The Old Bailey referred to the law of precedent to decide which sex acts constituted a crime. That got the attention of every English mind interested in the progress of their relationships, and the whole of Golden Life concluded that Seymour had raped the sales director's fiancée.

The Sunday Sport featured the trial appropriately in a centre spread:

'*This trial is evidence of a deliberate attempt by the Establishment to quell a counter-culture of open expression, not to mention the revolution against authority.*'

"I told you so!" Seymour insisted. "The judges are more interested in headmasters masturbating whilst beating schoolboys. Everyone knows the whole government is at it on their visits to Wales, not to mention the priesthood buggering the choirboys of Greater London on Sundays in the crypt!"

"All the while the Home Office has declined to disclose what happens in the schools of correction and even the hospitals up North," Dinah complained. "Sir Pure Scammer, head of the Crown Prosecution Service, has got over 200 complaints of child rape against his friend Jimmy Salivate and thrown them into the waste paper basket!"

"Anyway, Urina enjoyed it!" Seymour concluded, "And who's complaining?"

Then the trial of the publication 'Oz' set out to amend the Jurors Act of 1972, which legislated that jurors had to be property owners. This excluded mostly women, cohabiting gays and people living on the streets. The jury hearing the Oz evidence was, therefore, obliged to support the Establishment intent on shoring up its own barricades.

Marty Feldman, as a defence witness, insisted that the judge was a 'boring old fart' as he instructed the jury to uphold this requirement.

The public outcry caused an immediate appeal, which vindicated the three defendants. However, the cat was well and truly out of the bag, and it translated into an entire generation thinking jumping into anyone's knickers was now acceptable in public and even in mass gatherings in fields with music. This was not something to be confined to a Friday with the missus after work."

"You see!" confirmed Seymour. "Urina now can serve on a jury, happy that leaning backwards with her blouse open and her frock hitched up is consent!"

The Establishment's take was absurd. They contrived expressions that indicated they had won the case and shored up their right to rule. They cited the Industrial Revolution, empire-building and two world wars. They referred to the institutions of the land, the Royal Family, the Church of England, Parliament, the Civil Service, the judiciary and the police.

'We must stand shoulder to shoulder to protect the mysticism and authority of a hereditary political class', wrote Ewan Cry, the parliamentary journalist.

There was a refusal to look into the face of a popular vision of the future. Any modernisation of the old-style system of privilege without accountability had the enduring motto 'Born to serve'. The regulatory procedures would continue to be run vertically from Whitehall. There would be no cultural revolution!

Retrenchment after that trial prompted a backlash in the world of sudden wealth. Moreover, the insurance industry was too important to have salesmen in any position of control, perceived or otherwise. That was when the directors of Golden Life got scared. They were rich by accident, and the writing on the wall had taken them by surprise.

Sir Davy Lamp, chairman of Golden Life, saw the light and realised his big ticket would be if he could sell his shares.

Discretion was not part of Sir Davy Lamp's mindset, and the word got out that the greatest sales machine in insurance history was up for grabs.

"The dividend has doubled every year, and it's time to move on," summarised Jess Lapsed, confident that he would fill his own coffers from the share option scheme.

Jess needed to keep the machine running over the period of the negotiations so the potential buyer would see the sales force in action and evidence a continuity of sales.

Other than the directors, Percy, Mal and Roland were the only Golden Life people to attend Jess's wedding to Urina Trapp. They were glad they went as Urina's friends were all gagging for it at the reception.

It was a mistake for Jess to address the sales force in their own office because he was seen to be the architect of a betrayal.

"I'll make it my business to see you are all treated fairly!" he opened.

"We've got nothing to say to you," was all Percy could muster.

"I have something to say!" Seymour piped up. "Your wife's a lousy fuck!"

* * * * *

Behaving badly was an instinct that was part of the sales pressure at Golden Life. The lifestyle attracted a mix of dreamers and maniacs who saw huge earnings and guessed that they deserved whatever they could get out of life. Percy wanted to believe that his team was at the highest level of sales ability. He was also mindful that the enthusiasm to sell sometimes crossed the border into exaggeration and even lies. It was sometimes necessary when there was an objection that could not readily be put to bed, although it was a criminal offence.

Percy was contacted almost on a daily basis by people wanting to join from other insurance companies. He liked to think he designed his Wealth Plan to be a leader because of the attractive terms rather than his people beating the applicants into submission.

Percy consistently refused to let anyone else do the interviews, and he rejected most applicants for good reason. Those who got a second interview proved that caution was the best way ahead. Some were brilliant in sales but clearly dangerous, and the majority were useless in sales of financial products because they focused solely on the money, not on a career.

Then along came an Italian radio presenter speaking four languages with a massive following and an ego as big. He knew he wanted this job of commission selling, and no one could dissuade him.

Percy gave Sheridan Cox a second interview at the St James Club in the billiard room. Before they had even broken the ice, Sheridan picked up a cue and positioned two balls. He then took a shot, and both balls ended up in pockets on opposite sides of the table.

"So you play games?" asked Percy.

"Hire me, and I'll show you a game!" he said very seriously as a young waitress appeared and asked if they needed anything. She was about 24, and Percy guessed Sheridan was probably 28. He asked for a large Glenmorangie Signet Highland Single Malt Scotch with one cube of ice.

"I'll have the same", Percy said instinctively, not knowing what his next move would be.

Sheridan then started on his history – one huge mix of family disasters and personal achievements. Percy had difficulty in believing any of it, but there was something compelling about his assuredness - an ingredient that made sales automatically.

Percy was mesmerised, and after an hour, he agreed to take Sheridan Cox into his training program, but he would have to agree to an end-of-day summary for the first two weeks.

Percy drank his Glenmorangie, and it was so special that he signed without looking and walked out. He was a 5-minute walk away in the rain, looking for a taxi, when he realised he had left his diary behind, so he returned to the billiard room. He didn't knock and opened the door, and there was Sheridan with his trousers down by his ankles shagging the waitress against the billiard table.

"Please excuse me", Percy said calmly to the waitress as he retrieved his book and walked out.

"Amazing game of billiards going on!" Percy said to the doorman as he was in shock that Sheridan didn't miss a stroke.

At 9:00 a.m., Sheridan appeared immaculately dressed for his first day at work, and it was like a duck to water.

Percy invited Sheridan to join him after work every few days for an assessment, and Sheridan was introduced to whoever Percy was with during that time. There was nothing to suggest that this man was a lunatic until early on a Friday evening, when Percy had a phone call.

"I've got your girlfriend Olive Pipp here tied to a chair," Sheridan said calmly and without any hint of threat.

"I've often thought about doing that myself when she can't stop talking", Percy answered.

"I'm going to ruin her for you!" Sheridan smirked, so Percy knew it was serious. "And you'd better come here so you'll know what I want!"

"Can you untie her, and I'll come over if you tell me where you are?" asked Percy.

Then there was a scream.

"Get me out of here!"

"Come to Marble Arch right now, or I'm going to fuck her up!" Sheridan replied in a completely different tone.

The phone went dead.

Percy didn't call the police because he had no idea where they were, but he made it from Southwark Bridge, down the Embankment, to outside the cinema opposite the Marble Arch memorial in ten minutes. His car was screaming in and out between every other vehicle, and when he arrived, there they were standing like two tourists without speaking, except Olive's hands were tied with a length of nylon rope.

"Get out, I'm driving!" Sheridan ordered as he pushed the terrified Alla towards the car.

"I'm coming with you!" Percy said as bravely as he could as he noticed a knife in Sheridan's right hand.

Percy had the car key, and he walked around to the passenger side looking to see if there was any help at hand. No one was taking any notice, and he thought it better not to shout as Sheridan was clearly a maniac. He was standing behind Percy with the knife while Percy was getting into the passenger side with Olive.

Percy held the car key in the air and pushed himself next to Alla.

"Thank God you're a small Pipp!" he muttered as he squashed in and Sheridan slammed the door.

Sheridan got in the other side.

"We can't keep meeting like this, Sheridan, you fucking idiot!" Percy shouted as he handed over the key. "What do you want?"

Sheridan knew how to drive. Without saying anything, he floored the accelerator, and suddenly they were doing over 100 mph up Park Lane, changing lanes. Then Sheridan spun the steering wheel and accelerated and did a 360-degree skid in the middle of the road outside Grosvenor House. Without stopping, he accelerated towards the Hilton and then turned sharply left and skidded with screaming tyres into Curzon Street. In that moment, Percy thought they were dead. Olive was screaming in his ear as the car miraculously stopped facing the right way. Sheridan got out and ran down Curzon Street.

Percy then opened the door and took a breath, with Olive shaking like a leaf in a storm.

"And don't bother to come to work again, arsehole!" Percy shouted.

Hugo Away, the doorman at Aspinall's casino, looked up from outside the famous green door.

"Thank you, Mr Vere!" he shouted back.

"Why did Sheridan kidnap you?" Percy asked Olive as he undid the knots in the rope around her wrists. "What have you been doing?"

"I can't stay by myself tonight!" Olive pleaded.

"Suits me!" Percy replied as he turned to head off to the safety of his house in the country.

Percy was confused and looking for any explanation, but Olive was too scared to talk.

"I can't stop shaking!" she juddered.

"Then it's best if you go on top!" Percy concluded.

Sheridan didn't know where his house was, and Olive Pipp never told Percy what had happened or why.

Percy saw later that Sheridan Cox went on to establish a name for himself in Malaysia. He appeared in various local newspapers and on business television programs in share dealing. He seemed to be in bed with various officials and celebrities all over Southeast Asia.

Then a call from Olive confirmed that Sheridan had accumulated arrest warrants for a total of $1 billion fraud, variously in Belgium, Taiwan, Spain and Australia. He was traced travelling on one of seven passports, landing in his own jet in Taiwan, where he was convicted on 57 counts of fraud and imprisoned for twenty years. Despite being asked politely by his fellow convicts to tell where he had hidden all the money, none was ever found, and he died from injuries sustained in solitary confinement.

* * * * *

Then drama struck in London with a price drop in the client funds at Golden Life. There was no announcement, but it was easy to calculate that £1 million was missing from the fall in the unit price as recorded in the Saturday Financial Times.

Percy forced Jess to admit that £1 million of client money had been 'lost' by the investment director. This loss was inexplicably in a surging bull market, with the FTSE index of major shares soaring from 170 to 490. The investors were taking the hit.

The directors of Golden Life were not taking calls and were wrong to think business would carry on as if nothing had happened. In fact, nothing did happen - there was no enquiry, no scream.

"Why has the value of my investment gone down in a rising market?" came thousands of cries.

A directive came down from the board – *'the process of pound-cost-averaging is a bonus for savers who invest on a monthly basis. They get more units for their money when the price drops, so it's fantastic in the long term.'*

"Technically, that's true!" Percy concluded at a hastily convened advanced monthly meeting. "The reason the units are cheap at the moment doesn't matter!"

The day-to-day work plan of each salesman was originally structured in Canada around setting goals, believing in yourself and working hard. Percy followed that belief because, without that discipline in commission sales, even super-salesmen would spin off course.

'Today is yesterday's tomorrow within your grasp' would keep everyone on track in a team effort. Weaker colleagues would be incentivised and get a collective helping hand.

Then the deadly call came during the meeting.

"It's a double-whammy, boys", Percy announced as he put down the phone from Jess Lapsed. "The girls in the street stop as of today! It's in the public eye, and apparently, we're putting the company at risk! No more girls at the Tube stations!"

"Don't be ridiculous!" went up the universal cry.

"It's a statement, not a question!" Percy repeated. "We'll have to think up another way to bring in new clients."

After a silence, Percy was forced to admit this was not acceptable in the best investment climate for thirty years, plus the historic success with the in-house system.

"The company is not saying anything!" Percy admitted.

"They've stolen the savings of tens of thousands of investors!" Roland screamed.

"Well fuck them!" piped up Mal.

"Yeah, fuck them!" added Seymour.

"The board hate our guts!" Percy reacted. "Jess is covering the theft by blaming the publicity about the girls!"

"There were no complaints!" came ten voices together.

"We can get away with raping his wife, but Jess will blame us however he can to divert any possible attack on the company!" Lou Natic concluded. "The public standing of this company is far more important than a £1 million loss, and they'll bury it!"

"If any of you think you can keep your girls in secret, forget it," Percy emphasised. "Crimes in financial services are a death sentence, and this is our warning shot!"

"But all we do is sell their policies," remarked Yul Dye. "All the money goes into the company."

"We're attracting attention", Percy answered. "We're not a mainstream insurance company, and the directors can't afford a fallout in their own industry. We are going to get calls for the return of client money, and when the company refuses, it only takes one investor to go to a journalist. Then they'll fall back on the pound-cost-averaging answer and get away with it!"

"The journalist will have his four inches and call it mis-selling, and we'll get the blame!" came a voice.

"I'll give him nine inches!" Seymour blurted out.

"One way or another, we're going to get screwed", Percy concluded.

"So we've been feeding corruption in the City", Manley shouted. "We've done nothing wrong except sell their products. If they're no good, why does the industry offer them in the first place?"

"It's Golden Life who've taken the money," Yul insisted. "I heard that a director sold an office block he owned personally into the client fund at a vastly inflated price, so they're all at it. I'm not going to take the rap for doing what they train us to do. Fuck them!"

* * * * *

Roland Rock stood up and flicked the tails of his morning coat.

"It's clear that the directors of Golden Life are going to get complaints," he pronounced carefully. "This grief by our clients is about the charges and the falling value of the investments in a bull market. We know the investment manager churns buying and selling shares, and he gets a back-hander from the stockbroker's commission on a daily basis."

"Not to mention stockbrokers dumping shares into the insurance funds when they can't sell them anywhere else", added Yul. The regulators say nothing, but they know!"

"There's no point in staying here without my Joy Stick!" decided Roland, "and I'm not doing door to door in the evenings, so it's all over, and we lost!"

Roland flicked his tails back again before he sat down when Percy's phone rang. It was Norma Snockers.

"I know you're in the meeting, but you need to listen", she insisted. "I'm having a glass of vodka with Urina, you know, Jess's wife. "She just told me that Jess just came into £2.7 million from Golden Life share sales."

"He only has a few shares, so that's impossible", Percy confirmed.

"They've all exercised their options and got bucket loads of shares and sold them all!" she explained. "The share price is at an all-time high, and they've pocketed a million each."

Percy realised that it was inevitable because of their method of forward accounting – the embedded value.

"They're making a fortune and no one knows," drawled Hardy Breed in his seventh month of sales, last seen with £8,000 in a month. "The directors must know we'll bugger off without the girls and they'll be left with one per cent of fuck all!"

"Very eloquent, but you're missing the point", Yul responded. "The point is that Golden Life has 200,000 policyholders and under embedded value, there's £120 million coming in over the next 30 years. The directors know they're at a crossroads and their best way forward is to sell the company. It doesn't matter if they sell it or not. They'll make the rumour to keep the share price up while we bugger off!"

"They'll protect what they see as the fruit of their careers, mate," added Seymour.

"Why don't we expose them for what they are?" asked Mal.

"We're never going to win anything by taking on the company," reasoned Yul. "They'll deny knowledge of any manipulation of the client's money and say that fund values fluctuate. It's in the literature, and it's a legitimate disclaimer, and how do we prove the loss? They'll have it covered, or they would have kept it secret."

"It's a fucking miracle our clients have any money left", concluded Roland.

"What makes you think any client is getting any of their money back?" asked Hardy.

After a general outpouring of annoyance at their situation, Percy suggested they should wait a week to see how the management handled a situation if they kept the girls working. It was brinkmanship, and the directors would probably point to the new laws of '*soliciting for business'*.

"One thing's for sure," Percy summarised. "We're on our own."

The Golden Life salesmen who were connected in high places knew they had no rights in a case against the company and, if the process of retribution and point scoring started, every one of their sales team would be implicated. Worst of all was that their personal reputation and standing would be no defence, and that would kill any chance of a new job. The insurance industry would consign them all off for slaughter.

In that week of waiting, it was clear that the company was being groomed for sale. To maximise value, the practice of 'embedded value' took centre stage. Not one salesman could fathom how a business could be valued on the expectation of all monthly and annual premiums being paid for life or, at worst, to the age of 65.

'Embedded value' was already adopted by the merchant banks, a secondary level of banking championed by the likes of Keyser Ullman, Samuel Montague and British and Common Cents Bank, with a new attitude in risk taking.

The horror of 'embedded value' came to the attention of the public when British and Common Cents Bank acquired Atlantic Computers for £500 million. There was not one cent of profit since the Atlantic launch a decade before.

John Gunn, an entrepreneur described by *Private Eye* readers as a 'risky fuck', took control of Common Cents with the blessing of Keyser Ullman and Samuel Montague. Gunn promoted Atlantic on the basis of profits forecast on long leases of computer systems, with customers having the right to upgrade at any time. Every pub and club in England fitted itself up to broadcast live sport, and there was an avalanche of buying the Atlantic leases. They all had the right to upgrade the kit.

Atlantic were therefore guaranteed to be left with £ millions in scrap.

The trio of British and Common Cents and Keyser Ullman and Samuel Montague collapsed variously under the weight of lawsuits.

Case Closed, the partner at the accountants Spicer and Oppenheim, was responsible for the financial forecasts. Case Closed blamed the wet attitude of Terry Towel at Wrathchild for avoiding any part of the responsibility in clearing up the mess. It was Terry Towel who first recommended the Atlantic deal, and Case Closed was furious that Wrathchild refused to return the £ multi million fee for the introduction, leaving Case Closed in the dock for fraud and theft.

"Sons of bitches from the beginning," Case scorned in his defence. "Wrathchild started in business with the inside information of the result of the Battle of Waterloo. After their pigeon had arrived with the message of victory, they announced to the Stock Exchange that the British forces had been routed and Napoleon was on his way to London. Panic selling collapsed the market, and Wrathchild stepped in the next morning to buy up everything for pennies. After victory was known two days later, their £25 million outlay had become £4 billion.

Incredibly, it seemed that greed ruled the roost. Kiel Dover, the boss at Sound Alarm, valued his electronics business at an alarming total of all lease payments for 25 years, and that number was promoted by City stockbroker Lino Fire at Target Resources. The value of the business soared before it became valued for what it was, a pile of old wire.

'*Embedded value*' lived a charmed life, although it disguised a fraudulent intent.

This was the opportunity that prompted Mark Night-Hood to start the highly successful insurance and investment group Shabby Life. At

Shabby, policyholders who understood nothing paid for new offices, airfares, designer furnishings and entertainment. Shareholders saw insurance company share prices soar on the assumption that policyholders were blind. The fact was that they were blinded because the entire insurance industry would collapse if the truth came out. That truth was that the average life of a savings plan was seven years, and that was equal to the amount of the hidden fees.

Mark Night-Hood sold his shares and embedded £8 million in his bank account before starting the whole exercise again as the founder of Hambro Life. Then Mark was knighted by Her Majesty, although he had never been interested in benefits to anyone except himself.

"Are you aware that the founding fathers of insurance pledged to create '*a Society for equitable assurances upon lives for the benefit of the persons insured.*'" Asked Yul Dye. "Now the industry has become a £400 billion skimming machine, and Mark led the game.

* * * * *

At the same time, while trying to think of an alternative to the market survey technique of getting clients, Percy tried without success to keep his sales force together. It was useless to reinvent the reasons he had first identified to build the team.

"It's important that we remember what we're supposed to be doing and that we sell the value of insurance protection," Percy had always insisted. "We've all had clients die, and without the insurance we've sold them, the families would have nothing. Sure, some people have difficulty paying the premiums, and we give them a hard time. That's a legitimate part of our job. The widows may lose the breadwinner, but they can keep their home, and their kids can stay in school. Without us, they could be on the streets."

Percy often bulled himself up by looking at the 23 death certificates of his clients displayed on the wall of his office over the nine years he had been in the business. The coroner's summary in the middle of each certificate recorded the various reasons for death: '*shotgun injury of the brain,'* - '*fractured skull due to a vehicle collision,*' - '*death by drowning'* and several versions of '*heart failure.*' There was only one certificate with that section left blank. The unfortunate Johnny Golightly, speeding along on his motorcycle, hit a cement mixer, and firemen washed him down the drain.

"It's really morbid to frame them!" visitors to his office used to say as Percy pointed to his wall of death.

Percy would explain how he had handed over the insurance cheques to the widows personally, and this, more than anything else, continued to keep him in the business of selling insurance. However hard or manipulative they became, it was justified because o one voluntarily buys insurance.

"By the way," Percy would ask every prospective customer. "What happens to your children if you die today?"

"You can't get me like that!" some would say.

"Then you need to sign here," Percy insisted as he presented them with a disclaimer.

"On reading the will, I will say either '*We owe you £125,000',* or I will say '*He was a selfish bastard who declined looking after you and the kids'*."

Percy often told the story of how a widow received her husband's death certificate in the post. It was beautifully framed, but there was no indication where it had come from. The truth was that Percy's secretary had collected it from the framers to add it to his collection and left it on the train, and no one gave it another thought.

"Is this a new service?" the widow rang to ask.

"And what service would that be?" replied Percy.

"British Rail has framed my husband's death certificate, and I got it special delivery!" she explained.

Percy had to say how her husband's joining his 'wall of death' would encourage others to protect their families.

"It's the first time he's done anything useful!" she commented before hanging up.

* * * * *

"How many children do you have?" Percy had asked Detective Inspector Bokhara of the Rug Squad.

The police had arrived to investigate where the Persian carpet in their reception had come from.

"Three kids," Bokhara had replied easily. "And this looks suspiciously like the carpet from the hallway at 50 Park Lane, sir."

"And how old are you next birthday?" Percy persisted.

"What are you talking about?"

"If you die in the course of your investigations into this disappearing carpet, who will put your children through school?" Percy pressed him. "Have you introduced your wife to any of your workmates at Scotland Yard?"

"That's not your business!" he replied angrily.

"But that's exactly what my business is!" Percy continued. "Your wife may be forced into marrying one of your colleagues, and your children will have to call him Dad."

"I'm not here to buy life insurance," Inspector Bokhara insisted.

"Where else are you going to buy it?"

"The Police Service gives me all the insurance I need," Bokhara snarled. "And I'll be taking that rug with me."

"So if you die on the job, I must send one of two letters to your wife?"

That week, out of the blue, the Evening News started an exposé about 'soliciting' for insurance under the guise of a market survey and the name Golden Life was prominent in the article.

'*Girls on streets in new 'golden' profession,*' the headline read.

"I'll fuck whoever has done this!" shouted Mal as he threw the paper at Roland.

"I've had enough of this," mused Gary Deeds as he left the office and floored his new Ferrari up the ramp.

The seventy yards of rubber were the last thing he laid in the City of London. Gary slung his hook for a clean start without even saying goodbye to Anne Cillari, his beautiful Italian survey girl.

"He's going to look for fame and fortune in Geneva", mentioned his brother. "He can't work with this regulatory shit, and he's rented a magnificent chateau with its own dock on the lake. I have to admit I'm tempted to do the same."

Gary missed the follow-up in the Evening News featuring a semi-clad Norma Snockers with a clipboard outside Green Park underground station.

"Good God!" screamed Sir Davy Lamp, chairman of Golden Life. "I thought we stopped all that!"

Sir Davy kept the paper in his briefcase until the end of the week, when his driver reached his mansion in Hollow Bottom in the Cotswolds. He was planning a quiet weekend, and he took the paper to read while he soaked in an evening bath. He thought that would keep him calm. His faithful butler, Smithers, stood motionless beside the tub with a towel over his arm.

According to Smithers, Sir Davy developed a hard-on which rose through the suds as he studied the picture of the busty Norma Snockers in a half-open shirt and a very short skirt with a clipboard.

"Shall I inform her ladyship?" Smithers suggested.

"No, Smithers!" Sir Davy replied. "We'll break out the loose-fitting tweeds and smuggle this one down to the pub."

* * * * *

Jess Lapsed didn't want Sir Davy Lamp to realise the extent to which these incredible insurance profits were arriving on the bottom line of the annual accounts. On his three days a week on the golf course, Jess considered his main job was to keep secrets, and Sir Davy Lamp thought he was presiding over the bell-weather of business behaviour. After looking at the picture of Norma every hour and reading the Evening News article seven times on that Sunday, he was still in shock on Monday when he ordered his chauffeur to prepare for the drive back to London.

"The first stop is Green Park station!" he commanded from the back of a 1956 Silver Shadow.

It was Joy Stick's day at Green Park, and she was standing on the edge of the park with her clipboard when the Rolls pulled up next to her. Sir Davy got out of the car and approached her in a few seconds.

"Would you mind answering a few questions about savings and inflation?" Joy asked automatically as he stopped not a yard away.

Joy recognised Sir Davy as his picture was in the Golden Life brochure.

"You should be at home doing the dishes, my dear", Sir Davy had replied to her whilst staring at her ample cleavage, "and you stand a good chance of being arrested for indecent exposure of those assets."

"They're expensive!" Joy replied, looking at the open rear door of his Rolls.

Sir Davy retreated, shut his car window, and his chauffeur pulled away from the curb. He looked at his boss in the rearview mirror.

"She's one of ours!" the chauffeur announced proudly.

"One of our what?" Sir Davy asked abruptly.

Joy Stick went back to the office and told Norma Snockers how their ultimate boss had accosted her and, on Tuesday morning, the fate of the girls had been sealed in the Golden Life head office.

"It's Oz for me, mate," said Seymour, reading the situation clearly for the first time. "I've got my eye on a big chunk of land in Perth, mate."

"It was the girls," moaned Leo Tard. "They've killed the fastest-growing insurance operation of all time."

"See you around, guys," smiled Lou as he pulled his Ducatti racing leathers over his suit and gave Roland a high five.

"It's pathetic," complained Dinah Mite as the office gradually emptied. "Nine years on the way to multi-millions and now it's fuck-all because of one prick!"

"That's the nature of a bubble!" Percy reminded her.

Just then, the phone rang on Percy's desk, and out of habit, Percy picked it up.

It was Roger Ing, the Managing Director of Golden Life.

"We're negotiating the sale for £250 million," he announced. "You people left me with no choice!"

"We created this company out of nothing," Percy objected.

"And I rang to say it's not how I wanted this to end," Roger continued without listening.

"You said we were a family," Percy muttered deliberately.

"Wrong again!" Roger snapped. "If you're in the family business, get a dog!"

Percy opened the fridge and poured two glasses of Bollinger.

"I went to Roger Ing's house for a sit-down dinner two years ago," he reflected with a smile. "I'll always remember the smoked salmon still had the plastic sheets between the slices."

Percy sipped the champagne and looked over to the sales board. There was his record of 127 sales in one month in coloured chips running across the wall.

Dinah raised her glass.

"You all had a good time," she consoled him. "You were the best!"

Percy stood in his doorway for the last time and shouted down to the lone figure of the eccentric Dr Buck Trend sitting at the same desk he had occupied in the corner for his whole nine years. Buck turned slowly, removed the monocle he always wore and let it drop on its silk cord onto his embroidered waistcoat.

Buck Trend was a doctor of philosophy rather than of economics or medicine, and he used his qualification to leave urgent phone messages to members of professions like engineers, scientists, architects and sportsmen. Their contact details were listed on various membership registers, and the messages Buck left were all the same:

'Please ring Doctor Trend as soon as possible on this number.'

They all did, and Dr Trend did not need a marketing girl.

What no one knew was that Dr Buck Trend had bought his doctorate from Pacific Western University for $250. There were no exams involved, and the certificate on his wall was precisely the same as the one you get after four years at UCLA.

Buck's phone rang.

'Doctor Trend, I've got an urgent message to ring you,' said the caller hysterically.

"This is too tedious," Buck confirmed as he slammed down the receiver.

The phone rang again.

"Wrong number!" he shouted, pulling his phone jack out of the wall.

Jess Lapsed confessed to Urina that his override income had stopped, and he was going to get a lump sum from the sale of his shares.

"How much?" she asked.

After he told her the amount and added that it would be halved by tax, she screamed, '*What about the money we've been getting every month!*'

It took Mrs Lapsed a tenth of a second to collect her jewellery and her passport.

"This is going to cost you!" she alerted him as she headed off to the cottage of the golf professional at his club.

Seymour Clearly was arrested for being drunk and disorderly and apparently singing '*Don't cry for me Market Harborough*' in the police station of the same name. Seymour found himself in front of a magistrate.

"Do you have anything to say?" asked the court.

"Yes, mate," Seymour replied. "You make me sick!"

Percy collected Seymour eight weeks later from outside the gates of Market Harborough prison and dropped him off at London Airport.

"Do you have anything to say?" asked Percy in a final farewell at the Qantas check-in.

"Only goodbye, mate," he answered. "And remember that Magellan circumcised the world with only a fifty-foot clipper.

Chapter Nine
TWISTING THE TRUTH

Key Witnesses:

IAN SMEAR	*Smear Associates – Public Relations*
SPIKE UPWARD	*PR Account Director*
TED SHEATH	*Prime Minister*
BRETON AND BLUEBELL WOODS	*US Diplomat and his Wife*
SICCO PHANT	*Chairman – European Commission*
DOUGLAS NURD	*Political Secretary to Ted Sheath*
ALASTAIR MCSPINAL-JELLICO	*Treasurer – European League*
DREW STRAWS	*CEO – Taylor Woodcock*
FRANK TAYLOR	*Founder - Taylor Woodcock*
JOHNNY SMART	*Fairground Horses Collector*
GAUL BLADDA	*Manager of BONK – London*
ANTHONY FAUZI	*Micro-biologist*
LIZA LOTT	*Creative Director – Smear Associates*
PATTY O'DORS	*Film Star*
GUZZLA TANDOORI	*Driver – BONK*
IDI OTT	*President for Life – Uganda*
JEAN BENDAN BUCKASS	*Emperor - Central African Republic*
MENGISTU HAILE MARIAM	*President of Ethiopia*
HUGH HEIFER	*Chief Executive – Playboy*

GOBI ABADDI	*Founder Chairman - BONK*
AMANDA LING	*Madam*
MO HICAN	*Studio Boss – MGM*
SHEIKH NOTSTURD	*Ruler of Abu Dhabi*
WILBUR NISH	*Caretaker – BONK*
SHEIKH SQUALID WALID	*Chief Executive – BONK*
CINDY CATE	*Dealer – Rudolf Werewolf Securities*
JAMES CALLAGHAN	*Labour Foreign Minister*
MAZDA BAYSHUN	*Urban Development – Zimbabwe*
URIN ONITT	Urban Development – *Zambia*
WAYNE MOON	*Chairman – Commonwealth Institute*
SIR COFFIN DODGER	*Chairman – Institute of Directors*
CHARLES AZNOVOICE	French Crooner
ALBERT ROSS	*High Flying Advertiser*

"So, what makes you think you can work in Public Relations?" greeted Ian Smear, the shorter - but senior - partner of Ian Smear Associates.

Smear reached out and put his arm around Percy Vere's shoulder during the guided tour of their plush offices in London's Berkeley Square. He explained the difference between the work of his advertising agency and its political public relations subsidiary.

"Just as advertising designs a more attractive cheese to bait the mousetrap, public relations ensures that those who set the trap are perceived in the best possible light—by customers, the media, and within their own industry," he expounded. He then pulled Percy closer as they neared the boardroom.

Reel Life had refused all Percy's attempts to secure another assignment.

"And after your holiday on the Amazon, don't even think about waiting in reception!" Arty Farty had warned him. "There's nothing for you here!"

Out on the street there were no sensible jobs around, a phenomenon employers explained away as the 'baby bulge'. It seemed that every woman in England - including the Queen - had been jumped within twenty-four hours of the end of World War II, and no provision had been made for employing the resulting wave of school-leavers.

"We're politically orientated here, Percy," Ian Smear continued as Percy tried to wriggle free without telling him to fuck off. "Most of our accounts have a political bias - the Trade Centre development at St Catherine's Dock, the European Commission in Brussels, and the Bank Overseas National Kredit here in London. If we take you on, you'll work with Spike Upward, one of our senior account executives. He's been with us since the beginning and runs all three of those accounts. He's one of the family, if you know what I mean."

"Don't let him shut the door," mouthed a secretary as they passed her desk.

Percy stumbled over a hollowed-out elephant-foot umbrella stand, and Smear seized the opportunity to push him into the nerve centre and onto a Luigi Fagotti sofa.

Percy winced at the two monstrous elephant tusks mounted in silver on either side of the artificial coal fire as Smear adjusted the gold dimmer switches.

"You look quite ill. Are you all right?" Smear enquired, seating himself opposite.

"I've picked up a dose of dysentery travelling in South America," Percy replied, deploying his ultimate defence. "May I use your cloakroom?"

When he returned, Percy deliberately left the boardroom door open. There was no need for the three pretty girls in reception to get the wrong idea before he had even started.

Smear asked for a detailed summary of Percy's education and career.

"There's not a great deal to tell," Percy said, his bowels contracting at the thought, "but I know I'll fit in here."

This was Percy's sixteenth interview in two months, for work ranging from newspaper advertising to a gardening job at St Trinian's in Sunningdale—where, unfortunately, he couldn't answer the headmistress's only question.

"Mr Vere, why do you want this job?"

"I would have thought that was obvious," Percy had replied, as four long-legged teenagers in tiny pleated tennis skirts passed the window.

"This is a wonderful opportunity, Mr Smear," Percy urged. "I'm a quick learner, and you'll have no complaints once I get the hang of it."

"We're very close here, Percy," Smear insisted, leaning forward until a trace of spittle oozed from the corner of his mouth. "We'll be very firm with you."

"I have no doubt about that," Percy replied as his insides churned.

Smear leaned back and adjusted the immaculate Windsor knot of his tie, giving Percy a view of the individual black hairs protruding from his nostrils.

"The fact is, we depend entirely on our clients' income," he continued. "So we do whatever they want. If a client says black is white, then black is white, and the campaign reflects it. Am I clear?"

"Completely, sir," said Percy.

"The Englishman reading his morning paper is deeply sceptical of the self-evident, yet easily persuaded to believe a lie," Smear went on. "Try handing out five-pound notes in the street and people will refuse them. Print that a Venusian spaceship landed in Surrey and an eighteen-inch alien cock was rammed up a farm worker's arse, and they'll queue for the next edition!"

Smear's eyes sparkled as he rose and grasped one of the elephant tusks.

"No doubt," Percy agreed.

"Politicians are our bread and butter," Smear continued. "We entertain selected MPs and Cabinet ministers to appraise them of our clients' perspectives. We provide hospitality—and, of course, sufficient to cover their expenses, if you grasp my meaning."

"You pay politicians to protect clients' interests?" Percy asked, without thinking.

"'Pay' is the wrong word," Smear corrected him smoothly. "We organise lunches, holidays, parliamentary questions, and after-dinner entertainment. We're proud to have coined the term 'business affairs.'"

"I see," Percy lied.

"We'll let you know after the remaining interviews," Smear smirked, running a finger down the tusk.

Percy walked into reception with his buttocks involuntarily clenched.

"If God had wanted us to bend over, he'd have put money on the floor," Percy whispered to the receptionist as he fled.

A week later, Percy received confirmation that he had the job. The salary was £25 per week with a travel allowance and expenses. He would be under the direction of Spike Upward with the title 'Assistant Account Executive.' He was to start work on the first day of the following month.

Percy moved closer to London and slept on a mattress on the floor of a bedsit on the wrong side of Hammersmith. It was cheap. He celebrated his new job by buying a bed frame from the pawnbroker on the corner. In the yard at the back he noticed a battered red Mini.

"How old is it?" Percy asked.

"It must be one of the first," replied Al Cove, the effeminate owner, eyeing Percy appreciatively as he smoothed back his long hair.

"How many miles?"

"No idea, luv."

"How many owners?"

"Six or seven."

"What kind of people?"

"Are you planning to drive it or marry it?"

After twenty minutes of haggling, Percy became the proud owner of his first car for £18. The seats had collapsed, the radiator was punctured, the instruments didn't work, and the engine wouldn't start - but it had four good tyres, a new battery, and, as a real bonus, a modified Weber carburettor.

Percy rang Jack Hammer, the man who once converted a Jaguar's identity and who had oxy-acetylene-cut Philip Wayward's Rover in half to remove the gearbox.

"You still owe me," Percy said. "I've got a small job that'll square things."

"I thought Thelma House sorted you out?" Jack replied.

"Radiator leak and a fuel gauge on a Mini. No acetylene required."

"Alright. A fiver."

It took Jack five days to get the Mini roadworthy. It lacked comfort, but it went from A to B as fast as anything else, and with its straight-through exhaust it sounded gloriously aggressive.

Percy drove it as boys do, his confidence growing with every journey. Predictably, overconfidence soon followed - and disaster was not far behind.

He was invited to a weekend party at the Surrey estate of Breton Woods, an American career diplomat, and his wife Bluebell. Percy was friends with their son from university.

He arrived on time and eased the Mini through massive wrought-iron gates, parking between a beautifully restored Porsche and a classic Rolls-Royce from the thirties. He eyed both with envy.

"Want to try it?" his friend asked, appearing beside him. "Dad won't mind if you take it up the drive and back."

Percy hadn't even removed his overnight bag before climbing into the Porsche. The key was in the ignition. The engine started instantly.

"I won't go past the gates," Percy promised.

At thirty miles an hour the accelerator jammed.

Suddenly the brick gateposts loomed ahead - and the gates were shut.

Percy swerved too late.

The crash was violent and final.

"Christ Almighty!" he yelled as metal shrieked and stone exploded.

A concrete eagle toppled from its plinth, embedding itself in the bonnet as the windscreen shattered into a thousand pieces. The bird teetered, wings spread like a conductor mid-symphony, then fell sideways and crushed the Porsche's wing with a slow, terrible crunch.

Percy stood frozen for two minutes before turning back toward the house.

"How was it?" asked Breton Woods, emerging cheerfully.

"Words would fail me," Percy replied as Bluebell appeared on the steps, smiling.

"And where is the Porsche?" she asked her son.

"Down by the entrance," Percy answered.

The Woods shared a silent premonition and walked together down the drive. Percy followed at a discreet distance.

"Don't say a word," Breton warned his wife as they reached the wreckage.

"You must be lucky," Percy ventured. "I read this morning about a woman named Claire Voyant who was run over by the van delivering her eightieth birthday cake."

"How are we going to replace the eagle?" Bluebell screamed. "They were a matching pair!"

As Breton lunged for him, Percy ducked and ran.

"Good thing I didn't unpack," he muttered, fleeing into the night.

* * * * *

The following Monday was Percy's first day at Ian Smear Associates. He wore a white shirt, an Old Harrovian striped tie, and a new dark suit. He was now experiencing the reality of rush-hour traffic on the Hammersmith flyover.

On the elevated section the traffic had ground to a halt. At 8:45 a.m., crawling along at walking pace, Percy realised he was going to be late for his 9:00 a.m. start. Drivers were hooting; some had abandoned their cars to investigate the cause of the delay. Immediately behind him, a Costain twenty-ton lorry blew its hydraulic brakes. In his rear-view mirror Percy saw four beefy labourers squeezed across the front bench seat.

"Shit!" Percy exclaimed, glancing at his new—but second-hand—petrol gauge.

The needle was pinned hard against the upright of the "E" for Empty. He was running on fumes. He switched off the engine.

When the traffic edged forward, Percy turned the key and pulled the starter.

Nothing.

"Oh God, no!" he muttered.

The Costain driver leaned on his horn. The blast was biblical. Percy jumped—and at that moment, his half-digested breakfast erupted from his bowels in a dysenteric explosion that filled the seat of his new suit.

He sat rigid as heat spread beneath him.

"This isn't happening," he prayed. "It's a nightmare."

The horn blasted again, and whatever remained in his colon followed in a second convulsion.

Miraculously, the engine fired on the next attempt and Percy lurched forward. He tried to remove his jacket but it was too late. He flung it into the passenger footwell, loosened his tie, and felt despair wash over him as liquidised egg, bacon, and coffee soaked through his trousers.

As he wrestled out of his sodden clothes, Percy caught sight in the mirror of the four Costain men clutching their sides with laughter. For Percy, there was only the nauseating reality of filth everywhere - and it was already ten past nine.

"Please, God, don't let me run out of petrol," he pleaded aloud. "I'll do anything."

"Want mummy to wipe your botty?" shouted an Irish voice behind him.

Two girls in a Sunbeam Alpine with the roof down pulled alongside. One looked over and sniggered.

"This isn't happening!" Percy shouted, promising God he would enter a monastery for life if time could be reversed by fifteen minutes.

"I'm on my way to my first - and last - job!" he cried.

Suddenly the slip road appeared. It no longer mattered that it was the wrong direction.

Percy swung down the ramp and into a garage forecourt - only to realise it was a showroom without petrol pumps. He leaned on the horn at an Indian man behind the reception desk.

With his turban wrapped tightly over his ears, the man didn't look up until Percy's voice reached a shriek.

"Do you have a washroom?!"

"It is for staff only," the man replied calmly.

"Please!" Percy begged.

"This is not allowed. Do you not have a toilet facility at your home?"

"May your children be raped by a pork roast!" Percy screamed as he sped off to the Jaguar dealership a few hundred yards away.

"How many gallons?" asked the attendant, wiping his hands on a rag.

He looked up and recoiled.

"You appear to have a problem," he ventured, pinching his nose.

"I need a washroom and a gallon of petrol," Percy pleaded.

"The cloakroom's behind the workshop," the man said quietly. "Go through the showroom and if anyone asks, I never saw you."

"Thank you," Percy whispered.

"And don't worry about paying," the attendant added, eyeing Percy's hands. "Settle it next time."

Percy kicked off his shoes, peeled off his socks, and slid out of the car. Wearing only his ruined underpants, he made for the showroom.

"Oh God," he wailed as gravity took over.

Inside, a salesman was showing an elderly woman the latest Jaguar saloon when Percy burst in.

"Oi! Clear off!" the salesman shouted.

Percy bolted for the cloakroom, leaving a trail of footprints across the polished floor.

"I'm calling the police!" someone yelled as he locked the door.

Percy rinsed his underpants, washed himself at the basin, ignored the pounding on the door, mopped the floor with his underwear, rinsed them again, and put them back on.

"Hello!" he waved cheerfully as he emerged.

The old lady had gone pale and was clinging to a wing mirror.

"Don't worry!" Percy called. "It was an accident and you should see the other fellow!"

As the salesman lunged, Percy sidestepped and sprinted into the sunshine.

"I'll pay you later!" he shouted to the attendant as he jumped back into the Mini and drove off.

From the next phone box, Percy rang Ian Smear.

"It's unavoidable that I can't start until tomorrow," he explained.

"Don't bother," Smear replied, and hung up.

Percy rang again. The receptionist answered.

"Don't worry," she said kindly. "I'll tell him you'll be in tomorrow."

That day Percy hosed down the Mini, scrubbed the interior, threw away the carpets, and dried the seats. He washed his clothes at the launderette and bought a replacement suit for £3 from the charity shop next door.

The following morning, his shoes were almost dry and his suit passable. He even felt confident as he entered Smear Associates, thanked the receptionist for her discretion, and waited.

An hour passed. People nodded at him in passing. Percy understood then that professional life required surrender, humility, patience, and silence.

When at last he was summoned to meet his mentor, Spike Upward, Percy recognised this moment for what it was - his first true foothold in the real world.

* * * * *

Percy found Spike Upward to be a good teacher. As account director for public relations at the European Commission, Spike was a firm favourite of Ted Sheath, the Prime Minister. He also spoke daily with Sicco Phant, President of the European Commission. These two men were the principal players in Britain's initiation into the European Economic Community.

Spike's brief was simple: to ram the EEC down the British public's throat as palatably as possible.

"It's all in the wrist," he would say. "They can't afford to tell the truth about the long-term implications of European integration because they don't know them themselves. Whatever happens, it's the thin end of the wedge. We lose sovereignty, we're swamped by cheap labour and cheap goods, wages and property prices collapse—and before you can say Jack Robinson, we'll have Eastern European boat people paddling up the Thames."

"Who is Mr Robinson?" Percy asked, trying to look knowledgeable.

"So while this EEC is being put in place," Spike continued, ignoring him, "the government needs a grip on voters tight enough to stop them concentrating on anything else, but loose enough to let them catch the occasional breath."

He loosened his collar as he prepared for yet another round of Downing Street briefings.

This was a period of searching for a way to represent the people in a so-called democracy—one increasingly resembling a federal structure, beginning with a unified Europe. The stated purpose was to prevent another war between European nations.

"You don't do anything unless I say so, understood?" Spike ordered. "You'll attend meetings, but you won't open your mouth. This is delicate work. We're balancing European ideals with our own greed. You'll see that economic control lies in the hands of a few well-positioned families within our government. They represent heritage; we represent their influence."

"So our job is to influence the media in favour of our client's ambitions?" Percy ventured, smiling.

"What did I just say?" Spike snapped. "You listen - or you move on."

"One of our clients is the UK World Trade Centre," Spike continued. "That means getting the public comfortable with European globalisation and that is the root of controlling the population of the world."

"Surely, Europe controlling the world ended with the collapse of the British Empire?" asked Percy, confused.

"Wrong!" Spike retorted. "The start of a new world order started on May 1st 1776 when a group of wealthy families got together in Bavaria to prime the pump for a global initiative. They called themselves the '*Illuminati*' and now they're often referred to as the '*Deep State*'. They meet in secret each year to coordinate their progress and those meetings are referred to as the 'Bilderberg' conferences and that is supported by the World Economic Forum that holds its own conference in Davos each year. It's all about these *Illuminati* becoming one world government."

"You think that a European Union is a staging point on their journey?"

"When you read your newspaper have this agenda in the back of your mind" Spike suggested. "Then it will all make more sense as all the Press barons attend Bilderberg . They're making the narrative to condition you to their way of thinking - commercially and in all areas of religion and culture!"

"So the EEC aligns neatly with their plan and Ted Sheath, the former chorister and ocean sailor, fits into that narrative by getting into bed with strangers across Europe" Percy thought as he bit through his lip.

"There will be serious issues dividing national interests," Spike added. "We are paid to focus on the ones that demand a unified response."

"Is there an obvious example?" Percy asked.

"What did I just say?" Spike replied sharply.

"Sorry."

"Climate," Spike said at last. "It affects everyone. The Met Office raised it in *Nature* in 1973. In 1975, Columbia University published a study in *Science* suggesting that so-called greenhouse gases from industrialisation were heating the Earth exponentially. They concluded rising temperatures could extinguish life on Earth."

Percy sucked his teeth.

"There's never been any suggestion that humans could control planetary heating or cooling," Spike said, answering Percy's unspoken thought.

"So am I allowed to say there's nothing we can do and we're all going to die?" Percy blurted.

"The interaction between science and government has been hijacked by criminals," Spike replied. "Influencers setting up charities to harvest millions for themselves and it was the same with AIDS - billions vanished under the banner of compassion. I'm bisexual so I know! By the way, in case you didn't notice, Smear's a full-blown nutter and Ted Sheath's a peculiar prime minister. That's why you keep your mouth shut while I teach you how to survive with some integrity intact."

"I can tell you that science proves there's .04% of CO_2 in the atmosphere" Spike insisted. "Of that the same tiny amount, only .04% CO_2 is from human generated carbon emissions. So when they cite temperatures a million years ago, I'm not sure a thermometer deep in the ground is a safe way to judge that we're heating up outside the natural rhythms of nature. The Illuminati are carrying fear into every home and the politicians respond with £ billions to get their votes and the criminals rub their hands as they syphon off the government funding!"

Percy looked at Spike with newfound respect.

"It's worse in America," Spike continued, "$ billions flow through non-government-organsations – NGO's – and they receive monster money and there's no congressional oversight or any discussion when it disappears into thousands of scams with the Illuminati in the background claiming they can change Mother Nature when they're actually funding political support for their 'global ideas' to destroy national identity and culture. It's bollocks but we are part of promoting and spreading their version of the story. I want to write that there's no evidence that any intervention can stop them getting to their global finish line!"

"Ian said we're a political public relations agency," Percy murmured.

"The 'climate emergency' was born into politics," Spike smiled. "Politics will drown out the reality that billions of years of temperature fluctuation are unstoppable!"

"And our stance with clients?" Percy asked.

"We support anyone promising to reduce emissions, capture carbon, or make trees work harder," Spike replied. "None of it changes atmospheric CO_2 dynamics—nature compensates when it must."

At that moment, Ian Smear appeared in the doorway.

He had been listening.

"Short of a miracle," Smear said, "we watch the atmosphere and oceans warm. Thermal inertia. The poles gain and lose hundreds of billions of tons of ice at a time, sea levels rise, panic spreads and just before we all drown, nature resets the board. Our role is to monetise the panic."

"He means we suspend normal business to earn our share of the billions raised to 'fix' the problem," Spike added.

"Got it," Percy said.

*****

For the first few months, while making endless pots of tea, Percy listened carefully to Spike's presentations. Spike was persuasive, especially in promoting diversity and his dream of individual freedom and prosperity across Europe was under wraps. It was the opposite of the all-encompassing political, commercial, and social ambition of that '*Deep State*' he was crafting so effectively.

Government departments clung to his keywords and phrases carefully selected to maintain the illusion of coherence. Right or wrong, the job was done well. The media feasted on positive solutions born of guesswork, and the public surrendered to the inevitability of events beyond their control.

Percy began to understand that England had once presided over a global empire, culminating in a Victorian bureaucracy guided by elites who created an unparalleled commercial and financial footprint. That same bureaucracy now strangled progress with armies of regulators, administrators, inspectors, and clerks.

Workers saw their pay eroded by taxes, insurance, and faltering pensions, while banks and insurers gorged themselves. There were more clerks in the Ministry of Defence than soldiers in the army, and more administrators in the NHS than people living in Wales. At the empire's zenith in 1905, Lord Curzon governed India with the same number of officials who now ran Lord's Cricket Ground.

Percy recalled his research into the origins of power in Europe. He was still intrigued as he believed in hidden persuaders - networks with carefully guarded objectives. It may be they were still called the 'Cobras of Europe', or they were the same Knights Templar still existing through Freemasonry. Yet who truly orchestrated commercial control in a greater

Europe? Who had even been to Brussels? Wasn't that where sprouts came from?

If a secret collaboration existed, could any European nation challenge another within the same political and financial framework? Would domestic politics be reduced to bookkeeping and policing under European court directives? Would individual freedom shrink to the entitlement of a spring onion?

Douglas Nurd, Ted Sheath's political secretary, was so detached from ordinary people that he was said to have "the qualifications of a piece of turf." He championed Europe on the basis that England was better off prostrating itself before Brussels than dying slowly in isolation—an idea that would have had the war dead spinning in their graves.

"Don't give me the conspiracy theory," Spike insisted. "Britain is leading the creation of a Euro-market system. Authority will be handed willingly to a European Parliament, inevitably run from mainland Europe—Germany and France foremost."

"How can you have monetary union without fiscal union?" Percy asked. "That includes wages, hours, pensions, insurance—everything."

He struck a nerve.

Soon after, Percy saw a memo from Spike to Ian Smear:

It is reasonable to believe an intelligence system operates behind the scenes at the European Commission. Someone in our government is plotting—charting—the marginalisation of England.

The memo continued:

Even with limited involvement in Brussels, we detect an intent to wrest sovereign power from member states through centralised control.

And concluded:

Commercial overlords are mobilising for their own ends. This will undermine European society and create a new permanent poor.

Meanwhile, Percy quietly added his name to a guest list for a major EEC lunch at Buckingham Palace.

Inside, he avoided Spike and drifted into a group listening to an interminable soliloquy by former Prime Minister Harold Macmillan, whose nose ran unchecked until corgis burst in to announce the Queen's arrival, Princess Margaret close behind.

Beside Percy stood Dusty Nook, a television relic still hosting *Sunday Night at the London Palladium*.

"I am much loved by Her Majesty," Dusty smirked.

"I hear she shouts a lot and comes too quickly," Percy whispered.

Dusty glared and pushed ahead.

Percy retreated to examine a genealogical book detailing the Venetian Guelph family - Templars intertwined with European royalty, Hanoverians, and Queen Victoria herself.

Then Spike appeared.

"What the devil are you doing here?"

"I was invited," Percy replied calmly. "I sent my passport."

The next day, Percy wrote to Spike:

Sheath may believe he is uniting Europe, but he is presiding over the surrender of UK sovereignty.

That afternoon, Percy watched Spike orchestrate the celebration of Britain's first step toward federalism in the Great Hall at Hampton Court - beneath tapestries of English kings fighting to maintain power in Europe. When the curator cut the electricity to protect the fabric, Sheath carried on in the dark.

"These fears of losing sovereignty are completely unjustified," Sheath proclaimed.

"That's one of his greatest lies," Percy whispered. "And you wrote it."

The cameraman swore. Percy raised his Beaujolais.

"To Community spirit," he slurred.

The following day, Spike explained how the Information Research Department had covertly steered the media pro-Europe - until Sheath shut it down.

Now the operation continued under a different name.

"We're on Ted Alert!" Spike concluded.

"You're being moved," he warned Percy unexpectedly. "None of this concerns you anymore."

Back at the office, Ian Smear summoned Percy.

"Am I being sacked?"

"You're family now," Smear said warmly. "You're taking over press coordination for the new World Trade Centre at St Catherine's Dock - a landmark project and a feather in Frank Taylor's cap."

* * * * *

The London World Trade Centre was nothing if not ambitious. The complex beside Tower Bridge was being built under the watchful eye of Drew Straws, the hot-headed CEO of the property division of the construction giant Taylor Woodcock.

All meetings were held in the old lock-keeper's house at the entrance to St Katharine Docks. Drew's shouting echoed across the water as he wrestled with the local authority, attempting to negotiate a workable commercial balance between hotel accommodation, private housing, office space, and leisure facilities. Planning consent in this Labour-controlled borough depended on how much accommodation on the East Quay would be handed over for the homeless. There was no question of removing the Grade I listing from the enormous Warehouse B, which split the site in two. Unless the homeless received their share of this prime real estate, the deal was off.

"If you see anyone in a sleeping bag, throw him into the dock," Drew barked as his patience wore thin.

The final straw was Historic Heritage's insistence on preserving the rows of cast-iron bars dividing the cells beneath Ivory House, once used to hold prisoners awaiting transportation to the other side of the world.

"You idiots," Drew fumed at the planning officer. "Can't you understand that I can't build a World Trade Centre with half the space given to left-wing derelicts and the other half preserved as a museum to Australian convicts?"

As his dream of turning Ivory House into an ivory tower crumbled, Drew reported to the formidable Sir Frank Taylor that the entire project might have to be abandoned unless Warehouse B somehow vanished.

"I should bulldoze the fucking thing and issue a press release saying it collapsed," Drew muttered.

Frank Taylor responded only by raising his impressive eyebrows.

Later, Drew nudged him again, seeking endorsement.

"I never heard that particular stroke of genius, Drew," Frank whispered, nodding vigorously and raising his thumb.

From that moment on, Drew Straws walked with a lighter step and a noticeable glint in his eye whenever he gazed across at Warehouse B.

*****

Three days later, Percy went in to find Spike grappling with new Civil Service directives and an avalanche of regulations.

"More pen-pushers filling in forms and inventing new taxes," Spike groaned. "At the same time, we're giving away herring quotas."

"Learn to pass responsibility for your actions to someone else," he advised. "The government's only concern is to appear heroic in matters of accusation."

"Funny you should mention that," Percy interjected. "There's a small problem with Warehouse B. What would happen if it were knocked down?"

"Impossible," Spike replied instantly. "It's one of Queen Victoria's greatest monuments to the Industrial Revolution."

"But she's dead."

"Don't be fatuous."

"There are two massive bulldozers on site," Percy pressed. "If all four corners were hit, it would simply fall over."

"Rather you than me," Spike said coolly, examining his fingernails. "I've got friends to think about if I lose my job. I've never heard of this. Ian will go ballistic."

"At least help me with the press."

"Forget it. You're on your own. Just make sure there's no one inside."

"Thanks, Spike. See you later."

*****

Three nights later, after the site had closed and the Tower Bridge approach lay deserted, Percy met Drew Straws and two bulldozer drivers in the lock-keeper's house. Drew slipped each driver a thick sealed envelope. They nodded, took the keys from the hook, and headed out.

"Let's do it," one growled, exhaling a lungful of tobacco smoke and grinding the cigarette into the floor.

At 2:00 a.m., the roar of the engines shattered the silence. The huge machines lumbered toward Warehouse B, each fitted with a twenty-foot blade raised twelve feet high. In violent jolts, they smashed two opposite corners and backed away.

The building growled and groaned - but remained standing.

"It's not going down!" Percy gasped, hand clamped over his mouth. "No one will believe this was an accident."

"You can't leave it like that!" Drew screamed above the engines. "Finish the fucker!"

The drivers aligned their machines, lowered the blades, and attacked the two remaining corners and, with a final shudder deep inside the brickwork, the warehouse resisted for a last momentary hesitation. A final massive cracking and groaning noise of surrender tilted the roof before it disappeared in a massive tangle of brickwork, steel girders and wiring. Percy stood as if glued to the ground as a huge pall of dust rose like a mushroom cloud above the rubble.

The bulldozers backed away and rumbled towards the site entrance clearly not interested in admiring their handiwork.

Two low-loaders had appeared at the entrance in perfect time for the ramps to be lowered and the machines advanced slowly up onto the flat-beds. They disappeared in a synchronised growl of first gear heading towards the East End of London. Once there, it needed no imagination to know they would be washed and fifteen witnesses would swear they had been in the same yard on the Isle of Dogs all that time.

Percy was looking around for any sign of Drew Straws but he had arranged a private jet from City Airport up to Yorkshire. There had been no flight-plan filed.

Percy still stood in the same spot listening to a continuation of spine-chilling cracks and metallic screams. This was indeed a dying heart heaving out a message from a fifty feet high jagged mountain of granite, slate roofing, steel girders and glass.

Then Percy saw flashing blue lights getting close and he knew he had to disappear.

"Jesus Christ!" he muttered looking back with his hand over his mouth. "No one will believe this was an accident!"

As he was escaping over Tower Bridge, Percy's ears were still throbbing in tune with the diesel engines. He glanced back to see the altered skyline. Whoever shouted, *finish the fucker,* would be well pleased.

People in nightclothes had started to gather.

"I think Smear will need more than a press release," he muttered.

*****

The next day, Ian Smear slapped the early edition of the *Evening News* in front of Percy.

"Congratulations, you've made the front page!" he smacked the paper on the reception desk.

Percy looked at a picture of a fairground scene with a merry-go-round and the headline:

HORSES CRUSHED IN MYSTEROUTS DEMOLITION.

The print was in quarter inch type.

Percy blanched.

"What horses?" he blurted out.

"Get into my office and shut the door," Smear ordered, storming ahead.

Percy entered and opened the paper to see a photograph of the collapsed remains of Warehouse B. Smear was incensed.

"I've just spoken to Drew Straws. He's at a conference in Yorkshire."

"He's where?" Percy exclaimed, feigning astonishment while clearly knowing what that implied.

"Are you deaf?" snarled Smear.

Percy stepped back from the spray of spit.

"Apparently someone bulldozed the Trade Centre site last night and destroyed Warehouse B," Ian snapped, slamming the paper on the boardroom table.

He started jabbing the picture with his tar-stained index finger.

"This doesn't look good for Taylor Woodcock!" he reasoned.

"They've been trying every trick in the book to get the building de-listed" Percy replied.

"You'd better get over there and sort this out!" Smear ordered. "Spike will go with you then, when you get back, we'll need to issue a statement."

"I had nothing to do with this," Percy insisted. "It's the Taylor Woodcock show!"

"Don't be facetious with me!" Smear reacted.

Percy thought that if Smear suspected anything, he would have said so. He would be thinking automatically to respond to best protect his own firm.

"There's going to be an enquiry," Spike reasoned as they started out. "What did I tell you?"

"I've no idea what happened!" Percy answered sternly. "I didn't arrange anything!"

"You say nothing!" he insisted.

On the way to Docklands, Percy read the *Evening News* report that part of the warehouse had been rented by Johnny Smart to store the world's only collection of antique fairground horses. The journalist suggested Taylor Woodcock had bulldozed the place because Smart's lease still had a year to run and he had refused to leave.

"How convenient for you," Spike smiled, placing a hand on Percy's thigh.

Percy lifted it off and placed it firmly beside Spike. He noticed that Spike's fingers were shaped exactly like Smear's - skinny and carefully manicured.

Percy shuddered.

*****

At St Catherine's Dock, police, the Press and sightseers crowded the scene. Percy stood open-mouthed at the empty space where Warehouse B had stood for a century as a beacon for industry.

Spike identified himself and asked the police to clear the space and lock the gates.

"You don't do things by halves, Percy," Spike frowned a foot from Percy's ear.

Percy had to admit it was a thorough job and perfectly organised by Drew Straws. Moreover, it was darkest before midnight and there was no moon and a slight mist from the river, enough to disguise identification of what was happening. Also, the nearest residence was over 250 metres away.

Apparently, the bulldozers had been heard but not seen and Percy decided to phone the Taylor Woodcock head office from the lockkeeper's office.

"Sorry, Mr Vere," the security operator said. "There's no one here who knows anything."

"Well, who is there?"

"Don't misunderstand me," the man replied carefully. "No one is – I mean everyone and anyone - if you get my meaning!"

Then he hung up.

Within a week, Drew Straws had paid an undisclosed ex gratia sum to Johnny Smart, and the site was cleared. Warehouse B had been consigned to history along with any vagrants who were sheltering there. Drew Straws publicly blamed 'homeless vandalism' and announced that housing for the poor would be included in the new scheme.

*****

Ian Smear summoned Percy the moment they returned.

"For reasons we both understand, you're off the Taylor Woodcock account," he barked. "You're being reassigned to Bank Overseas National Kredit. No more stunts or I'll have your guts for garters. Now get out!"

Percy felt a wave of relief until the receptionist handed him a message. Frank Taylor wanted him to call.

"Hello, Mr Taylor," Percy began.

"I hear you lost your job," said the god of British construction cheerfully.

"It was educational," Percy replied.

"Well, Drew Srtraws says we wouldn't have a Trade Centre without you."

"You nearly didn't have one *with* me!" Percy admitted.

Frank Taylor invited him to dinner at Mark's Club, London's most exclusive gentleman's refuge.

Percy arrived early and crossed into the Footman pub opposite.

"Enormous vodka and Coke, please, Gloria."

"You look happy," she observed.

"I'm dining at Mark's Club," Percy said proudly.

"The likes of you won't get in there," Gloria laughed.

* * * * *

Mark's Club was the height of tradition in the greeting and the courtesies. Frank was already seated.

"It all started on 1st July 1967 when the treaty between the UK and Europe to merge behaviour came into operation" he opened. "The UK was ready to share the laws of the European Assembly and even their court orders."

"And you're happy with the implications for sovereignty?" asked Percy, accepting a glass of 1968 Dom Pérignon.

"Why else would I build the UK World Trade Centre?" Frank smiled. "It's going to be part of a chain reflecting World Trade in a process of eventual globalisation of banking and commerce."

Percy frowned.

"Is it better to fuse customs and regulations with open borders and eventually a world police force?" he asked.

"Drew Straws told me you used the expression '*When needs must, the devil drives*'" Frank replied as he raised his glass.

"Some families in history take matters into their own hands to survive" Percy smiled. "My own family was blessed with Ethelred the Unready so we learned from an ealy age to be better prepared. The fact is I don't know if I can side with globalisation putting power in the hands of puppet-masters?"

"So you think I'm the devil driving?"

"Not at all," Percy laughed. "You've let me lay the cornerstone of your World Trade Centre. It'll be on my CV for life as my contribution to globalisation. I like it when nations fence for their identity but now I see the beginnings of a conflict that will sweep away identity and custom. I can't agree the concept of one world and I'm happy to have been fired. Now I won't be batting on the wrong team."

Percy sipped his champagne and let the austerity of the location sink in.

"Globalists dictating what happens to every culture and religion leads to horror" he concluded.

"I'm on the cusp myself," Frank admitted.

"How so?"

"On 1 July 1967, the European Community Merger Treaty came into effect and the World Health Organisation conducted the first trials of a vaccine to beat any virus like the Spanish flu that wiped out millions" he admitted. "A trial audience was assembled in England with a modified coronavirus. It was a breach of every biological weapons treaty. Pfizer funded Anthony Fauzi to developed the vaccine at the University of North Carolina. It was tested on pigs and dogs. They all developed gastro-infectious diseases and tumours and most died."

"And they kept the results secret?"

"Coronavirus mutates too fast for it to work!" Frank Taylor explained. "Pfizer shelved it because they knew some maniac globalist could use it to depopulate the world!"

Percy stared, speechless.

"The virus they were fighting doesn't occur naturally," Frank continued. "It has to be engineered so they knew a specialist like Fauzi would co-operate because he filed the patent."

Percy felt cold.

"The WHO is part of the globalisation objective," Frank said. "Fauzi will keep the vaccine until the WHO gives the go-ahead to jab millions."

"When needs must, the devil drives," they said together.

* * * * *

Over the following three days at Smear Public Relations, Spike gave Percy the lowdown on his new account Bank Overseas National Kredit.

"Before you start, you need to learn the language of Third World banking," he instructed. "It starts with *Foreign Aid* which is mostly handed out to the former British colonies who are supposed to buy British goods with it but 100% of foreign aid is stolen by those in power. *Development Funding* means an under-developed nation needs a new road which they never build, and *Local Custom* means a backhander. *Free-Election* means that the outcome is known in advance, but you'll pick up the language as you go along.

"Thanks, Spike."

"The most important thing with these darkies is that their values are at an earlier stage of development," Spike continued. "To them, stealing is acceptable because we've stolen everything they've ever had. They've now developed sophisticated answers like 'That's not my hand you see in the till' and 'I don't know how that cash register got into my van!'. Go with the flow, Percy. It's called politics."

Percy reflected on how 'politics' must have been how his grandfather had brought all those tea-chests full of jade out of China.

"Listen to what they say and how they say it," Spike concluded, "and you'll discover what I mean as every bank uses its customers' money. The only difference with this bank is they haven't even discovered the difference between using it and stealing it."

Ian Smear, on his way out to lunch, passed Spike's desk and instructed Percy to invite Gaul Bladda, the BONK London manager, to an in-house lunch.

"Bring in a few of our advertising people," he suggested. "Bladda is a Pakistani but he has the lips of an African and I get the feeling we can expand this account if you know what I mean."

* * * * *

Gaul Bladda was surprisingly coherent and charming. He did not scratch his crotch and his only two lapses were blowing his nose on his napkin and mopping up his bearnaise sauce with a bread roll.

"He's probably hungry," Percy said behind his hand to Liza Lott, the voluptuous blond creative director from advertising.

Liza Lott smiled as Gaul was busy extolling the virtues of the Third World.

"Bank Overseas National Kredit will be the emerging force in international banking," Gaul prophesied. "We bring together the Third and First Worlds by utilising the petro-dollars of the Middle East where we have friends. Alongside this, we have nurtured relationships with banking customers in the West and projected a humanitarian and ecological bias to our business projects. Most of all, we have special accounting talents in Pakistan, where we acknowledge our duty to do the Prophet's work."

Liza smiled some more while Gaul focused on her.

"And with your creative talents," he had added, his eyes fastening on her ample cleavage, "I can see a great opening."

Percy had been out with Liza, and her creative abilities were not restricted to advertising and Percy had been stroking her leg under the tablecloth. She had opened them deliberately almost as an invitation as Gaul leaned towards her.

"You wouldn't?" Percy whispered in horror in her ear.

"Maybe."

Before Ian Smear had a chance to offer Gaul a brandy and a cigar, Gaul rose and held out a moist brown hand. It was a deliberate movement in slow motion for Ian to see a diamond-faced Patek Philippe, half hidden by body hair on his right wrist.

"Please arrange an appointment with one of our secretaries at Leadenhall Street so I can introduce you to BONK personally," he said directly to Liza.

Gaul cleared his throat, took his silver topped walking stick out of the elephant's foot stand and walked out jauntily.

"Well done, Percy," Spike Upward concluded sarcastically. "The first public relations man to land an advertising account."

Spike Upward then turned to Liza.

"You'll get on well with Gaul," he taunted. "Seeing that you always have an eye on the future."

"At least I have one," she laughed before sweeping out of the room.

"Little bitch!" muttered Spike.

"Well, I suppose I'd better arrange the public relations appointment with Gaul's office before advertising swipes the limelight," Percy suggested.

"If you want a future, I'd say that was a pretty good idea," Spike agreed.

* * * * *

In his excitement at his new account, Percy was tidying up his belongings and he found a cricket ball in amongst his socks and dropped it. The ball rolled across the landing and over the top of the wood staircase. The sound was bonk, bonk, bonk, bonk, bonk and a final bonk when it hit the wall in the hall.

'It's a sign!" Percy exclaimed to Zebedee, his blue Persian kitten. "BONK here I come!"

Percy was summoned to a final briefing in Smears office.

"Don't you ever forget this is a Smear Associate account!" Ian insisted.

"I'll run over what to expect!" Spike volunteered as he led the way to his own office.

"Before you start, learn the basic language of Third World finance," Spike instructed as if this was the most important lesson. "*Foreign Aid* means money that's going to be stolen. *Development Funding* means money for a project that's never leaving the drawing board. *Local Custom* means a backhander. *Free Election* means the outcome's known in advance. You'll pick it up!"

"Thanks, Spike."

* * * * *

BONK's Leadenhall Street headquarters office was a display of wealth. Four black Daimlers sat outside the imposing façade.

Percy and Liza arrived separately at 3 p.m. but were kept waiting an hour until Gaul ushered out four guests: three in immaculate Italian suits, one in a flowing white robe with three gold *gutras* circling his headdress. They laughed boisterously as they crossed reception.

"Happiness is a great BONK," Liza whispered.

Gaul ignored them until twenty minutes later when the receptionist finally showed them into his office.

"BONK opened officially for business at the Phoenix Hotel in Beirut in September 1972," Gaul began over the clatter of a chattering telex. "We now have six offices—Beirut, Dubai, Abu Dhabi, Sharjah, Luxembourg, and London. Image is vital. We must be seen as offering a superior banking service. Our PR must develop a customer base first, then our loan book, then private banking into corporate finance and investment management, and eventually replicate this across England, the UAE, Turkey, Saudi Arabia, Hong Kong, Zimbabwe, Colombia, and beyond."

Percy presented a skeleton PR programme. "If you are to become a centre of influence," he advised, "we must forge links with the UK Establishment. Effective PR will introduce you to influential people, get BONK noticed in the corridors of Whitehall, and cement your reputation."

Liza drove her stiletto into Percy's shoe, a silent warning not to overreach.

"Politicians and newspapers are key," Percy said through gritted teeth. "We'll need BONK to be seen around town and photographed with Establishment figures."

"I'll need to see your list of account holders," he added. "We can expand it with known personalities - press coverage follows naturally. We'll hire our own photographer to make sure you look the part."

"I can guarantee the right coverage," Liza confirmed.

Guarantee!" Gaul exclaimed. "How many pictures of me do you want each week?"

"That depends on the advertising budget," Liza said. "We should build the BONK brand. That's up to Percy - you have to hammer away until BONK is a household name."

"That's what I hope we'll be doing," Gaul admitted, his gaze homing in on Liza's bosom.

"I'm sure you are," Liza replied, uncrossing her legs so he could see a little more.

"And what would you do with my business, Miss Lott?" he asked.

"I'd get my teeth well and truly into it," Liza purred. "And please - call me Liza."

Gaul coughed loudly, flustered.

"I've come up with a television campaign," Percy suggested. "A young Indian businessman drops cricket balls down a staircase. It goes BONK BONK BONK BONK. He takes his secretary into his office and closes the door. It's subliminal but it has a certain momentum!"

Liza stared at Percy, realizing his angle. She adjusted herself deliberately, giving Gaul a pointed look.

"I'm interested in more exposure," Gaul said, scratching his chest through an undone button in his shirt. "By the way, how do I meet Patti O'Dors, the sex goddess?"

"That's easy," Percy replied. "Charity balls. BONK can take a table. I'll introduce you. Alan Lake usually escorts her but he drinks, fights, and passes out. He's a mimic, a voice on many TV ads. Be careful who you talk about because Alan will reply to you in their exact voice. He does a hysterical Imran Khan impression."

"The playboy and our captain of cricket?" Gaul salivated.

"I'll include charity donations in the budget," Percy confirmed. "And then there's Ascot, Wimbledon, Henley ..."

"Yes, yes, we like all that," Gaul winked at Liza. "Maybe later?"

Liza raised her eyebrows, extending her hand.

"Shall I issue the appointment letter and begin the advertising thrust?" she concluded.

"Of course," Gaul said. "Ring me tomorrow to set a time to do business."

Gaul rose, took a Romeo y Julieta No. 2 from a carved walnut box, slipped it into his jacket, and gave a lingering look at Liza as she strode out.

* * * * *

"Playboy Club, Guzzla," Gaul ordered his driver, who had been asleep for five hours outside in a new Mercedes 500.

"Guzzla Tandoori has been my driver on three continents," said Gaul. "If you need to reach me urgently, just ask Guzzla where I am."

As they moved through traffic, Percy noticed a gold Rolex hanging loosely on Guzzla's wrist.

"Amazing watch!" he said casually, aware he had to play the game carefully, keeping pace with their strange mix of business and leisure.

At Curzon Street, Gaul was instantly recognized by the doorman. He signed the book and, along with Percy, was escorted by two full-bodied costumed rabbits up to the gaming room. Gaul slid each of them a £20 note. The rabbits ignored Percy. They knew instinctively it was more than he earned in a week.

Gaul's game was roulette. He sat at the end of the table, pulled out a cigar, and nodded at the croupier:

"Marker £5,000."

A rabbit returned with a chit on a silver salver. Gaul signed it, and £5,000 in £100 pink chips were piled in front of him. He dribbled the chips across the numbers surrounding zero.

"Thirty-two red."

Percy stood politely behind him. Gaul clapped his hands and smiled. He handed Percy six chips off the top of the piles.

"I can't accept these," Percy protested.

"The first rule of business in my country is never to refuse money," Gaul confided. "Take it—life is short!"

Percy wasn't sure whose life he meant.

The wheel spun. Percy placed a pink £100 chip on EVEN; Gaul spread his chips over all numbers except 12, 23, 27, and 34. The ball landed on zero. Gaul's face fell. Percy's bet was wiped out.

"Marker £10,000," Gaul spluttered. The croupier delivered a new set of chips. Gaul rearranged them meticulously. Percy put his remaining chips on RED. The ball landed on 2 black. Percy lost again.

Gaul smiled at a win on 20 black, cashing out six purple slabs marked £10,000, and distributed a few chips to Percy. Percy beamed, realizing he had made a small profit while Gaul continued to dominate the table.

Later, Percy counted the crisp notes in Hyde Park and began planning a series of lunches and cocktail parties at BONK's head office, including arranging Gaul's introduction to Patti O'Dors at the Save Bangladesh Ball at Grosvenor House. Alan Lake wandered off mid-dinner, leaving Gaul next to Patti for twenty minutes.

"This woman is a true sex goddess!" Gaul whispered on his return.

* * * * *

Over the months, Gaul became impressed with Ian Smear's protégé and took Percy into his confidence. Percy became more knowledgeable about the workings of BONK in every department with the exception of what happened in the locked room on the second floor. Only the chief executive of BONK, Squalid Walid, had a key.

Guzzla Tandoori drove Percy to his many meetings at Gaul's North London townhouse, where a group of mediocre-looking girls were always parading up and down the stairs in dressing gowns.

"The prices keep on going up," complained Guzzla as a rather pale-looking girl with a red rash on her right thigh staggered by mistake into the boardroom. She clutched the back of a chair and staggered out.

"The price of what?" asked Percy.

It was Guzzla who, in that indiscreet moment in the boardroom, explained that the girls coming to the house had to satisfy Gaul's sexual preferences. To ram home the point, he disappeared, came back with a holdall and tipped a tangle of handcuffs, chains and whips onto the boardroom table.

"What are the padlocks for?" asked Percy.

Guzzla seemed surprised and opened a drawer of the bureau. He pulled out two packets of photographs and handed them over.

"Why is Gaul wearing high heels and suspenders?" Percy mused as he flipped through some ridiculous pictures, including Gaul thrashing a naked girl handcuffed to the washer-drier.

"This is called public relations," said Guzzla calmly, pulling a stack of calling cards out of a drawer. "My cousin Goussi collect these out of London phone boxes!"

"You are confusing public relations with pubic relations," suggested Percy without considering what it might lead to. "There must be a better way to organise these things."

"You let me know how we get better-looking girls," answered Guzzla as Percy was winced at the sight of Gaul with an enormous hard-on in front of what looked like three undressed cleaning ladies from Slough.

"And I'm forever having to buy bits of jewellery for them," Guzzla moaned.

"They should be paying you," commented Percy as he looked at another picture – it could have been a Polish gypsy dressed in black thigh-length plastic boots topped with a tangled mass of pubic hair and wearing a spiked, metal collar.

"That one was really good," smirked Guzzla. "Gaul had to leave early and she asked me '*who's next*', so I stepped in to help out!"

In the following weeks, Percy was out of his comfort zone as it seemed that these girls were prepared to do weird stuff. They were housewives, waitresses, secretaries and even some sixth-form schoolgirls with an eye on building a future.

"These are on a different level from street girls!" Guzzla insisted.

"You mean, up a notch or in the bargain basement ?"

It was by accident that Percy stumbled on Amanda Ling and her very unusual model agency. Percy had met a girl in Morton's who called herself Janine. She was signed to Models One, an agency supplying extras on film shoots and Percy saw an opportunity. He invited Janine to dinner, and they were joined by her flatmate, Yvonne. After two bottles of champagne, Janine had opened up to explain how Amanda Ling worked and the background of her girls. Many were rescued by Amanda from off the streets, cleaning them up, giving them a place to stay and finding them work as film extras or in crowd scenes. That was infinitely better than the alternative offered by the government that guaranteed they return to exploitation.

Yvonne looked directly at Percy as if to apologise for something.

"My mum died when I was ten" she said carefully. "My father broke me in the same night and, afterwards he abused her until I was fifteen. It only ended when he went to prison for armed robbery and I was taken into care. The social workers took over where my father left off and Amanda was the saint who saved me."

"Christ!" Percy replied after a sharp intake of breath. "That's such a sad story."

Janine looked at her watch and mentioned they had an engagement at the Carlton Tower at midnight.

"Is it a party?" asked Percy.

Both girls started sniggering.

"You've got a lot to learn," replied Yvonne. "Everyone starts with a few drinks and these guys are in from the Middle East so they're just looking for a bit of company - so why don't you come along?"

*****

The penthouse suite at the Carlton Tower opened onto a private lounge with a bar. Most of the guests were staying in the hotel and part of a multinational team engaged in the oil industry from across the Middle East and North African. These were business people with families at home and there was no hint of any rough stuff. The introductions were professional and conversation was simply where they lived and went on holiday and how much oil they were pumping out of the ground.

Percy had intended only to watch the situation unfold but he was soon invited to drinks. He studied the way the girls' skilfully teased their hosts.

Percy spotted an American attempting to put his hand round one of the girls. She excused herself. Another American put his hand on Yvonne's backside and she calmly tugged his hair and he apologised.

Percy slipped across the room through the mix of Arabs and Africans and some of the ladies chatting to them. He reached the bar where an obvious American was standing eying up his choice out of the ten girls circulating. He made a clumsy patting the bottom of the girl closest to him. She broke free and excused herself to go to the bathroom. Then the American put his hand on Percy's shoulder.

"Amanda's girls are great!" he ventured.

He went on to explain that he rings up when he gets to London and Models One send round a book of the girls' agency cards and he simply makes a choice and pays the courier.

"I understand the girls are between filming engagements?" Percy answered as he asked the waiter for a vodka and grapefruit.

"Large?" the barman asked.

"Is there any other kind?" Percy smiled as he watched the scenario unfold with these attractive girls playing this collection of wealthy men.

Then another large man, also American, sitting back on a deep sofa at the side shouted to the waiter for a double Canadian Club. It was Yvonne who joined him when his drink arrived and as he was grasping the drink, he pushed his hand up Yvonne's skirt.

Yvonne coolly grabbed his hair and, to her obvious surprise, it came away in her hand.

"You bitch!!" he screamed for everyone to hear. The entire party paused.

"Jesus!" the man on Percy's right whispered. "That's Mo Hican, studio boss at MGM in LA!"

"MGM?" asked Percy, taken aback at the situation.

"Does Metro-Goldwyn-Mayer ring a bell?" he replied, while Mo covered his bald patch with his hand as if it was top secret.

"Bitch!" Mo repeated under his breath as he struggled to stand. "I'll make sure you're finished in this town."

"But Mo, this isn't your town," Yvonne replied calmly as she threw Mo's toupee, like a frisbee, across the room and, by an accident of fate, it went straight out of the slightly open window.

As Mo continued to swear, Janine took Percy to one side and explained that the girls might be on their uppers but they still deserved respect.

"No one is here for fun" she explained. "We're here for survival."

"I have an early start" Percy replied, "and I hope I see you girls again."

Percy slipped and down through reception into the street.

He smiled when he noticed Mo Hican's hairpiece in the road seconds away from being run over by a bus.

At 3.00 in the morning, he woke with a start, imagining whether this was an opportunity for Gaul Bladda. If Gaul was abusive then it was a big danger for him.

He got up to check the card in his jacket pocket which confirmed Amanda Ling was the agency director at Models One.

The truth was that Amanda had rescued these girls who were on the streets at the end of their rope with nothing but pain and confusion. Amanda had built a platform that offered them protection and potential work hopefully for a transition to a better life.

Percy made himself a cup of tea and it occurred to him even that it might be possible to introduce Amanda Ling's agency to Liza Lott to provide all kinds of 'models' for their own advertising campaigns. Maybe not but Gaul was a certain upgrade from what Percy had seen of the telephone box dates or what Guzzla had said he recruited from graveyards in the night.

* * * * *

There was no internal public relations programme at BONK so Percy saw the opportunity to plan every part of a professional interface in the banking sector.

Percy underestimated Gaul Bladda in this ambition as he started to attract well-heeled depositors in the UK. He was offering a good deal for their account-opening and promising business funding on preferential terms. These few then recommended BONK to their associates, mostly Pakistani and Arab traders in the Midlands and the East End of London. Surprisingly, the BONK customer base was expanding all on its own.

Gaul had started by concentrating on Islamic attendances at the local mosques. These were mostly Pakistani businessmen settled in the UK. Some of them were already using foreign exchange desks and commission houses so they were a natural target. BONK made remarkable progress and their fee income for client custodian services escalated because the novelty of secret accounts never to be disclosed was attractive.

BONK was a particular favourite of Rudolf Werewolf Securities, where Gaul Bladda had formerly been a leading trader. No fewer than eleven commodity traders now handled the BONK account, taking a few percentage points on every trade. Percy would sometimes sit in Gaul's office and watch the secretary coming in and out all day, steadily adding to the piles of trade confirmations. Gaul flicked through them briefly before they disappeared.

On occasion, Percy sneaked a look. He noticed the trades were divided between two accounts: one in Grand Cayman, the other in the UK. The division aligned suspiciously neatly profitable trades only to Cayman, while losses were directed to the UK address. It was a crude but effective way of deciding who received the profit and who absorbed the loss.

As Percy's confidence grew, he began organising cocktail parties in BONK's marbled reception area, beneath the watchful gaze of a large portrait of Gobi Abaddi, the founder. Percy was instructed to invite influential guests - particularly politicians and industry leaders who would be encouraged to make speeches.

At the opening of each new BONK branch in the UK and overseas, especially across Africa, senior government officials were invited to cut the ribbon and address a carefully assembled business audience. This provided Percy with the opportunity to launch a monthly magazine and appoint himself editor. Percy loved to write, and the role fitted neatly with his broader plan to build influence.

The first print run was 50,000 copies. That soon escalated to 100,000 as BONK expanded into sixty-seven branches across seventeen territories.

At the end of each speech, the dignitary would be invited to nominate a favourite local charity for a BONK donation.

The resulting magazine exposure triggered what appeared to be a miraculous surge of donations, sponsorships and free publicity. Apart from praising BONK, the coverage extended to the dignitaries and to the donors. Full page photographic spreads would appear as promised in each issue. The publication also conveniently alerted BONK's growing audience to humanitarian projects in every area in the expanding branch network.

The truth was less noble. Most of the recommended charities, particularly those in Africa, were in severe financial distress. Donations were received by BONK but rarely recorded properly. Donors enjoyed their photo opportunity, while the charities received a token sum - just enough to prove that giving had occurred. Grateful for anything, the charities remained silent.

No accurate record was kept of how much money was raised or where it ended up.

A completely separate revenue stream flowed from advertising celebrating BONK's supposed humanitarian mission – featuring their house model irrigation scheme and medical projects. Every advertisement began with the same declaration: *THANKS TO BONK*.

Percy was close enough to see the financial balances inside the machine he had helped construct. He witnessed the backhanders, the inducements and the girls while forcing himself to write glowing accolades for the people who enjoyed the money that was gifted.

* * * * *

In little more than three years, BONK was being spoken of in the same breath as the prime banks in nearly every capital of the Third World. Governments bestowed extraordinary political acclaim upon it. Their ambassadors in London were briefed on how the British Empire had created a financial stranglehold over half the world, and how Bank of England strategies might now be replicated.

BONK recognised the strategic importance of the drugs trade and deliberately expanded into the Far East and the Caribbean, establishing a banking presence capable of absorbing money that was otherwise difficult for lower cartel tiers to place.

Foreign embassies in London were encouraged to forge closer ties with BONK, using its financial leverage to benefit their focus on foreign exchange, on banking for their nationals and even for some Treasury transactions recommended by dishonest ambassadors who had grown to positions of authority by stealth and family connections. Diplomats were invited to open undisclosed personal accounts to receive their own foreign reserves as a commission for opening the association with B

ONK. All along, BONK would quietly transfer a 'token of appreciation' to their 'fixers'. That appreciation would come from the pool of donations collected for worthy causes.

Gaul Bladda was suddenly appearing at charity events, not as an anonymous attendee tucked away in a corner, but as a prominent guest alongside royal patrons and celebrities. He attended prestigious occasions such as the Lord's Taverners' annual celebrations with Prince Philip and the Sir Cyril Yorker cricket match.

A few phone calls to Pakistan later, and to the horror of the MCC membership, BONK directors packed Lord's with their account holders cheering on the three finest batsmen in the world. As if that wasn't embarrassing enough, BONK fielded its own team, thrashing the Bank of England by eight wickets.

Gaul was feted in the private boxes of racehorse owners at every major meeting. His photograph even appeared behind the Queen Mother at Royal Ascot. Society columns of glossy magazines regularly featured him credited as a client of Smear Associates. Ian Smear took credit for his elevation from 'eating maize' to ordering caviar.

As BONK became a household name, customers flooded in, generating massive organic growth. Branch expansion accelerated as ethnic communities switched allegiance. The established prime banks became obliged to acknowledge the newcomer.

"How refreshing it is for this fellow with huge lips to be treated as an equal," remarked Ova Draft, wife of the boss of the top drug cartel in Jamaica.

When celebrated cricketers in Jamaica rushed to become BONK customers, their fan clubs were featured in a special issue of the BONK magazine. During the English Test season alone, this attracted over 100,000 new accounts, lured by the promise of '*a preferential service of an unsecured overdraft facility available to club members*.'

"Can we have a page in your magazine?" asked the chairwoman of the Kingston Bowls Association.

"If your members switch their bank accounts to BONK," Percy replied, "you can have a whole page - free of charge."

"If a customer has assets, why not lend them money?" Gaul boasted to journalists. "At BONK, we don't take a mortgage on the wife and children. Our business grows by word of mouth. The top five UK banks are so far up their own bottoms that we're stealing their customers without lifting a thumb."

Percy explained that English banks promoted managers from lifetimes spent counting other people's money. By the time they reached management, the chips on their shoulders were so large they needed salt and vinegar. Taking their business was irresistible.

"English bank managers have never been capable of being in business themselves," Percy observed.

"So how is BONK different?" the journalists asked.

"All our managers are already successful Pakistani businessmen," Gaul replied. "The money business is in their blood. You English don't understand customer business. When you see a problem, you just call in the overdraft!"

"That should make interesting press," Percy smiled, knowing how much Gaul enjoyed admiration.

Despite everything, Percy felt uneasy about BONK's corner-cutting and complete absence of accounting discipline. But no regulator had raised an eyebrow so why resist the flow? Smear Associates required no progress reports as long as their fees arrived monthly, alongside Percy's salary and modest expenses. It was cheaper to keep him housed inside BONK, complete with office and secretary, than back at Smear's headquarters. With his own office and secretary in Leadenhall Street, Percy was just fine.

Percy remained in the shadows as an undisclosed but invaluable guide. He deliberately allowed Gaul to take the credit of deposits pouring in. In this wholesale garden of corruption, Percy felt a dangerous temptation to investigate and report but who to? Everyone was blissfully swimming in their own success.

If you become a crook, that's your life over, he reminded himself, catching a sudden glimpse of reality.

“You wait and see how this unfolds,” Gaul declared. “We’ll soon be taking over councils and conducting meetings in Urdu - the national language of Pakistan. You might want to invest in a course of ‘*Urdu for Beginners*’.”

* * * * *

On the third anniversary of Percy taking over the BONK account, Gaul summoned him to an unscheduled meeting in a ‘neutral’ location. Percy assumed it would concern overspending on after-hours entertainment. The accounts now carried a footnote noting that BONK had spent eight million pounds on gratuities in the UK alone during the previous year. These monies were covered by a handful of receipts from the House of Caviar because nobody bothered with receipts anymore.

“Alright,” Percy replied. “If it’s private, shall we go round to the Claremont?”

Instead, Gaul waved him into his office. As Percy entered, he saw the same man in white robes he had noticed on his very first visit to BONK seated in the upholstered armchair.

“This is Percy Vere,” Gaul began. “Percy has been responsible for our public relations campaign. Percy, this is Sheikh Squalid Walid, representative of Sheikh Notsturd, ruler of Abu Dhabi. Sheikh Notsturd is our most important shareholder and one of the founders of the bank. He is also our largest depositor, at six billion dollars.”

It was well known that Gobi Abaddi had introduced the funding and was therefore accorded due reverence. Nobody mentioned that Abaddi had taken fifteen per cent as a fee, insignificant apparently, for a man with personal income from Abu Dhabi oil revenues at twelve billion dollars a year. The deposit had conferred on bONK instant credibility and worldwide political clout.

“Mr Vere,” Sheikh Walid said courteously, “Gaul has told me much about your work, and I thank you. I understand you have arranged a lunch for us next month at the Institute of Directors. You will accompany me, and I shall hear more of your plans.”

"Thank you, Sir, and please convey my gratitude to His Highness," Percy replied, bowing slightly. "I'm glad to have been of service."

Without responding, Sheikh Walid turned back to Gaul and began speaking in Farsi. Gaul replied fluently, often switching to Dari and Persian. Percy assumed they avoided Urdu deliberately as they likely suspected Percy might understand enough to follow them. Some secrets were best kept sealed.

Gaul picked up an envelope from his desk and handed it to Percy.

"This is for you," he said briskly. "We'll speak tomorrow."

Percy retreated, bowing backwards until he reached the door. Once outside, curiosity overcame him. He opened the envelope. A set of keys dropped onto the carpet.

Attached was a red-and-yellow Ferrari key fob.

Inside the envelope lay a vehicle logbook for a newly registered Ferrari 512 Berlinetta Boxer. Percy stared at his own name printed beside the registration number: **BB 512**.

"Are you looking for something, Mr Percy?" asked Wilbur Nisch, the caretaker, polishing the brass banister.

"Yes," Percy said faintly. "You haven't seen a Ferrari around here, have you?"

"Only the one outside, Sir."

Guzzla Tandoori stood by the kerb, next to a gleaming red Ferrari 512.

"Is this serious?" Percy blurted.

Guzzla shook his wrist so his Rolex slipped into view.

"Gaul is a very generous man," he said, opening the driver's door and releasing the intoxicating scent of new leather.

The door shut with a heavy clunk. Percy waved weakly as Guzzla stepped back. He turned the key. The engine exploded into life.

"Incredible," Percy mouthed, easing down the stiff clutch and guiding the gearstick through its chrome gate. He edged into traffic near Great Queen Street. Seeing Guzzla wave in the mirror, Percy pressed the accelerator. The Ferrari lunged forward with a roar. He braked instinctively, stopping inches from the rear of a red double-decker bus.

* * * * *

Percy felt rewarded - validated. It felt like winning a Pulitzer Prize for duplicity. The Ferrari was a clear signal he could not ignore: it was time to leave Smear Associates and join BONK outright. As a consultant, he would be free to continue his duplicity in plain sight. There would be no tax deductions, '*plausible deniability*' would be called upon as necessary and air travel, petrol and insurance and hotel accommodation could be charged to expenses on his own company with BONK picking up the monthly tab!.

It was a miracle he reached Hammersmith without incident. Other drivers longed to test him at the lights, but restrained themselves as Percy was clearly not taking the bait.

That night, Percy knew he had a month to secure his position at BONK and give Smear Associates his contractual one month notice. Sheikh Squalid Walid was the decision-maker so Percy needed to wait until he returned to London. Gaul's secretary would keep him informed for the earliest opportunity.

* * * * *

Percy had dressed for the meeting in a pressed white shirt and polished shoes.

"What do you want?" Gaul asked tersely as Percy knocked and entered his office.

Percy already knew Squalid was there with him.

"Just a moment for an important question that affects us all" Percy answered carefully.

"We're focused on giving smaller businessman an overdraft facility and the depositors getting a better rate of interest" Percy said as a compliment. "By understanding the customer, we can suggest business ideas that they never dreamed possible!"

"Yes. It's going well, but this is only the beginning," replied Sheikh Walid, knowing immediately that there was more to come.

He wasn't to be disappointed.

"During the time I have spent at BONK, I have worked with Gaul to put the programmes together that will give BONK market position," Percy continued slowly. "However, some of the programmes, whilst creating valuable publicity, have given rise to questions about how BONK can afford to break the normal banking procedures. Questions are being asked and we need to prepare to answer should it be necessary."

Squalid was paying close attention but he was showing signs of impatience so Percy repeated that whilst BONK was recording exponential growth and unmatched facilities, extreme vigilance was necessary if comparisons with normal banking procedures arose.

"We need to avoid enquiries and also be ready to answer them" Percy confirmed as a warning.

Squalid was suddenly alert.

"I recommend you create an internal PR department," Percy concluded. "All sensitive documents should be kept here."

"You want us to replace you?" Gaul snapped.

"No," Percy replied evenly. "Smear Associates hold records of our approaches to MPs and industry leaders. They have a history of '*cash for questions in Parliament.'* Any enquiry would be disastrous!"

Squalid stiffened.

"A cleaner at Smear could access our files," Percy continued. "If regulators see them, the Bank of England will ask awkward questions about your licence."

"So we fire you to retrieve our files?" Gaul asked.

Squalid went pale.

"I'd also be unemployed," Percy added. "A personal catastrophe!"

"We could hire you permanently?" Gaul asked slowly.

"I think just a three-year contract would be fair," Percy suggested. "We will need to pay Smear a months notice and then I can get all the files!"

"Write your agreement now!" Squalid barked.

Percy went to his office and picked up the draft agreement he had prepared on a new Vere Associates letterhead. It was for three years;

twice his Smear salary; annual inflation-linked-uplift; expenses, car, travel, health insurance and discretionary Christmas bonus.

Neither Gaul nor Squalid read it or even thought about a legal opinion.

"Go!" Squalid shouted as he scribbled his signature and Gaul's secretary came in with the final cheque plus a month's notice.

Half an hour later, Percy was in Berkeley Square asking to see Ian Smear.

"It's over with BONK," he announced as he stood in his boardroom doorway. "You'll be pleased that I have a final cheque which includes the contractual one month notice."

"That's not how it works!" Smear objected. "It's a matter of protocol and I arranged Squalid Walid as a speaker at the Institute of Directors next week. I have to introduce him and there's nothing you can do about it. Sir Coffin Dodger is the chairman of the Institute and he's a personal friend."

"That's up to you" Percy recoiled. "I'll just pick up my personal stuff if that's all right with you?"

Ian waved him out of the door and slammed it shut.

Spike was not in evidence so Percy grabbed his old briefcase, opened Spike's filing cabinet and simply lifted out all the BONK files and snapped his briefcase shut.

On the way to the exit, he spotted Spike cowering in the photocopier room and he went in.

"What size engine does your Mini have?" Spike asked.

"Why do you ask?"

"BONK sent over your expenses already and they included £93 for petrol?" Spike smiled.

The boardroom door opened ad Ian rushed over.

"Right now, you're still my employee," he fumed slinging an arm round Percy's shoulders. He was so close Percy could smell boiled eggs. "I know you've been up to no good, and I want an explanation!"

"I really haven't got anything to say!" Percy replied.

"I expect you at my flat tonight," Smear hissed. "Seven sharp!"

"I can't," Percy lied. "I've got tickets for Sadler's Wells."

"Then maybe you should try Pentonville Prison next door to the theatre," Smear snarled. "You think you're untouchable, Vere. You're not. You're a disgrace. You're jeopardising this firm for the last time. The police and the Inland Revenue will be very interested in you. I'm giving you the contractual one month notice. No reference. Now get out!"

Smear's legs vibrated like a pneumatic drill.

"I assume drinks at seven are off?" Percy asked politely as he jingled the Ferrari keys in the air.

In that moment of leaving, Percy felt he had betrayed Spike and he paused to sit on the familiar bench in Berkeley Square. His hand started to vibrate although he felt good that Smear would never go to the authorities. He had too much to lose and BONK held accounts for innumerable of Smear introductions. That was the ultimate insurance.

"Never be dependent on anyone in business," Percy swore aloud to the pigeons when Spike appeared beside the bench.

"I'll make sure he pays your own notice!" Spike assured him. "Your mistake was the Ferrari petrol, as he went berserk!"

Percy hugged him, genuinely moved and suddenly aware that there was a grim responsibility attached to his new freedom - he no longer had the defence of working for Smear Associates!

"I learned so much from you!" he said quietly. "I'll never forget!"

As he walked to the car, Spike read his mind and called after him: 'Don't forget to fall back on your '*plausible deniability*'."

* * * * *

Percy had first met Cindy Kate when he was in his Mini and he had no chance with her as her passion was fast cars. They were both at Jamie's wine bar opposite the iconic Michelin building on the Fulham Road. Separately, they knew Jamie, the owner, and they had screamed with laughter as he did his famous house stunt climbing round the whole lounge area in his boxer underpants without touching the ground. At various stages he was upside-down with his balls hanging out as his left foot was up on a window ledge and his right toes gripping a wall-light fitting.

"It's the splits!" came a cry as Jamie reached ten feet away from the finish on the bar.

Jamie didn't make it and crashed onto the bottles and glasses on a table underneath. Two astonished German businessmen sat with solemn faces as Jamie landed in a heap on the floor beside them. Cindy was in hysterics.

"Let's go back to my place," Percy had volunteered.

"No!" she insisted looking outside at the wreck of his Mini. "I'll get a cab to mine."

Now it was different as he was a confident Ferrari owner, albeit in name only. He had yet to get used to the unusual ways the car performed and he had been unable to get insurance or afford the petrol until the switch to BONK was completed.

Percy saw Cindy again by chance again in Jamie's. Her parents lived in Leicestershire and had bought her a flat overlooking the Thames in Cheyne Walk. She obviously did not need to work for a living. A painting on her hall wall of a stately pile in untold acres vouched for that.

Cindy was determined to make her own way in life with a career, and she was working as one of the only female traders at Rudolf Werewolf Securities.

"They're one of the world's largest firms of commodity traders dealing for some 50,000 private clients internationally," she confirmed.

"That I know," was all Percy said at that point.

After his first month with the car, Percy reunited with Cindy and in view of his new status, she was nearly treating him as an equal. The Ferrari had played its part and she invited Percy to Leicester for the weekend.

"I don't know if my parents will be there," she warned him.

Percy picked Cindy up in Cheyne Walk after the rush hour to drive on his Ferrari's first major trip and he lost sight of the speed as the car cruised past Watford at 120 mph. It felt like 30 mph.

"Slow down!" Cindy urged him. "Keep it below 100 mph and I'll keep quiet."

Cindy stretched out her long legs and lay back with her blonde hair flowing over the soft cream upholstery.

Percy took the opportunity to find out about BONK dealing with Rudolf Werewolf.

"I assume you operate 'discretionary' accounts where Werewolf do whatever trades they like?" Percy mentioned. "I always thought it was a bit dangerous letting the broker have control so they can dump losing trades on a client and there's no comeback? Who can tell if their profits are being allocated to a favourite client?"

"You have to trust your broker," Cindy mused without turning her head. "Otherwise, the whole system breaks down."

"Is anyone in your firm in a position to decide who gets the profits and who gets the losses?"

"You have to understand how the futures markets work," Cindy answered dreamily against the hypnotic whine of the car at 130 mph. "The clients gamble on the future price of all commodities - wheat, barley, sugar, gold, silver and so on. I'm on the metals desk, so we deal with copper, lead, aluminium, tin, and that sort of thing. Clients only have to put down 10% of the value of any contract, so if the price goes up or down only 5%, they gain or lose 50% of their money. It's called 'trading on margin.' It's a big risk and only the big boys should be in it."

"So, if the price moves 10% either way, they're either wiped out or they double their money," confirmed Percy without saying he knew BONK had eleven traders dedicated to their account. "That's nice if the trader is your friend and not so nice if he doesn't like you!"

"Yes, but most clients don't survive for long," Cindy continued. "They 'day trade', which means they're in and out the same day. They only get charged half commission on a day trade."

"How on earth can you tell if copper or lead prices are going up or down on any one particular day?" Percy persisted.

"You can only guess," muttered Cindy, her guard down. "A few of the huge clients know what they're doing and take a longer view but the majority are simply gambling, but don't forget, for every winner, there's a loser. The price fluctuates all the time from the original miners and farmers until it gets to the users. The market takes in the production of all commodities on paper until physical delivery. It's a good system. The seller gets the price he wants and the buyer gets a fixed price he will pay all in advance of unknown uncertainties. In the middle is a fluctuating market. It's all very sensible."

"That doesn't explain why some clients have two accounts, one for profits and one for loss" Percy asked.

"Mostly, they do it to put profits in some overseas account where the tax man isn't involved" she explained. "Losses can go into an account which is used to offset business profit and capital gains. Werewolf doesn't care, and it's easy with 'day trades' because they are only allocated after the trade is closed. The client can tell us which account to use. You can imagine some profitable trades are included in an all-losing account or Her Majety's Tax Office would smell a rat!"

"That's useful," Percy surmised.

"That's nothing, darling," she responded drowsily. "Some of the professionals buy and sell the same commodity at the same time on two separate contract notes. That way they get to match the profit and loss. They keep the profit and allocate the loss all at the same time. I guarantee they're stealing from their own clients and these trades can be in the hundreds of thousands or even millions of pounds in government and industrial accounts. We can't see when they do that because they get both contract notes at the same time."

Percy braked hard and then accelerated to jolt Cindy awake.

"Surely Werewolf doesn't allow profits and losses to be separated like that after the event?"

"We wouldn't know," she answered. "We've got one client who acts for a bank. The bank takes all the losses, and the manager gets the profits in an account in his cousin's name – and slow down!"

Percy's foot came off the accelerator for at least thirty seconds as he realised that the two accounts he had seen in Gaul Bladda's office were mirror images of a buy and sell and a sell and buy. Someone was taking the profit and BONK was getting the loss and who was to know?

Percy decided he would distance himself from discussing BONK trading.

Percy accelerated and drove in silence until he reached the motorway turn-off and he needed directions.

After a few lefts and rights down narrow lanes, they were in front of some pretty impressive wrought-iron gates. They opened electronically as Cindy pressed a key fob and there was a long driveway leading up to a magnificent stately home.

"Go round the back," instructed Cindy as they were driving slowly up a continuation of half mile of crunching gravel.

"Everyone's asleep," Cindy whispered, to stop Percy roaring the Ferrari engine.

Percy carried their bags down flagstone corridors and up a sweeping circular staircase into a far bedroom. Cindy turned on the light to reveal a beautiful four-poster bed with lace drapes, a Louis XIV bureau with gilt-scrolled legs facing the windows and magnificent tapestries hanging on the walls round them.

"This is some room," Percy exclaimed, looking out over manicured lawns in the moonlight.

"Shut the curtains, Percy darling, I'm really tired," Cindy asked as she pulled her sweater over her head. "You can see outside in the morning."

Percy couldn't sleep. He tossed and turned, worrying about what Gaul Bladda was doing. Surely it was only a matter of time before someone at BONK would question every major trade being a loss, and there would be an enquiry as to where the profits had gone. No one lost ten trades in a row – or did they?

Gaul would be caught taking the profits abroad in another name - what about all the money they had given to charity? - what about all BONK's expenditure on politicians and escorts and, oh God! - what about his Ferrari?

Percy sat bolt upright in a cold sweat in the dark. He could hear Cindy breathing evenly and peacefully.

And what about Cindy? Percy's imagination was running wild in the dark. Would all the traders be arrested?

Percy threw back the bedclothes and fumbled blindly across the room, bumping first into the bureau. His hands felt the blotter as he pitched forward and blindly knocked over the silver-framed pictures but managed somehow to stop the overturned inkstand from falling off the edge. He thought he had stood it up again, so he edged carefully round the desk and moved forward until his hands felt a tapestry.

He heard the howling of the wind as he moved one hand at a time across the ancient weave. He then felt his way along until he reached a second tapestry and then paintwork where he tried to find a light switch. Feeling his way, he then felt the bathroom doorway, found a switch and flicked it on.

A standard lamp in the corner threw light across the room.

Percy froze in disbelief. His hands were black with ink, and the inkwell was overturned on its side on the desk. Worse, there were black, inky finger marks across the tapestries and on the wall in between.

"Fuck me gently, Lady Kate!" Percy whispered in anguish as he wiped his indelible Quink-stained hands on a white bath towel.

"What on earth are you doing, Percy?" squinted Cindy.

"Having a nightmare," Percy replied quickly, turning off the light.

"Well, come and finish it in bed," she ordered.

In the morning, Cindy opened her eyes and, four seconds later, she was bolt upright in horror.

"Those tapestries survived two centuries and two World Wars and were smuggled out of France by the Resistance at a cost of four lives," she choked. "My mother is going to have a heart attack!"

"It won't be so bad," Percy comforted her. "Don't tell her until after we've gone!"

"She'll kill you!"

"These things are always better handled on the phone!" Percy concluded.

* * * * *

Ian Smear got the call from Cindy's mother, and Percy was jolted into the importance of Spike's 'plausible deniability' - in this case easily as Percy was history at Smear Associates.

"Get a grip, madam!" Ian Smear responded with glee to Cindy's mother's urgent call. "Who is this Percy Vere? We've never heard of him here!"

"Aren't you Smear Associates?" she insisted.

"They left this business before we moved in after the War!" Ian replied.

"Are you certain?" Mrs Kate asked, definitively off balance.

"I should know!" Ian Smear retorted. "I'm here with my partner, and he's been with me all this time. In fact, we're just doing a jigsaw together of some naked Greek wrestlers, if you'd like him to confirm anything?"

"That won't be necessary, Mr Smear," she apologised, "and I'm sorry to have troubled you."

* * * * *

The pre-arranged speech for Squalid Walid at the Institute of Directors was a big deal for BONK, and Percy had to avoid any of the potential disasters that could fuck up everything - and that meant everything. He had worked for three years on building the platform to give BONK a global presence, and even a minor indiscretion at such a publicised event could take BONK back to the Neanderthal age of public relations.

"Just use your head," he said out loud as he crossed Berkeley Square for a cup of coffee at Morton's with the much-loved manager, the forever ebullient Simon Drummond Brady.

'DB' was in a jovial mood as he wandered, wishing the early-morning faithful 'have a great day!' This greeting was welcomed by his close friends, Simon and Helen Ponzi, who were sharing a boiled egg - after a High Court conviction for stealing £237 million from 11,600 investors and spending it all on themselves.

Percy had followed their issuance of the Ponzi mini-bonds, which carried a coupon of an 8% return from a fictional London Oil and Gas entity. The Institute of Directors had been prominent in the regulatory investigation for such a high-profile fraud. It was an act of Almighty God that Helen Ponzi saw Percy that morning and screamed 'you fucking rapist!' across the room.

"Why are you smiling?" asked a horrified DB.

"Who'd rape an ugly cow like that?" Percy replied. "However, we were going to announce a new mini-bond issue from BONK at the IOD today, and God has just warned me to shelve it!"

The Ponzis had only one way to repay bondholders, and that was by attracting new bondholders.

"Think of the life you have lived as over," DB suggested to Simon and Helen. "Then you will be able to see the years ahead as a bonus to be lived differently—and, by the way, your membership is cancelled!"

* * * * *

Guzzla Tandoori arrived to pick Percy up as arranged from outside Morton's. Percy was looking across Berkeley Square towards his former office, just in case Ian Smear or Spike Upward could see him.

Percy uttered the usual pleasantries to Guzzla and sat back as they drove to collect Sheikh Squalid Walid from Claridge's.

Percy button-holed Squalid as soon as he was sitting in the car. Percy was holding his arm to make sure he was paying attention.

"Please listen to me carefully, Squalid!" he opened. "Have you got the speech I sent to you?"

Squalid pulled it out of a pocket somewhere in his white robe, almost fearfully, and Percy grabbed it, pulling out his pen.

"What, by the grace of Allah, are you doing?" Squalid asked as Percy crossed out three paragraphs and scribbled over them until they were an unreadable mess.

"There is no mini-bond issue!" Percy insisted. "You must not even say the words 'mini-bond'!"

"But it is an important way to take in money from every one of our depositors!" he objected. "It was your idea, and we have people all over the world waiting for the launch!"

"We have to shelve this for today!" Percy was still insisting as Guzzla turned into Pall Mall and pulled up outside the IOD building.

The gatherings at the IOD were always a pompous affair, and Squalid, in his robes, made an immediate impact. Then Ian Smear came out of the crowd of guests and grabbed Percy's shoulder.

"I am introducing Sheikh Squalid!" he muttered, baring his teeth. "Smear Associates do this for a living, and you can take a back seat for a change!"

"Sheikh Squalid is our keynote speaker for this morning," said the authoritative voice of Sir Coffin Dodger. "Are we ready to invite the guests to take their seats?"

Sir Coffin guided Squalid onto the staged area and then beckoned to James Callaghan, to join them.

"Ladies and gentlemen," Sir Coffin started as he tapped the microphone to make sure everyone was settled. "May I introduce the leader of the Labour Party, Baron Callaghan of Cardiff - the only person to have held all four great offices of State: Chancellor of the Exchequer from 1964 to 1967, Home Secretary from 1967 to 1970, Foreign Secretary from 1976 to 1979, and, of course, Prime Minister."

Ian Smear grabbed Percy's shoulder.

"Have you sidelined me?" he insisted. "I have to introduce Squalid Walid as a matter of protocol."

"Don't worry," Percy assured him. "You are mentioned in the order of procedure but James Callaghan is the shining light behind BONK and he's chairman of the Oxbridge Commonwealth Trust."

Sir Coffin continued. "James Callaghan has been an inspiration to our first speaker, His Highness Sheikh Squalid Walid, founder of Bank Overseas National Kredit. He has introduced BONK to the Commonwealth countries, and I'm pleased to announce that BONK has today been awarded a £1 million grant by James Callaghan. This award is for projects in Zimbabwe and Zambia through the initiatives of Mazda

Bation, Minister of Urban Development in Zimbabwe, and Urin Onitt, his counterpart in Zambia."

Callaghan stepped forward to universal applause and thanked his long-standing friend Sir Coffin Dodger. He then introduced Squalid Walid as a pioneer in banking, bringing funding to the underprivileged and helpless across half of the planet.

Squalid swept up to the lectern to more applause.

"It is with great honour, in this austere gathering, that I address you," he read from Percy's double-spaced speech. "We have never set up a new financial institution before and we have never even designed any complex financial structure so this is new ground for us. It has not been an easy process because we are feeling our way forward in areas of the world that have not known democracy. In fact, a 'show of hands' was a colonial order to stick them out front to have them chopped off!"

"That was a joke!" he added as Percy waved to stop him going off-script.

"We all suffered from totalitarian regimes before fighting for independence" Squalid went on as he tried to find his place on the script. "Our journey has been difficult, but we are now building upwards on strong foundations to achieve our dreams of inter-racial government on a global scale."

They was a smattering of applause.

"However, even the best of dreams in business will not succeed on top of a single pillar" he was arguing. "Weight has to be spread and we are grateful for your support to follow us in making change possible."

There was a definitive shift in attitude, with a ripple of applause and even appreciation.

"BONK has expanded rapidly across the Third World, particularly in Africa," he continued. "We follow Islam so we know that the West will investigate any hairline fracture to discredit us and that attitude can lead to a collapse back into the old ways. I have seen the future and connected with the leading firms of attorneys and auditors to evidence integrity in our management."

The portraits along the walls of the IOD, glorifying those who had first colonised and raped the Third World, looked down in astonishment.

Squalid spoke for forty minutes, and Percy's text, although interspaced with Squalid ad-libbing, received a rare standing ovation and there was a sea of eager hands clambering to touch the tool of Sheikh Notsturd, surely one of the world's most generous men.

Percy was well pleased at the part he had played. No one suspected that the donations and government grant monies never left the BONK account until $30,000 of the $1 million Callaghan grant was transferred to acquire second-hand earth-moving equipment from a scrapyard in Holland. On arrival at the entry point in Maputo, Mozambique, the bulldozers were transported to districts far away from the Zimbabwean and Zambian capitals.

"Where are the keys?" asked the near-naked villagers excitedly.

"You will not be needing any keys," answered Mazda Bation as he was photographed to celebrate the arrival of the bulldozers for the latest edition of the BONK magazine.

"And here are some picks and shovels," commanded Urin Onitt in a collection of mud huts in a barely accessible village on Zambia's southern border with Botswana.

The balance of $970,000 was appropriately transferred internally into Squalid's personal account at BONK, and he, in turn, transferred $10,000 to each of the BONK accounts of Mazda Bation and Urin Onitt.

After the morning session and an exodus for lunch for specially invited guests to the Athenaeum Club opposite, James Callaghan spoke again and congratulated Squalid Walid for being coherent and even impressive.

"Every member of the Labour Party is delighted to help a bank that does so much for our friends in the Commonwealth communities," Callaghan concluded, with his bushy eyebrows hovering as the words cruised out on automatic pilot.

"It is nothing, really," replied Squalid. "We must all do our share. I am sure that, if you return to government, you will continue your support and we will be able to do even more."

"Percy is a smart cookie," Gaul Bladda whispered to Squalid as he enjoyed the poached salmon. "We should make more use of him!"

The speaker at the end of the lunch was Wayne Moon, the Chairman of the Commonwealth Institute whose farm had been seized in the Eastern Highlands and his daughter had been raped in gaol by Mugabe's Zanu PF security forces. Wayne had been agonised not just by his own loss and pain but by the dysfunction across the whole of Zimbabwe following the departure of Ian Smith, the Prime Minister of the former Rhodesia.

"We must all learn a lesson about decolonisation," Wayne started. "If natives are to rule themselves, every gain achieved over centuries of guidance will vanish. Infrastructure will collapse, roads will be impassable, trains will be abandoned, hospitals will be closed, farms like mine will be grabbed so there will be no food for the people. After they reduce themselves to life with sewage in the streets they will believe it's normal!"

"When we secured you as the keynote speaker, I asked Sir Coffin not to let Wayne loose!" Percy whispered to Sheikh Walid.

"My country, Rhodesia, was hugely successful in every respect," Wayne kept going. "We built a unique and beautiful culture while also ensuring living standards and economic growth for blacks. Then Mugabe arrived and wrecked everything with his racist communism. It has been the same with these Marxists insisting they are the new way forward in the Congo, Kenya, Sudan, Ethiopia, Mozambique, Nigeria, Ghana, and South Africa. We must make sure that their horrendous version of the truth is seen by everyone as a comprehensive destruction of civilisation."

"Shame on you!" came a call from the other end of the table.

"You may believe that all black men are equal not only in the eyes of God but in human capability," Wayne shouted back. "That is undoubtedly false and utterly ridiculous, but it is the basis of your present system. That's why peoples across Africa are now ruled by contemptible buffoons!"

There followed unease and calls for order.

"The wages of race communism are death!" Wayne shouted.

Then Sir Coffin Dodger stood up and started clapping. At the same time he called security.

"The ideology of race communism is now not only across the whole of Africa but spreading to Europe and even to the United States" Wayne was shouting as two beefy coloured security guards were hauling him out of the room.

That created the most applause of the day.

Percy took note that BONK was a perfect fit into the mould of Marxist communism.

"I have to take my hat off to you," Percy muttered to Sheikh Squalid behind his hand as they walked out onto Carlton Terrace to where Guzzla Tantoori was waiting. "You caught the mood of the room!"

Percy looked up at the line of buildings. So many like it were built by George IV as London residences, and it caught his idea of legacy perfectly. George IV was a compulsive romantic. He had multiple long-term mistresses, including Mary Robinson (the actress), Grace Dalrymple Elliott, and Maria Fitzherbert. He had a secret illegal marriage to Maria Fitzherbert (a Catholic) and he married Caroline of Brunswick for political convenience.

"I believe you are fast surpassing the sexual pursuits of George IV" Percy suggested.

"I've taken a leaf out of Cecil Rhodes' book," Squalid announced as Guzzla pulled into the traffic. "Rhodes bribed everyone in government through his Chartered Company to get control over a vast area of central Africa. As the elected Prime Minister of the Cape, he had assumed control of the Kimberley diamond mines. He built a life of greed, arrogance, and exploitation. He annexed provinces for his personal supply of slave labour and young women. Wherever he didn't find gold or diamonds, he stole the cattle. When they rose up, he got imperial troops to slaughter them."

"Some role model!" Percy admitted. "It's almost like BONK as Rhodes handed out directorships and share options in his companies to his associates!"

"I'm following the same patriotic endeavour in inseminating virgins in every branch of BONK!" Squalid grinned as he stroked his crotch.

"I always wondered where the word 'bonking' came from!" Percy questioned. "I would hate to think that London was not playing its full part in your selfless efforts in that regard!"

Percy was utterly taken aback but he stopped himself from saying that Squalid was a racist plunderer amassing a fortune for himself.

Squalid slumped back comfortably in the back of the car and beckoned Guzzla to drop Percy off.

"The hypocrisy of the British government was their moral outrage at apartheid," he whispered. "You British collaborate to get a safe supply of migrant black labour."

"You know your history!" Percy replied in surprise.

"In 1948, the Afrikaners simply copied the national socialism of Germany to replace the British Jewish stranglehold," Squalid concluded. "You know the 'panga' is one of the few words of African origin in the English language. Every few weeks, you had communities being hacked to death all over the African continent with the panga, but the tribal blood is strong. It bred rebel groups who wanted power at any price. That's why the killing and corruption will never stop. There's a pathological indifference in Africa about the future, and until that changes, BONK will do anything we want!"

* * * * *

It was a normal working day at BONK before Percy gathered his thoughts after the IOD experience.

'The truth is there for everyone to see,' Percy reasoned. 'BONK was heading for suicide in Africa after the donations stopped. As for protection, this was a no-condom business leading to a wave of still births.'

Squalid didn't miss a beat in confirming the African mind had become brutalised.

"When children die, it's of no particular consequence," Squalid had reasoned. "They just have another one because their communities have experienced such vile sexual behaviour over centuries that there is no limit to their retribution. Idi Ott, president of Uganda, fills his fridge with human limbs; Jean-Bédel Bokassa, emperor of the Central African Republic, spent £2.5 million on a crown for his wife, and he eats babies and drinks the blood of young children to extend his own life. Mengistu Haile Mariam, the Stalin of Africa, tortures his political opponents to death while famine is killing half of Ethiopia. Look at how Africa spends $ hundreds of millions annually on stupid wars. It has no end because the victors are siphoning off all the humanitarian aid, and they all say – 'it might as well be us, heh?'

"Aren't you worried about how the Press might expose this kind of attitude?" Percy responded in a quiet, sickened voice.

"Don't worry about that," boomed Squalid. "We've just paid for our computer technicians from Karachi to upgrade the computers in the Conservative Central Office!"

* * * * *

Squalid stayed on in Claridge's and was ferried to the office each day by Guzzla and they chatted in secret. Percy often went with Squalid to have a cup of tea with him at the end of the day. This kept Percy in touch with BONK priorities and allowed him to think through their plans in context. This also provided the bulk of the editorial in the monthly magazine.

Guzzla would wait and drive Percy to wherever he wanted to go and then. One evening, Guzzla raised the flag Percy had been waiting for.

"Sheikh Walid wants you to arrange two girls to come up to his suite," Guzzla announced on the eve of his departure back to Karachi. "He has a few hours before the flight!"

Guzzla reached into his pocket and handed over a sealed plastic envelope full of fifty-pound notes.

"Do yourself a favour and make sure they're not dogs," he ordered.

Percy's mind flashed back to the night at the Carlton Tower when he first got the Amanda Ling escort agency phone number.

He had put the card in the back of his wallet, so he took it out and dialled from the car phone.

Amanda Ling answered the phone personally.

"I'll send someone round with the book to meet you in Claridge's in an hour," she agreed. "You make a selection of two but you'd better ring me straight away if you want them this evening and don't forget we only take cash."

Percy looked at the plastic envelope in his lap. It had "Playboy Club" printed on a sticky label which was embossed with the amount £5,000.

"Back to Claridge's please, Guzzla!"

Percy walked through Claridge's reception and to the left of the lounge into the more private alcove. He ordered a large vodka and grapefruit and sat back. This was going to cement his position inside BONK and that fitted with his longer term plans with access to BONK money.

Amanda's messenger arrived with a stack of pocket-size Z cards introducing each girl. None of these candidates would have been more than twenty-five years old and all of them could honestly be described as attractive after their makeover of a wash, a make-up specialist, a hairdresser, a dentist and a decent photographer.

"It's short notice," the messenger explained. "Let me give you a run-down on those available immediately."

Percy looked to make sure no one was looking before he flicked through the pages for a tour of the flesh. When he passed Yvonne and then Janine, Percy again had a flashback to that extraordinary night at the Carlton Tower.

"I will only be a few minutes," he mumbled as he headed for the lift. "Please wait for me in the lobby."

Squalid's personal butler opened the door to his suite, and Percy identified himself. Sheikh Squalid quickly appeared and started drooling as his plump fingers caressed the plastic-coated cards.

"Will they do what I want?" he asked immediately.

"It's short notice," Percy replied as he indicated his two trusted choices. "This is Janine, who will give you a show with Jacqui and, since you're short of time, they'll both do you together."

"But will they do my business?" Squalid asked as if he was ordering something to put on his toast.

Percy assumed he understood what Squalid wanted and moved on appropriately.

"Tania likes it up the bottom for an extra five hundred," he guessed. "As for Yvonne, she will hum you a tune with your balls in her mouth. This is Zola in reserve, and she will beat you half to death with a rubber truncheon, and you might not make it to the airport. Then, as a standby, there's Candida who will tie you up and piss all over you."

"This is wonderful, Percy," Squalid dribbled as Percy grimaced. "I am not surprised Gaul Bladda speaks so highly about you!"

"You must hurry if you want them now," replied Percy.

"Okay, so I'll have Tania and Yvonne together!"

"That's an interesting mix!" guessed Percy. "You're probably the first to try it. Anyway, I know they'll be happy to make you happy!"

Percy had not forgotten the envelope in his pocket, but he didn't have to refer to it. Squalid snapped his fingers, and his butler moved over to the desk and pulled out a briefcase. It was chock-full of cash. Squalid just plucked out a wad of notes and handed them to Percy.

Percy could see there was more than £2000 in new fifties in that one stack and he shoved it into his pocket before going back down to reception

"How much for Tania and Yvonne?" he muttered.

"A monkey!" he replied assuming Percy knew his Cockney slang for five hundred quid and its origin from the monkey on the 500 rupee note in 19th-century India.

"Each!"

Percy passed over £1,000 with an extra £100 for the messenger so he still had the balance around £1,000 from upstairs and the £5,000 packet in his inside pocket.

"I made up a lot of stuff they will do to him, but they can work it out," Percy frowned. "It's the Prince Alexander suite for an hour?"

The messenger went outside to make a call and was back in two minutes.

"Okay, Mr Vere," he confirmed quietly. "It's all set for eight o'clock."

Percy was grinning as he remembered Yvonne recollecting her first six months with the Amanda Ling agency. She made up for her years of abuse by being a waitress at School Dinners. The restaurant was always full of sensation-seeking advertising folk who survived the disgusting food to be publicly flogged by suspender-clad St Trinian's look-alikes. Years of venom were given an outlet, and Dick Head, boss of Head and Swallow Advertising, at monthly intervals, had lunch there. Each time he refused to eat all his greens, Tania beat him so severely that he was hospitalised. When Dick was released from surgery the first time, he offered Tania a photographic test for an in-house shoot. That day she beat the shit out of all three senior partners in the boardroom at Head and Swallow. Her repertoire culminated in dropping each of their balls into her mouth and humming a tune for a few minutes to relax them. Then, in an ultimate act of revenge for her miserable upbringing, she clamped her teeth round them.

Percy couldn't understand why she was so popular.

* * * * *

Percy was aware that integrity is something one only loses once and Amanda Ling, in her genius, had gone far beyond that criticism because she had laid a path into a new space of respect for that oldest profession. Each girl was immaculately made up and dressed in Chanel and Saint Laurent. Moreover, they had intermittent assignments as film extras with even an occasional feature in the glossies, often with more front than Harrods. Top photographers were unpaid to work their magic and enjoyed a happy intimate moment if there were to be any decent photographs at the end of an afternoon.

The two girls walked straight through reception, into the lift and up to the Prince Alexander suite.

Squalid Walid was knocked out.

"By the Prophet Mohammed, such beauty!" he started as Percy made the introductions and the butler opened the champagne and withdrew.

"I am short of time," Squalid announced abruptly as he ushered the girls into the bedroom area.

"Enjoy!" Percy replied with a grin as Squalid closed the double doors behind them.

The messenger phoned Percy to report that the assignment had been a success, including an almighty scream reported by a maid.

Guzzla had arrived back at Claridge's to collect Squalid to go to the airport and the girls appeared at the door ready to leave.

Tania and Yvonne were laughing out loud as Squalid appeared in his robe, quivering.

"Book my flight for tomorrow," he choked.

* * * * *

"He liked the girls," Gaul Bladda said in thanks to Percy the next morning. "It's important to keep him sweet."

"You're picking up English expressions from somewhere," Percy replied. "And it's not from me!"

Gaul checked that Squalid was still at Claridge's and had not so much as ordered breakfast. Gaul wanted to know nothing was going to backfire from the entertainment.

Percy had added £6,100 to his stash under his floorboards as he pondered what to do next. There was clearly money to be had if he played his cards carefully and left no fingerprints in the spaces where the money was flowing out of BONK if and when the balloon went up? He was helped by the absence of any detailed financial records so how much risk could that be?

Percy made a decision to tell Gaul there was a danger in a trail of bank transfers. A policy of cash only payments for all their extra-curricula activities would be wise and that included his monthly expenses.

"That's ok with me" Gaul reminded Percy. "An accounting issue would not only be serious for BONK, it would end your career in public relations before it had got into its stride!"

Gaul clearly thought they were covering the risk but he wanted confirmation from his boss.

"The way to handle this is for you to come with me to collect Sheikh Walid to go to the airport," Gaul announced as he telephoned Guzzla.

"Collect me before you get Sheikh Walid from Claridge's" he instructed.

So it was that Squalid moved slowly out of the hotel with his butler holding him up. Then Guzzla set off with the three of them not speaking until they were halfway to Heathrow on the Hammersmith Flyover. Gaul nodded to Percy to shut the glass division to the driver.

"Mr Vere has approached me with a situation that needs some thought," he said guardedly to Squalid. "I have suggested that he explains it to you directly."

Gaul looked at Percy and nodded.

"BONK has to be careful with its present way to record your financial dealings" Percy started. "The auditors won't be able to account for your transfers out of the company as legitimate expenses and they'll question the recipients of the money. It could become a big headache and, frankly, you can't trust the auditors to keep the discussions about it private. They are bound by law to report where the money is coming from and where it is going.

Percy already knew this would be a nerve as regular payments were going to their private accounts and to their families."

"So what do you suggest?"

"A separate account for public relations expenses in my name" Percy answered. "Then payments are a legitimate expense and there won't be any questions. How I prepare my accounts is not relevant."

"So we give you the money in advance for you to pay our bills?" asked Squalid defensively.

"Not quite!" Percy replied. "You open an account for me at BONK, you make an advance deposit, then you give me an overdraft facility. At the end of each month, I give you a list of your expenses, you check it and see I'm not cheating you and you pay it leaving the deposit intact. Of course you rip up my list of expenses because it's no longer your business."

Mercifully, the limousine went into the dark of the Heathrow tunnel at that precise moment. Percy knew he must not say one more word until Squalid replied, otherwise the moment would be lost.

Percy didn't realise the tunnel was so long. It went on and on with the tyres humming and the lights on each side flashing as they passed.

Percy was suddenly thinking of Yvonne's gurgling 'Jingle Bells' with Squalid's testicles in her mouth.

Gaul and Squalid now spoke excitedly in Urdu before they emerged into the light. Squalid was leaning back and smiling.

"Agreed, but only on two conditions," he said. "The first is that you will make Gaul's secretary the secretary of your Vere company which I believe is in Luxembourg where BONK is also registered.She will complete your accounts. Secondly, on January 20th, you come as my guest to Karachi to attend a BONK strategy meeting."

"Agreed," Percy replied, holding out his hand.

Gaul got out of the car with Squalid.

"We have things to discuss," he nodded to Percy. "You take the car."

Percy pressed a pre-prepared invoice into Gaul's hand. It was an invoice for a £250,000 advance payment for Vere P.R. Services in Luxembourg, his educated structure. He knew Squalid would agree after a night with Tania and Yvonne. There would be multiple further bookings.

Percy opened the glass divide, slouching across the back seat.

Guzzla started to look relaxed.

"Brilliant!" Percy shouted, knowing that Squalid Walid would torture his mother to save himself.

"You sound happy," said Guzzla.

"More than you know," said Percy.

"So, you got a deal?"

"You heard?"

"I hear what everyone says," Guzzla admitted. "That's why Gaul always asks me to take his business visitors back to their offices after meetings. I record what they say on their phones!"

"You sneaky shit!"

On the plane, Squalid tossed off his sandals, adjusted his bruised balls into his first-class seat and smiled as he considered his momentous schematic to be unveiled in Karachi in the New Year.

Gaul Bladda also smiled because he had learned a big lesson about record keeping and Percy had protected him. Moreover, the £250,000 advance to Vere P.R. Services was a drop in the bucket of what he had planned with Squalid.

Percy was happy because, under sharia law written in their military manual the Quran, these Islamics were not only permitted to lie through their back teeth, they could cheat and steal and get married to pre-pubescent girls, they were forbidden to charge interest on loans. Percy's expenses for BONK could go up to £250,000 a month and the balance would disappear in his holding structure. BONK could never complain. Percy's fees would be recorded as an interest free loan and that was just the beginning.

The phone rang and it was Gaul.

"You are one smart mercenary fucker!" Gaul muttered.

"Are you speaking to me?" asked Percy.

www.ingramcontent.com/pod-product-compliance
Lightning Source LLC
LaVergne TN
LVHW041059080826
845145LV00007B/1637